EXCHANGE
Weathersfield Commons
Schaumburg, IL. 60193
(312) 529-5305

EARLY PRAISE

"THE DELICATE DEPENDENCY is rich with period detail and extraordinary insight. The tension builds page by page to a stunning climax, and the sense of creeping, subterranean horror is truly awesome. I doubt that I will ever forget it."

Whitley Streiber

"The past half-decade has seen a glut of vampire novels, but few as ambitious and seriously intended as this one....an impressive book, unflaggingly interesting."

Publishers Weekly

KEVINS BOOKS EXCHANGE
81 Weathersfield Commons
Schaumburg, IL. 60193
(312) 529 - 5305

Avon Books are available at special quantity discounts for bulk purchases for sales promotions, premiums, fund raising or educational use. Special books, or book excerpts, can also be created to fit specific needs.

For details write or telephone the office of the Director of Special Markets, Avon Books, 959 8th Avenue, New York, New York 10019, 212-262-3361.

THE
DELICATE
DEPENDENCY
A Novel of the Vampire Life

MICHAEL TALBOT

AVON
PUBLISHERS OF BARD, CAMELOT, DISCUS AND FLARE BOOKS

THE DELICATE DEPENDENCY is an original publication of
Avon Books. This work has never before appeared in book form.

AVON BOOKS
A division of
The Hearst Corporation
959 Eighth Avenue
New York, New York 10019

Copyright © 1982 by Michael Talbot
Published by arrangement with the author
Library of Congress Catalog Card Number: 80-69887
ISBN: 0-380-77982-x

All rights reserved, which includes the right to
reproduce this book or portions thereof in any form
whatsoever except as provided by the U. S. Copyright Law.
For information address John Brockman Associates, Inc.,
2307 Broadway, New York, New York 10024

First Avon Printing, March, 1982

AVON TRADEMARK REG. U. S. PAT. OFF. AND IN
OTHER COUNTRIES, MARCA REGISTRADA, HECHO EN U. S. A.

Printed in the U. S. A.

WFH   10   9   8   7   6   5   4   3   2   1

This book is dedicated to
Paul Van Antwerp,
without whose support, patient ear,
exchange of ideas and contributions
this book would never
have been written.

Table of Contents

"If there ever was in the world a warranted and proven history, it is that of the vampire."

—Jean Jacques Rousseau

Book One

Niccolo

I

When I was very young I had a vision of an angel, or at least I thought it was an angel then. My father was a physician, as his father was before him, and we lived in the very heart of fashionable London, in Mayfair, on Bond Street. Our house was a dark-brick Victorian terrace house with turrets and oriel windows and it surrounded an enclosed garden shared by the other terrace houses around the square, but closed to the street.

To the best of my recollection the incident took place in the spring of 1856, when I was seven years old. I was able to determine the date many years later because Queen Victoria had just visited the Paris Exhibition, and French bonnets placed very far back on the head had become the rage of the fashionable ladies of London. I had quarreled with my father, although I'm not quite sure over what anymore, and had run into the garden to collect my thoughts. The garden was a mystical place. To begin, the mere fact that it was completely cut off from the bustle of the street gave it an almost religious tranquillity. But it was the cool evening fog wrapping around the chestnuts and lilacs that completed the other-worldly atmosphere. It was here, beneath the huge wrought-iron astrolabe that stood in the middle of the court, that I first saw the angel.

I recall quite vividly that I was neither in any sort of reverie that might have evoked such a vision, nor was I given to even the vaguest religious thought at the moment. Instead, my mind was still reeling from the angry words of that argument long forgotten, when suddenly I realized there was a young boy standing before me.

He arrived so suddenly and quietly I scarcely would have noticed his presence had it not been for the slightest rustle of his black silk waistcoat. Naturally my first impulse was to run, but when I looked up and gazed at his face for the first time. I was entranced by his unearthly

3

beauty. He had a thin and delicate face with a fine straight nose, chiseled cheeks, and an angular chin. In fact, the delicacy of his features was so striking he might have been mistaken for a woman were it not for his masculine attire. The unsettling quality, a quality I later came to know as androgynous, was only heightened by his reddish-golden hair, which fell in small fleecy ringlets to his shoulders, gently framing that pale and fragile face. I must add that my first impression of this being was that he was a boy, but there was an ineffable something about his presence that suggested he was older, possibly seventeen or eighteen. Perhaps it was the dreamy and almost sad intensity of his immense dark eyes. Or perhaps it was the regal and deathly still way he held his head as he returned my gaze.

As I stood mesmerized by the stranger I slowly realized that I had seen his face before. However, there was something odd about this sense of recognition. I was certain I had never actually stood in the presence of the young man until this very moment. My recognition was more like the familiarity you feel when you see a famous person on the street whom you've only previously known from newspapers or daguerreotypes. And then it came to me—the long, curly hair, the pale, androgynous face. This was the countenance of an angel, none other than the angel in Leonardo da Vinci's *Madonna of the Rocks*. I knew it well for I had spent many hours standing in front of that haunting masterpiece in the National Gallery. The Virgin is depicted kneeling in a gloomy enclosure of jagged rocks with her right arm around the infant St. John the Baptist. Her left hand is extended protectively over the head of the seated Christ Child, before Whom John's hands are folded in prayer, and to the extreme right of the painting is a beautiful kneeling angel. The most disarming aspect of the London *Madonna of the Rocks* (for Leonardo painted two versions of the work—the second hangs in the Louvre) is that the entire landscape is pervaded by a ghostly and supernatural light. The twilight upon the pallid complexion of the young man created exactly the same effect, and I knew beyond doubt he was the angel in the painting.

I have no idea how long we stood facing each other.

Before any words passed between us the young man
vanished. In the dim and misty light of the garden I could
not tell whether he actually faded away or merely crept
into the shadows. If he did steal away by natural means he
did so with a skill and stealth unmatched by any human
being I had ever encountered. One moment he was there
and the very next instant he was gone. No crunch of
gravel betrayed his exit, no rustle of lilac.

I was so thrilled by the appearance of the angel I immediately ran into the house and made my way upstairs.
Without realizing what I was doing I burst through the
doors of my father's bedroom. The moment I stepped
inside, the impropriety of my deed dawned upon me and I
found myself confronted by all the overwhelming things
which comprised the presence of my father. My father's
bedroom was large and dark, save for a small circle of
light cast by the fireplace on the opposite end of the room.
The air was musty and cool, and heavy with the dry,
burned-cork smell of my father's Fribourg and Treyer pipe
tobacco. The walls were a dark reptilian green and
sparsely scattered with bleak and gray watercolors
painted by aunts in the Highlands, and a bed occupied
most of the area in the center of the chamber—an
immense dark bed, a monster, a tomb, shadowy with dusty
and ancient bed-curtains.

The first thing I noticed was that there were several
evening visitors in the room, old friends and colleagues of
my father. My father was ill and they often met with him
in his bedchamber. They either sat or stood around the
fireplace in casual but dignified poses. Some boasted gold
watch chains and others possessed huge beards, beards
like old Russian patriarchs. I always disliked my father's
friends. Like his bedchamber they stank of pipe tobacco.
They were always calm and smug and they greeted
everything with a sort of priggish amusement.

In the midst of the crowd loomed a chair different from
all the rest, a tall chair of elaborately carved black oak,
which enclosed its occupant like a huge seashell. The
chair was positioned with its back facing me, but through
its cabriole-leg hooves I could see the dark green brocade
pillar of my father's evening robe.

The group had been laughing, but after I burst in they

all grew silent and gazed in my direction. I padded across the room and stood before my father's green-robed legs. In the dark alcove of the chair something rustled.

"Step closer so I can see you," he said solemnly.

I obeyed.

As I took an intrepid step forward I became aware of another smell mixing with the heavy aura of tobacco.

"Closer still."

I moved into the very womb of darkness, just inches away from my father's cool presence, and the other smell enveloped my face like a warm mist. It was a different smell, not at all like old tobacco, or the distinctive animal scent of my father. It was oddly pleasant and I recognized the familiar aroma of red Bordeaux, an encircling fog of fine claret that often hovered about the darkness where my father sat. I noticed several of the men held large round glasses. Everyone was silent.

"Have you come to apologize?"

"No, Papa."

Nothing . . .

"I've seen—"

I cut off abruptly and gazed into the darkness. No eyes or face. No glimpse of large and powerful hands. Only the warm, wet fog of claret. And silence . . .

"I've seen an angel," I managed to blurt out.

For a long time there was no answer, and then, without a hint of emotion his voice asked, "Where?"

"In the garden. Beside the astrolabe."

Once again I stood in the stony presence of an unseen judge. I shifted my weight nervously and felt my palms grow damp. From the darkness one of my father's friends chuckled derisively and there was movement. Here a foot scuffed across the carpet. There a glass tapped against a table.

"And how do you know it was an angel?" my father asked dispassionately. "Did he have wings, and if he had wings, did he have teeth? Were they very large wings?"

There was more laughter.

"No!" I exclaimed. I proceeded to relate the entire incident. I breathlessly described the young man with exacting detail and explained how magically he had both appeared and vanished. I told him he resembled the angel in the *Madonna of the Rocks* and how unearthly the moonlight seemed upon his face. Indeed, I was so excited by the occurrence that I'm sure I glowed with the fiery conviction of the visionary, and when I finished there was an uneasy silence in the room.

With this Father quickly sat forward and for the first time his face entered the circle of firelight. He had a hard face, thin and drawn, with closely cropped white hair and a small, graying mustache above his solemn lip. He was handsome, but age crept in around the corners of his face. His eyes were pale, pale blue, almost gray, like drops of dew on the edge of a razor, and the heaviness of wine crept in his breath.

"There are many incredible things in the world," he said with slow and measured breath. "Dr. Livingstone's crossed the Kalahari. We can inject medicine beneath the skin with a hypodermic syringe and they've crisscrossed the country with railroads." He glanced around the room at his friends, seeing that they waited quietly for his judgment.

". . . but there are no angels."

I was stunned. I could scarcely believe that he was so blindly disregarding what I had seen, experienced. "No!" I cried, but my voice was quickly swallowed by the stale air and the crackling of the fire. Again there was an anxious silence in the room.

"There are no angels," my father repeated and finally broke the spell. I looked into his eyes. He gazed back at me. The greater will had won and the other men in the room began to chuckle once again.

"Admit it. There are no angels."

I burst into tears and struggled to shake my head.

"Admit it!" he repeated again, and slowly, agonizingly, I nodded.

I turned and quickly left the room as my father resumed his phlegmatic silence. The glass of claret lifted into the darkness.

Later that evening I managed to locate a book of my father's containing an engraving of the *Madonna of the Rocks* and I stared at it for hours. There was no mistake: The face of the young man in the garden was exactly the same, down to every last line, as the face in the painting. I

fell asleep that night telling myself over and over that I
had seen Leonardo's angel in the garden, but I never
mentioned the incident to anyone again.

II

In the years to come I learned that there were many more simple facts of life than the one my father tried to teach me that evening—that the sons of prominent physicians did not see angels. So many layers of Victorian propriety were placed upon me. So many rights and wrongs. I suppose you have to have lived in genteel society to understand how pervasive and intimidating all of its rules were. Veneer upon veneer of propriety. I believed in the rules because everyone else seemed to believe in them, until two very different people altered my faith in two very different ways.

The first, oddly enough, was the same person who had created my faith, my father. For a long time I respected my father. He was tall and stolid; without desires or complaints. I was hurt by his decisions and his cruelties, but I trusted that he knew more than I did.

One day I was playing outside the east room of the house when I discovered a small low window I hadn't really noticed before. Originally some sort of pipes had entered the wall through the opening, but now a small square of paper had replaced one of the tiny panes. Numerous layers of paint had made the paper hard and shiny like a lacquer box and on impulse I reached out to touch it.

I must have pressed too hard, for one of my fingers inadvertently poked through the surface. It was as thin and fragile as an egg shell and as I stepped closer to examine what I had done I noticed I had a clear view of my father's office from a vantage point about twelve inches above the tiled floor. Through the peephole towered glass cabinets of medicaments. There was a bent-wood hat rack with a white jacket hanging on it and a padded and buttoned black leather examining table.

To my surprise, as I watched, my father entered the room followed by one of his prim and stately Victorian patients, a woman with a bird on her immense hat. Her bodice and brown velvet jacket were tight and from her high collar and neck blossomed a cavalcade of white ruffles. Her deep maroon dress fell in voluminous tiers of lace and frills and the bulk of it revealed the presence of numerous petticoats and undergarments.

I would have turned away except that I knew Father was not going to examine her. Father never examined his female patients unless his nurse was present, and he had just sent the nurse to the chemist's.

The woman daintily stepped upon the metal footstool and when she did this I noticed she wore frilled pantalettes on her legs and tightly laced brown suede boots. She paused for a moment, gently lifting her skirts a little, and then she sat down on the table.

Neither she nor Father said anything.

To my surprise, Father seemed to be ignoring her. He busied himself from cabinet to cabinet, but when he turned back around his hands were always empty. Even when he approached her and briefly placed his hand upon her shoulder, he did not look in her face or speak. Then he clumsily dropped a small metal container on the floor and fell to his knees to search for it.

What happened next was very strange. Even though the metal container was in full sight under the table, Father continued to grope around as if he could not find it. He muttered something, and then, awkwardly, his shoulder became entangled in the woman's capacious skirts.

I watched terrified, hypnotized, as he grumbled and lifted one of her legs to free himself. The kind lady remained sedate through all of this, and gazed blankly off into space as if nothing were happening. Then he lifted her other leg and in a slow and breathless ritual he began to peel back her slips.

I remained frozen with uneasy fascination as he lifted each one of her petticoats. I was amazed, delighted, appalled, as layer upon layer of fabric was drawn back. And then, in the ample billows of her clothing, I caught a glimpse of sweated hair, and father's powerful hands on the inner surface of her pale, smooth legs.

He moved slowly, pressing in to the copious undergarments.

She continued to gaze off into space, oblivious.

They finished quickly and it wasn't until the woman stood to leave that I became aware of something else. Indeed, every time I returned to peer through the fragile hole in the egg-shell window I noticed it. It was faint, languorous, a gentle but oppressive whisper of my father's stale tobacco smell. It delineated his territory. It warned, like blackbirds impaled on a fence around a field of rye.

There is one other incident I always remember when I remember my father. It was a simple incident. Very simple. Just a fragment. It occurred one night when I was absentmindedly peering out my bedroom window and happened to notice Father rushing out into the garden. It was strange. I knew something was wrong because Father's shirt was unbuttoned and half off him. Throughout my entire life I don't think I ever saw Father with his collar button undone, let alone his entire shirt. Not only that, but he also seemed to be looking for something. He madly circled the astrolabe and searched the bushes. Had he imagined he'd seen something, something that had alarmed him? He turned about, clenching his fists.

When he glanced up past my window and I saw his face for the first time, I became truly frightened. It wasn't Father's face that I saw. There was something strange in his expression, something furtive and anxious, like an animal being stalked. The wind ripped at his shirt, and he struggled to stand against the wind as he continued to search, scanning the chimneys and the treetops.

Dare I consider it? Deep inside him had he always believed and feared? Was he looking for something, someone, he dared not admit existed? Perhaps he had imagined it. Seen a shadow. Watched a tree branch grow into a man. Whatever it was, it had triggered more than just alarm in Father. It had broken a wall, released a flood of dark and monstrous fears, and now as he stood there he was in momentary danger of being swept away.

It is Father's eyes that I remember the most. They were

wide and not quite human. And, yes, deep in those pale
and omniscient eyes was an unmistakable terror.

My father's facade of propriety taught me many other
things besides the fact that children don't see angels. Oh,
yes, it taught me the decorum required when dealing with
a viscount or a baronet to ensure their patronage, the
proper investments to make, how much money to donate
each year to the Salvation Army, and the discipline and
ambition to go on to medical school. In short, it taught me
everything necessary for material survival. For this I
thank him. But my father was so adverse to anything
outside the beaten path of tradition that his fear instilled
in me a constant watchfulness and concern. I was never
against going along with tradition and using it, but I
never wanted it to use me. I never wanted to be afraid to
do something because it wasn't proper and I never wanted
to forget the face of the angel.

My father died when I was in medical school and
although I loved him in a way, I have to admit a burden
was lifted from my shoulders. The huge Victorian terrace
house became mine and for the first time in my life I was
completely unafraid to enjoy myself. I suddenly found I
was an "eligible young gentleman," as the old matrons
put it, and not only that, but an eligible young gentleman
living in Mayfair. To comprehend the full meaning of this
you must understand that Mayfair was one of the two or
three most exclusive regions of mad and electric London.
Fashion was dictated from those narrow, twisted streets
with their dignified houses and vast, lugubrious blocks of
flats and ornate hotels. Even the very name of Mayfair
evoked visions of red carpets and hothouse flowers, of
parvenus and great courtesans, of ermine and white satin
and even whiter shoulders.

It was a wonderful time to be alive and made even more
wonderful by the fact that this was when I met my
Camille. If there ever was an exhilarating experience that
even came close to my vision of the angel, it had to have
been my first glimpse of Camille. To be quite honest I
have considered lying and saying that the first time I saw
her she was stepping down from some beetle-black four-
wheeled carriage in front of the Baron Alfred de
Rothschild's or the Maison Dorée, but truthfully, Camille

was what society of the time impolitely referred to as a
soiled dove, or an *houri*, one of the dark-eyed nymphs of
the Moslem Paradise.

I met her at a dance hall, one of the notorious night
houses of King's Road. She was a radiant creature with
auburn hair and raven eyes and the smallest, most
delicate hands I have ever seen. She reminded me of a
character created by Edgar Allan Poe, the American
poet so admired by the French: Ligeia...the lady
Ligeia, whose haunting face caused one to shiver with
the same luminous wonder as "the ocean...the falling
of a meteor...and the glances of unusually aged
people."

But she was not Ligeia. Camille was small and pale and
she drew one to her, but there was nothing deathly in all
of this. No, in fact Camille exuded life. She was always in
movement, dancing or rushing to see something. Even
when she paused for breath, there was a fire in her, and
beneath the carefully learned Victorian gestures and
expressions there glimmered something unspeakably
sensual. Camille was, indeed, an *houri*, but in the antique
sense. She was a rare flicker of life amid the dark and
shallow creatures of the London night. At once fragile and
wild, like a newborn colt. And yet, disconcerting, even
magical, like a haunted china doll.

In striking contrast to this was where Camille lived. My
memories of the place are fragmentary and troubled. Her
flat was above one of the night houses, with a narrow
gaslit staircase and peeling cork linoleum floors. There
was a rustling in the place and here and there a fragment
of muffled conversation. There was also a terrible smell, a
smell that might have been mistaken for an animal smell
were it not so distinctively human. It was an unpleasant
smell, but morbidly interesting in its human*ness*, like the
smell of childbirth only without chloroform or antiseptic.
Most repellent of all was Camille's dingy little room, and
here my recollection fades. I dimly remember only a brief
glimpse of a cot whose canvas was polished gray from use,
a shabby blanket.

I only mention these things to emphasize how unlike
Camille was from the squalor of her existence. She, too,
seemed to recognize this and there was something very

detached and innately aristocratic about her. I'm sure
Father turned in his grave when I married her.

It was not easy making Camille a lady of Mayfair. For
months we struggled refining her natural grace and
bringing out the inborn melody of her voice. Most
difficult of all was the myriad of incidental information
she had to learn to survive in society. There were rules of
conversation and certain table customs, operas to become
familiar with, and nuances of language. The Duchess of
Sutherland was wearing magenta to help the textile
workers, and so magenta was *distingué*. And everyone
must know the quadrille.

In an effort to enrich Camille's background I decided to
read various books and poems aloud to her. On one of these
occasions I chose a free adaptation of a work by an
eleventh-century Persian, *The Rubáiyát of Omar
Khayyám*. I had purchased the work in the form of an
anonymous pamphlet, but its imagery was being so
touted by the likes of Dante Gabriel Rosetti and
Swinburne that its translator, a Suffolk poet named
Edward FitzGerald, was becoming quite famous in
London.

On the occasion of my reading it we were in my father's
bedroom—or, rather, my bedroom, then. It was strange,
taking over the master bedroom. The burned-cork smell
was gone and the fireplace burned a little warmer. I also
kept the gas jets on just a little so that the place wasn't so
gloomy. But the huge green bed was still there, and the
watercolors painted by aunts in the Highlands, and the
foreboding seashell chair.

Camille sat stiffly in the window seat. She wore an
ample white nightgown, very frilly about her neck and
falling in voluminous pleats. Her auburn hair had just
been brushed out by her French servant and was
unusually full and wavy. There was something almost
animated about it, sinuous, like vines wrapping around
the base of a tree. Each rivulet of hair, each wave and curl,
caught the shimmer of the gas jets, bringing out a rich
copper color not always present in Camille's hair. Her tiny
white hands were folded motionless in her lap. Her face
was blank.

She was beautiful, but I have to confess she looked a

little silly. She was so small and frail she seemed lost in the immense nightgown, her small, round face a little overwhelmed by so much hair.

"Camille," I said. "I'm going to read you a poem."

"Go on," she said.

I cringed a little at her choice of words. "Please don't use that expression."

She drew in her breath and sat a little more upright. "Pray, read me a poem," she said in more rounded syllables.

"Much better," I commended, thumbing through the pages. I stood a few feet in front of her and held the book at eye level. I read her several verses.

I glanced up from the book. "Now, there, wasn't that lovely?"

Camille remained unmoved.

I read her another verse. I paused again to get her reaction, but she seemed more bored than appreciative. I was about to begin again when one of the gas jets in the room began to flicker and I crossed over to adjust it.

"No, leave it."

I turned toward her with pursed brows. "Why?"

"Don't you think *that's* lovely, just the flicker of the gas jet?"

"I suppose it is," I grunted and once again lifted the book to my face. But this time Camille quickly jumped up and snatched the book from me. She thumbed from page to page looking at each as if they were blank and there was nothing there to see. Suddenly, she returned her gaze to me as she assumed an expression that in time would grow all too familiar to me. Her head was tilted back. She regarded me with an air that for all the world could have been a silent, contemplative fury. Except that it wasn't. Or didn't seem to be. At least, Camille never followed it with anger, but usually some sort of mild agreement with what I was saying, a nodding of the head as if to say she had given in.

Her body acquired the same air. For a few seconds it was very rigid and tight. Her small hands seemed to press upon the book with unusual pressure. And then she came out of the spell, became a little dreamy and murmured, "It is very lovely."

"Come here, Camille," I said.

She took a step and the white nightgown caught around her feet. This made her very angry and she gave the gown a sharp tug. She sat down heavily beside me and once again seemed overcome and very small within all that white fabric. She might have remained ill-tempered from tripping in her gown were it not for the fact that she had once again been captivated by the flickering gas jet.

"Is anything wrong, Camille?"

She looked puzzled, as if honestly pondering the question, and then she pulled back the bedcover and slowly stroked the white linen. She smiled. "The sheets are so starched and white . . . too white." She looked at me and there was the devil in her eye.

"Come on, now. Are you teasing?"

"No, I'm quite serious." She regarded me with a quiver of amusement. She shifted in her nightgown, twisted and leaned toward me a little and as the fabric pulled tighter it revealed the delicate contour of a nipple. Also revealed was the pinkness of the aureole around it, distinct from the hidden white of her breast.

She looked down, slowly rubbed her hand over the nipple, pulling the fabric even a little tighter, and then gazed silently at me. She inched closer and once again became brooding. " . . . much too white," she said with a low and contemptuous voice.

And then, just as she was pulling the robe back over my chest, she laughed and pushed my leg off the bed. In a frenzy she tore back the bedcover and began loosening the sheets. As she darted about, her hair seemed especially dark and tangled and parts of her nightgown became translucent in the flickering amber light.

"Camille, what are you doing?" I demanded, but she ignored me. She gathered up the sheets and actually began to leave the room with them.

"Camille!" I shouted. I ran after her.

She fled down the stairs and hesitated at the front door. *No, she couldn't,* I thought, overwhelmed by visions of her bursting out into the street, neighbors and passersby aghast—a mad little wraith dressed all in white, holding the bottom of her nightgown in each hand and bundles of

bedsheets under each arm. Possessed, like one of the nuns
of Loudon. *No, she couldn't, mustn't!*

To my slight relief she glanced at me briefly and then
ran to the back door, sprinting out into the garden. She
rushed past the dark wet lilacs and I heard the familiar
creaking of the stable doors.

That was worse. Did she plan to ride out on a horse?

But when I arrived at the stable I found her engaged in
furiously rubbing the crumpled white sheets all over the
back of one of the deep brown carriage horses. The animal,
a young but gentle stallion, was frightened at being
plucked so rudely from his sleep and began to stamp and
snort. Camille was delirious.

I wanted to grab her, but I could not get near her for the
rearing horse. Then, just as quickly, she finished and
returned to the house. I caught up with her in the
entranceway at the base of the stairs. The sheets were
dirty and smelled of the stable, resinous and heavy. She
flung them out and bit my leg as she pulled me down into
the disheveled mass. I was filled with anger and
restrained myself from using my strength. The soiled
sheets were close around my face and I recoiled, trying to
shut out all awareness of the smell, the dense and
penetrating smell, but Camille was all about me. Just as I
was about to sit up she gently held a single hand,
outstretched, against my chest. The white nightgown
slipped from her shoulders and she was golden once again
in the faint light from the stairs.

III

We had been married a month when I read Camille the *Rubáiyát*. We did not know it then, but we conceived a child that night. We were much too concerned with other things to suspect it. I was busy fashioning Camille into a proper wife. It took another two months of rigorous drilling to separate the last wheat from the chaff. It is difficult to say how Camille felt about the changes she had to undergo. It was obvious she wanted to live up to my expectations, for she accepted the constant corrections of her speech and manners calmly and courageously, but I sometimes suspected she was enduring more of an inner struggle than she let on. She had lost a little of her effervescence. On occasion her smile seemed just a bit forced. Still, all things considered, she adapted to her new life with amazing facility.

Naturally, London society would never have tolerated such an intrusion of the classes, and so it was necessary to fabricate a mysterious past for Camille. There was a suggestion of a wealthy father dying when she was a child, an invalid and reclusive old aunt, an estate in Yorkshire. It was very simple, really, but quite expectedly Camille was uneasy. When at last the time came for our first social appearance I chose the Lyceum. I knew an evening at the theater would provide only brief opportunity for social contact and give Camille a chance to feel more at ease. Because of my overwhelming love for Camille I could not fathom that anyone would feel any differently. Camille did not share my utter confidence.

The moment we stepped down from the brougham I sensed her prickle. She tried to conceal it. She moved with grace. She smiled just enough, but there was a nervousness in her eyes.

I surveyed the crowd. It was typically genteel. The gentlemen all wore dress coats with black waistcoats, and very narrow, inefficiently tied white ties. There was a profusion of top hats and canes. The women, what few women there were—for society women attending the "legitimate" theater were the exception rather than the rule—all wore billowy evening dresses with very small, tight waists. At a distinct level of the crowd fluttered a handful of fans like so many cabbage butterflies.

I didn't see anything that should have caused Camille's apprehension. As we passed through the majestic gilt arcade of the Lyceum and into the lobby I spied one of my professors. He was a man named Hardwicke, Dr. Cletus Hardwicke, a piteous fellow. Polio had twisted his frail and diminutive little form into a most trollish figure. Through his thinning, reddish hair, freckles and age spots dotted his bulbous forehead, and his long, yellowed fingers bulged with veins. In his top hat and suit he looked like old Nick, and so he was in the lecture hall—a hellish professor, as feared for his vitriolic cross-examinations as he was esteemed for his knowledge. There was even a sort of a mystery about him. He always seemed to be up to something, although no one was quite sure what. For stretches of time he would spend every free moment in the library, but he never published, or revealed any fruits of his research. He had a habit of asking sudden odd and personal questions, but it was a credit to his discretion that no one ever apprehended why. On top of everything else, his private life was equally enigmatic. He was always seen gadding about, but never with friends or acquaintances. No one knew how he spent his leisure time.

When he spotted me he nodded and gave a brief smile. Restrained but cordial. When he saw Camille he nodded again. This first hint of acceptance by a stranger from my class calmed her a little, but a host of other worries plagued her. As we sat in our seats I noticed she was still shifting about skittishly and I asked her what was wrong.

"It's just very new to me," she said.

I looked around again and although I didn't notice anyone gazing at us boldly I fancied the eyes of the women in the crowd, and a few of the men glanced our way with more than chance regularity. Was Camille's paranoia contagious? Were these people really staring at us, or was I just imagining it? I tried to dismiss it, but the feeling persisted. The fans concealed, the monocles glinted, and like frogs nervously peeping out of water, heads turned and quickly looked away.

Why was it, I wondered, a lady of society could never be without her fan? To the Japanese the fan was the symbol of life. The rivet end was the starting point and as the rays expanded, so the road of life widened out. Thus fans were decorated with armorial bearings and the totems of families. In some strange way, the history and honor of ponderous generations were represented on those totem fans of the Japanese.

It was at the beginnng of the play, a performance of *Antony and Cleopatra,* that it happened.

Demetrius and Philo had just walked out onstage and as the royal couple approached with their band of eunuch attendants, Philo gave his opening lines. When he finished he gestured at Antony and his Egyptian queen and proclaimed: "The triple pillar of the world transformed into a strumpet's fool: Behold and see!" With that last line, every paper and ivory fan in the theater snapped shut.

It was a rude interruption, but who could say it wasn't just a coincidence, that there was a judgment in those fans?

Camille said nothing.

In the days to follow such occurrences continued to happen. An old matron would give a deadly smile. A carriage wheel would come just a bit too close to a puddle. Each time the action was indirect enough we could not be sure whether we were being overly sensitive, or whether somehow society was able to see through our ruse and chose to make their condemnations in hostile but subtle ways.

The most forward incident took place just two weeks after our evening at the Lyceum. It was at the reception of an opera singer given by one Lady de Grey in her Georgian home in Belgravia. The reception was the largest social function Camille and I had attended together. I don't remember the name of the opera singer (she was a massive German woman with hundreds of tiny scarlet ribbon bows encircling her immense white bosom like a wreath around a racehorse). I vividly remember

where the reception was held. It was in the conservatory
of Lady de Grey's stately home. Lady de Grey's conservatory was a sight to behold, a huge glass and white-
frame structure like a transparent miniature Gothic
cathedral. The floor was of white and black marble with
various tiers and fountains and pools inlaid with Florentine mosaic. Aside from a verdant jungle of palms and
ferns, one other type of plant dominated the wondrous
room, lilies. There were white lilies and moon lilies, and
most of all, orange and salmon-colored tiger lilies.
Everywhere and everywhere, tiger lilies. Clusters and
explosions amid terra-cotta *putti* and the trickle of a
dozen fountains. Tiger lilies.

After the old German opera singer finished shaking the
glass with her thundering arias, wispy cricketlike men in
black tails quickly clattered the chairs away, and the
orchestra turned to lighter music. The rapid strains of a
waltz swept through the room and the floor filled with the
élégants of London—whaleboned and waistcoated couples
spinning stiffly like so many music-box dancers.

Amid this stood Camille.

Camille was a ghost, a small pale vapor of a woman, but
in her pale peach evening gown she acquired a powerful
and beautiful presence. Her tight-fitting bodice revealed
what would later be known as the Edwardian Profile, and
years before her time she was not unlike that other
Camille, Camille Clifford, the famous Gibson Girl.

I recall Camille rushing weightlessly across the floor
and into my arms. She laughed, spun around. She was
becoming much stronger and more at ease in public.
"John?" she asked in a mock-innocent tone of voice that
was all too familiar with me.

I stared down into her dark eyes. "What do you want,
Camille?"

"Will you dance with me?"

"Camille, it isn't proper for a lady to ask a gentleman."

"Then you ask me."

I smiled.

"Will you ask me now?"

She was so exquisitely beautiful.

She raised her eyebrows hopefully, knowingly. "Will you
ask me in a little while?"

I smiled again and she read the message in my eyes.

"Very well." She lifted her dance card to consult her list of partners. "I've been asked by that jabbering old fool, Lord Langtry, to dance, and I'll dance with him first. But after I've danced with him, and perhaps the second cousin of the Duke of Marlborough, I expect you to seek me out and be a proper gentleman."

"Yes, Camille," I conceded.

And instead of laughing coquettishly, she dropped the silly girlish façade and tilted her face back in an expression that was frightening in its emptiness. The dark eyes leveled upon me, vacant and yet infinite. The mouth fell open to reveal a slight glimpse of small white teeth, a red tongue. The tongue moved ever so slightly in a gesture that was so suggestive, I blushed.

"Camille!"

She continued the silent gaze for a few seconds, like a snake captivating a sparrow, and then she came out of it, throwing her head back in her familiar flirtatious manner, as she laughed and resumed her former self.

She hurried off, her dress rustling upon the marble like a piece of paper in the wind.

In moments she had grabbed an old walrus of a gentleman—Lord Langtry, I presume—and went virtually flying around the dance floor with him amid the slow and surprised crowd. Apparently refreshed by the spectacle, the orchestra picked up tempo and a livelier waltz surged up through the room.

I have to admit, I was slightly embarrassed by Camille's behavior and I didn't notice someone had ambled up beside me.

"A gentle bird," a raspy voice murmured and I gave a start. I turned to see old Hardwicke standing to my right. His black coat, waistcoat, and trousers fit his deformed little body with perfect neatness. His white cravat was carefully tied, and his lavender-colored kid gloves might have adorned the hands of a clergyman. Since I had seen him socially at the Lyceum he had been just a little more cordial toward me in his lectures.

"Oh, I'm sorry. I didn't mean to frighten you."

"It's all right," I returned. "What was it you said?"

"A gentle bird," he repeated. "Pardon my saying so, but your wife is very beautiful."

"Thank you," I said, somewhat surprised at his friendliness.

With lurching movements Dr. Hardwicke lit a Laurens Egyptian cigarette and awkwardly circled around to my other side. He seemed very deep in thought.

"Where did you meet your wife?" he asked presently.

"I was introduced to her by one of my aunts at the Richmond Horse Show." The lie rolled glibly off my tongue.

"I see," said Hardwicke, impressed. "And after you graduate, you intend to set up practice on Bond Street?"

"Yes."

"Ah, good. You'll make a fine living for her following in your father's footsteps."

"Did you know my father?"

"I knew of him, a fine physician, a very successful physician."

"Thank you," I said, nodding.

Hardwicke gave a big puff of blue smoke and clicked his feet together. "Do you know what made your father such a successful physician?"

"What are you getting at?" I asked.

"Not that he wasn't a fine doctor, as I've said. But do you know what made him so successful as a society doctor?"

Images from the past swept through my mind. "Yes, I know," I said dryly. Hardwicke did not seem to hear.

"He carefully cultivated his clientele. He cultivated them and he pampered them."

"Yes, indeed, he did."

"And you must do that."

"What?"

"What I mean, my boy, is that sometimes you are going to have to be a hypocrite. You are going to have to lie and put up a façade because those people out there are going to be your future patients." He wafted a gnarled hand at the crowd. "Those people out there will be your bread and butter, my boy, and no matter what you feel inside, you are going to have to please them to insure their patronage."

"I understand," I said, smiling. I was amused because

Hardwicke was so smug and pompous about everything I imagined he must have given that little speech to a hundred former interns.

"Do you?" he said with a curious edge to his voice. I looked at him and for the first time I realized there might be more than boastful chitchat on the little gremlin's mind. He was clearly watching my reaction. I turned to the crowd. Yes, these would be my future patients, a very fat woman in white and covered with jewels; a man with a monocle and goiter. I turned back to Hardwicke.

"Yes. Yes, I do understand," I repeated, but Hardwicke only frowned and grew quiet.

Finally, to break the silence, I surveyed the room until I spotted Camille spinning about the dance floor. After exhausting the old walrus she danced with another gentleman, and then another. And each one, snatched out of his zombielike state by a whirlwind, seemed to enjoy being part of the spectacle.

The music-box dancers, however, did not. One by one they backed off the floor and gazed on with frigid disapproval.

"I think I should dance with Camille," I said and tried to pull away from Dr. Hardwicke.

"Nonsense, my boy. She's enjoying herself. And besides, I want to talk to you about something."

I glanced back at him.

"I've been thinking. I have a lot of work to do with both my research and my teaching. And, well ... I need an assistant. I was wondering if you might be interested. It would be very good experience; look very good on your record with the board of review—"

"I—" I began abruptly, wanting to jump at the chance. But then prudence demanded I maintain my composure. I was about to accept when suddenly I noticed Lady de Grey walking haughtily around one corner of the dance floor. Lady de Grey was a large woman, in her midthirties, and pretty in a sort of puffy way. She had blond hair meticulously styled with the aid of a pair of hot tongs and alcohol lamp into numerous rolls and side curls. She also boasted an aesthetic fringe of curls stuck firmly to her forehead with spirit gum. Her face was round and white, completely without makeup, and her lips were thin and

downward cast. Around her neck was a heavy malachite
necklace and she wore a shimmering green satin gown.

"I would be most happy to be your assistant," I replied,
and continued to watch Lady de Grey. She elegantly held
up the train of her gown as she stalked by Camille and
muttered something to her.

Camille, a dark fury, spun about and apparently
returned the insult, whereupon an audible gasp rose from
the crowd. Even the old walrus of a gentleman looked on
with indignant horror.

"—and you promise you will come talk to me about it,"
Dr. Hardwicke ended as I pulled away.

By the time I reached Camille's side a large crowd had
gathered around her. Before her stood Lady de Grey, and
the circle of onlookers tried desperately to maintain their
dignified air as they breathlessly ogled the two oppo-
nents.

"Mr. Gladstone," Lady de Grey said, turning to me, "I
demand your wife apologize."

"Well," Camille defended, "the kind and respected Lady
de Grey made a comment about my manner of dancing
and told me I was frightening other guests off the floor."
Her small white breast rose and fell rapidly. "I'm not
keeping anyone else from dancing."

A scornful murmur rippled through the crowd and the
female onlookers noticeably increased the flutter of their
fans.

"I—" I began. I looked at Lady de Grey, the carefully
groomed blond hair, the thin, cruel lips. The green satin of
her gown shimmered against her doughy skin. If she had
been a man I would have struck her. I looked at the
encircling crowd. They exuded an air of condescending
disinterest, but the fire in their eyes showed that beneath
their dignified exteriors they were as fascinated and
jeering as a mob in a Roman coliseum. I was about to
defend Camille when I noticed Dr. Hardwicke standing a
short distance away and watching attentively. A feeling
crept through me, the same cool emptiness one
experiences at the news of an unexpected death. He was
right. He was quite right. One day these gout-infested
skeletons would be my patients, my bread and butter, *our*
bread and butter. What sort of life could I provide for

Camille if I openly insulted them? It couldn't be, I thought to myself. Fate could not have designed a more hellish decision. I was wrenched. Something tightened in my throat. "My dearest," I said stiffly, "it is Lady de Grey's party. She has every right to make such a request."

Camille turned to me, stupefied.

Lady de Grey raised an approving eyebrow.

I thought, perhaps, Camille might understand, but she continued to search my face. I had never seen her look so hurt.

"Well?" Lady de Grey prompted.

At last fire rose up in Camille as she gazed at the hideous creature. "I'm sorry," she said unconvincingly. "I beg your pardon."

Lady de Grey nodded vaguely as the orchestra diplomatically began another waltz. As the older woman turned to walk away I detected something in Camille's eyes. Before I could do a thing she strode up behind the other woman and with the full of her strength gave her a mighty push and sent her tumbling into the fountain among the lilies and the terra-cotta *putti*. There was a mammoth splash followed by an astonished uproar from the crowd as they saw what had happened. As if following some secret stage direction the female onlookers were overcome with that most favorite of Victorian feminine afflictions, the vapors, and one by one began to faint into carefully chosen arms and couches.

For a moment I was entranced by the horror of the scene that was transpiring and when I turned once again toward Camille I saw that she had retrieved her wrap and was rushing toward the door. I followed after her and noticed Dr. Hardwicke standing near the door. His eyes were filled with sympathy. He nodded briefly as I left.

That evening Camille cried. I found her sitting curled up in the window seat of her boudoir, framed by the red velvet curtains, and wrapped only in a black embroidered shawl.

"Camille," I began, but then quieted as I sat beside her. After many long moments I whispered, "Is there any way I can ever make you understand I did it only for you?"

She shook her head and turned toward the window.

Outside, the huge elm tree brushed against the pane and
through the branches Orion's belt twinkled. A faint beam
of moonlight shone through the clouds and caused an
oblique shadow to fall over Camille's face and down her
slender neck. It neatly divided her cleavage into an area
of shadow and pearly white and for a brief moment I
fancied she was somewhere between two worlds—half
lady of society and half fairy nymph. I imagined her
among Moslem princes, dancing and laughing, and then
suddenly bound up by the corsets of my world.

A chill ran through me.

She turned and her expression was once again terrifying and vacuous. I stared into her eyes for many long
minutes.

"John," she finally said, "I can't bear it. I must be
myself." And with that she turned away. I left her quietly.

I had been asleep for several hours when I felt
something move across me. At first the presence was so
measured and snakelike I sat up with a start, but then I
saw her face in the moonlight. Dark hair fell about my
shoulders. The black shawl trailed softly over my arms
and enveloped me. Her hands kneaded my flesh and I
smelled her familiar scent. And then, for just a brief
moment in the moonlight, I saw the red tongue moving
serpentine, framed by the small white teeth.

Camille and I never spoke about that incident. From
that day forward without a word said between us, we
scrupulously avoided the subject and the necessity to
maintain a fiction regarding her past. We shunned social
events and took in few guests. It was Camille who
suffered most from this. I could tell she felt uneasy, bound
hand and foot by the seemliness of me and my world.

Dr. Cletus Hardwicke became most friendly toward me.
After lectures he would call me up to the podium to
commend me on my answers or the thoroughness of my
reading. When he saw me in the corridors he smiled and
always took the time to say hello. He did not mention the
assistantship and I assumed he was either deliberating or
had forgotten it. He was very kindly and I even grew to
suspect his interest was more than just professional, but
paternal in an odd sort of way.

One sunny afternoon and several weeks after Lady de Grey's party I passed by one of the lecture halls and recognized his familiar hunched form at the base of the steep and empty amphitheater. The amphitheater was a treacherous canyon of rickety seats, metal pipe railings, and porcelain-tiled walls. Sunlight flooded in the tall, narrow windows and brightly lit the chalkboard, the numerous immense and yellowed anatomical charts, and the seven grinning, partial, and complete human skeletons surrounding the main table.

Dr. Hardwicke sat on a high stool behind the table. He was surrounded by a number of alembics, beakers, distillers, and flickering Bunsen burners. A faint miasma of uric acid filled the chamber and on the table were several large metal enameled trays containing human brains and livers, kidneys, and stomachs. In very large trays were two human cadavers, one, the large gray corpse of a man, and the other, only a spinal column and pelvis, disarticulated at the neck and hip, with most of the flesh and internal organs removed and half submerged in formaldehyde.

"Dr. Hardwicke," I called from the upper door.

"Mr. Gladstone. Come down. Come down." He wafted his hand excitedly as I made my way down the precipitous steps. Have you come to talk to me about what I think you've come to talk about?"

I smiled. "The assistantship?"

"Oh, yes," he returned excitedly and I felt flattered he should be so happy about it. "I'm so busy, you know, there are many things you could help me with, my boy. Are you free evenings?"

"Yes."

"Good. Good. There's a lot of work to be done in the evenings. Of course, I must warn you, if you decide to accept my proposition and work for me, there will be many nights you'll have to work alone. Will that be all right?"

"Quite all right."

"Good. And you accept my offer?"

"Of course I do." I gazed warmly at the strange little man, marveling at his willingness to offer me such a precious opportunity. "But I must ask you, Dr. Hardwicke: Why have you chosen me for this position?"

The little man regarded me with a strange smirk. "Because I like you, my boy. Because I like you." He gave a throaty chuckle and slipped on a pair of rubber gloves. "How's Camille?" he asked abruptly.

"Camille?"

"Oh, excuse me. Mrs. Gladstone, I mean. For some reason I don't think of you and her according to your last names."

"She's quite fine," I said curtly.

Hardwicke grunted. "Quite fine, yes, indeed." And then he glanced at me and once again he was curiously amused.

I smiled, not quite understanding the joke and he drew in his breath.

"You ask me why I chose you?" he said and suddenly reached over and lifted the partial cadaver out of the tray. The smell of formaldehyde filled the area. "Because you're clever, my boy. See here. See this remnant of a human being. Trunk. What little soft tissue remains shows some putrefactive changes. Spine's been severed in the upper lumbar region. No rib cage. The entire pelvis is here and its organs, with the exception of the genitalia. Question: Is it a male or a female skeleton?"

"From the bone configuration it's obvious it isn't female," I said. "And besides, the amount of adherent prostatic tissue clearly reveals it's a male skeleton."

"Yes..." he said slowly. "The amount of adherent prostatic tissue. You see, you are clever." He glanced at the hulk of flesh and bone and back at me. "Can you tell me anything else?"

I leaned forward and scrutinized the mass. The formaldehyde caused my eyes to sting a little, but I tried not to flinch. I examined the rivulets of grayed flesh, the dull blue vascular bundles. It was a decaying hunk of meat, the ignominious remains of extensive dissections. It was the work of one of two possible perpetrators—medical students or wolves. Other than that I was at a loss as to what he was looking for.

"I'm afraid I do not see anything else, sir," I said reluctantly.

"Don't be afraid, Gladstone," he returned. "That's exactly what I was looking for. Outside of a limited number of possible chemical differences, there's nothing to distinguish this remnant from any other remnant. We're all the same here." His gloved hands squeezed the flesh like a sponge and little rivers of formaldehyde trickled between his fingers. "One cannot distinguish between the internal organs of a baronet or a beggar." He allowed the portion of spine and pelvis to slide back into their murky bath.

After that little exposition he ran through a list of duties and scheduled the evenings I would be working. My responsibilities consisted of various mundane tests and the tagging of anatomical specimens. When he had finished I said, "May I inquire, Dr. Hardwicke, does any of this have to do with your research?"

"No," he replied.

"May I ask what your research entails?"

He turned to me and his expression became utterly serious. "No!" he snapped. "I never divulge what I am working on." He continued to glare at me for a moment as if my question had been so improper he was considering some further reprimand. I was about to beg for pardon when, just as swiftly, his frown melted. "I'm sorry, my boy. It was a harmless question. Please excuse me for being so flammable." He smiled amiably and offered me his hand.

Word that I was Dr. Cletus Hardwicke's personal assistant spread quickly and I was soon the envy of my peers. Elder professors seldom took on such youthful assistants, and when they did it was a most prized distinction. It established reputation. I felt very warmly toward the strange little man for this. In the trial-by-fire world of academe, reputation was the most important passport.

True to his word, Dr. Hardwicke was often absent from his laboratory. I, however, was not. I often stayed well into the night and when I left, the streets were foggy and deserted. I did not mind. The stroll by the majestic pillars of the university was relaxing. The darkness was tranquil. Only the distant whistle of the commissionaires hailing cabs from the rank by the river disturbed the calm. It was often well past midnight when I got home.

It was one evening about a month after I had started
the assistantship that I found myself confronted with a
list of duties unusually long. I had not gotten much sleep
the night before and the prospect of staying up all night
was far from attractive. I hit upon a plan. I knew that Dr.
Hardwicke's first lecture wasn't until the afternoon of
the following day and if I returned early the next morning
I would have plenty of time to complete the allotted tasks.

When I arrived home unexpectedly, I discovered him
there in my house, dressed in his usual attire, the black
coat, waistcoat, and trousers. The white cravat carefully
tied. The lavender-colored kid gloves. He appeared to be
imploring Camille, hands outstretched in an entreating
gesture. Even more horrifying, there was a glint of
warmth in her dark eyes, a desperate fascination born of
her utter isolation and loneliness. She looked up blankly.
The twisted little man showed more surprise. Veins
bulged through his thinning, reddish hair. His face puffed
crimson. "Gladstone!" gasped the voice.

I was furious. I moved toward him, but in an instant he
was gone.

That night we fought as we had never fought. Although
Camille had no awareness of the incident, Cletus had
apparently seen her at one of the dance halls. Perhaps he
had hoped ultimately to blackmail her. I don't know. All I
knew was that he had visited her with intents of gaining
more than her favor. She had not succumbed to his
immoral entreaty, but the mere fact that she seemed to be
flattered by it, still took his hand warmly, sickened me.
How could she stoop to trifle with such a disgusting little
man? As soon as she had discovered his intent, why hadn't
she had him thrown out? My pride was hurt, but there
was more. I knew that she was faithful to me, but
somewhere deep inside I always wondered what she had
secretly wanted to do, what would have happened had I
not intervened?

After I left her I paced for hours in my room. I was torn,
torn because my intellect told me I had no right to judge
her. It was I who had brought her into a world where she
didn't belong. I knew what she was. I even understood the
starvation that had glimmered in her eye for a visitor, any
visitor, even that malformed and repulsive little

blackguard, but my emotions overwhelmed me. No amount of intellect could ever banish the pain that sprung within me. I was controlled by the pain. Whenever I recalled the image of his gnarled appendage reaching for her sweet hand... It was the pain that caused me to allow her to believe I blamed her when secretly I blamed myself.

That evening I also began to understand something that I had never quite understood before. I had always thought of myself as a sort of rebel against propriety. When society wrongly judged Camille I had always held her to my heart as an innocent victim. However, there were sides to my beloved, things that both allured and repelled, that even I could not condone. I was loath to admit it, but at certain times I found myself inextricably on the other side of the fence. There were certain issues in which she was quite blameless, but there were also certain issues in which she did stray too far from the norm. I thought I had hated propriety. I knew its hypocrisy, but at long last I realized I too had to believe there were things that simply weren't done.

It was well after midnight when I found myself standing before the elaborately carved seashell chair, listening to the echoes its darkness contained. And then, slowly, falteringly, I sat down, encompassed in the alcove of black oak. For the first time I felt oddly comforted by the chair, protected. My legs melted and became one with its cabriole-leg hooves. My arms sank heavily into the worn and polished hand rests. I don't know how many hours I sat in my father's chair.

From that day on I had as little to do with Dr. Hardwicke as possible. As might be expected, some contact with him was necessary, but I resigned my assistantship and shunned any contact with him that wasn't absolutely necessary for the attainment of my degree. Toward the end of our first year of marriage two things happened that brightened our world. I graduated from medical school and Camille gave birth to our first daughter, Ursula. From the very beginning Ursula was such a perfect child I often found it difficult to believe she was a product of the two of us. Not only was she even more

of a beauty than her mother, but also she was precociously
intelligent. By the time she reached fourteen, in a day and
age when young women were supposed to modestly
pretend not to know that animals were of different sexes,
Ursula had mastered French and Latin, learned to
recognize the major constellations and recite their myths,
and had raised two litters of champion whippets. As for
Camille, she was never truly happy, but the child helped.
As the years wore on Camille hid her discontent behind a
proper smile, and looked quite regal in her chinchilla
toque and her muff with a tiny bunch of violets on it.

It goes without saying I was pleased at Ursula's passion
for life, at her mettle and ardor. I realized she was far
from being the prim and delicate granddaughter my
father would have demanded, and this delighted me. At
the same time I was filled with a subtle and yet terrible
fear. When I searched myself I realized it was because of
my experience with Camille. My intellect told me this
was silly, but the feeling remained. No matter how hard I
tried to suppress it, every once in a while the poison would
leak into my veins and I would yield to a painful fear that
the child conceived on the night of the *Rubáiyát* reading
might somehow become "fallen" like her mother.

Two years before Ursula's coming-out party I accepted
a position on the faculty of Redgewood University
Hospital. For the first time in my life this afforded me the
resources to undertake the medical research I had
yearned to do for so long. During this period Camille also
became pregnant with our second child and it looked as if
everything was going right in our lives. It was in the
winter of 1887 that Camille became ill. There was an
influenza epidemic sweeping London, and when she
showed the first symptoms I put her directly to bed. I was
not worried at first, for Camille had always possessed a
strong constitution. She could dance all night if I would
let her and for the first few days those tiny hands gripped
the edge of the bed defiantly. But then meningitis set in
and my reserved concern became obsessed terror.

Memory of those terrible days is foggy. When I try to
recall them I see gauze-masked policemen in snow-
flurried streets, pots of eucalyptus boiling on the stove,
and Camille's sweat-beaded face, motionless in the deep

recesses of her pillow. Her fever raged. I went insane, cursing myself. It seemed the greatest irony that of all the occupations I could have chosen, I became a doctor and still was powerless to help her. At last the tiny hands went limp. It was only by performing a caesarean that I was able to save the child.

There are no words to describe the pain I felt. I'm sure I would have lapsed into shock if it weren't for the child. Because she was born two months prematurely it was necessary for me to keep a constant vigil over her and this, at least, kept me occupied. I named the baby Camille. She wasn't as striking a child as her sister, but I cherished her nonetheless. The first indication that something was wrong came when she was about ten weeks old and had still not learned to focus her eyes properly. Initially I attributed this to her prematurity, but her failure to register even the faintest hint of recognition when I held a candle up to her eyes revealed she was completely blind. At the age of two it became evident she was severely mentally retarded and incapable of all but the simplest of communications. Her only avid interest in the external world was a peculiar fascination for sounds. She would sit for hours listening to the cook shelling peas, or to the rhythmic clacking of the carriage wheels on the bricks of the street outside.

Although I have never told a soul, I was at first repulsed by Camille. Perhaps it was my grief and guilt, but I viewed her imperfection as somehow connected to the imperfection of that little man. I knew it could not possibly be, but some irrational part of me kept suggesting her mother's long-ago association with Hardwicke had somehow laid a blemish upon the child. Worse yet, even though she did not physically resemble her mother, there were times in her constant stupor that she struck the same vacuous expression that had so unsettled me about Camille. Was it fate? Was it cruel justice that I would come into the room and find her standing there in her white little frock and black knee-stockings, with her small pink mouth opened dumbly and her hazel eyes in that same vacant stare? It was coincidence, but it was her mother's gaze.

I could not be cruel to the child. I forced myself to show

this poor little creature the affection that innocence and
helplessness rightfully deserved, but it was a struggle.
Limited though Camille was in her reasoning faculties,
her acute hearing enabled her to recognize the weight
and rhythm of my step. Whenever I stooped she would run
and lovingly wrap her arms around me. The pressure of
her tiny hands against my back seemed more than the
pressure of a child's hands. There was a firmness in her
grasp, almost a passion that reminded me uncannily of
her mother. It took all of my will to conceal the uneasiness
the touch of those innocent little hands caused in me.

I only revealed my feelings once. It was late one night
as a terrible thunderstorm shook the house. Camille had
become anxious over the vibrations, and Ursula brought
her to my bedroom to be comforted. It was more than I
could take. The moment those helpless hands pressed
against my nightshirt—the nightshirt her mother had so
often pressed with her own tiny hands—my feelings got
the better of me and I lost my temper. I yelled at Ursula
and told her she could just as easily have comforted
Camille. It had never been my nature to lose my temper
and Ursula was stunned. That was the first evening I
became aware of the music.

I had just been lulled asleep by the storm when I was
awakened by the strains of a beautiful waltz. For the first
few moments I lingered on the edge of my dreamy state
listening to the music, but then my curiosity became
aroused. I did not recall owning a gramophone disc of that
particular waltz. I sat up in bed and listened. Against the
background of the storm someone was playing the piano. I
slipped on my robe and made my way to the upstairs
drawing room. I pushed the massive walnut doors aside.
The flashing of the lightning through the French
windows intermittently lit the room. There was no one at
the ornate gilt and rosewood pianoforte.

The mysterious music repeated. I heard it when I came
in late one evening, but by the time I ascended the stairs
it had stopped. I even heard it in the daytime. On one
occasion it met my ears when I was strolling through the
garden. I looked up at the French windows, but I could not
see anything through the glare.

One afternoon I was napping in the study when the

music began. There was no mistaking it. The muted tinkle was coming from the room over my very head. I rushed in my stocking feet to the upstairs drawing room. When I pushed the doors open my eyes were greeted with a miraculous sight. There, framed by the golden sunlight streaming through the French windows and seated at the gilt and rosewood pianoforte, was little Camille. The small china face looked up at me, the mouth agape. At first she seemed frightened, but when her large hazel eyes turned toward me and encompassed me with the infinity of their emptiness, I sensed a change in her. She was hesitant, but she resumed her playing. Her face remained blank and expressionless, but her small, delicate hands melted into the keys with such skill and emotion I was overwhelmed. I looked down at the hands.

The thin, rapid music filled the room. The waltz she played sounded familiar, and then it came to me. Cook often hummed it as she was working. Somehow Camille had memorized it and had learned to play it upon the pianoforte. Still overcome with amazement I placed a red wax disc upon the gramophone and one of Mendelssohn's simpler melodies from his *Songs Without Words* issued scratchily from the large horn. As soon as it had finished, Camille returned to the keyboard. Without hesitation she tapped out the plaintive melody precisely as it had been arranged in the recording. In complete awe I played a Bach fugue, and then a Mozart sonata, and each time she played them back, note for note, measure for measure, exactly as they had been written.

By some stupendous fluke of nature, Camille, the idiot child who could not perform the simplest of everyday tasks, possessed a genius for music unequaled by even the most accomplished virtuoso. Although she could not see to read a single note or even express the slightest comprehension of the word "music," it was only necessary for her to hear a composition once, any composition, and she could play it perfectly, with inspiring expertise. In psychological terminology she was what was known as an idiot savant, an individual who was retarded or subnormal in intelligence, but who possessed an incredible skill or talent in one specific area. Several of my colleagues urged me to put little Camille on tour and profit from this

talent, but I could never bring myself to exploit her. For
the first time in my life I realized I could not view Camille
as a deficient human being. She may not have been a
normal child, but a talent like hers belonged to no mere
mortal. In some ineffable way Camille was very special.

In time, my repulsion for Camille, for that poor, sweet
child, began to fade. Instead of the empty infinite, I began
to see innocence in her face. I grew to love the child with a
love I would never have thought possible. As I worked I
would find myself thinking of her face. It was not a
striking face. It was plain. Her eyes were ashen. I would
find myself smiling when I thought of how her chestnut
hair curled around the tiny, perfectly formed little ear. It
might have been the face of any urchin on the street, soft
and round, unmarred by experience, a simple face plucked
from the ocean of children, and yet it was captivating
merely because it was a child's face. I took her frequently
on walks. I held crickets to her ear. Slowly, cautiously, I
abandoned myself to the haunting touch of her hands. In
time I even grew to look forward to her artless embraces,
the pressure of her fingers against my back. I comforted
her when it thundered. I warmed beneath her touch. It
was her only expression outside of her music. Her hands.

Understandably, Ursula was surprised by my change in
attitude toward little Camille. Ursula never mentioned it,
but I could tell she was mystified by my conversion. She
did not seem jealous. Indeed, it was often I who was hurt
by her aloofness and independence. In time she grew
accustomed to my new closeness with Camille. Only once
or twice did Ursula's gaze reveal that perhaps she was
hiding something, that she was a little more deeply
affected than she let on by my special love for her sibling.

IV

These were the events that shaped my character, and the events that left me on the doorstep of something I was not quite prepared for. I did not know it then, but the series of occurrences that followed would ultimately change my life. After Camille's birth *Haemophilus influenzae* became the consuming passion of my life. I spent all of my free time either in my office at the university or in the laboratory I had set up in my home. I was obsessed with deciphering all the intricacies of the killer and had published several papers on the subject. The success of the experiments that followed these papers was so promising I was certain I had made an important scientific breakthrough. I was keeping all of my newest work secret because the project had become a very personal vendetta with me. I didn't want anyone to beat me to the discovery of a cure and this was becoming a growing fear. Since the epidemic many of the senior faculty at Redgewood were concentrating their efforts on *influenzae* and several of them had hinted they were making dazzling discoveries.

It was shortly after Camille's fifth birthday that a most disconcerting thing happened. One of the older faculty members at Redgewood, a Dr. William Chiswick, announced at a trustees' meeting that he had made a great discovery and was going to publish his findings within a very short time. For several weeks the university buzzed with anticipation, but when Chiswick was approached concerning his coming revelation he became irritable and strangely apprehensive. He had the locks changed on the door of his office and even had wire grates placed over the windows. When more time passed and he showed less and less inclination to release even the tiniest bit of information, the trustees became nervous. They approached Chiswick, but this only caused his peculiar paranoia to rage completely out of control. The next night

he took a hammer to all of his equipment and tore his
office to shreds, burning every file, book, and paper he
possessed. And then, strangest of all, he vanished,
completely, and after following every lead Scotland Yard
could offer no explanation for his mysterious disappearance.

A rumor spread about the hospital that Chiswick hadn't
actually made any discovery, and rather than admit his lie
to the trustees, had destroyed everything. Those of us who
knew him found this hard to believe. William Chiswick
was a very respected physician. The notion that he would
end his illustrious career in that way was out of the
question. Something very strange had happened, but
certainly something that was no stranger than the
incident that befell me scarcely a week later. It was a very
rainy and cold spring night in April. I was riding in the
brougham along Coventry Street on my way to the
hospital when suddenly I heard the horses rear up, and
the carriage careened to a stop.

"What's wrong?" I shouted, pounding on the glass.

"I've 'it 'im," the driver stated breathlessly as he
jumped down from his seat. I wiped the steam off the side
window and peered out. There, lying facedown on the wet
cobblestone, was a man in a blue evening coat with gilt
buttons sparkling faintly on the sleeves. I quickly stepped
down from the brougham and raced to his side.

"What happened?" I asked the driver as I examined the
man. His dark trousers were sticky with blood. I could see
that both of his legs were badly broken.

"He just stepped out of the shadows," the driver
returned. "I tried to swerve to miss 'im, but he must have
fallen under the wheel."

I shook my head as I carefully turned the man over on
his back, and it was then that I saw. It was he, the young
man, the angel from the *Madonna of the Rocks.* There was
no mistaking the pale, angular face and the reddish-
golden curls. What was most startling of all was that
although forty years had passed since I had first seen him
in the garden, he still possessed the face of a young man
only seventeen or eighteen years old. I hesitantly touched
his cheek to see if he were real. My shock must have been
written all over my face.

"What's wrong?" the driver asked. "Do you know 'im?"

For a few moments I remained silent, filled with disbelief, and then I nodded. "Yes, I know him."

The driver helped me place him gingerly in the backseat of the brougham and we sped on to Redgewood. After we arrived at the hospital I searched the young man's pockets in hope of discovering any clues to his identity. All I found were several crisp hundred-pound notes, a small vial containing a fragrant oil, and a gold pillbox containing a number of shiny black pills. Because of the severity of the fracture it was necessary for the nameless young man to undergo surgery, and this I insisted upon performing myself.

Under the bright lights of the operating table I examined him carefully. His hands were as sleek and youthful as a child's. There wasn't even the vaguest hint of a wrinkle upon his smooth face. When I saw this, I realized it was impossible that he could be the same young man I had seen in the garden. I dismissed the resemblance as an uncanny coincidence, but I remained captivated by the haunting familiarity of his face.

As I began to set the bones I discovered the cause of the young man's pallor. His blood was more of a straw color than red. It was apparent he was in the last stages of leukemia. His pupils were also so incredibly dilated I suspected he had very recently used some sort of atropic drug, perhaps cocaine or belladonna. When I had completed the operation I accompanied the intern as he wheeled my strange young patient to a private room.

I remained by the young man's bedside for the next three hours, partially out of a sense of responsibility for the accident, and partially, I confess, because his resemblance to the angel still held me transfixed. When he finally stirred from his slumber I almost froze with excitement. I grabbed his hand and patted it gently. "Don't worry. It's all right."

His grogginess faded and he stared at me questioningly.

"You're in safe hands," I continued. "There was an accident. You walked in front of my carriage. The driver couldn't stop."

"I remember everything distinctly, *signore*," he stated with a thick Italian accent.

"Your legs were pretty badly broken," I went on. "I spent almost two hours operating on you."

"How convenient to have stepped out in front of a physician," he returned as his eyes searched the room. "Where is my evening coat?"

I pointed to the chair by his bedside and he reached into the pocket. He withdrew the gold pillbox and placed one of the shiny black pills in his mouth.

"May I inquire as to what those are?"

"No," he stated simply as he swallowed the pill without water.

"Are they for your—" I hesitated "—are they for your leukemia?"

"You mean, are they morphine to ease the pain from an advanced state of Virchow's leucocythemia, characterized by the abundance of white corpuscles in my blood?" he questioned dryly.

"Why, yes," I said, marveling at his technical grasp of the disease.

"No," he answered again. I straightened slightly as he stared directly into my eyes. Once again I was struck by the familiarity of the very tilt of his head. The manner in which he pursed his brow made me realize he knew I was examining him closely. "You are very anxious about something, *Dottore*. What is it?"

"What makes you think I'm anxious?"

"The rapid beat of your pulse in your temples."

I nervously allowed one finger to brush against the side of my forehead. "You're very observant to notice that."

"You have not begun to imagine how observant I am," he replied. "For example, I can tell you that they are mopping the floors directly above this one. I can smell the carbolic acid, and the fumes are coming from above, from the transom, not from beneath the door. From the gait of their walk and the pressure of their footsteps I can tell you a woman is in the room directly to the right of us, a very old and frail woman, and to the left a rather heavy man is deep in slumber." Then, with a strange melancholy, the young man withdrew the vial of aromatic oil and flung a few drops into the air. The room became perfumed with a sweet and pungent odor.

"Whatever are you doing?" I asked.

"It's oil of lily and palm," he explained. "I can smell death in this hospital. I can smell death very close by. If I were to venture a guess I would say that the heavyset man will die within a day or two. The lily and the palm represent death. I always sprinkle a little of this oil when I know that death is very close."

I shivered a little at the young man's ghoulish eccentricity when his penetrating gaze once again caught my eye. "But tell me, *Dottore*," he continued, "why does your pulse beat so rapidly when you look in my face?"

"It's nothing," I dismissed.

He continued his icy stare.

"Well," I conceded, "it's just that very long ago, when I was a little boy, I once met a young man who looked very much like you."

"How long ago?"

"Almost forty years."

He chuckled slightly. "Well, it couldn't have been me then, could it?" Without waiting for an answer he threw the bedsheets back and deftly lifted himself up against the headboard. "Would you be kind enough to get me a wheelchair so I can get out of here now?" he said as he struggled to control a grimace of pain.

"Where are you going?" I asked incredulously.

"I don't know," he returned. "I have no home or friends in London, but it would be completely out of the question for me to stay here tonight."

I was a little taken aback. "But you must stay here; in fact, you must stay here for many nights to come. I told you, your legs were very badly broken and you'll be very lucky ever to—" I stopped myself short.

"—ever to walk again," he filled in and laughed a light and airy laugh. And then, with a voice so wrought with self-assurance it frightened me, he said, "I'll walk again."

"Yes," I returned. "Perhaps you will, but nonetheless it would be completely impossible for you to leave the hospital tonight. You must stay in bed."

At this the young man became visibly upset. *"Per piacere,"* he pleaded, "you don't understand. I cannot stay. You just don't understand!"

"I think I do," I said and he eyed me suspiciously. I held the lamp up to his face and he uttered a little cry as he covered his eyes. "You're afraid you won't be able to continue your habit. What was it, cocaine?"

He glared at me. "If I stay you must make perfectly sure no sunlight comes into this room."

"I'll make sure the blinds are kept drawn—"

"—not enough!" he snapped.

"I'll have the nurses put sheets over the windows. We do that with patients who are acutely sensitive to light."

"No!" he shouted and gripped my arm. "Boards!"

I regarded him sternly. "My good fellow, I think putting boards over the window is a little extreme. I guarantee you, we can keep out all of the sunlight by simply nailing a few bedsheets up."

"Lei non capisce," he said as he sank back heavily into the bed. "It is not because of any cocaine habit that I am so against staying here."

I looked at him inquisitively. "May I inquire as to what it is then?"

His expression became deadly serious. "My dear *Dottore,* if you have ever believed anyone, you must believe me now. I am not safe here. People fear me and if I am forced to stay here very long they will begin to hate me."

"What reason do they have to fear you?"

He shrugged. "Because I am different, I guess."

"Come now—" I began, but he only shook his head with solemn resignation.

"Trust my words, *Dottore.* Watch and listen very carefully, and you will see for yourself." With that he ended and drifted off into a troubled silence.

I was struck by his words. I was still convinced he was using some drug that dilated his eyes and suspected his worries were no more than eccentricity and perhaps momentary confusion from the shock of the accident. Nonetheless, the gravity of his expression moved me, tugged at something deeper than my proper and traditional common sense.

"Do you have a wife or family I should inform of your accident, or any other affairs I should handle for you?"

"No," he sighed, "there's no one."

I nodded. "In that case, I think you should be getting some rest now. I'll look in on you tomorrow afternoon to see how you're doing." As I turned to leave I remembered one more thing. "I'm sorry, in the excitement of your waking up I completely forgot to introduce myself. My name is Dr. Gladstone." I smiled at him once again and he nodded slightly. "Could I inquire as to what your name is?" I prodded.

"Niccolo," he said, and a faint flicker of pride spread across his worried face. "Niccolo Cavalanti."

V

When I left Mr. Cavalanti's room that evening, curiosity
possessed me to check the occupants in the rooms on
either side of his. I was impressed to find there was,
indeed, a frail and elderly woman in one of them and a
heavyset man deep in slumber in the other. I was not
surprised when I mounted the stairs to the third floor and
was greeted by the fresh antiseptic smell of carbolic acid.
So he was right in these matters, I thought to myself. He
was a very keenly observant young man, as he had said.
But what I did not know at that time was that he was also
very correct about people fearing him. I saw to it that no
sunlight came into the room, as he requested, and this in
itself created a certain degree of notoriety. But what
really set the sway of opinion against my ethereal young
acquaintance was that he refused to touch a drop of food
or drink. Whenever a meal was placed before him he
would inhale the aroma of each dish carefully, as if
absorbing some nourishment from the vapors, and then
push the plate aside without touching a thing. After
three days of this absolute fast he had developed quite a
reputation among the internes and staff of Redgewood,
and not a favorable reputation at that. For some reason his
odd habits were interpreted as sinister and malevolent.
The nurses on duty started avoiding his room, and a low
form of gossip began, alleging that he was *different*.

At first I greeted this chatter as ridiculous. When I
confronted Mr. Cavalanti on the matter he insisted he
never ate. I humored him in this assertion and took it as
another example of his eccentric paranoia, but as the days
of his fast continued, and he revealed no sign of weakness
or deficiency, even I became suspicious. On my way to
Redgewood one afternoon I paid a visit to the National
Gallery, and when I set eyes on the frail and delicate
being seated beside the Virgin, I felt a cool chill of
adrenaline rush through my body. There was too much

coincidence, I told myself. Had I encountered a being who was truly of a different substance, a different vibration? Had my carriage actually injured an angel?

By the seventh day of Mr. Cavalanti's fast the entire hospital was in an uproar. By some stretch of the imagination he might have remained unharmed by his abstinence from food, but everything medical science taught us said he could not have survived that long without water. Disregarding normal body functions, even the amount of water lost through the lungs in every exhalation of his breath should have left him dangerously dehydrated. Such a loss should have resulted in an abnormal thickening of the blood—what little of it Mr. Cavalanti had—and cyanosis, a bluish coloration of the skin caused by lack of oxygen in the blood, should have set in. Nonetheless, Mr. Cavalanti did not suffer from cyanosis. He remained as anemically pale and animated as ever.

I begged him to take some sustenance, or to allow me to have him fed intravenously, but he adamantly refused. With this I was left with the choice of either putting him under sedation, or allowing his deadly fast to continue. It was a decision I found impossible to make. To put him under sedation I would have to use force, and I could not extricate myself from the fear that perhaps this was the wrong thing to do. After all, his metabolism obviously was very different, and he already had survived an impossible seven days. If I did give him an injection, would I be saving a strange young man from his own madness, or if he was something unearthly, a being with a more sublime body structure, would our coarse and material medications rip through his veins like molten lead? I found myself trapped in an insurmountable state of indecision, a state that my colleagues neither understood nor approved of. There was talk that I was flagrantly ignoring my responsibilities as a physician in catering to Mr. Cavalanti's "condition," and I became more and more uneasy about the possible consequences of this disapprobation.

On the morning of the eighth day when I entered Redgewood I discovered a name on the assignment sheet that filled me with panic: Hardwicke. Dr. Cletus Hardwicke had nobly assigned himself to this case. The audacity! I was outraged. Fate had assigned us to the same institution, but we avoided each other like old tigers. After all these years why should he suddenly want to confront me? I rushed to the second floor. As I neared Mr. Cavalanti's room I noticed that the door next to it was open. Inside was a figure draped in a sheet. The heavyset man had died.

Outside of Mr. Cavalanti's room itself a small group of nurses and internes had gathered. As I struggled to push through them I became aware of the sickening odor of paraldehyde. My alarm increased. Before I had a chance to reach the door I rushed headlong into the bloody little man. It was the first time in many years I had had occasion to scrutinize him so directly. Age crept in his ugly features; his thinning, reddish hair was streaked with gray, brown spots dotted the bulbous forehead. Bluish veins embroidered his fingers. His brow was bushier, and his eyes, even more piercing.

"Why?" I demanded as I took his arm and pulled him away from the door.

At first he was frightened, but when his gaze met mine he calmed. He knew me all too well. He knew I was not capable of violence of any form. As we stared at each other that same familiar and inscrutable amusement drifted into his expression.

"Gladstone," he said placidly, almost amiably.

"Why have you seen my patient?"

"I thought it best."

"I smell paraldehyde."

"We tried to put your Mr. Cavalanti under sedation."

"Tried?"

"It's the damnedest thing, Gladstone," he said shaking his head. "I've never seen anything like it before."

I watched his face closely. What was he up to? What was he orchestrating now?

"After three internes and a nurse struggled to hold that young man down I administered enough paraldehyde to knock out a man twice his size—"

"And?"

"And he got awfully sick, but after he finished coughing and retching he just sat there and looked at us,

cursing in Italian and saying we were fools." He shook his
head.

"Why were you giving my patient paraldehyde without
my permission?"

He regarded me with surprise. "Your patient? Dr.
Gladstone, all I know is that there's a young man in there
who hasn't eaten in eight days, and if you weren't
considering intravenous feeding, somebody had to." He
looked at me incredulously. "But come now, John. That's
not the point. I gave that young man enough paraldehyde
to knock out a man twice his size. Do you hear me? Twice
his size!" Something fanatical glimmered in the eyes of
the little man before me, something that for the slightest
mote of a second seemed to overwhelm even him. He
ruffled his feathers as if once again regaining control.

The internes nearby shifted nervously.

Dr. Hardwicke glanced at them and then back at me. I
could see in his expression that he was not dismissing
what he had just witnessed, a medical enigma of no small
import. He was much too clever to allow a flare of human
irrationality to jeopardize a situation pregnant with as
yet unknown possibilities. He looked again at the internes
watching and judging our every word. His smile returned.
"... but come now, Dr. Gladstone, you seriously wouldn't
allow a patient to continue to refuse intravenous feeding
without prescribing paraldehyde yourself, would you?"

"Well ..." I stammered nervously. Of course I objected,
but the last thing I wanted Cletus to know—anyone to
know—was the fantastical belief I had allowed to take
root in my mind. It was impossible, but for some unknown
reason something within me asserted with increasing
conviction that there was a linkage between the angel of
my childhood and the helpless creature in the room
beyond. It was not out of any fear over my own future and
reputation that I wanted this absurd and desperate notion
concealed. It was concern for him, the boy.

Hardwicke looked at me searchingly. "Something
strange is going on, isn't it?" His voice was self-assured,
but I could tell he was merely fishing. "How much do you
know about this Mr. Cavalanti, anyway?"

"Nothing."

"Well, people just don't exist without food."

"Obviously not, Dr. Hardwicke. He must be secretively obtaining food and water—his secrecy due to his psychological condition. I have not previously prescribed paraldehyde because I never seriously entertained the notion that Mr. Cavalanti had survived eight days on absolutely nothing." I looked at the internes and the nurses. My vision returned to the little man. "In the future I will thank you to follow respected and ethical medical procedure and consult me before you administer any treatment to one of my patients."

With that I finished. Several of the internes began to nod slowly, appeased for the moment by my explanation, but Cletus simply glared. He had no retort, but he had read the meaning in my pause. He knew I was hiding something. I could feel his eyes burning into the back of my head as I turned the doorknob in its brass collar and entered the room. As usual the blinds were drawn and several bedsheets stretched tightly over each window kept all but a faint hint of sunlight from entering. According to Mr. Cavalanti's directions the room was illuminated by two or three dozen candles arranged over the tables and ledges. It gave the room an almost ecclesiastical glow and in the midst of the flickering golden light rested the boy. Nature could not have chosen a creature more diametrically opposed to the man I had just left. The boy's gentle face was flushed and beaded with perspiration. His hair was disheveled. An acrid trace of paraldehyde still lingered in the air.

He gave a terrified start as I entered and then sank back heavily against his pillow. "Oh, it's you," he gasped weakly. "I'd thought you'd forgotten about me."

"I would never do that," I said quickly. "I'm so terribly sorry about what happened."

"I told you! I knew I shouldn't have stayed here." He turned toward me desperately; his eyes flashed. "Do you know how awful it was, me being helpless while those men held me down, and that little gremlin came at me with his furious eyes?"

For a moment I imagined this fragile boy thrashing wildly as the internes surrounded him, the candle flames flickering in the commotion. I could see Dr. Hardwicke hobbling about, leering with the satisfaction that he was only doing his duty as he plunged the hypodermic down and the angel emitted a pained and agonizing cry.

"What will the paraldehyde do to you?" I asked inquisitively.

"What does it do to you?"

"It would make me go into a very deep sleep."

"It has made me sick, but I will not sleep."

I nodded as I approached the bed and began to undo his bandages. He drew back at first, but then he huffed and relented. As I removed the gauze I discovered with a mixture of awe and expectation that the flesh had already bonded together. Miraculously, the discoloration had already started to fade, and only a faint pink line remained where I had made the incisions. "And the bones?" I asked.

"They have already set," he replied. "It will be a day or two before they're healed completely, but I could walk on them if it meant my life." He fumbled for the gold pillbox and popped one of the shiny black pills into his mouth.

"You won't be very safe here after this incident," I conceded. "As soon as my colleagues ponder the implications of your surviving their massive dose of paraldehyde, they'll be back. A few of the more noble ones might bring needles and scalpels, but most of them—" I stopped abruptly as I heard the floorboards creak outside the door. I imagined Dr. Hardwicke just happening to drop a cigarette near the keyhole and stooping to pick it up. My young friend glared intently at the open transom.

"Most of them will be medieval," he said in a hushed and distraught voice. "You don't know how they'll be, but I've had to deal with this sort of thing before. Anything that people don't understand, they fear, and anything people fear, they hate. You'll see a side of—" He was becoming so anxious and frightened I had to gesture for him to be quiet.

He lowered his eyes as I walked over to the night table.

"I'm a transgression," he continued as he shook his head slowly and drifted off into silence.

While he was distracted in his thoughts I carefully slipped one of the black pills out of the little gold pillbox and placed it in my pocket.

"Niccolo," I said abruptly. He looked up at me, his eyes

wide and curious when he realized I had called him by his first name. "Are you sure your legs are healed enough that you could walk a little?"

He nodded slowly.

"Well, then, when I come back on my evening rounds," I whispered quietly, "I'll bring you one of the interne's uniforms. At ten o'clock sharp the nurses change shift and for a few moments no one will be paying much attention to your door. If you slip out then I'm sure you could make it to the back receiving door undetected."

He gazed at me unbelievingly as I sketched him a map of the hospital.

"I'll have a carriage waiting for you there," I ended. "Do you think your legs are strong enough for you to make it that far?"

He nodded yes.

I shook my head with amazement. "Even if you do arouse a little suspicion, no one would dare consider that the unusual young patient in room 214 could be walking on his own accord for many months to come." I glanced once again at his legs.

"Dottore," he said incredulously, "why should you alone be so different? Why are you doing this for me?"

"Let's just say I'm trying to make some amends," I returned as I stood to leave. I reached for his hand and he drew back reluctantly, as if for some inexplicable reason he did not want me to shake it. His eyes met mine as I clenched his hand reassuringly. The poor dear boy was so flushed with worry his hand was actually cool to the touch.

That afternoon I went to a chemist's I frequented on Piccadilly, and waited for the tall, thin wren of a fellow to come from the back room. The shop itself was dark and brooding with walls cluttered to the ceiling with boxes, bottles, and apothecary jars filled with every imaginable pill and tonic. A row of stuffed birds lined the perimeter of the ceiling, and two immense mirrors in Chinese frames behind the counter gave it an illusion of space.

"Good day to ya, Dr. Gladstone," the shopkeeper greeted when he appeared. "Peevish weather we're havin'."

"Peevish, indeed, Mr. Sedgemoor. I wonder if you might oblige me in a rather unusual request."

I laid the shiny black pill on the counter. "One of my patients is taking this medication, and refuses to tell me what they are. I was wondering if you could try to track it down for me?"

"There won't be any problem in that, Dr. Gladstone," he replied. "Of course, if it's a home remedy and not in any formularies, it might take a couple of weeks to test it."

"Whatever," I returned. "Just get in touch with me as soon as possible."

He smiled and slipped the pill into a small brown envelope as I turned and left the shop.

The evening was warm and muggy and midge swarms hovered in haloes around the gas lamps. I drove the brougham myself so that it would not be necessary to fabricate any explanations for my driver. I did not want anything surrounding Niccolo's escape to lead to me. I know I sighed with relief when I saw the white-coated figure walk carefully down the steps, and I caught a glimpse of the shining face in the lamplight. The ride to Bond Street was uneventful.

When we finally reached the house I led Niccolo directly to the study, and he sank heavily into one of the two padded and buttoned black leather armchairs in front of the fireplace. Even though he remained silent I could tell he was carefully scanning the details of the room. The walls were of black paneling, and a deep scarlet Axminster carpet covered the floor. Huge aspidistras towered everywhere, and dark walnut bookcases shimmered in the light of the fire. A gilt pendulum clock upon the chimneypiece ticked loudly under a glass dome supported by a red, plush-covered plinth, flanked by two other domes containing carefully mounted African grasshoppers. In the corner by the door sat my desk cluttered with papers and inks, and between the chairs by the fireplace was a huge mahogany table containing an epergne, a pair of wine coolers, candelabra, and innumerable salvers, mugs, coasters, goblets, and other silver articles covered with *repoussé* work.

I poured Niccolo a cognac without stopping to think

that he never drank, and he accepted it greedily, rolling it slowly in the snifter as he savored the aroma. "Ahh, brandy," he sighed. "It has been so long since I've sniffed brandy."

I poured myself one and sat down in the chair opposite his when suddenly a rustling in the corner caused Niccolo to lurch forward in his seat. "It's all right," I said as a brown, furry creature crept out from behind one of the aspidistras. "It's only Deirdre, our hedgehog."

He eyed me inquisitively as the little animal nosed along the baseboard and waddled out through the partially open door. "She eats beetles," I explained, and Niccolo sank back into his chair. "Many English households have them."

After many long moments he finally stared directly into my eyes. "Signore Gladstone, I . cannot express enough gratitude for your assistance, but I must ask you again: Why did you do it?"

"Help you escape?" I replied, and contemplated the question for a moment. "I suppose I did it because you were in trouble. You were quite right: People were beginning to fear you, and besides, what is that old saying? Be not forgetful to entertain strangers, for thereby some have entertained angels unawares."

The faintest hint of a smile crossed his face only to be crowded out once again by his continued uneasiness. "Is that the only reason, because you think I'm an angel?"

I took a long sip of my cognac before I answered. "I have to admit that you pique my scientific interests as well. I mean, the fact that your metabolism heals itself so miraculously fast is of more than a little interest to the physician in me. And, of course"—I hesitated—"I want to know why you haven't aged a day since the first time I saw you."

"Signore Gladstone," he said chuckling evasively, "I have no memory of this meeting. And, besides, how can you be so sure it was me? How long did you say it was? Almost forty years ago?" He continued to laugh quietly, and sniffed the brandy again, but still he did not drink it.

For the first time I grew uneasy, even frightened in the young man's presence. I stood up and got a large red book bound in Russian leather from one of the walnut cases,

and quickly thumbed through it. When I found the
engraving of the London *Madonna of the Rocks* I offered it
to him. He hesitantly accepted it. "It's no coincidence," I
said once again, gazing intently into his dark and
deceptively innocent eyes. "Every line, every delicate
contour is exactly the same." I leaned closer and placed
my hand upon his shoulder. "I helped you escape, Niccolo.
The least I deserve is to know who and what you are."

At this he hissed the same outraged hiss of a cat before
it strikes, and pounced upon me. It was then, as the
terrifyingly angelic face was only inches from my own,
that I saw he had filed the canine teeth on either side of
his mouth into points. "You're such a fool," he shrilled,
and although he had not touched his drink his breath was
warm and moist with brandy. He continued his exhala-
tions slowly, even passionately, as his lips drew close to my
flesh.

I screamed and struggled to escape, but the slender and
frail hands held me with unusual strength. Then, as
suddenly as he had leaped up from the chair, he threw me
down and walked over to one of the windows. "Aren't you
going to run now?" he asked bitterly.

I gasped and tried to compose myself. "Why should I?"

This remark startled him greatly. "My teeth! Look at
my teeth!" He stepped forward and opened his mouth,
revealing the teeth he had filed down.

"Why on earth would you do that to yourself?" I asked
as I stepped forward and scrutinized them. They had been
filed into tremendously sharp points. Moreover, they must
have been abnormally long to begin with, for they
protruded a good eighth of an inch below his other teeth.

I might have been mistaken but he seemed amused. I
reached up and gingerly touched one of the canines,
making sure not to puncture myself. As I slowly withdrew
my hand I recalled the peculiarities of his metabolism, his
refusal to eat, and his miraculous ability to heal. A
shudder passed through me. "You're awfully strange," I
said.

"Stranger than you suspect."

I chuckled. "What are you, a vampire?"

He smiled.

I felt as if all of the wind had been knocked out of me by

a heavy blow. Every fiber of my being doubted even the remotest possibility of such a preposterous notion and yet at one and the same time I realized it was absolutely true. "Am I in danger?" I asked.

"You are in the presence of the vampire!" he hissed and began to pace furiously.

I wanted to run but I summoned all of my courage and remained. "But am I in danger?" I repeated.

At this his expression softened, and he regarded me imploringly. "Couldn't I have taken you in the garden? Or couldn't I just as easily have killed you now?" He shook his head sadly. "Signore Gladstone, I have never had any intentions of ever hurting you. Indeed, I have given you a trust that I seldom give any human being. It is very rare for a vampire ever to reveal himself. It is too dangerous."

"Then why are you confiding in me?"

"Because you are different from all others," he answered. "In you I sense a curiosity, even an admiration. You knew I wasn't human. You knew it in the hospital, and yet you had compassion instead of ignorance and fear. But tell me, Signore Gladstone, now that you know exactly what I am, what are you going to do about it?"

"I don't rightly know," I returned. "You're not well enough to be put out on the street, but—" I stopped abruptly.

"—but you have your family to think about."

"My two daughters are away visiting, but they'll be home in a couple of days."

"*Mio caro*, Dottore Gladstone, you are so naïve. Do you think vampires are so crass as to go around biting children?"

I blushed. "Isn't that what people say?"

Niccolo folded his arms indignantly and sat back down in his chair. "That's what the rabble says. But what does the rabble say about medicine, about disease? What superstitious prattle circulates about anything that people don't understand and are afraid of?" He paused and reached for his cognac. "That isn't to say that there isn't a basis to the legend. We do subsist primarily upon blood, but we don't just go around leaving conspicuous marks on random necks. That's dangerously flagrant. It starts panics and witch-hunts, and innocent people end

up with silly things like stakes in their chests. The first
law of survival in the world of the vampire is never to
attract attention, and besides, we don't have to worry
about where we get what we need. There are many
individuals who offer themselves freely to the vampire."
There was a rustling and we both noticed that Deirdre had
once again entered the study and was nosing along the
baseboard. A large wood spider scurried out and she
gobbled it up greedily. Niccolo chuckled and swirled the
golden liquid around in his snifter as he continued to
inhale the bouquet. "Oh, no, there are other things that
the vampire is much more concerned about than blood."

"And what are those?" I asked, returning to my chair.

He smiled. "Well, first there's pleasure and the delights
of the senses. The older you get the more you realize you
should drink life's liquors before the cup goes dry, as
friend Omar puts it. Once you're no longer afraid of dying
and not getting into heaven you become numbed with
abandon. Yes, pleasure is always a concern, but come now,
Dottore Gladstone, you're an intelligent man, can you tell
me what the most important thing is to a vampire?" As
he regarded me the firelight made strange patterns upon
his face. "Think about it. If you were a vampire, what
would you feel? What would be important to you after you
watched the entire folly and pageant of humanity pass
before your deathless eyes? Well, I'll tell you: You would
soon realize that being a vampire is a very special thing.
Of course, at first it's frightening because you've been
taught you're one of the undead, a monster. But then you
realize you've changed in ways that don't seem monstrous
at all. Yes, your metabolism becomes so refined that you
can digest only blood, and that may seem a little
monstrous, but there are many wonderful things as well.
Your senses become incredibly acute. You can smell what
kind of hard rock candy a child has in his pocket, and you
can sense the heat of a man's footprints hours after he has
paced a carpet. You no longer get colds in the winter, or
sneeze from the goldenrod, or get cholera when an
epidemic ravages everyone around you. And when you get
hurt, your wounds heal as if touched by saints. Cuts don't
bleed and scars fade like mosquito bites. And you know
what else?" His voice lowered to a reverent hush. "You

can see many things other men don't see. You can watch the sharp lines of cliffs grow soft, religions that people once died for, die themselves and be forgotten, and great cities rise and fall, for you see, my dear Dottore, you never grow old.

"Now contemplate that, Dottore Gladstone. What would be important to you if you had all the advantages of being a vampire, and you realized you were immortal? Not blood, or helpless young women wandering into dark old castles. Knowledge would become your Holy Grail, knowledge and all the learning you could glean about this phenomenon we call humanity, about a universe awesome enough to create such a thing as a vampire."

After many long moments of silence I shifted my weight excitedly in my chair. "Is it you, then? Are you the angel in the painting?"

Niccolo drew in his breath very slowly, and then nodded. "I was the model who posed for the master, Leonardo."

To my amazement his confession didn't surprise me in the least, and I realized that I, or some part of me, had known how old Niccolo was from the very first time I set eyes on him. As I glanced at the smooth, youthful hands I noticed all of his cognac had evaporated, and I proffered him more. He accepted it eagerly.

"Were you a vampire when you knew Leonardo?"

"Oh, yes."

"Was Leonardo a vampire also?"

"No."

"How did you meet him and what was he like?"

"Our meeting was planned," Niccolo said, and paused before he added, "by Lodovico."

As he murmured the name I thought I noticed an almost imperceptible trace of sadness in his voice.

"You see," he continued, "I am not the only vampire. There are many others, and many of them are much older and wiser than I. The oldest and the wisest one I've ever met was Lodovico." Niccolo tilted his head back against the chair as he gazed dreamily off into space. "Ahh, Lodovico," he sighed. "What do I tell you about Lodovico? He was as mysterious as he was overwhelming. Not only was he as clever and conniving as a pope, but he was wealthy and dashing as well. All of the young women of

Florence were in love with him, not to mention a number
of the young men.

"At that time Lodovico was obsessed with discovering
what he called the enigma of the vampire. What did the
existence of vampire mean? Were we devils? Were we
genetic mutations, or were we some strange and
mysterious facet of that entire collective organism we call
humanity? Lodovico became convinced we were some sort
of evolutionary experiment being performed by the
collective being of the race, and set out to discover clues to
substantiate this theory. In the incredible genius of
Leonardo he discerned, perhaps, another evolutionary
mutation. That is why he planned our meeting. He knew
Leonardo was very fond of beautiful young men. Lodovico
wanted me to allure him, to be accepted into his
confidence so that I could observe him. However, as with
all of the missions Lodovico sent me on, the aesthetics of
our meeting had to be striking, even surreal. This was
intended to disconcert Leonardo, and keep him on
unsteady ground so there would be less of a chance of his
figuring out our meeting was anything other than
accidental.

"He was a very young man then," Niccolo continued.
"He had just moved to Florence from his father's house in
Vinci, and had been accepted by the workshop of the
master, Andrea de' Cioni Verrocchio. It was at that time
that he also expressed his first interest in detailed
anatomical studies, and joined the physician's guild of St.
Luke. As a member of this guild he was afforded access to
the morgue in the hospital of Santa Maria Nuova, and
was able to perform extensive dissections of the human
body.

"On one of the evenings Leonardo was planning to visit
the morgue, Lodovico managed to dispose of the cadaver
intended for his dissection, and I took its place." Niccolo's
voice became oddly passionate. "I still remember the first
thing he murmured as he lifted the sheet and found me
resting motionless on the slab. 'Amantissimo,' he
whispered, 'most beloved.' I scarcely breathed as he gently
caressed the musculature of my ribs and shoulders. His
long, thin hands carefully examined every bone and
ripple, and finally, almost hesitantly, he allowed a single

finger to brush across my lips. Then he stood admiring me
for many long moments. It was only when he finally
picked up the knife and touched its cool blade against my
flesh that I sat up quickly, feigning terror.

"That's how I met the master, Leonardo. I told him that
the last thing I remembered was being thrown from a
horse, and that I had no memory of who I was or how I had
gotten there. He cursed himself for nearly destroying me,
and took me back to his single room over Verrocchio's
studio. He wanted to employ me as a model, but I told him
I could never visit him when the sun was shining. Of
course, this puzzled him greatly, but he respected my
wishes. And so, night after night, he would sit in the
moonlight for hours scratching his red chalk over vast
sheets of yellow paper.

"I learned a lot about Leonardo for Lodovico, particu-
lars of his diet, how many hours a day he spent on his
work, and even the time between each beat of his heart.
However, it was his accomplishments which most
impressed Lodovico, for Leonardo had an energy that
would take most mortals many lifetimes to develop. In
time Lodovico decided to do what he chose to do only a few
times throughout his long life. He chose to make
Leonardo a vampire."

Niccolo gazed directly toward me. "You ask me what
Leonardo was like," he said abruptly. "Well, I'll tell you
what the most uncontrollable force in his life was, what
feeling dominated his every unguarded moment. He was
tortured by his passions. He never once repeated the words
to me that he had whispered when he thought I was dead."

With this last remark Niccolo drifted into a lengthy
silence.

"What happened?" I finally interrupted. "Did Lodovico
turn Leonardo into a vampire?"

"No," he replied. "I'm afraid other circumstances
intervened. You see, at that time in Florence the Ufficiali
di Notte e dei Monasteri, the ruling council, had
instituted a system of anonymous denunciation to control
vice. In front of the Palazzo Vecchio there was a box
known as the *tamburo,* in which anyone could anonymously accuse anyone else of any crime, and the mere fact that
the accusation was placed in the *tamburo* meant that it

was automatically brought to trial. On April 8, 1476, an accusation was found in the *tamburo* accusing four young Florentines of pederasty with a seventeen-year-old model. One of the four Florentines was listed as Leonardo, the son of Ser Piero da Vinci, living in the house of Andrea del Verrocchio." Niccolo paused for a moment before he added, "And I was the young model."

As I finished the last dregs of my cognac I noticed Niccolo glancing apprehensively toward the crack in the curtains. "I must leave before dawn," he said suddenly.

"Don't worry," I returned, "I'm watching the clock for you."

He fidgeted nervously.

"It's still several hours before the sky begins to get light," I continued. "You must tell me what happened to Leonardo."

"He flew into a rage, of course, and threw me out the next time I visited. He returned all of my letters, and even pretended not to know me when we passed one another in the evening streets. As for the *tamburo* incident, his accuser never showed up in court, and consequently Leonardo was exonerated. Nonetheless, the allegation insulted him deeply and he never forgave Florence for that libelous observation of his personal life."

"But who made the accusation and why?"

"Can't you guess?" Niccolo asked somberly. "It was I. You see, being a vampire is a very difficult thing, for in the eyes of humanity you are forever more something to be feared and loathed. The accusation in the *tamburo* was a test designed by Lodovico. Obviously, if Leonardo was so vulnerable to public opinion, it would be impossible for him to withstand the abhorrence the rabble directs against the vampire."

He once again glanced uneasily toward the curtain as he stood and crossed the room. "There's not much more to tell. I ended my evening visits to Leonardo and this seemed to be quite all right with him. Indeed, I thought he had completely forgotten me until I saw the *Madonna of the Rocks*. So he did remember, even captured the bluish tint of the moonlight in the first version of the work. He made me, *amantissimo*, an angel, but he refused ever to set eyes upon my face again."

"But now, Dottore Gladstone, I must end my revelation. I'm afraid the hour is growing too late and I must leave before dawn."

I paused for a moment, considering the situation. "No, Niccolo," I said. "I can't let you leave. I'm sorry if I insulted you, but you must forgive my fears. I've never had to deal with a vampire before. If I have your sincerest word as a gentleman that you'll never harm either me or my two daughters as long as you remain in my house, I would like you to stay as my guest."

His expression softened. "You would not tell anyone about me?"

"You have my word."

"I must have a room with total darkness."

"I can close the shutters in the guest bedroom and put heavy velvet curtains over the windows."

He walked toward me and gently gripped my arm. "And why would you do all this for me, Dottore?" he asked.

"Can't you figure that out for yourself?" I retorted. "You have the metabolism of a superman, and you ask a physician why he would want to have you as a guest in his house or give himself a chance to observe you?"

He smiled and nodded. "You are like Lodovico, always wanting to figure out the enigma."

He allowed me to put my arm around his shoulder. "That is very true, Niccolo," I said as I walked toward the door, "but I don't want you to think I view you as merely a medical curiosity. I do not fear or hate you. I want you to know that I am your friend."

He continued to smile, but I noticed a trace of sadness in his expression. "I believe you, Dottore Gladstone," he murmured softly. "I only fear that you will find it difficult to remain my friend—"

"No," I interrupted.

He shook his head. "You may be above the mistrust and the venom now, but few mortals ever really trust the vampire. Perhaps it is a part of the aura we exude, perhaps it is a part of the enigma. In any case, I have never run into a human who has ever trusted me completely."

"And do you ever give anyone reason to mistrust you?" I asked falteringly.

"I don't believe I do," he ended as I turned out the light. "But then again, I didn't believe I had given Leonardo any reason." As I shut the door to the study I noticed Niccolo was secretly observing my reaction out of the corner of his eye, but when I turned in his direction he once again lowered his head disconsolately.

"We shall see," I murmured half under my breath as I led him toward the stairs.

VI

That evening I lay awake in my bed, unable to sleep. My mind was in ferment. Just a few rooms away slumbered a boy, wayworn as the humblest traveler. The air around him was cool. He would leave the white cambric sheets as cool as he found them. Was this the creature who had inspired the blood-sucking demons, the Ekimmu, of the ancient Assyrians, the decomposed and taloned ghouls of the medieval bestiaries? Or were vampires, indeed, the victims of superstition, mortals who had undergone some unknown but natural process? I, like most of my colleagues, was a scientific positivist at heart. If vampires existed, there had to be an explanation, a physical mechanism, and it was the dazzling implications of this thought that obsessed me as I drifted into sleep. It was during the last few hours of the early morning that I awoke in a cold sweat. Gripped by an inexplicable terror, I slipped on my robe and made my way to his room. When I cracked the door he was sleeping peacefully, curled like a child beneath the coverlet.

The next day when I went to Redgewood I checked in on Niccolo as casually and normally as I always did. It was with a smug and concealed satisfaction that I ran into one of the nurses and allowed her to tell me breathlessly how the mysterious Italian gentleman had faded into thin air without a trace. "It was vedy odd," she said, pausing with strange delight over the phrase. "Vedy odd." He would have to have been moved out in a wheelchair or stretcher, but the floor matron had noticed nothing. A young man with two broken legs certainly couldn't just walk out on his own accord, could he? I shook my head with perfunctory amazement.

I saw Cletus only once during the morning. We spotted each other at opposite ends of one of the corridors and both stopped dead. First, we looked each other straight in

the eye, but then we glanced away sheepishly. Neither of
us revealed anything in our expressions.

As the day wore on I continued to disavow any
knowledge of the "enigmatic Italian gentleman," but
thoughts of Niccolo kept reeling through my mind. What
would I tell Ursula about Niccolo? Camille would accept
his presence as quietly and obliviously as she accepted the
world. Ursula, however, would not be so detached. Not only
would she think I had taken leave of my senses, but also, if
I did convince her, would she be thrown into a panic? If
she grew accustomed to the fact, would she ever be able to
contain such an incredible secret? Would she be able just
to shrug it off when one of her friends asked about the
handsome young gentleman staying at our house? Or
wondered why he's only seen at night? Or why he never
takes his meals with us? To be sure, thinking of a suitable
subterfuge to tell Ursula would be difficult. My only
comfort was that I could put off the task for several days.

Other questions took precedence. I wanted to know
more about Niccolo's Renaissance mentor, Lodovico, and
whether he had ever discovered anything about Leonardo
or the condition of vampirism. On my way home from
Redgewood I stopped at a book dealer and purchased
several books on vampirism.

I sat reading them before the fire in my study.
Something brushed against my leg and I noticed it was
Deirdre. I gently lifted her up into my lap. She went limp,
pretending to be dead. I turned her motionless little body
over and tickled her stomach. She maintained her deathly
repose.

"Good evening," Niccolo greeted as he paused in the
open door.

"Good evening," I said. "Did you have a good"—I
stopped and checked myself before making the error—"a
good day's sleep?"

Niccolo smiled. "Oh, yes." He gazed at little Deirdre for
a few moments as he shifted his weight. "I was
wondering, Dottore, I am really so tired of being locked
up. Would you be interested in going for a little stroll?"

I was stunned. "Do you think your legs are well
enough?"

"It might have to be a very short walk."

I nodded as I gently placed Deirdre on the floor. As Niccolo moved away I observed his gait. He did not limp, but there was something most peculiar about his movements. I had never seen anything like it. It was neither feminine nor masculine. It was different, a subtle, almost weightless undulation. I wondered if it were due to his injury, or if it were a movement peculiar to the vampire. I went to put on my Wellingtons.

It was raining, a fine, light mist, and the slippery granite paving stones shimmered in the light of the gas lamps. The streets were pervaded with the brown, dun-colored fog of London. After some time we passed through a Georgian building, and we could hear the pigeons cooing uneasily in the wrought-iron balcony as we walked beneath it.

"I'm interested in something," I said as a black hansom sped by us and we had to step out of the way. "Did Lodovico ever figure out the enigma of the vampire?"

"Alas, no," Niccolo replied. "He could find no mythological or physiological reason. But the fact that he could not discover such reasons only made him continue to believe that we are the product of the collective soul. However, he didn't pursue this theory very much after I met him. Other things intervened."

I glanced at him inquiringly.

"The Medici," he explained simply. "You must understand, the Medici was a very special family. In a time when most wealthy merchants were bringing in cargoes of spices, almonds, and sugar, Cosimo de Medici, the *pater patriae,* was sending scribes to Greece and Alexandria for manuscripts. Lodovico was delighted. The patronage of the Medici was the first time since antiquity—since the burning of the library of Alexandria—that the human race revealed any interest in the awesome erudition of the past.

"And so Lodovico arrived in the Medici court one day, pretending to be a mortal scholar interested in reviving the ancient learning. It wasn't long before the dazzling and mysterious young nobleman became a confidant of Cosimo, himself. He encouraged him to found a group of study known as the Platonic Academy, and once again the classics were read and discussed. If you look through the

old records today you might still find the name of
Lodovico." Niccolo wiped the rain off of his neck as we
passed a strumpet in a green alpaca skirt and a black
straw bonnet trimmed with beads. She clutched her black
cloth jacket with an imitation fur collar as she eyed us up
and down. Niccolo tossed her a disdainful glance as we
passed.

"After Cosimo died, Lodovico instilled the same love of
the past in Cosimo's grandson Lorenzo, Il Magnifico, and
together they would put on huge festivals, or *trionfi,*
dedicated to literature, poetry, and love. Leading artists
were engaged to design the chariots and costumes, and
Lorenzo himself composed the music. At the height of the
carnival a cavalcade of garlanded floats representing
mythological events, accompanied by processions of
beautiful maidens and richly garbed youths on prancing
steeds, came over the Ponte Vecchio to the spacious
square before the cathedral.

"Ah, Florence," Niccolo said, drifting off into a
daydream. "How many times I wandered down its ancient
and twisted streets lined with countless artists'
workshops, glassblowers, and goldsmiths. How often I was
lulled by the musky scent of horses and the pungent smell
of bronze being cast. It was the Renaissance, and Florence
was the throbbing heart.

"It was shortly before one of these carnivals, when I
was seventeen years old, that I first set eyes on Lodovico. I
was walking through the streets one evening at twilight
when Il Magnifico came riding through on a glorious
chestnut Arabian stallion and called out to me. I
recognized him immediately. He was an ugly man, with
swarthy skin and a large, flat nose that overhung his
upper lip, but his presence was electrifying. 'Signore,' he
said, 'my friend thinks you have the countenance of an
angel and we most humbly request that you participate in
the pageant we are organizing.'

"It was then that I noticed the second man accompanying him. He was tall and handsome, with dark hair and
delicate androgynous features . . . and such eyes." Niccolo
shuddered. "If you ever meet Lodovico you'll see what I
mean. His eyes sometimes seem to vanish in their very
sockets, and all that's left is darkness. In Italy we have a

word for that, *jettatura*, or the eyes that transfix. They're terrifying, and yet they seduce you, and once you've heard the foggy laughter that comes from that beautiful face, you remain a prisoner of those eyes.

"Lodovico wanted me to be one of the Greek gods on the floats and I agreed. The evening came, we mounted our perches, and across the Ponte Vecchio the horses dragged our barques. It was at the height of the carnival, when the bonfires were burning bright and the wine and the sounds of the crowd formed a hypnotic farrago that I felt Lodovico's cool hands upon my naked back. His breath was cold upon my neck, and the tiny pinpricks of pain I felt melted into a pleasurable dizziness as he caressed my shoulders. Ahh, what an infection," Niccolo purred as he tilted his head back into the mist, and his face was momentarily lit by the aureole of a nearby gas lamp. "What an insensate bliss."

Suddenly we heard the sound of muffled shouting coming from a narrow alley, and Niccolo turned with obvious curiosity. "A shilling on the little blighter!" cried a rough voice, and there came the sound of raucous laughter. The alley, which stood beside a blacking factory, was dark and cluttered. It exuded a heavy smell of rotting punk and mackerel, and only a faint light gleamed from a basement grating at the far end. I was about to walk on when I noticed Niccolo carefully sniffing the air.

"Do you smell it?" he asked.

I reluctantly inhaled, and detected a faint trace of another odor. "Gin?" I returned.

"No, not the gin. There's another smell, even fainter."

As I started to take another breath Niccolo vanished into the darkness. The gilt buttons on his evening coat twinkled faintly as his silhouette approached the grating. When I caught up with him I saw that the basement room was full of people. Most of them were ragged and coal-smudged, but there were a few incongruously fashionable gentlemen scattered among the riffraff. They formed a circle around one mangy brown-and-white terrier who was delicately licking a small gash on its leg. A trickle of blood showed up vividly against the white fur.

"That," Niccolo hissed as he flared his nostrils. I realized he was staring intently at the wound. For a brief second I caught a glimpse of his fangs as the corners of his mouth twitched excitedly.

"Another shilling!" shouted one man as he waved the coin above his head.

A low murmur ran through the crowd as a decrepit old man came hobbling in with a filthy burlap sack slung over his back. His greasy white hair was tucked haphazardly beneath a tight flannel cap, and his protruding chin was covered with a gray stubble. A trickle of tobacco spittle ran through his broken teeth. It was only after several seconds that I realized the side of his sack was moving as if a thousand tiny feet were squirming and kicking to get out.

With a raspy crackle the old man suddenly flung the contents of the sack on the floor, and half a dozen rats scattered as the terrier let out a savage growl. Most of them hovered about the edge of their enclosure, but one unusually large rat froze when it saw the terrier and bravely stood its ground. It was obviously an old rat, with most of its tail and part of its hind leg missing, but it bared its long yellow teeth with ferocity. The terrier lunged. The rat squealed and sunk its fangs, and the bets were on.

As I went to pull Niccolo away he accidentally tipped over a stack of boxes. The movement revealed one of the evening's earlier hopefuls, a grimy little white dog. Its eyes were wide open, frozen in a vacant and deathly gaze, and its neck was a mass of bloody gashes. I shrunk back with horror, but I noticed Niccolo was leaning forward with a peculiar interest.

"Please," I beckoned. He looked at me with wild and excited eyes. He hesitated for a moment, torn between two loyalties, but upon seeing my disgust he tried to compose himself as he reluctantly drew away. After several minutes of uneasy silence he glanced up at me sheepishly.

"My legs," he said. "I think we'd better go home; my legs are beginning to throb a little."

I nodded and pointed in the right direction, but it was obvious that the quiet tension was still very much present. It started to rain a little harder as we made our way back to Mayfair, and we pulled our collars a little tighter around us. "Niccolo," I finally blurted out, "how many vampires are there?"

"In round figures?" he asked. "Oh, maybe a couple hundred in most countries."

"Do you know others here in London?"

"No, not really. I am new to this part of the world and I haven't had time enough to seek out friends."

"And what are you doing here?"

"Traveling."

I nodded and then resumed the stony silence for a few more minutes. "Can I ask you one more question?"

He glanced up at me and in the light of a nearby gas lamp he was once again an angel. "Yes?" he said and his face was wrought with innocence.

"Whatever happened to Lodovico?"

"He's still alive, of course."

The remark took me a little by surprise. "From the way you talked I gathered he might be dead."

Niccolo chuckled and I detected something sad and distant in his amusement. "No..." he said slowly. "Lodovico will never die. If you must know, he is very much alive and well. He still resides in Italy, but I really couldn't tell you where."

This last remark also caught my interest because from the ever-so-slight quaver in Niccolo's voice I got the distinct impression he was lying.

"Oh," I returned quietly.

As we approached our address on Bond Street I noticed he was dropping back about ten or fifteen paces behind me and appeared to be taking in the architecture. As I turned the key in the lock I saw him quickly slide an envelope into a nearby letter box and then come running back.

"Could I be so bold as to ask you who that was to?" I inquired.

He looked at me with reproach. "Certainly not. I still have a right to my privacy, Dottore."

I felt myself blushing at my own presumptuous behavior, but the fact he'd obviously tried to conceal the action still bothered me. "Would you tell me why you were so secretive then?" I asked.

"No," he snapped again as I shut the door behind us. "That is a private matter also."

It was sometime in the afternoon of the next day that I detected the pungent odor of Niccolo's oil of lily and palm. I was sitting in the breakfast room in one of the white peacock-backed rattan chairs at the glass-top table supported by carved and gilded water lilies when I noticed the familiar scent. It was only moments later that Cook came rushing in, her face filled with disquiet. She was a short, plump woman with a round red face, and a nose that betrayed one too many teacups full of gin. Her disheveled, fleecy hair was pinned haphazardly atop her head, and a few stray strands dropped down into her china-blue eyes. In her hands she held a bundle of glazed butcher's paper. It was from this that the scent of Niccolo's oil seemed to be emanating.

"Whatever do you think could have 'appened?" she asked in her thick cockney accent as she held the bundle out for me to see. I caught a familiar glimpse of quills and saw that it was Deirdre. When I touched her I realized she was stiff and cold.

"I don't know," I said. "Perhaps she just died of old age." I took the little bundle from her hands. "I'll dispose of her in the laboratory."

"Dear, dear," Cook purred as she left the room.

When I reached the laboratory I placed Deirdre on the counter and examined her carefully. She seemed smaller than usual, as if she had lost quite a bit of body weight. It couldn't have been old age, I thought to myself. I knew the life span of hedgehogs distinctly and Deirdre was still in the prime of her youth. But there were no other markings or signs of injury over her body I could discover. For a moment I became afraid that perhaps a strain of one of the viruses I kept in my laboratory for my experiments had escaped, but as I pulled back her quills I saw. There, on the nape of the neck, and so tiny so as nearly to escape my attention, were two small holes.

VII

That evening I reprimanded Niccolo for killing Deidre and he was duly apologetic. He explained that the sight of blood at the rat fight had made him feverish and anxious, and later that evening when Deirdre had wandered carelessly into his bedroom it was simply too much for him. From that day forward we made an agreement that every two or three days I would supply him with a brown rabbit, and this made him quite happy. He informed me that the vampire didn't require much food. A larger animal such as a baby lamb would keep them satiated for a week, not unlike the anaconda, and, indeed, the blood of an even larger creature might last well over two weeks.

As for his eating habits, after the incident at the rat fight he never allowed me to see him indulging in his strange predilection. He even kept his fangs carefully hidden when he spoke, and, to my great unhappiness, under no circumstances would he allow me to examine them. About the only thing Niccolo would allow me to check was his pulse and body temperature, both of which were impossibly low. However, under no circumstances would he allow me to take any blood samples. He explained that long ago Lodovico had warned against it. This was all Niccolo would say about the matter. No amount of persuasion would convince him otherwise.

Naturally, I was upset. There were few truths I held so fervidly as the belief that the pursuit of scientific knowledge was a universal good. All the teeming peoples of the world may prove themselves wretched, but the wonders of their creation will remain. Even if a man fails in life, if he makes one contribution to the betterment of society, he has fulfilled his purpose. I tolerated the frustration, for I thought I understood it. What a feat of survival this boy had perpetrated. He certainly hadn't done so by trusting the world. For brief moments I thought I could actually see through his eyes, not for long, a fleeting but lucid second of perfect vision. I saw what an inhospitable and dangerous world he must live in. I felt with curious depth how cautiously he must view my scientific interests.

Until I gained his trust I was forced to confine my curiosity to other arenas. I scoured all of the details contained in the books on vampirism. I discovered few facts. Here and there were reports that suggested possible cases of vampirism: an extraordinary account of an epidemic on the island of Mykonos in 1702 as recorded by a Jesuit father; the many cases collected in Hungary by the Benedictine abbot, Dom Augustin Calmet, in 1746. However, all of the supernatural aspects and legends about Niccolo's kind turned out to be completely false. He was reflected in mirrors. He did not sleep in a coffin or require a handful of his native soil to be with him. He was not repulsed or disturbed in any way by Bibles, crucifixes, or garlic.

My observations led me to quite another possibility. All of Niccolo's unusual aspects, from his sensitivity to sunlight to his immortality, smacked of having physiochemical explanations. It was my growing belief that vampirism was a medical condition. This notion led me inevitably to the next glistening possibility, that perhaps Niccolo's incredible immunity might provide a key to the guiding force in my life, the search for a cure to *Haemophilus influenzae*.

All the next day at Redgewood I thought of nothing but this possibility. My thoughts were still so pervaded with ideas when I arrived home and went into the garden to compose myself, I completely forgot it was the day of Ursula and Camille's return. It was that strange interim between sunset and dusk when the last rays of sunlight remained frozen for a brief moment at a low angle through the ivy trellises, and the shadows of the hedges were at their longest point, stretched across the courtyard. Everything seemed strangely becalmed, frozen in one final shimmer of gold before the ghostly blue of twilight set in.

I was so lost in thought as I strolled around the wide perimeter of the astrolabe, I almost didn't notice the shadowy figure standing beneath the chestnuts.

"Ursula," I gasped, "is that you?"

"Yes, Father," she said and stepped out into the light.
She was a beautiful young woman with fervent dark eyes
and pale skin. Her face was round, not unlike a Botticelli,
but her chin was strong and determined, and her dark red
hair, drawn tightly behind her head, made her seem
stronger, even harsher than her young years should have
allowed. Her thin lips also betrayed a sort of melancholy
in the way they were turned slightly downward. It was not
a weak or passive melancholy. It was a sad reticence that
held behind it a self-assured strength, even a reserved and
noble beauty. She was tall for a woman, almost as tall as I,
and she wore a white chemise with fashionable puffed
sleeves. However, she also wore riding breeches, which
were certainly not fashionable attire for a young woman
to wear so casually, but they only added to her self-
confident, slightly mannish presence.

"I forgot completely that you were coming home today,"
I said. "Just out for an evening stroll?"

She shrugged.

"Is anything wrong?"

"Not really," she replied and her moody silence startled
me. Even when Ursula was deeply troubled she usually
confided in me. It wasn't like her to be so evasive. There
was only one other time that I remembered something
sending her into such a hushed disquiet. It was during an
evening several years before at the home of one of my
fashionable colleagues when a young woman of social
inferiority manipulated her crinoline, purposefully, but
without obvious jostling to get through the dining-room
doorway ahead of Ursula. It wasn't that Ursula minded so
much that the ridiculous, but nonetheless rigid, protocol
hadn't been followed. It was what the young debutante
had murmured so quietly and dispassionately beneath her
breath. *"Bad seed,"* she sniffed. *"Bad seed."*

"It's a nice evening, isn't it?"

"Very nice."

Ursula tilted her head back and admired the darkening
sky. The sunbeams coming through the ivy trellises were
gone now, clipped off suddenly by the inexorable advance
of twilight. "It's turning out to be a very warm spring. It
should mean wonderful weather for May."

"Yes," I agreed.

"Do you know where the name 'Mayfair' comes from?"

"Why, yes . . . yes, I do. Because the celebration of May Day has always been held here." Visions of a raffish festival of scamps and pickpockets with their doxies rollicking round maypoles filled my mind.

"But do you know where the celebration of May Eve comes from originally?"

I shrugged. "From the old ritual of welcoming in spring?"

"Yes, spring," she repeated and then her voice became distant. *"Through the rowan and through the keep, spare the horse and spare the sheep. Spare the fox and spare the hen, but throw the woman in. . . "*

"Throw the woman in?" I said with a puzzled smile.

"Aye," she continued the old Celtic litany. *" '. . . but throw the woman in.' "*

"What's wrong, Ursula?" I asked and for the first time a flicker of emotion crossed her face. "Oh, I don't know," she said. "It's all so formless and confused. All these worries."

I put my arm around her. "Try to tell me."

"Well . . . here I am. Everything given. What I mean is, I know who I am. I know my 'station' in life, and what is proper and what is not proper. I know that at dinner parties I must talk to the gentleman at my left until the soup is removed, and that I must contrive to wind up the conversation in time to turn to my other neighbor the moment the fish arrives. I don't mind playing the games, so much. But here I am, already getting glances because I'm a spinster, and I'm scarcely into my twenties."

"That's never bothered you before," I interrupted.

"Well, it doesn't bother me now, so much. I know I'm not going to live my life according to the deadly smiles, but what I don't know is what I am going to do." She regarded me imploringly. "I can't help feeling I don't fit in, Father. I have luxury and position, but I feel trapped in the world, and I don't know what I want to do with my life."

"My poor Ursula," I said as I guided her once again toward the chestnuts. "You know what I wish you would do. I wish you would get married and settle down happily, but, as I've always told you, you can do whatever you want to do. There's the university or travel, but we've been through all of this before. I don't understand why you are so unhappy all of a sudden."

She looked me straight in the eye. "I know what you're going to say to this, Father. I know the very reply that will pass your lips, but I want you to think about it and answer with every bit of truth and conviction that's in you."

I released my grasp upon her as I gazed into her dark eyes and saw something familiar there, a fire and intensity that reached back to another person, another time.

"Very well," I said, swallowing.

She drew in her breath slowly. "Do you think there was something wrong with Mother? I mean, do you think she was bad?"

I paused for several moments before I answered. "Of course not. No . . . of course I don't."

I noticed Ursula's expression fell ever so slightly, as if it was the answer she was hoping I wouldn't say, the answer she knew was a lie.

"Of course not," she repeated hollowly. "I guess it's just that sometimes I worry. Sometimes I think it's bad that I'm different."

"No," I told her sharply, "it isn't bad, and I don't want you to ever think that again." I once again placed my arm around her shoulder and hugged her tightly. "Whatever brought this on, anyway?"

She shook her head and I could tell that she was still deeply upset. "I suppose I should tell you. I didn't sleep very well the other night. I had a dream." Once again she drifted into a troubled silence. "You know, the celebration of May Eve wasn't always people dancing and laughing with garlands and hawthorn and a May Queen."

I nodded.

"It's a rite of spring, an ancient fertility ritual. Last night I think I dreamed about May Eve as it must have been celebrated when people still believed in the old ways." She shivered. "I was here in Mayfair, but I could see through all of the blocks and ornate flats as if they were only phantasms, reflections in a shop window. And through the shadow buildings I could see many strange things. I could see the land, rolling and green, unviolated, save for a few rugged thoroughfares. And standing still and silent within each ghost of a building I could see all the ancient cairns and cromlechs like insects within their chrysalises. There were people, too, and everyone was running, celebrating the May Eve. I was running with them, but I didn't realize at first. The people weren't dressed in silk or velvet, or even wool or flannel. They were almost naked, and their robes were coarse. Their faces were shining in the moonlight and I could see that they were smudged with grease and ash." Ursula allowed one hand to caress the rough bark of the chestnut as she continued.

"We may have maypoles and bonfires today, and it all may be very happy, but a long time ago it was different. When we burn the old witches today we don't realize what their rag and wicker bodies really mean, what they represent. I realized it all the other night, in the dream, when I noticed the people had a leader, a dark and ragged man, and I noticed he was pointing toward me." Her face paled and I squeezed her tightly.

"I ran, but they chased me, and the dark and ragged man began the chant as he grabbed at my nightgown with his suet-covered fingers: *'Through the rowan and through the keep, spare the horse and spare the sheep!'* They continued the chant as they backed me up against an immense bonfire, and I could hear the flames roaring and crackling in the wind. *'Spare the fox and spare the hen,'* they shrilled, *'but throw the woman in!'* I began to scream when I realized I was the ritual maiden, the sacrifice, but they just continued. *'But throw the woman in, aye, and throw the woman in!'* I felt cold and empty with terror as they lunged at me, and I woke up in my bed covered with..."

"There, there," I comforted. "It was all just a bad dream. What makes you think it has anything to do with your mother?"

"I don't know," she said somberly. "It just set me to thinking, I guess. I know it was all just a bad dream, but somehow I can't get it out of my mind that the dream meant something."

"And what do you think it meant?"

"I think it means that when May Eve approaches, something's going to happen." She turned to me quickly. "Oh, I don't think the people of Mayfair are going to run me out or anything. I just think I'm going to have to change, make a few decisions about what I'm going to have to do with my life. Perhaps I'll meet that dark and ragged young man." She gave a grisly chuckle.

"Well, I don't think he's the dark and ragged young man of your dreams, but we do have a house guest I've been meaning to tell you about."

She regarded me inquisitively.

"He's a young Italian gentleman named Niccolo Cavalanti, and he arrived very late a couple of evenings ago. I don't know how long he'll be staying with us, but I must warn you. We're going to have to make some special allowances for him. He has a very unusual medical disorder, and is acutely sensitive to sunlight."

"Will he be joining us at dinner?"

"I'm afraid not," I explained. "Because of his medical disorder Signore Cavalanti requires a very special diet, and I'll have to take care of all of his meals."

"My goodness," Ursula broke in, "what is wrong with this Signore Cavalanti?"

"He suffers from a rare disorder of the lymph system," I said glibly. "The technical name for his condition is phototropic leucocythemia." She pursed her brow and I wondered for a brief moment if she knew I was making the term up.

She nodded her head slowly. "How did you meet him?"

"I knew his father," I continued. "The young man has come to London to visit a specialist, and I told him he could stay here until he found out whether he's going to have to move to London permanently or not."

"How very interesting," Ursula murmured, and I could see a sparkle of interest in her dark eyes. "How old did you say this young man was?"

For some reason, even after I had lied so fluently, the question caught me completely off guard. I stood dumbfounded for several seconds.

"Why don't you judge for yourself?" a voice said suddenly from the direction of the astrolabe. I looked up to see Niccolo standing there exactly as he had been

standing when I had first set eyes on him. Once again he
was an angel in the shadows of the garden. When I
glanced at Ursula I was more than a little surprised to see
she was completely cold and expressionless.

He swiftly crossed the courtyard and elegantly kissed
her hand. "And you, I presume, are Signorina Gladstone."

She nodded, coolly unimpressed by his gallant gesture.
"And you must be Signore Cavalanti."

He smiled and gave a slight flourish with his hand.

"Signore Cavalanti," she repeated, "I'm so sorry to hear
about your unusual medical disorder."

Without raising an eyebrow he smiled and nodded.

"It must be dreadful to be so sensitive to the sunlight."

"One gets used to it after a while," he said, shrugging.

"Well, I hope that the specialist you've come to see here
in London can cure you of this awful condition."

"Ahhh . . . yes," Niccolo returned. "Actually, I was hoping your father might offer some solution."

Ursula regarded me curiously. "But surely he's told you
he spends most of his time doing research on *Haemophilus
influenzae.*" From many long hours of assistance in my
laboratory she had learned to pronounce the words
perfectly.

"Oh, yes," Niccolo agreed.

"Has he shown you the laboratory yet?"

"No," he answered with growing interest.

"Father!" Ursula burst out, "I can't believe you haven't
shown Signore Cavalanti the laboratory."

"Indeed, Signore Gladstone," Niccolo added, "I would be
very interested in seeing your work."

They both regarded me excitedly, and I conceded to
their wishes. I motioned toward the back door, and
gestured past the study. The laboratory was a large
circular room in the east tower of the house, and more
than half of its walls were covered with windows that
normally overlooked the huge astrolabe in the garden.
Now, however, all of the shutters had been closed and the
twilight passing through the louvers splayed the room in
an eerie skeleton of light. A faint rustling sound betrayed
the presence of numerous test animals in unseen cages.

I slowly turned on the gas lamps and Niccolo gave an
audible gasp. *"Scusa,"* he apologized, "but I am a being of

the senses, and the magic of the flame always entrances me." He waved his hand at the jungle of glass tubing, distillers, and flasks that covered most of the counters. They captured the flickering light of the gas jets and reflected it like luminous blood through so many scintillant emerald veins. After he stepped into the room I noticed that something else had caught his eye. To the right of the door there was a small alcove set off from the laboratory, lined with window seats and green leather cushions. In the very center of the tiny space stood a huge glass cubicle with an ornate brass frame and cupola housing a single brown rabbit.

"Most impressive," Niccolo said, nodding. "So this is where you do your work on—"

"*Haemophilus influenzae,*" I filled in.

"Forgive my naïveté," he continued as he walked up to the cubicle containing the rabbit. "Understandably I am rather ignorant on diseases. Would you mind explaining to me exactly what that is?"

"There's not much to say," I began.

"Don't let Father fool you," Ursula said as she crossed the room and pulled out a terrarium containing an Asian viper. Next she plunged her hand beneath the counter and came out with a dangling brown mouse. She casually tossed it into the terrarium and pushed it back against the wall. "Father can go on for hours and hours about *Haemophilus influenzae* if you trick him into it."

"That may be true," I conceded, "but what I meant to say is, of all the things I can tell you about *Haemophilus influenzae,* I still can't tell you what causes it."

"Was Dottore Pasteur wrong?" Niccolo asked.

"Oh, no," I returned, impressed by the erudition of his question. "As you apparently know, Pasteur discovered that many diseases are caused by microorganisms known as bacteria, and this has enabled us to make stupendous advances. However, even though *Haemophilus influenzae* possesses many of the properties of a bacteria, no such bacteria has ever been found under the microscope."

"Another enigma," he said, smiling.

"Of sorts," I answered as I tapped the cubicle, and the brown rabbit stirred slightly in its sleep. "But as T. Bryant stated in *Practical Surgery*, published in 1878, 'It should never be forgotten that it is the virus that attacks the system." We don't know for sure what viruses are, but they behave like microorganisms even though they must be incredibly small—so small, in fact, that they cannot even be seen under the microscope. According to our current way of thinking, *Haemophilus influenzae* seems to be just such a virus."

"You see," Ursula said smartly, "with a little prodding you've already got Father convinced he's in the lecture hall."

I blushed as I turned to Niccolo, but his eyes were steadied upon the little brown mouse as it pawed furiously at the glass walls of the terrarium. There was an unmistakable expression of horror on his face as the viper languidly tilted its head to one side. Ursula also noticed his horror, and across her face flickered first shock, then regret, and finally a strange sort of smug arrogance. An electricity passed between the two as Niccolo, in turn, watched Ursula's expressions, and both of them finally tilted their heads, haughtily and knowingly, as if each had discovered something about the other that they' neither liked nor felt was worthy of verbal criticism.

"There are several other things Father could tell you about *Haemophilus influenzae*," Ursula continued with a subtle and chiding contempt. "For example, it is infectious and can easily be transferred in test animals by injecting the blood of a stricken animal into the blood of a healthy one. This fact, of course, substantiates the viral explanation. In medical terminology the attacking virus is known as the 'antigen.' Now, in response to the attacking antigen the lymphatic system produces specific chemical substances known as 'antibodies' to combat the particular offender. Do you have that? The invader is the antigen; the defenders are antibodies."

Niccolo remained expressionless as she removed a white rabbit from a cage beneath the counter. "About a week ago," she went on, "Father injected this little fellow with blood infected with the *influenzae* virus. Needless to say, he became quite sick, but his system continued to create antibodies, and he survived the disease. Then an interesting thing happened. The rabbit had so many antibodies in his blood that he developed an immunity to the particular strain of *influenzae* Father injected him with. If Father were to inject him again he would remain healthy and active, for he is now completely immune."

"Ursula—" I began, but then quieted. Etiquette demanded that I stop her, but somehow I felt Niccolo would be able to handle himself.

"It's the same with human beings," she said, putting the rabbit back into its cage. "Once we have had a particular strain of *influenzae* we become completely immune to it. The odd thing is that *influenzae* epidemics continue and people do get *influenzae* over and over again. Why? Because the virus appears to be very malleable, genetically, and has the ability to undergo what we call an antigenic mutation. In other words, every year or so, it changes its chemical structure slightly, and it becomes increasingly more difficult for our antibodies to ward it off. Even stranger, medical science has discovered that about every ten to twelve years *influenzae* becomes an entirely new disease. That is why periodically there are worldwide epidemics of the virus."

"And is your father working on discovering a cure?" Niccolo asked.

"Ultimately," she returned. "Of course, finding a cure is Father's long-range goal, but at the moment he is more interested in *influenzae*'s ability to undergo such radical mutations. Father's reasoning is that if he can discover what causes these antigenic mutations to occur naturally, perhaps he can find a way to stop them."

"And what does cause them to occur?"

"No one knows."

Niccolo regarded her piercingly as if he knew she were lying, and for the first time I saw Ursula's nerve falter for a brief moment. "Your father does not know what causes them?" he asked with a rise in his voice. Ursula looked at me entreatingly, and I nodded in consent.

"Well..." she said falteringly. "I will tell you a secret. Father doesn't know what causes the natural antigenic mutations to occur every ten to twelve years, but he has discovered a synthetic way to cause *Haemophilus influenzae* to mutate in the laboratory."

"And what good is that?" he asked.

"Not very much good at all," she replied. "In the test

animals he's caused the disease to mutate dozens, even hundreds of times, each time hoping to glean some clue to its cure from its kaleidoscopic mutations. Usually, however, he just ends up with another typical strain of *Haemophilus influenzae*."

"Usually?" he prodded.

Ursula once again glanced in my direction, and I nodded with hesitant approval. I was very covetous of my scientific discoveries because of the unscrupulously competitive world of academia, but I couldn't fathom that Niccolo would have any reason or motive to steal any information.

"Well, since you are so curious I'll tell you another secret," she said as she walked toward the glass cubicle containing the brown rabbit. "In one of the tests Father performed not too long ago, he created a rather unusual strain of *influenzae*. After he injected it into the blood of a test animal he discovered that, unlike all the previous strains, the organism did not begin to generate antibodies. Thus it had no chance of ever surviving the disease. The virus raged in its system unchallenged, and within two days the animal was dead. He infected another animal, and the same thing happened, and another—"

"And this little rabbit in the glass cage," Niccolo interrupted. "He has injected it, also, hasn't he?"

"Why, yes," Ursula replied, obviously a little surprised by his remark. "How did you know?"

"His heart beats so very fast," he returned sadly, and pressed his hands against the glass.

"Can you see it beating in its fur?" she asked skeptically.

"I can hear it. I can hear it beating like waves pounding against a rock, only very rapidly."

She regarded him quizzically. Then her voice became very cold and hard. "He'll be dead within a day or so. You see, in medical terminology the strain of *influenzae* Father injected him with totally lacks antigenicity. In other words, the body is completely incapable of combating it and consequently it will always prove fatal."

Niccolo shuddered as he stepped back from the glass. "And what will your father do with—"

"With *Camillus influenzae*," she filled in. "Study it.

Look at it from every angle in hopes of discovering some
new information from our lethal little friend. He's already
published several papers hinting at his discoveries that
have caused quite a stir in the medical world, and soon
he's going to publish his complete findings. After all, in
another ten to twelve years it will mutate on its own and
be lost to science forever."

I was touched by Ursula's words, but I did not find it
easy listening to someone boast about my findings. I
made an excuse to leave for a moment and passed through
the door. It was after I was in the hall that I heard Niccolo
say something that caused me to pause.

"Your father is very blind."

I heard Ursula turn abruptly as if to rush to my
defense, but Niccolo apparently quieted her with a
gesture. "Your father is an honorable man," he continued,
"but the world is filled with dishonorable men. Your
father does not see in *Camillus influenzae* what a weapon
of destruction it could become if it fell into the wrong
hands."

"You're just upset because you think you're very noble
and aristocratic and view death, even in the name of
science, as unnecessary and distasteful," she retorted.

"That isn't true," he countered. "I am more familiar
than you might suspect with the necessity of death."

With this last remark I grew alarmed and rushed back
into the room. Both of them looked at me briefly,
wondering why I had been gone only a moment, and then
Niccolo once again turned sedately toward Ursula. "What
I find distasteful is that you are so dispassionate when
death is a necessity. What this tells me about you,
signorina, is that you are very unhappy with the world,
and you don't know how to deal with this unhappiness."

Ursula straightened. "You—"

"Hush," he said and quieted her with a finger. "You
needn't argue, for it is all too clear that it is true. And you
needn't be ashamed, for I, also, am not at all happy with
the prejudices and ignorances of the world. But at least I
would never treat death so casually. There are better ways
to deal with one's unhappiness."

"And what is your way?" she snapped.

"Me," Niccolo returned with a humble shrug of his

shoulders. "Because I've realized that I cannot change
this world, I lose myself in my senses. Of course, there are
other ways, like your father's—to lose one's self in one's
work. To lose one's self in one's work and one's senses are,
perhaps, the two most common solutions to the reality of
the world. I simply find that my senses give me more
solace."

"What do you mean—?" Ursula began once again. The
sudden change in Niccolo's expression made her realize he
was not paying any attention. Instead, he was tilting his
head back contemplatively, as if listening to something
far away. "What is that?" he questioned as he knitted his
brow.

"What is what?" Ursula returned. We both listened
very carefully. I could hear nothing.

"Squisito!" he cried as he quickly left the room and
Ursula and I followed. As we passed the study we became
aware of a distant tinkle of music, and we finally realized
what Niccolo had been hearing. When we reached the
drawing room I pushed the massive walnut doors aside,
and there in the darkness was the familiar silhouette
seated at the gilt and rosewood pianoforte.

"It is my other daughter, Camille," I whispered.

"You are blind?" Niccolo stated immediately. She tilted
her head in our direction and the silhouette of her tresses
tumbled over her tiny shoulder. "No, no... please continue to play," he implored and turned to me. "She is blind
and mentally distant, is she not?" he asked in a hush.

"Why, yes," I gasped in surprise. "How could you tell?"

"That she is blind is obvious—the way she holds her
head, the fact that she plays with such facility in a
darkened room. That she is mentally distant is more
subtle, but nonetheless apparent. When we entered the
room her playing remained unaffected. The playing of any
normal pianist would have undergone minute changes
due to the fact that they would have been distracted to a
very slight degree by the realization of our mere presence.
The pressure they applied to the keys would have changed
more, or their tempo would have increased by a tiny
fraction. But Camille's playing did not change until I
spoke, and this could only be explained by two things.
Either she is deaf, but what deaf person at such a tender

age can play the piano? Or she was not distracted when we entered the room because her thoughts are not in this world."

"You are extremely perceptive," I complimented. "Camille is both blind and mentally distant, as you put it."

"Is it as a result of her mother's death by *influenzae*?" he inquired.

"Why, yes!" I gasped again. "How did you know that?"

"Really, Dottore," he returned, "you must think I am very simple not to be able to figure all of this out. It is so obvious—you name your daughter Camille, and your deadly strain of *influenzae, Camillus;* you are so prepossessed with discovering a cure to the disease.... Do you think the personal vendetta is so difficult to discern?"

"Yes, I do," I answered. "I think you are an abnormally clever young man."

He smiled slightly. "There are others more clever than I. One thing that I do not know is, how did you teach Camille to play the piano so beautifully?"

"You ask the only question that I cannot answer," I replied. "You see, no one taught Camille how to play the piano. As far as I can discern she has always known how to play. All she has to do is to hear a composition once and she has total recall and can play it back perfectly."

Camille lifted her tiny fairy hands and brought them crashing down in deep sonorous chords as Niccolo let out a gasp of amazement. *"La bellezza dei lampi e dell' arcobaleno,"* he murmured with passionate admiration as he turned his fiery gaze toward Ursula. *"'What do you mean?'* you ask me, *signorina,* what does it mean to be blissful and abandoned and completely immersed in one's own senses? That is what it means," he finished, thrusting a finger toward Camille.

VIII

Of all of the members of the household I think Niccolo
got along best with little Camille. He revealed a voracious
interest in both her ability and her condition and asked
me many questions about her. In answer to his numerous
inquiries I explained to him that Camille was not without
medical precedent. There were many examples of idiots
savants throughout history. Usually, they are human
calculators, or individuals who can do complex
mathematical calculations in their heads. For example, a
little boy who can scarcely talk and who has been raised
as an animal because he is subject to strange convulsions
might be able to tell you instantaneously that 1729 is the
lowest number that can be expressed in two ways as the
sum of two cubes: $12^3 + 1^3$ and $10^3 + 9^3$. A little girl
who never learned to recognize her own mother and father
might be able to multiply two twelve-digit numbers faster
than the hand could write the solution on a blackboard.

Another variation of human calculators are date
calculators. Without batting an eye they can instantaneously tell you that June 17, 1257 fell on a Sunday,
and September 29, 412 B.C. was a Saturday. Date calculators have been found to have a correct knowledge of what
day of the week a particular day falls on extending
beyond seven thousand years, even though, to the best of
my knowledge, the longest perpetual calendar that has
currently been calculated only extends to about twenty-
four hundred years. And yet you ask them what a leap
year is and they say they're not sure, or you ask them how
they compute the dates and they say they don't know, the
answer is just inside their heads.

I informed Niccolo that one of the most interesting
idiots savants I encountered in my reading was an
American slave boy in the 1850s known as Blind Tom.
Like Camille, although Blind Tom was mentally retarded
and completely incapable of learning on any other level,

he could mimic any piano piece played to him. His owner, a man named Colonel Bethune, realized that the boy was a potentially lucrative phenomenon and began touring with the unusual virtuoso, consequently making a fortune in numerous concert tours both in the States and in Europe. Blind Tom became world famous and played for numerous world leaders, including the American President, James Buchanan, in 1860. At the height of Blind Tom's career it was estimated that he had committed over five thousand compositions to memory, including works by Beethoven, Mendelssohn, Bach, Chopin, Verdi, Rossini, Donizetti, Gounod, Meyerbeer, and countless others—although his vocabulary and verbal capacity were limited to a little over a hundred words, and he was described as behaving "more like an ape than a human."

As for Camille, she made no explicit acknowledgment of Niccolo's increasingly frequent presence in the drawing room, but she did add a strange and hauntingly beautiful melody to her musical repertoire. Niccolo seemed to recognize that this was his theme, and a peculiar and silent understanding formed between the two. The odd thing was that the melody was completely unfamiliar to me and as far as I could determine she had composed it herself. If this was the case, it was the first time I became aware that Camille's talents included original musical work.

As for how Niccolo was getting along with Ursula, this was another story entirely. As the days passed, the interactions between her and Niccolo grew more and more like a snake biting its own tail, a constant repartee. The more negatively he reacted to her character, the more chiding she became. The more chiding she became, the more calmly he accepted it. His solicitude only kindled her outrage, whereupon he would once again calmly point out her faults—that is, her propensity for becoming outraged so easily—and the circle began again. More than once Ursula would storm out of the room in seething and frustrated silence, leaving Niccolo sitting and flicking lint off of his evening jacket with cool disdain. Nevertheless, at the heart of every battle was a fiery game of chess or a fervent discussion of Renaissance art. I didn't doubt for a moment that each was enjoying their dislike for the other immensely.

It was nearing the end of Niccolo's second week with us that I found out a most interesting bit of information. I was making my normal rounds at Redgewood when I became aware of the familiar form of Cletus. He was in his laboratory coat and came hobbling out of the receiving ward. He looked at me sharply, and then, to my surprise, he boldly approached. I was astonished. Something rather heavy had to be weighing on his mind to inspire such audacity.

He stopped directly before me and we stared into each other's eyes with territorial steadiness. If he was nervous he was artfully concealing it. He gracefully lit a Laurens Egyptian cigarette. "Well, well," he said, "have you heard the news?"

I bristled.

"Chiswick," he said simply.

For a brief second the name took me by surprise, but then I remembered. "You mean they found Dr. Chiswick?"

"Yes, indeed," Cletus returned as he rolled his thin lips pleasurably over his teeth. "And you'll never guess where. . . ."

"At the Blue Post Saloon," I quipped.

"In a closet," he said solemnly.

I pursed my brow.

"It seems that about a month ago an English gentleman checked into a little resort in Interlaken, Switzerland, and after a couple of days he vanished. Of course, no one seemed to notice until his bill came due. In investigating they discovered one of the closet doors in his room wasn't working properly, and so they had it forced open. Well, the reason that it wasn't working was because William Chiswick had nailed it securely shut . . . from the inside."

"And was he dead?"

"Oh, lord, yes. He'd been in there for weeks. But it's a damned odd way to commit suicide, isn't it, to lock one's self in one's closet and slowly starve to death." He gazed at me intently.

I suddenly wondered why the little man had approached me with this information.

"Oh, there's more," he added quickly. "You see, papers found in the hotel identified the body as our Dr. Chiswick, but he had checked into the resort under the name of C. William. Following that up, Scotland Yard was able to follow his path as he left the country. It seems that he made a beeline from Dover to Calais and all the way through France and Switzerland *without stopping until he reached Interlaken.*"

"Without stopping?"

"Not once. It seems that Chiswick was in a very great hurry." Cletus lowered his head and clasped his hands behind him as he began to pace back and forth in a space about five feet long. "Several people remember him from that first evening, the maître d'hôtel, the desk clerk when he asked for the hammer and some nails. He apparently sealed himself in the closet shortly thereafter."

"There's no chance it was murder?"

"None whatsoever."

"Do you think he killed himself because he was lying to the trustees about making an important discovery?"

"Certainly not!" he snapped angrily. "You don't put grates on your windows and new locks on your door to cover up a lie. Chiswick was frightened by something, and he was racing madly out of the country to get away from it. I think he nailed himself in that closet because whatever it was that made him crazy with terror showed up at that resort."

"And what, pray tell, could that have been?"

Cletus stopped pacing and looked at me. There was a knowing glint in his eye. "The only fragment of anything that Scotland Yard has been able to turn up about the case is that a visitor from Italy showed up that evening and asked for him at the desk. They don't know anything else. They don't even have a description." He puffed his cigarette. "I knew William Chiswick for a long time. I saw him walk into houses where smallpox epidemics were raging and I saw him overpower men twice his size so he could cauterize their wounds. I never saw him back down from anything, and if it was that Italian visitor who caused him to go insane with fear, let us hope you or I never confront him, for he was nothing of God's world."

With that he stared rudely and directly into my eye. "I know there's no real evidence, but every intuition in my body tells me there's a connection between Chiswick's Italian visitor and the arrival of the mysterious Mr. Cavalanti one week later."

I felt a chill run down my spine. "You think Niccolo had something to do with it?"

"Niccolo?" Cletus asked as he continued to eye me curiously. "Yes, I think Niccolo had something to do with it. Two very strange events have occurred within a very short space of time and I think we're naïve to think they're not related."

For a moment I was almost believing his words, but then I realized Cletus was succumbing to the same irrational fear that Niccolo had warned about. "Don't be absurd," I dismissed. "Granted, this Chiswick thing is most peculiar, but there are millions of young Italian gentlemen. The fact that one puts in a brief appearance a thousand miles away is a ludicrous reason to assume that Mr. Cavalanti had anything to do with it."

Cletus drew back. "Tenuous and circumstantial, yes! But you mark my words, Dr. Gladstone. You just mark my words." He swelled his chest self-assuredly, and then turned around and strode off.

That afternoon I found a small card in the letterbox with the words *J. Sedgemoor, Esq., Chemist,* embossed upon it. Scrawled in a crowquill was a brief and simple message: *Please come in for consultation.* I obliged the request on my way home from the hospital.

I was still both angry and amazed at Cletus's accusation when I stepped into the little shop on Piccadilly and saw the tall and wispy proprietor standing behind the slate counter, carefully counting out small brown capsules. He was putting them in a glass vial with a rubber stopper. In front of him was a dithery little old woman waiting impatiently. When he finished she took out a neatly folded pound note and stuck it securely into his hand. As an afterthought she asked, "Do you have lemon grass for sachets?"

"No, mum," Sedgemoor replied. "I'm afraid you'll have to go to Butler's, the herbalist, right down the street."

She took her change, nodded, and left.

"Good afternoon, Mr. Sedgemoor," I greeted.

"Ahh, Dr. Gladstone," he returned. "I'm so glad you came right in."

"Do you have the information I required?" I asked.

"I'm not sure," he answered oddly. He turned around and opened a small cherry cabinet, not unlike a card catalogue at the library. He pulled out a yellow card with a brown envelope clipped to it and emptied the few crumbled remains of the black pill on the counter. "I can't exactly tell you what it is," he explained, "but I can tell you what it isn't. It isn't in any formulary, and it isn't anything that any apothecary in the country knows about. I've tried everything, but this little pill has a very complex chemical structure—too complex, in fact, for me even to begin to tell you what it is composed of."

"Does this happen very often?"

"If it hadn't happened in this instance I would have told you it was impossible. I mean, the English race has a finite knowledge of chemistry and any pill manufactured within the realm of this knowledge can be deciphered by anyone else within the realm of this knowledge. But this pill..." He became contemplative. "Either someone stumbled onto a very strange and complex compound by accident, or they have a brilliant knowledge of chemistry that far exceeds what they're teaching in the universities."

"I see," I said quietly. "Well, Mr. Sedgemoor, if you had to venture an opinion, do you think the pill was an accidental creation or the product of a more advanced knowledge of chemistry?"

He stroked his pointed chin as he nervously poked the fragments of the pill around on the slate. "There's no doubt in my mind that it's the product of a more advanced knowledge of chemistry," he said. "You see, when I was unable to decipher the pill I sent it to a friend of mine at Oxford. He didn't have any luck either, but he ran a few other tests on the pill, and he's discovered that it is a phenomenal healing agent. It causes a wound practically to suture itself and it seems to safeguard against infection as well. In short, it is a medicinal substance any chemist in the country would give his eyeteeth to be able to duplicate." Mr. Sedgemoor's voice became very hushed as he leaned over the counter. "But come now, Dr. Gladstone, let's drop this 'patient of yours' nonsense and level with me. I could be very helpful, you know."

"Whatever do you mean?" I gasped.

"I know the business," he said. "I have the legal acumen and the connections. If you'd only come clean with me we could make a fortune." His pale hazel eyes became insane with excitement. "You made the pill, didn't you? Come on, you can tell me."

"No, I'm afraid I didn't," I returned. "I'm as much in the dark as you are, Mr. Sedgemoor."

"I wouldn't ask for much of a profit."

"I didn't make the pill."

"Twenty-five percent. That's not much. One quarter and I'll do all the work from here on out."

"How much do I owe you?" I asked briskly.

"Oh, nothing," he answered. "It's free, just tell me—"

"Good day, Mr. Sedgemoor," I said crisply as I scooped up the remaining fragments of the pill and left the shop.

The revelation about the pill left me with an odd mixture of excitement and apprehension. I was excited, as any physician would be, with the discovery of such a compound, but it raised many questions in my mind. Who made the pill? Niccolo? Lodovico? And if they possessed a knowledge of medicine that far exceeded what we were teaching in the universities, what else did they know, and perhaps more importantly, why were they keeping their discoveries to themselves instead of sharing their knowledge with humanity?

When I arrived home that evening I discovered Niccolo and Ursula alone in the parlor involved in one of their fiery discussions. I asked Niccolo if he felt up to going out for a little walk, and Ursula politely realized I wanted to be alone with him. It was raining, a particularly spectacular rain. The sky was wracked with lightning and the pretentious mummery of thunder. The wind tugged at our umbrellas as we passed a cast-iron street lavatory crowned by a gas lamp. I noticed that a playbill for Oscar Wilde's *Salome* was about to be ripped off by the storm. The lightning flashed and for a moment the head of St. John the Baptist was revealed in garish detail before it was swept away in the muddy waters of the gutter.

"You are troubled, aren't you, Dottore?" he finally stated as the wind died down.

"You don't have to be overly perceptive to see that, do you," I returned.

He shrugged. "You won't tell me what it is?"

"Well," I began slowly, "today I went to the chemist's. I had one of those black pills of yours tested...."

"And?"

"And it turns out they're a very sophisticated healing agent, much more sophisticated than our medical science could currently produce."

"So?"

"So, who made them?"

"A brilliant chemist living in Paris—a vampire, of course. But it was Lodovico who devised the formula."

I straightened with amazement. "And is Lodovico a genius when it comes to chemistry?"

"Probably," Niccolo answered naïvely. "Lodovico's a genius in just about everything. You know, he is very old, much older than I, and it's difficult to have lived as long as Lodovico has and not acquire an incredible wealth of knowledge."

"Are all vampires as knowledgeable as Lodovico?"

"Many of them. I told you, knowledge is our Holy Grail, and I daresay the wisdom possessed by the vampire would boggle your imagination. You see, we don't have political allegiances to worry about, or religion, or differing mores. We all work together for one purpose: to further our achievements and our learning."

"Why don't you share your learning with the common man?" I snapped angrily. "This healing agent alone could save countless lives."

"Why don't we share our learning?" Niccolo repeated bitterly and laughed. "We're feared and hated. Do you know what happens when a being who is obviously not human comes up to the rabble and says, 'Look, I've invented a machine that will take generations for your scientists even to come close to understanding; here, let me help you with it'? Well, I'll tell you what happens: witch-hunts and inquisitions. I can open the history books and find you the names of hundreds of vampires who were tortured and burned as heretics because they tried to 'share' their learning with the common man."

"But surely that was during the Dark Ages—"

"You're hopelessly stupid—" he began shrilly, but then lowered his voice as he struggled to maintain his composure. "We're still in the Dark Ages. The scared and the superstitious savage still lurks behind the mask of civilization and he will remain there for untold generations to come. If wondering why we won't share the science that created that pill is all that was troubling you, we can consider our conversation ended." Niccolo pulled his evening coat more tightly around him as his pace quickened and he began to move ahead of me. He struggled to hold his umbrella firmly in the oncoming wind.

"No, wait!" I called as I ran to catch up. "It's not all that was troubling me."

He regarded me haughtily.

"You see," I explained, "shortly before our carriage accident one of my older and respected colleagues at Redgewood vanished. He went insane, as if he were very frightened by something, and Scotland Yard just discovered he committed suicide at a little resort in Interlaken, Switzerland."

"What does this have to do with anything?"

"Well, it seems that a visit from a mysterious Italian gentleman spurred him into taking his own life, and Dr. Hardwicke, you remember, the physician with the furious eyes?"

He shivered.

"Well, Cletus, the old fool, tried to convince me that you had something to do with Chiswick's tragedy."

"How clever of him," Niccolo murmured dryly.

"Even though I didn't believe it for a moment, I guess it just sort of put me into a frame of mind. . . ."

"And you just got to thinking, perhaps my presence in your house is a little more than accidental—"

"No, I—"

"Perhaps Lodovico has just sent me on another mission. I mean, if he would have me wake up under Leonardo's knife in the morgue of Santa Maria Nuova, why couldn't he just as easily have me throw myself beneath the wheels of your carriage? I mean, a couple of broken legs aren't all that serious to a vampire...."

"No."

"And after such an accident, you certainly wouldn't dream of suspecting I had actually been sent to infiltrate your household." He tilted his head back in a cruel and fraudulent contemplation as the lightning momentarily lit the rain-slicked street.

I straightened with fear as I felt my pulse quicken. He was delivering his words facetiously and with a strange sort of pretended guilt, but I fancied that I discerned a hidden edge of truth in the parley. Was it actually there, I wondered to myself? Was Niccolo trying to give me some sort of cloaked warning, and if so, was he doing so because of an unconscious concern and affection, or simply to torture me with a cruel puzzle?

"Perhaps," he continued, "the same thing that happened to this Chiswick of yours is in the process of happening to you."

"Niccolo!" I gasped. "It's true, isn't it? You did have something to do with Chiswick."

"What do you think?" he retorted cuttingly. His face was filled with anticipation.

"I think it's true!" I cried and he flung his hands into the air.

"Dottore, don't you see how easy it is to make you turn against me? I said all of those things just to test you, and now I see. You are as suspicious and filled with fear as all mortals are. I thread a few outrageous lies together and you allow them to throw you into a panic."

I sighed as I wiped the rain off my forehead. "Niccolo, you can't blame me—"

"No," he snapped and released his breath. "I can't blame you, but I can see that the time is drawing near when I must leave your household."

"No!" I said.

He merely shook his head. "Don't bother to try to change my mind, Dottore. Whether you like to admit it or not, I can tell that the first germs of mistrust are already growing within you. As I told you, it is inevitable that you will grow to hate me. I think it is better that I leave your household very soon before that happens."

I felt my emotions welling up inside me, but Niccolo's pained and distant expression sent me back into silence. For many long minutes we did not speak. I was so lost in my thoughts I almost didn't notice we had wandered into a small courtyard adjacent to the British Museum; the courtyard contained numerous pieces of Greek and Roman statuary flickering eerily in the lightning. The thunder rumbled as Niccolo paused beneath the statue of a man with his hand outstretched a few feet above our heads, and it looked as if he were offering some blessing.

"Do you know why I ran so clumsily in front of your carriage?" he finally asked.

I regarded him questioningly.

"I was running from Lodovico."

My eyes widened. "Lodovico's in London?"

"No . . ." he said slowly and sadly. "Lodovico doesn't have to be in London for one to be running from him." He paused. "Did I ever tell you whom Lodovico had me portray in the *trionfi?*"

"No."

"He had me portray Endymion. Do you know who Endymion was?"

I shook my head.

"In Greek mythology Endymion was a most beautiful young man, so beautiful that the moon herself fell in love with him and came down in the form of the goddess Selene to court him. As with most mortals loved by divinities, Endymion found only fatal peril in her attention, for when Selene kissed him her kiss sent him into a deep and eternal sleep. That way she could always possess him, and he would remain forever the never-waking lover of the moon." He paused again. "*Jettatura . . .*" he murmured and grasped the foot of the statue. "Look at the face." He made a sweeping gesture over our heads and as I looked up a crackle of lightning allowed me to see the stone visage of a Roman patrician with a straight and delicate nose and a strong, square chin. Also, for just a brief second as the marble flickered electrical blue, I noticed there were no eyes in the sockets, only an impenetrable darkness, and then the night closed in once again with a rumble of thunder.

"Lodovico?" I gasped.

"Yes," he returned slowly. "This is Lodovico."

With trembling hands I struggled to shield a match from the rain and gazed at the inscription. The small bronze plaque informed me that the figure was a facsimile of a Roman work, a statue of an Alexandrian scholar from the Arch of Constantine, dated at around A.D. 315. I straightened with amazement as I dropped the match and it sizzled in the wet gravel.

"I loved Leonardo," Niccolo said distantly. I realized he was thinking out loud more than addressing me. "If I would have only known Lodovico always likes to make his move during a celebration, a carnival. I didn't know then. How could I?" He spat in anger as he let go of the statue and took a few steps, slowly shaking his head. "It's not that I didn't love Lodovico, but that I couldn't love anyone else. How could I knowing that I would see their sweet young faces become embroidered with wrinkles, see them grow old and die, while I remained unchanged in their frightened eyes? But there's always Lodovico. Oh, yes, forever and ever, no matter how far I run, there's always Lodovico." He turned madly about until he found a rock beside the walkway, and then he flung it with his full strength at the statue, neatly snapping the outstretched hand at the wrist.

"Niccolo!" I cried as he vanished into the night. In helpless confusion I picked up the stone hand and noticed for the first time there was a large scar across the top of it, sculpted in gory detail into the marble. For the first few seconds of my bewilderment I hesitated, wondering if I should leave the broken hand. But then, on some strange impulse, I kept it and fled into the darkness to look for Niccolo.

IX

After the revelation that the vampire possessed a body of learning that Niccolo asserted would dwarf the accomplishments of the human race, I begged him incessantly to tell me more, but he remained silent. He also refused to reveal any further glimpses of Lodovico, save for the disclosure that his mysterious mentor had, indeed, been alive at least since the time of Constantine, the first Christian Roman emperor. From this I began to understand why Lodovico must have been so delighted with the interest of the Medici in the works of antiquity. If he had been an Alexandrian scholar he could very well have known the authors of the ancient classics firsthand. He had walked the colonnades and papyrus-lined corridors of the library of Alexandria itself. Nonetheless, when I suggested this to Niccolo, he still said nothing. Even when I showed him the scar on the stone hand he only shrugged.

I immersed myself in everything ever written on the Arch of Constantine, but I could find no more than the briefest mention of the disfiguration. None of the books offered either a clue to the origin and meaning of the scar, or a hint of the scribe's identity. I developed a strange aversion to touching the object. It was not that it didn't fascinate me. I would sit for hours gazing at it as it rested upon the black velvet table shawl on the tea table in the study. What deeds had it wrought? What shoulders throughout history had it rested upon?

To my dismay, little Camille took an unnatural interest in the hand. Several times I came upon her staring off into space while her hands, embued with a life of their own, turned the object over like a puzzle box. Of the precious few times Camille had made contact with the nonacoustic world around her, I was at an utter loss to explain why she was fascinated by the cold marble hand.

After the incident in the courtyard all communication between Niccolo and me became very strained. He grew increasingly reluctant to allow me to check his pulse and body temperature, and even mentioning the taking of blood samples became a *bête noire*. We had several heated arguments over this issue, and I could tell he blamed his unwillingness on me, although he said nothing to this effect. I made a further observation. Impossibly, Niccolo's legs had completely healed, but the peculiar rhythm of his walk remained. There was a ghostly cadence to his step. I asked him about this as well, but he only flared with anger. It was more than apparent that my accusations and suspicions had hurt him deeply. Nothing could persuade him that the disintegration of our mutual trust was not imminent. This, of course, caused me no small amount of anguish. I realized more and more I had to penetrate the world of the vampire, not only because of the medical knowledge they already possessed, but also because unraveling the secrets of their incredible condition offered, perhaps, unfathomable medical advances for the world of men. I had to hold on to Niccolo, for he was the bridge, the only tie I possessed with a dark and unbelievable world.

The only thing Niccolo did seem interested in pursuing was his relationship with Ursula, and as the days continued to pass this took an unexpected turn. They still indulged in vehement, even passionate debates, but it was undeniable Ursula was beginning to mellow. Her counterattacks became softer. Instead of storming out of the room she tended more and more to lapse into periods of rapt attention as Niccolo prattled on eloquently in French and Latin. In itself, I did not mind this change. What I did mind, what disturbed me greatly was that Niccolo was just a little too conscious of my presence during these victories. After he had caused her to gasp or smile over some magnificent point he had just made he would invariably throw a glance my way as if to make certain I was aware of the tiny bit of influence he was gaining over her. At first I thought I was reading too much into the situation, but then his parleys became too obviously staged and directed for my benefit. He would dazzle her with a closing line of his argument just as I was coming out of my study, or extract a word of admiration from her at the very moment I started to descend the stairs.

As for why he was doing this, I assumed it was his way of getting back at me for hurting him with my accusations. It was more than obvious I disliked his cruel game. He seemed to bask in my uneasiness. As for Ursula, to my surprise she was completely blind to his manipulations. She was much too involved in her own rôle in the situation to notice Niccolo's words were for anyone else but herself. Although this saddened me, I did not look unkindly at Ursula's blindnesses. It was Niccolo and Niccolo alone whom I blamed, and the rift between us grew greater every evening.

It was one night toward the end of April that I knocked on Ursula's door and opened it to discover her sitting in the middle of her pink and gray Persian carpet. Her boudoir was cluttered, in accordance with the most contemporary tastes, with a large mahogany bureau and vanity, various rosewood occasional tables, gimcrack chairs of black lacquer inlaid with mother-of-pearl, and small tables of fretted teak brought from Burma. Heavy rose velvet curtains covered the windows and walls, and everything was decorated with voluminous drapes of velvet, plush, and brocade, and trimmed with fringes, tassels, and chenille baubles. It was a cacophony of styles, and in the middle of the room sat Ursula in a Japanese kimono illuminated by several large silver candelabra. She was surrounded by several branches of white hawthorn, which she was carefully weaving into a garland.

"Good evening, Father," she greeted, threading a needle through one of the blossoms.

"Whatever are you up to?" I asked.

"Fixing my costume for the celebration of May Eve. You know it isn't that far off."

The remark startled me a little. "You're going to go through with the celebration?"

She regarded me quizzically. "Why not?"

"After your dream, I thought maybe you would be a little too afraid."

She chuckled as she momentarily positioned the garland upon her head and casually glanced at herself in the mirror. "I told you, Father, I didn't take the dream literally. I just thought it represented some sort of major change in my life."

"And do you have any idea what that change might be?" I asked as I sat down gently beside her.

"No," she murmured unconvincingly. She removed the garland and once again began threading blossoms. "You know," she began, "Mr. Cavalanti may be a smug and supercilious young man, but I have to admit, he amazes me sometimes."

I gazed at her inquiringly.

"Well, the other afternoon when I arrived home he told me I deserved to be called a dirty name if I had the nerve to lead a young man on by going to tea with him and then slap him in the face when he made an advance. He further added that it served me right for picking such a crude and rough young man and then asked me who my dark-haired gentleman caller had beat up the night before. The odd thing is that I had just been to tea with young Mr. Wooland, the umbrella salesman from Briggs in St. James Street. I confess I guess I did lead him on in that a young woman can't even accept an invitation to tea without the young man thinking it's a flirtation. He said something vulgar to me. I slapped him and he called me a high-class rump. Of course, I left, but the odd thing is that during the course of our tea he boasted he had beat up a young man just the night before. And," she added, "he's certainly not my suitor, but he did have dark hair."

"You went out with an umbrella salesman?" I asked in surprise.

"Oh, Father," she huffed and then continued. "I was so amazed. I asked him how on earth he knew all of that, and, of course, he said it was all very obvious. He said my hair smelled faintly of cigarettes, not Turkish or Egyptian, but Benson and Hedges, and since young women don't smoke I must have been out with a gentleman. He deduced that it was too late for lunch, and whether I liked to admit it or not, I was too proper to do anything else, so I must have been out to tea with a young man. As for my slapping him and his making a vulgar comment, Mr. Cavalanti conceded that this was an educated guess. He pointed out that my face was flushed and my heartbeat was very rapid, as if I had just been either frightened or embarrassed. He further noted this," she said, holding up the blouse she had been wearing and pointing to a faint blackish streak on the sleeve. "He said he couldn't be sure, but it looked very much like a cigarette had brushed against my clothing. Judging from the regularity and angle of the smudge it seemed more than apparent that the cigarette had probably flown out of the young man's mouth after his head turned swiftly to one side, as if rebounding from a hard, firm slap. Taking these several bits of information along with a knowledge of my character, Mr. Cavalanti said it wasn't too difficult to imagine my leading the young gentleman on in what he called my usual 'feigned naïveté,' he making an advance, I slapping him, the cigarette flying from his mouth, and he saying something vulgar, causing me to blush."

After she had finished I stood in mute awe for a few moments and then asked, "How did he know that this Mr. Wooland had dark hair and had been in a fight the night before?"

"It's too incredible," she said and held her open hand for me to examine. "Do you notice anything?"

"A sort of reddish tint to the fingers," I murmured, "but what does that mean?"

"*Papiers poudré*," she said, "makeup of the type used in Madame Rachel's shop down the street on 'wild' young men who come to have their black eyes and other marks of fist encounters repaired and *maquillé* so that they might be presentable for a social occasion. I must have gotten it on my hand when I slapped him. As for the black hair, Mr. Cavalanti confessed that was merely a lucky guess." She shook her head in amazement.

"Mr. Cavalanti can be very clever when he wants to," I said sardonically, but she did not seem to notice my contempt.

"You know what else?"

I stared blankly.

Ursula went to the mahogany bureau and withdrew a small white glove. "Do you recognize it?"

Of course I did—the tiny white satin fingers, the delicate beadwork. It had been Camille's.

She saw my answer in my eyes. "Well . . ." she started

carefully, "the other evening I sat here while Mr.
Cavalanti examined this glove and then told me its entire
history, from the very first time it clutched a violet to the
last time it was worn. He told me it was the glove of a
woman who loved to dance, who enjoyed petting
greyhounds and throwing snowballs. And"—her voice
trailed off as a faint trace of sympathy crossed her
normally emotionless face—"and he told me it was the
glove of a woman who died in a sickroom because there
was still the faint smell of medicaments, of camphor and
eucalyptus . . . and of death."

I glanced at the tiny glove as my throat tightened. "So
what is the purpose of telling me all of this?"

"Oh, don't you see, Father? Mr. Cavalanti may not be
able to go out into the sunlight, but such a world is opened
up to him, such a marvelous universe of nuances and
kaleidoscopic facets."

"So?"

"So, I want that world opened up to me."

I straightened. "That would be quite impossible."

"Why?"

"Because phototropic leucocythemia is not contagious."

"Mr. Cavalanti says it is. He says we could transfer it to
me in the same way we infect the rabbits in your
laboratory, by injecting a little of his blood into my veins."

I stared dumbly at the round, pale face, the dark red
hair tumbling gently over the kimono.

"Oh, Father, I want to *see* the world as Mr. Cavalanti
sees it. That is the change I want to go through this May
Eve."

I was horrified. I had not realized it before, but there
was an undiscovered dread within me. The thought of
someone I knew becoming a vampire, my own daughter,
supping on crawling things, her face transformed like a
rat or viper, carnivorous and necrophilic, filled me with
sudden disgust. "Ursula, I can't allow it—"

She seemed shocked. A question trembled on her lip.
"Why? Is it not my own decision?"

"No," I said falteringly. "No, it is not."

Anger flushed her face. "Why?" she demanded again,
and then her expression changed. The rapid scanning of
her eyes revealed a tumult of thoughts, thoughts perhaps

even she did not realize she possessed. "Is it because it's all right for you to be different, for you to help Mr. Cavalanti escape from the hospital when everyone feared him, but it's not all right for anyone else?"

"That's not true," I said, realizing Niccolo had been talking to her.

"It isn't?" she continued, still possessed. "It isn't true that you married Mother because you wanted to be different, but then you turned around and punished her for it?" Her face became unusually cold and hard. "You know why you're so against my infecting myself with Mr. Cavalanti's disease? It's because you're jealous. You're hurt that he's opening up a world to me that he's closed off to you. You'd infect yourself if he gave you the opportunity, but you'd damn me if I did the same."

I was shocked and hurt by the attack, but I struggled to maintain my composure. "I think you'd better consider what you've just said," I advised. "It's true that photo-tropic leucocythemia intensifies the senses, but we know very little about the disease, about what untold physiological and psychological side effects it may have. It would be completely out of the question for you to be a guinea pig for such an experiment."

Ursula crossed her arms defiantly.

"One more thing," I said as I turned toward the door.

She regarded me scornfully, her white knuckles gripping the hawthorn.

"I don't want you leaving the house during May Eve," I stated with all the self-restraint I could summon.

For the next several days I spent most of my time working in the laboratory. I tried not to think of Ursula's words, but simply allowed myself the luxury of feeling a blind and unarticulated hurt and anger. As for Ursula, when we passed each other in the halls, and even when we sat across from each other at the breakfast table, we remained completely silent. Even though her quiet contempt was agony for me, I took some solace in the fact that she wouldn't be feeling such anger if she didn't intend to obey my wishes.

It was shortly after sundown on the eve of May that I went into my laboratory and discovered for the first time

Niccolo in the act of indulging in his fiendish practice. He
stood facing the door with his face buried in the nape of
the neck of one of the brown rabbits I had provided for
him. The rabbit's sable eyes were wide with terror, its
mouth agape with the rictus of approaching death. As I
entered, the vampire looked up, the blood still moist upon
his canines.

"Niccolo!" I gasped and then stuttered, not knowing
what to say.

"Dottore," he apologized, "there wasn't time for me to
finish before you came in."

"It's all right," I said, trying to calm myself. "It's just
the first time, I guess, I've actually seen you—"

"Killing something," he filled in, and I thought I
detected a slight smile when he realized how revolted I
was. He gently placed the animal upon the counter, and
then removed a hair from between his teeth, smugly and
with aristocratic delicacy. The rabbit twitched. It was not
quite dead.

"Poor thing," he comforted and stroked its fur. "At least
it's lost enough blood so that it's deep in slumber."

I shuddered as I approached the counter and made some
semblance of looking busy. "Niccolo," I finally began,
"I've been meaning to talk to you about something."

He looked in my direction.

"I don't like what you've been doing lately."

He remained expressionless.

"Come now, Niccolo, you know what I'm talking about.
You've been playing some sort of game with Ursula, for
my benefit, to get back at me for my accusations."

"Ahh," he said and casually padded over to the glass cubicle
containing a gray-and-white rabbit. The brown one that had
had *Camillus influenzae* had long since died, and the gray-
and-white one was the newest living receptacle for the deadly
virus. "Well, Dottore, I've noticed that you've been taking it
that way, but trust me, I did not consciously intend to cause
you any discomfort. My only motive was to—"

"I don't trust you," I interrupted angrily.

Niccolo abruptly glanced in my direction.

"I'm tired of you lying," I said in desperation. "You may
calmly and coolly deny everything, but damn it, you're up to
something."

"You see!" he shrilled. "I warned you. I warned that the day would come when you would turn against me."

"Yes, Niccolo, but not because I am one of the superstitious rabble, as you so eloquently put it. You've used that ploy to keep me in a state of constant indecision, but it won't work any longer."

"Just like all the others!"

"'Just like all the others!'?" I mimicked harshly. "'Just like all the others!'? Then why did you tell Ursula you would infect her with your disease?"

"You're the one who told her I have a disease," he countered. "I was just playing along." And then, in a flurry of exasperation, he turned to me. "All right. You are correct, Dottore. It was a parlay, a stratagem in a game, and now that you have confronted me so violently with your suspicions, you have forced my hand."

His words struck me like a sword against my flesh, and for a few moments I stood stunned. "What do you mean?"

His eyes widened with fury, but then a strange smile crossed his face. "I am leaving," he said simply as he lifted the brown rabbit up to his lips and finished it with gusto. As I shrunk back he turned to me one last time. "I am leaving and going back to my own world, my own kind," he ended as he stormed out the door.

I stood there for several minutes after he had left, trying to sort out my thoughts from the confused emotions of the situation. At first I felt only elation, as if some danger had passed and I could finally breathe easily. But then I became filled with a growing sense of remorse and profound disappointment. If only I could have handled it differently, I thought, and once again made some feeble attempt to go about my work. As I continued, as each painful minute passed, I became more and more aware of the implications of Niccolo's leaving. What an opportunity I had allowed to pass through my hands. No . . . I corrected myself, not just an opportunity, an entire unexplored world. Finally, and almost without thinking, the anguish became too much and I found myself racing to his room to see if he had left yet.

When I arrived I discovered I was too late. Niccolo was gone. The wardrobe was empty and on the neatly made bed was a crisp hundred-pound note and a gracefully written message. It read: *"The money is some meager payment for all you have done. The end has come."*

I uttered a little cry of pain as I crumpled the message and stuck it into my pocket. I walked blindly into the hall and along the balustrade overlooking the foyer, and al ost didn't notice that Cook was standing at the foot of the stairs.

"Lord Almighty," she gasped. "Are you in another world, sir?"

I glanced dazedly at the puckish red-cheeked face with its tousle of white hair. "What?"

"I've called to you several times," she continued. "I said, 'You 'ave a visitor. 'E's in the drawing room.' Shall I tell 'im you've taken ill?"

"No, no," I said, shaking my head and wondering who it could be. Cook cast me a worried glance as I descended the stairs.

When I pushed the massive walnut doors aside I noticed the familiar odor of Egyptian cigarettes. Then I saw Cletus's dwarfish form silhouetted in the light from the streetlamps shining through the French windows. The sounds of a crowd could be heard faintly from the street below.

"What are you doing here?" I demanded.

"Quite a mob forming out there," he said, motioning toward the window.

"You didn't come here to talk about May Eve."

"No . . . no, I didn't."

"So why?"

"I've been thinking, that's all"—he bit off the end of his cigarette and spit it into a parlor palm—"about *Niccolo*." He said the name with a peculiar rise in his voice.

"What about *Niccolo?*" I mimicked.

"Oh . . ." he said as he paced around the gilt and rosewood pianoforte and casually tapped a solitary note, "I was just thinking, if his metabolism were truly as, shall we say, preternatural as it seemed to be, you might have been very interested in—"

"Studying him," I filled in and gazed sternly at the little gremlin. "I might as well save us both a lot of fancy footwork and tell you that I helped Niccolo escape from Redgewood. But so what? He left of his own free will. He just wanted to get out without anyone knowing when he was leaving or where he was going."

"So!" Cletus snorted. "If he did have something to do with Chiswick's disappearance we might have been able to have extracted some information from him about the matter."

I threw up my hands. "You bloody fool, how often do I have to point out to you that there's nothing to tie Niccolo with the disappearance of Chiswick? Indeed, I foolishly allowed myself momentarily to become persuaded by your wild suspicions, but when I confronted Niccolo he was completely shocked and denied everything."

Cletus eagerly hung on to my every word. "And what is this young man, this Niccolo?" His voice became very low. "Is he something—?"

I regarded the little man with complete sincerity and calm. "He is a vampire," I replied simply.

"Oh, come now."

"Don't believe me if you don't want to."

Cletus raised a bristling eyebrow as his face revealed he was searching my eyes for the truth. He puffed rapidly on his Egyptian cigarette and I could tell the machinery was working full speed behind his fierce little eyes. "Where is he?" he said without a hint of his acceptance or disbelief. "I want to see him."

"You can't."

His lip quivered truculently. "Why not?"

"He's gone. We had an argument today and he left." In self-righteous anger I explained the entire story, Niccolo's refusal to allow me to take any blood samples, how I told Ursula he had phototropic leucocythemia, the way he toyed with her, and how our friendship finally disintegrated in a strange interchange of mistrust and cruel games. There was nothing Cletus could do now and I wanted him to share in the helplessness I felt. In my telling, I wanted to rid myself of the little man once and for all.

After I finished I slowly walked over to the French windows and gazed out at the expanse of Bond Street. Branches of hawthorn had been attached to most of the gas lamps, and lengths of ribbon and brightly colored swatches of flannel formed a macabre spiderweb over the street. People milled about everywhere, and the crowd of dodgers and tawdry women formed an odd contrast against the somber and stately façade of Mayfair. Here and there children bandied effigies of witches, and raffish men carried torches. I knew that somewhere in the distance a huge bonfire was being built.

"What else?" Cletus finally interrupted.

I turned around.

"Something else is bothering you. What is it?"

"It's Ursula," I said, unable to fight any longer. "She had a dream a couple of weeks ago that she was a Druid during the ancient rite of May Eve, and that she was sacrificed in the fire."

"So?"

"So, she's certain that something is going to happen to her tonight. She was convinced, even hoping, that Niccolo would infect her with his *disease.*"

Once again Cletus raised an eyebrow. He was about to say something when we both became distracted by the muffled strains of a familiar chant. *"Through the rowan and through the keep, spare the horse and spare the sheep."*

"May Eve," he huffed disdainfully and flicked an ash into the palm. "In any case, I trust you set Ursula straight."

"Of course," I retorted. "I told her that under no circumstances was she to leave her room tonight."

"Spare the fox and spare the hen," the litany continued.

"And you're completely certain she's there now?"

"Well, of course—" I began, but then a strange sensation crept over me. I thought I was sure. But as Cletus stood there holding me down with his tigerish gaze, I became uncertain. It was true I hadn't seen Ursula since well before my blowup with Niccolo, but I couldn't fathom she would go against my word. "Come and I'll show you," I said as I opened the huge walnut doors.

As I gripped the balustrade on my way up the stairs I realized my pace was unconsciously quickening. There was even a trace of sweat on my palms. Cletus hobbled behind me. When we reached the boudoir I tapped loudly on the door. No answer.

"Ursula," I called, and there was still no reply.

I flung the door open and a gust of wind caused the heavy rose velvet curtains to billow on either side of the window. The room was empty. As I glanced about madly at the mahogany bureau and the black lacquer chairs I became aware of something else. It was then that I noticed the broken vial and the small glass rod on the table of fretted teak. The air was redolent with the smell of lily and palm.

"No!" I cried as I pushed Cletus aside and raced down the stairs. I ran headlong into Cook.

"Ursula," I exclaimed, "have you seen Ursula?"

"She went out," Cook gasped in surprise. "Well, my goodness, it's the May Eve—" She swung around in addled confusion as I ran by her and out the door.

Outside, the street was a swarming mass of shouting and frenzied people. Some were brightly dressed with garlands and scepters of ribbons and flowers. Others were shifty and ragged. Many of them carried cattails soaked in paraffin and set aflame. The multitude of little fires cast grotesque shadows on the looming buildings.

"Through the rowan and through the keep," they chorused and a cry rose from the mob as one young doxy was hefted upon the shoulders of several rowdy men. As I burst through the crowd a horse reared, and I realized I had blundered directly into the path of a shiny black barouche filled with fashionably dressed people. A monocled gentleman shouted something at me but his voice became lost in the din of the celebration. I became dimly aware that Cletus was struggling to follow me, but I soon lost him in the turmoil of the crowd.

I ran and ran and here and there people oblivious to my panic tried to catch me up in their circles as they laughed and danced. "Spare the horse and spare the sheep!" I pulled away from them madly as I tried to discern the flow, the inexorable ebb of the crowd as it swirled and eddied through the streets and slowly made its way to the bonfire.

At last I saw the conflagration, a swirling pillar of yellow and vermilion engulfing an abatis of trees and broken chairs as the swirling, sooty mass twisted up into the inky blackness of the night. The bonfire crackled and roared and all the faces of the crowd were lit in the flickering yellow light. "Spare the fox and spare the hen, but throw the woman in!" they shrilled as they flung the crumpled straw body of a witch into the flames. "Aye, and throw the woman in!"

I turned about in a frenzy and then at last I saw. Standing amid the Doric columns and white portico of a Georgian mansion across the square was Ursula. She wore a long white dress and the garland of hawthorn was slightly askew upon her head. In the bright circle of light from the inferno I could tell that her expression was silent and dazed and she peered into space with a glassy stare.

"Ursula!" I screamed as I rushed to her side and sharply turned her shoulders about. "Where's Niccolo?"

She remained blank for a few seconds as if she hadn't even heard the words, and then suddenly her expression crumpled and she burst into tears. "He's gone," she sobbed. "Oh, Father, I knew he was a vampire. He asked me to meet him here and I begged him to make me a vampire, too, but he refused. He just said good-bye and then he left." She buried her face in my chest and continued to cry. I hugged her tightly and led her through the crowd.

On the way back to Bond Street I was so swept up with relief and the emotions of the situation I didn't even stop to wonder why Niccolo had to call Ursula out into the celebration to say good-bye, or why he erroneously left the vial of aromatic oil in her boudoir. When we arrived home Cook came running out to greet us and I noticed that she, too, was frantic and crying.

"Oh, Dr. Gladstone," she gushed, "they came while you were gone."

"Who?" I asked with a puzzled expression.

"Mr. Cavalanti and another gentleman, a little older, with the most penetrating and frightening eyes. It was 'orrible." She shook her head madly. "Simply 'orrible. They rode in a 'earse, of all things, a Neapolitan 'earse, windowed in black plate glass with black-plumed stallions!" She flung herself at me as if making some pitiful gesture for mercy.

"Why, Cook, what is it?"

"They took her," she gasped and gazed up at me with her china-blue eyes. "I tried to stop them, but they took little Camille."

Book Two

Hespeth

X

My world had crumbled. The only thing I had ever touched without ruin was gone. Why had they taken her? I could not imagine Niccolo hurting Camille, hurting a child, but the image of that tender face sucking the life out of the rabbit was still vivid in my mind. Would they hurt her? It did not make sense. Why would they go to such lengths for such a small and innocent creature? I did not know. That was the agony, the unknowing.

The days that followed the abduction brought a relentless barrage of outsiders into our home and lives. Not a morning passed that Scotland Yard wasn't knocking at our door. I told them everything it was safe to tell about Niccolo Cavalanti and Lodovico—about the carriage accident and Niccolo's stay in my home, about my interest in his 'rare medical condition,' and how I knew nothing of his immediate past, his family, or where he lived. I judiciously recognized that the authorities were far from being able to consider seriously the supernatural in their investigations. Even the mentioning of Niccolo's immunity to paraldehyde and the Neapolitan hearse brought raised eyebrows from Scotland Yard. I cautioned myself not to put too much hope in their investigations. Still, it hurt when they uncovered nothing.

Camille's abduction made front-page headlines in the city's newspapers, and not a day passed that some reporter wasn't snooping around our door. In my first encounters with the press I was cordial and issued brief statements about my remorse over what had happened. They also kindly printed a public plea for anyone having any information that might help us, and to my surprise hundreds of letters poured in. At first I greeted these letters with excitement. Some even blamed the vampire. Once again my hopes were crushed. After I examined them I realized they were only from crackpots. I suppose it was the Neapolitan hearse that inspired the wretches.

The theories that blamed the vampire for the kidnapping were as puerile and uninformed as those that blamed Jack the Ripper, the Whigs or the Tories, and even Prince Edward. After their initial sympathy the newspapers soon realized it was the lurid details of the case that sold copy. *The Times* ran headlines like "Prominent Physician's Daughter Taken by Body Snatchers," and *The Illustrated London News* ran hideous lithographs of every possible atrocity that might be performed upon little Camille. They were stories for the "penny dreadfuls" and they made life nearly unbearable.

As for Cletus, the only bright spot in those dark days was the fact that he was visibly shaken by the event. Although he had come to warn me about Niccolo I don't think Cletus ever really believed any of his theories or concerns. Now that something had actually happened, he had taken on an entirely different attitude. He was very quiet and ill at ease when I saw him in the corridors of Redgewood.

It was one week after the incident that two inspectors from the Yard, a Captain McClough and an Inspector Inglethorpe, came to tell me of their first break in the case. Both had visited my home several times previously. Captain McClough was the chief officer of our local precinct. He was a large man with caterpillar eyebrows and a full gray mustache. His demeanor was more apologetic than proficient. It was clear from the first he was one of those typical and very traditional English gentlemen known as "a good ol' boy." Inspector Inglethorpe was a younger gentleman, of medium height, polite and good-looking, with black hair and a black mustache.

The maid brought them to my study.

"Dr. Gladstone," Captain McClough greeted.

"Yes."

"We wonder if your cook is at home."

"Yes," I returned, wondering what possible need they had of her. Three different groups of inspectors had already asked her every imaginable question twenty times. It seemed cruel to go through the list once again.

"Is your schedule very busy today?"

"Is there some news?"

"We think we've located this Neapolitan hearse of yours," Captain McClough said with obvious pride over his revelation.

"In London!"

His face fell. "I'm afraid not, sir. It's in Dover."

"And Camille?"

Once again he lowered his eyes disconsolately. "I'm afraid there's no luck in that either, Dr. Gladstone, sir. The hearse was discovered abandoned. There was no sign of the blokes who took your daughter."

I sighed and stroked my forehead as both Captain McClough and Inspector Inglethrope shifted their weight uneasily.

"We were wondering," the younger man continued, "would today be a convenient day for you and your cook to accompany us to Dover so that a positive identification could be made?"

"Yes, we can go with you," I said.

After explaining the situation to Cook we made our way to Victoria Station. The train ride to Dover was uneventful. Once there we were led to a rundown storage lot in the waterfront area, near the piers where the passenger ferries leave to cross the Channel to France. The storage lot was filled with numerous large crates and piles of metal pipes, all covered with huge tarpaulins. As the police wagon approached the lot I noticed a number of policemen standing around one of the rows of crates. It was only after we came to a stop that I noticed the hearse. It was large and elegant, with gilt inlay on the huge spoked wheels. The carriage housing was black and shiny with decorative carved knobs at each of the four upper corners. The plate glass was blackened from the inside and as shiny as a sheet of obsidian.

Cook, prim and dignified in her black woolen shawl and cap with a bit of netting hanging from it, began to shift about excitedly, trying to get a better view.

"Glory," she said, "but if that isn't it!"

We stepped down from the police wagon and approached the abandoned hearse.

"Can you be absolutely certain?" Captain McClough asked. Cook began to cluck and shake her head as she touched a small handkerchief to her eye.

"Oh, yes, Constable. I'm quite certain of that, I am. The image of them taking the little mistress away—it 'as been burnt in my mind." She dejectedly turned toward me. "I'm so sorry, sir. I—"

"It's all right," I hushed and put my hand upon her shoulder. The wind from the Channel swept around us. I looked at Captain McClough. "So what has happened to them? Did anyone see them leave the hearse here?"

Captain McClough began to bluster something when suddenly Inspector Inglethorpe stepped forward and cleared his throat. "In answer to your questions, I'd say it's pretty obvious they went to France. They apparently abandoned the hearse so as not to attract attention on the ferry. We're trying to trace the hearse and the horses, but we don't think that's going to result in much. Unfortunately, we have very little to go on. There's no record of Mr. Cavalanti buying a ticket, but that doesn't mean anything. They most assuredly traveled under assumed names.

"In answer to your second question, yes, someone did see them. We did a lot of legwork and asked a lot of people up and down the piers if they saw anything. We've come up with a dockworker named Herg who remembers two men and a little blind girl answering their description."

He motioned toward a group of policemen standing a little ways away from the hearse and for the first time I noticed a large man, crudely dressed, with his sleeves rolled up over his powerful arms. He was young, with short brown hair, a large red nose, and clear blue eyes. He seemed very humble and willing to please and held his cap in front of him in his hands.

I felt a pang of hope.

"Dr. Gladstone, may I introduce you to Mr. Herg."

The man nodded and meekly came forward. "Dr. Gladstone," he said, continuing to nod.

"Mr. Herg," I returned. "They tell me you have seen my daughter?"

"The lil' blind girl wi' brown 'air an' large green eyes?"

"And wearing a plain white smock with black knee stockings?"

"Aye, I belie' so, Dr. Gladstone, suh. An' t'other men as well; a red-heidit young boy wi' curly hair, an' the aulder man. I saw 'em drive up into the yard, and belie' me, suh, I began to watch. I wondered who would be comin' in a 'earse. An' lo', these two blokes get out wi' the lil' girl."

"Were they mistreating her?"

"Noo, suh. They seemed most kind. An' the lil' girl, she was as 'appy as could be, playin' wi' ... well, yew know. . . ."

"Playing with what, Mr. Herg?"

Herg glanced around nervously. "That awful object, suh. The sever'd 'and. The 'and made o' stone, wi' the scar across its back." He gripped his cap diffidently as Inspector Inglethorpe stepped forward.

"Do you know anything about that, Dr. Gladstone?"

"No, nothing," I said, wondering if they knew anything about Niccolo's vandalism.

Inspector Inglethorpe continued. "Well, this is a strange case, an abduction in a hearse and giving a little girl a marble severed hand to play with." He looked uneasily at old Captain McClough, who was busily straightening his tie.

"Oh, yes. Quite, quite," he said.

Inglethorpe turned once again to the dockworker. "Was there anything else of note that you should mention to Dr. Gladstone?"

"Jes' that I am sorry. I 'ave a daughter o' my own, an' I know 'ow it must be." He glanced at me sympathetically.

I nodded.

"Jes' the 'earse, the three o' them, an' the sever'd 'and. An' tha's all."

Herg went back with the other group of policemen.

"So, Inspector Inglethorpe. What will you do next?"

"Continue our investigations here, of course, but I think we'll have more luck across the Channel. I've already contacted the French authorities and we're proceeding with every possible effort. Still, Dr. Gladstone, there's one thing that bothers me a great deal. It's been quite a while and they still haven't sent you any hint of a ransom note. What would such criminals want with the daughter of a wealthy physician if they weren't after ransom?"

I felt helpless. "I wish I knew, Inspector Inglethorpe. I wish I knew."

* * *

When I arrived at home I went to the study. The hand was, indeed, gone. Camille must have wandered in and retrieved it. Such a strange fascination she had with that curious *objet d'art.* I wondered what Lodovico thought of seeing the little girl playing with the facsimile of his hand, his scar, and what had caused the scar?

I was still deep in thought when Ursula broke into the room.

She wore a bright scarlet shawl and her flesh was waxen against its brilliance. "Oh, I'm sorry," she said. "I didn't know anyone was in here."

"It's all right," I returned.

A tension prickled between us. Ursula strolled casually to the fireplace and admired the African grasshoppers. We pretended not to be overly aware of each other, but we were. I expected Ursula to apologize. As I have said, it was rare for us to fight. I could tell she was deeply disturbed over the rift that had developed between us. She seemed anxious and involved in her thoughts. Finally she turned toward me. Her eyes were searching.

"Father?"

"Yes?"

"You blame me, don't you?"

"You disobeyed me. If you hadn't disobeyed me this might never have happened."

She regarded me sadly. "Did you never disobey your own father?"

Had I? Had I ever really disobeyed him? Only in my thoughts. "No," I replied solemnly.

Again her eyes searched mine. There was a strange mixture in her gaze. There was remorse, but there was something else. Was it anger? Anger at what? Not at me. A question lingered on her lips. I knew she wanted to dispel the uneasiness that existed between us. Only her intense pride held her back. Was it the soft word I waited for?

Her lips began to move. "Why do you think they took Camille?"

The question surprised me. I frowned at her, distraught by my own bewilderment. "I don't know."

She stepped forward and allowed a single white hand to grip the back of the padded and buttoned black leather armchair. The pressure of her grip and the knitting of her brow indicated it was a question of unexpected importance to her. It was strange. It was not an easy thing for me to say. Ursula had always been very compassionate about Camille. Ursula had comforted her and rocked her to sleep, perhaps even more than I had, but there remained a certain streak of coldness in Ursula. Naturally, she was concerned about Camille's welfare, but I could not help feeling her curiosity was of a deeper vein than mere sibling affection.

She looked directly in my eyes. "Do you think they will hurt her?"

I shrugged. I remembered Niccolo's indignation at being accused of "biting children," but I also considered how deliberately he had lied to me and created the subterfuge to kidnap Camille.

"I don't know," I gasped impotently. "Do you think he will hurt her?" In the ensuing seconds I realized Ursula's answer was much more important to me than I might have expected. I found myself watching her anxiously, waiting for her answer as if I secretly felt it was somehow more valid than my own perceptions and feelings.

"I'd like to think he won't," she replied. "I'd even like to hope he won't," she stressed, "but when I search the farthest corner of my feelings I find that I simply don't know."

There came a tap at the door and we both turned to see Cook standing there. "There's a woman waiting in the drawing room who wishes to have a word with you," she informed.

"You let her in before consulting me?" I asked, a little piqued.

"She insisted," Cook blustered. She wafted a lock of white hair out of her eyes. "She told me her name was Lady Dunaway, and as I turned around to fetch you, she pushed right in and made her way into the drawing room."

"Well, I'm going out," Ursula said as she quickly left without even saying good-bye. I cast her a quizzical glance as I shook my head and proceeded to the front of the house. As I entered the drawing room I realized for the first time that it was a particularly sunny June day. Golden light flooded through the French windows and the gilt on the pianoforte glistened brilliantly. Indeed, everything shimmered, the deep red brocade wallpaper, the brass standard lamps, the bright chintz sofas and chairs, and even the mellow green and gray Constables on either wall glowed as if filled with a new atmosphere. In front of one of the Constables stood Lady Dunaway.

She turned the moment I entered the room.

Lady Dunaway was a sight to behold. She was very tall, fully as tall as myself, and she wore a plaid ulster and cape, with a two-peaked Sherlock Holmes cap. At first when I examined her face I thought her features were unusual. Her cheekbones were a little too high, the angle of her chin a little too sharp. A pair of small and froggish gold-rimmed eyeglasses rested precariously on her long and very straight nose, and the lenses magnified her deep brown eyes ludicrously. As I continued to look at her, the eyeglasses were so incongruous with the broad white face that my mind's eye blotted them out. It was only then that all the awkward jigsaw pieces of her features melded into a strange harmony, and I saw how striking a woman she actually was. She was beautiful, but in an aquiline, even alien way. Her raven-black hair was drawn tightly into a knot behind her head, and it made her face look very smooth and chalky, like a piece of statuary. Her presence was exceedingly dignified, and I guessed her to be in her early thirties. Her hands were large, and she wore prim suede gloves.

"Dr. Gladstone?" she inquired and the smoky contralto of her voice startled me. It was deep for a woman's. It did not go with the delicate little eyeglasses, but it formed the perfect counterpoint with the powerful bone structure of her face. In the distance I heard the front door close as Ursula left for her undisclosed appointment.

I smiled. "Lady Dunaway?"

She nodded, but did not smile. "Lady Hespeth Dunaway," she said as I motioned for her to have a seat. Even though she was large for a woman, I could tell she was svelte and graceful beneath the folds of her ulster and cape. She sat down on the bright chintz sofa.

I sat down in one of the nearby chairs.

"You have a lovely home," she said, toying with the locket around her neck.

"Thank you."

"Is this the pianoforte?" She gestured at the window.

"The pianoforte?"

"The one the little girl played."

"Is that why you're here?"

She did not answer.

"So tragic. Please let me offer my sincere condolences." She gazed at me intently. Even through the large spectacles I discerned a warm and deeply felt sadness.

"Thank you," I muttered.

"May I ask you something? Did you like the young man, that Niccolo Cavalanti?"

"My dear Lady Dunaway, why are you asking me these questions?"

She gazed at me blankly. "Well, did you like him?"

"With all due respect, I'm afraid I cannot answer unless you explain to me why you are here and why you want to know all of these things."

"I'm interested," she said simply and tilted her head back, gazing at me with indignation.

I started to think she was one of the sympathetic and doting women who had written me. That was it, I thought, just another one of these silly women. But all of a sudden her peculiarity, the pallor of her complexion, and the power and authority with which she spoke struck a chill into me. Had Lodovico sent another emissary to my home? Was this creature a vampire?

With a sweeping gesture she threw her plaid cape behind her shoulders, stood, and walked toward the pianoforte. I was ready to jump up when I noticed something. There was a gleam about her hair. It was in the middle of the afternoon. She was standing in the full flood of the sunlight pouring through the windows.

At just that moment Cook clattered in with a tray of tea and scones and placed it on the mahogany table amid the chintz furniture. She glanced at me with nervous curiosity. As always, her eyes revealed she was dying to know what was going on. I did not know what was going on. I shrugged and she clucked her tongue in exasperation as she left the room.

Once again Lady Dunaway turned around.

"You must have liked him to have trusted him in your home. I'll wager you were even fond of him."

The words struck a note within me and I felt an odd urge to answer.

"Did he give you any reason to suspect he might kidnap your little daughter?"

"No, but—"

"No, he wouldn't have. You're obviously an intelligent man. You observe what is going on around you. It would be difficult not to arouse your suspicions." She stopped for a moment. "Did he tell you incredible stories of his past?"

"Yes."

"And you say he looked just like the angel in that painting?"

"Yes."

"I never knew that painting, but I looked it up after I read all of the articles in the newspapers."

"Lady Dunaway," I said harshly, "you must tell me what all of this has to do with you."

"I will," she said crossly, "but first you must tell me one thing."

I suppressed my temper one last time.

"Did this Mr. Cavalanti sleep during the day?"

I realized I was in the presence of an utter lunatic. I stood up quickly. "So you've read about the hearse, and you have this theory that Niccolo Cavalanti was a vampire. Is that it?"

For the first time my words seemed to have some effect on her and she looked at me with shock. She was obviously an eccentric English noblewoman, not unlike the frenzied letter writers. I suddenly imagined the two-peaked Sherlock Holmes hat was of obvious significance. Lady Dunaway, if she was a lady, had read the papers and had decided to go sleuthing.

"I'm afraid I'm very busy," I snapped. "Please pardon me, but I must ask you to leave."

She stiffened. "You think I'm crazy, just like the rest, don't you? You think I'm crazy?"

"No, no," I said calmly as I approached her.

She drew back in a huff.

I was afraid she was going to fly completely off the handle, but she abruptly composed herself. With self-assured calculation she stared directly into my eyes. Her breast rose and fell. She was on the verge of saying something. I could tell she was deliberating, hoping. And then she took hold of herself as a single word passed through her lips. *"Jettatura . . ."*

It swept through me like a bolt of lightning. I had not mentioned it to anyone. It was not to be found in any of the newspaper articles. "Why do you say that word?" I demanded.

"Because I am not crazy," she returned and grasped my arm tightly. Her eyes were wide and entreating. "And because I, too, have seen an angel."

XI

My heart leaped.

"Won't you please sit down," I beckoned and we both returned to our seats. I almost shook with excitement as I poured her a cup of tea, and once again our eyes locked.

"My good Lady Dunaway, you must tell me more. Do you know Niccolo Cavalanti?"

She took a sip as she composed herself. "I *knew* him."

"You do not know where he is now?"

"I'm afraid I do not."

"But how ... why?"

"You must let me explain. You see, after I read about your daughter in the newspaper, and after I saw the name, there was no question that it was the same young man. But I was afraid. I thought it was a trick, some sort of hoax. I thought ... well, the vampire was trying to lure me in. They're very tricky, you know. You can never believe or trust them."

I nodded.

"But please, Dr. Gladstone, tell me what you know. How did you become involved with, well, with *them?* Tell me, and then I'll tell you how I met Niccolo Cavalanti."

I proceeded to explain the entire incident to my newly found confidante. At every twist and turn of the story she was gasping and nodding excitedly. "Oh, yes, Il Magnifico. Yes, yes." She sat her cup of tea down. *"Lodovico!* Oh, yes ... Lodovico."

Finally, when I had finished, Lady Dunaway literally squealed and embraced me heartily. "Yes, oh, yes," she kept repeating. I was astonished to see she was crying ever so slightly.

"You must excuse me," she said, wiping her eyes with a handkerchief. "It's just I am so overwhelmed finally to find someone to talk to. Someone who won't think I'm crazy."

The last words touched me and I began to catch a

glimmer of the sadness hidden behind her dignified demeanor. When she had once again regained her will, she cleared her throat. A faraway look shimmered in her eyes.

"My meeting with Mr. Cavalanti was somewhat similar to yours," she began. "But first I must tell you a little about myself. Have you ever heard of my husband, Lord Lucien Dunaway?"

I shook my head no.

"No matter. I often wish I hadn't heard of him myself. In any case, we live in Cornwall. We have an estate, Dunaway Hall, on the cliffs overlooking the English Channel. As you might gather, I don't get along well with my husband. I am not the type of wife he really wants. He is not the type of husband I want." She sighed. "I'm going to be perfectly honest with you, Dr. Gladstone. I know it is highly irregular to be so talkative about family matters, but I never talk. No one ever listens, and I must confide in someone."

"I understand," I said quietly.

"Well . . ." she said slowly, "Lucien . . . there's just no tactful way of putting it. Lucien is a monster. He's much older than I and he doesn't want a wife. I mean, he doesn't want a human being, a thinking and feeling woman. He wants something vacuous. Something pretty, and"—she paused—"he wants something that won't fight back. A possession, a chattel that he can level abuse upon whenever alcohol and rage sweep his mind. But as soon as the storm is over he wants his chattel to stand up again and smile and greet dinner guests as if nothing has happened."

I offered her more tea but she declined.

"It isn't so bad, really. I'm a strong woman and I find that I can survive. I seek solace in the sea. The land where we live is beautiful in a desolate sort of way. Dunaway Hall is an aerie on the cliffs overlooking the beach. There's always the beach, the rugged beach. Here and there on the cliffs are disused mines, you know. They look like tiny abandoned castles. There are always the abandoned castles . . . and the gray and omniscient sea.

"It was on the beach that I first found Niccolo Cavalanti. He was ragged, and looked every bit as if he had just washed ashore from some terrible wreck. Now

I'm sure it was just another ruse, like dashing in front of your carriage. But then I was fooled. I thought the ocean had given me an omen, a shining and beautiful boy. I had found another creature ravaged by a thoughtless and mindless storm, and I took him into my heart.

"Oddly enough, Lucien didn't care. He seemed to glean some amusement from the way I nursed this strange boy. I expected Lucien to be jealous, but I guess one has to love to be jealous. I think Lucien viewed Niccolo as something that would keep me happy, appeased, and Lucien was actually relieved that my heart was going out to him.

"Of course, it didn't take long before I found out the bits of the story. As soon as Niccolo realized I needed him, he revealed he was a vampire. As soon as I accepted this, he told me about Lodovico. Niccolo captivated me with tales of Florence and the Medici, and after I had breathed the opium of his words, cleverly, unobtrusively, he began to take an interest in my son."

"Your son?"

"Yes, that is what made me so excited when I read about you in the newspapers."

I leaned closer.

"You see, Lucien and I have a little boy, Ambrose. Ambrose is one of the reasons Lucien hates me so much. Ambrose isn't the type of son Lucien wanted. He's nine years old. He'll never carry on the family name with honor. He'll never manage the house or the finances. Ambrose is an idiot, at least in Lucien's eyes. And, yes, he may stick his hands in candle flames, and fail to understand the complexities of opening and closing doors, but Ambrose is no idiot."

"He has a talent?"

"He doesn't play the pianoforte, but he has an interesting hobby. We didn't discover it at first. I think Ambrose was six when the cook first started complaining that someone was unraveling her knitting. As time went on the nanny began to notice that spools of her brightest thread were missing. Then came the gardener. He swore up and down that a brand-new roll of twine had simply vanished from his bag. It wasn't until a very expensive brooch of mine disappeared that we searched the entire house.

"We had no luck. The gardener, the nanny, the cook, the maids—we looked everywhere. It was Lucien who discovered the brooch. He was searching Ambrose's room when he accidently bumped into the bureau and heard a clicking sound. There, in the scrollwork, was a secret drawer that no one knew about except Ambrose. Inside was my brooch, and do you know what else?"

I was hypnotized by what she was saying, but I managed to shake my head.

"Knots. Dozens of knots. Not just simple bows or square knots, but the most beautiful and complex knots you have ever seen. Mathematical sculptures. Knots as big around as oranges, but made up of thousands and thousands of strands of the finest thread. They were works of incredible intricacy, and yet each one was different. Like snowflakes. Lucien rumbled into a slow rage, but I begged and pleaded with him to understand. How could he be angry at the boy? Couldn't he just look at those knots and see that each one was a cosmos?"

She reached into one of the inside pockets of her ulster and withdrew a cream-colored ball about the size of a doorknob, and handed it to me.

As I examined it I must admit I was impressed. At first I didn't immediately realize that the hard little object was a knot. It was more like a piece of carved ivory with ripples and whorls all laid out in a dazzling symmetrical design. Only when I looked at it closely did I see that it was made up of sewing thread, spools and spools of sewing thread, meticulously braided and crosshatched into a knot of breathtaking complexity.

"Can you imagine the mind that can conceive that design? Can you imagine the little boy, withdrawn and silent as a frightened sparrow, who can spin a creation like that somewhere in the universe behind his empty blue eyes?" Her deep voice cracked sadly. "In Greek mythology King Gordius of Phrygia possessed a knot that was so complex no one could unravel it. An oracle told him that if anyone ever did undo the Gordian knot, that person would become the master of Asia. Alexander the Great solved the riddle. He sliced the knot in two with his sword—a barbarous solution to a puzzle of such gossamer complexities. Lucien would draw the sword. Lucien would cleave the knot without ever seeing the meaning of the design."

"So Ambrose is also an idiot savant?"

"Yes."

"And Niccolo, did Niccolo take your child as well?"

Lady Dunaway looked at me, but her eyes passed right through me. Her face was empty, without even the vaguest hint of what her answer might be.

"You liked Niccolo, didn't you?" she asked slowly.

"Yes, very much."

"You didn't even have to tell me. As you must realize by now, Niccolo is one of those rare beings whom it is impossible not to be completely enraptured by. He truly is an angel, an earth angel to be sure, but something celestial glows in that face of his. That's why Lodovico chose him, you know." Lady Dunaway became even more dreamy. "Oh, I'm sure Lodovico fell in love with him, as you and I, but I'm also sure Lodovico realized what use such a shining youth could be put to. A candle for so many moths." She toyed listlessly with the handle of her teacup. "And you felt betrayed, didn't you?"

"Of course I did."

"Yes, betrayed because such a youth could lie so guilelessly. But don't judge him too harshly. You must have noticed how tortured he was." She looked at me.

I thought back to the sad reveries he used to drift into, and the rage with which he threw the rock at the statue of Lodovico. "Yes," I admitted.

"And why? Because Niccolo is unlike most men. He is both male and female; an androgyne, and like a woman he is vulnerable. He cannot pretend to be friends with someone without getting attached. I'm sure he had true affection for you, Dr. Gladstone."

I listened, but said nothing.

"I'm sure he had true affection for me as well. Just a short time before he left, he tried to warn me. I could see it in his eyes. He loathed what he was doing. I'm certain he almost came right out with the whole affair. We were walking along the beach and he stopped and turned about madly. He wanted to speak. He wanted to tell me what he had been sent to do."

"But did he tell you?"

"No," she replied sadly, "he didn't. But he told me something else. Something very strange."

"And what was that?"

Lady Dunaway's expression became at once remote and deadly serious. "He told me he was worried I would be drawn into the world of the vampire. He said they were a very clever society existing hidden and within our own culture, and if I was swept up into their world I must remember one thing: *Never trust the vampire, for everything they say and do is for some other purpose. They will play a cruel and enigmatic 'game of the mind' with you and it will be up to you to solve the puzzle, unravel the Gordian knot.*"

She motioned once again at the ivory-colored ball.

"What happened?"

"One evening Niccolo came and told me Lucien had fallen on the rocks of the beach and was hurt. I rushed to look for him, more out of hope that I might be rid of him, than fear for his safety. But when I arrived there, Lucien was nowhere to be found. I think I instantly understood what had happened, for I was gripped with terror as I ran back to Dunaway Hall."

She became a little distraught.

"It was too late. Niccolo . . . my dear, lovely Niccolo was gone. And he had taken Ambrose with him."

She began to weep again, and dabbed her eyes with her handkerchief.

"Oh, this is silly," she said, pulling herself together and straightening a little. "I'm a strong woman. I have to be. When Lucien returned from town, where he had been all along, I told him what had happened, and I think he was actually relieved Ambrose was gone. The local constable made a halfhearted attempt to find the boy, but I'm afraid I made a mistake you were intelligent enough not to make, Dr. Gladstone. I told the constable all about Niccolo and the vampire. I even wrote to Scotland Yard, but everyone thought I was crazy, a lunatic. When no ransom note ever came they gave up all hope of finding Ambrose, and I guess I was expected simply to forget the entire thing. Can you believe that, Dr. Gladstone? I can see in your eyes that you are a man of some emotion. You love your daughter, I can tell. Can you believe they all wanted me simply to give up my son?"

"I'm so sorry," I tried to comfort.

"That's why I came to you. After I read about your daughter I realized the same thing must have happened to you. I hoped. I prayed. I knew you would help me. We can help each other."

"My dear Lady Dunaway, I would love to help you. There's nothing more that I would like to do but to get my little Camille back. But how are we going to do that? I have no idea where they have taken our children. Do you?"

She slumped a little. "I don't know where they have taken them, but I have some information."

I leaned closer.

"When I arrived back at Dunaway Hall that fateful evening, the nanny said that another man had come to fetch Niccolo and my little Ambrose, a tall and handsome man with deeply set eyes. They explained to her that they were taking Ambrose to me, and so she did not object. But she did overhear them talking. She told me that they had mentioned France. She got the distinct impression they were planning on going there soon, and she also overheard something else. They kept repeating a curious expression. *Days*, something, and then a long *a* sound. And then *son*, only accented as if they were actually saying *saun-* in the word *saunter*. *Days a son*, they said. *Days a son*. Do you have any idea what that might mean?"

"*Days a son*," I repeated and shook my head.

"I thought, perhaps, there might be someone out there named *Daysa* or something, and, perhaps, they too might have a remarkable child, a son. Do you comprehend? At this very moment Niccolo and Lodovico might be plotting to take Daysa's son. It's horrible. They must be stopped. Even if they will play a cruel 'mind game' with us, we must do something to try to get our children."

"But once again, Lady Dunaway, we really have nothing to go on. Are we just supposed to travel to France and hope that we stumble into them? And even if they went to France, how do we know they weren't just passing through and continuing to Italy? That's where they're

from, you know. I know I just can't stand waiting around
while nothing happens. We must do something. Do you
know anything I don't? Do you have any clues? The only
thing I can think of is that there is a statue of Lodovico
here in London, at the British Museum."

Her eyes lit up. "A statue?"

"Yes, Niccolo showed it to me one evening. It's a copy of
a Roman work, a statue of an Alexandrian scholar from
the Arch of Constantine, dated at circa A. D. 315."

She became very excited. "That fiend! That horrible
creature. Why didn't you tell me about this statue
sooner?"

"You've been talking."

"No matter, no matter. I must see this statue."

"Well, it's getting rather late. We could go tomorrow."

She nodded eagerly. "Yes, tomorrow." She paused. "Is
there anything else you might tell me?"

"Well, yes. There's one thing. In a fit of temper Niccolo
flung a rock at the statue and broke one of its hands off. I
never reported it to the authorities, and I don't know why,
but I kept the stone hand. It had a scar across the back of
it. If we ever run into Lodovico we will be able to identify
him."

"Wonderful," she returned. "Do you still have the
hand?"

"No, I'm afraid little Camille took a morbid liking to it.
She took it with her when they abducted her. In fact,
Scotland Yard has just located the hearse in Dover, and a
witness there says he saw her playing with the gruesome
object."

"Dover!" she pounced. "You see! Why would they be
going to Dover, but to travel to France?"

"We may know that, Lady Dunaway," I repeated, "but
that still tells us very little."

Lady Dunaway gathered her ulster and cape around her.
"Yes, but we have each other. And, perhaps, together we
will be able to retrieve our children."

"Perhaps," I echoed, hoping there was promise in her
words. She was about to leave when I thought of one last
question. "Lady Dunaway?"

She looked at me.

"Did you notice anything strange in the way Niccolo walked?"

"You mean his light footfall?"

"No, not that. It was more, a very subtle but distinct modulation to his walk."

She pursed her brow and thought about it, but then she shook her head. "I am sorry, Dr. Gladstone, but I never noticed."

"It's all right," I ended with a shrug. I accompanied her to the door.

"I thank you for your time, Dr. Gladstone. It's been a very encouraging afternoon. I'm staying at the Great Eastern if you need me. I will call upon you at three sharp tomorrow."

"Three o'clock," I ended as I showed her out.

XII

That evening as I lay in my bed I thought about everything Lady Hespeth Dunaway had told me. I pondered again why Lodovico would want two children, both mentally deficient but with unusual talents. Did he want them for their genius alone? It seemed unlikely. Little Ambrose could create fantastic knots, but surely that was more of an oddity than a useful skill. Ambrose and Camille were not scientists or doctors who might be kidnapped for their knowledge. They were curiosities. Freaks. Did Lodovico want them simply as entertainment, as kings collected dwarfs and hunchback jesters? I dismissed that thought as well. If idiots savants were merely collectibles to the old vampire, why would he go to such elaborate schemes to steal them away? Why have Niccolo throw himself beneath the carriage? Why have him stay and gain our friendship instead of just breaking into the house one evening and taking them? No . . . what Lady Dunaway had said seemed correct. Their abduction was a puzzle, perhaps even a challenge. What disturbed me the most was it was a challenge we had no choice but to pursue.

The more I thought about it, the happier I became that Lady Dunaway had come to me. Suddenly I had a kindred spirit, a true compatriot in whom I could confide who was confronted by the same bizarre set of circumstances as myself. By late afternoon of the next day I found myself anxiously awaiting her arrival. When I heard someone at the front door I rushed from my study to see who was there. To my disappointment it was only Ursula. She was dressed in a light summer blouse with a large white hat and carrying a parasol.

"Hello, Father," she greeted.

"Hello," I said smiling as I turned to go back to my study. But then I noticed something, a faint but familiar smell.

"Where have you been?" I inquired.

She looked at me innocently. "Out to tea. Why do you ask?"

"Because I smell Egyptian cigarettes."

"There's nothing unusual in that. I've been to tea with Dr. Hardwicke."

I gave a start. "Why?"

She wrinkled up her brow. "He invited me. What's so odd about that? Dr. Hardwicke has been a friend of the family for quite some time. Is it so unusual that he should ask me out to tea?"

"Did he ask you any questions about Niccolo?"

"Of course he did, but you needn't worry. I didn't tell him anything you wouldn't have told him yourself. In fact, if anything, I made him suspicious with how mundane my story was."

I wrung my hands together and began to pace. "That old devil."

Ursula gave a light and airy laugh. "I don't know why you and he don't get along. He was ever so kind to me. And," she added, "he spoke very highly of you, asked about your research and all that."

"You didn't tell him—"

"No, Father," she said rather sharply. "I didn't tell him a thing about your discoveries. Really, I think you've misjudged Dr. Hardwicke."

I snorted.

"No, really. I think Dr. Hardwicke is one of the kindest—"

I turned upon her grimly. "You do not know Dr. Cletus Hardwicke as I know him."

Ursula frowned, a little angry that I would not explain myself more fully, and then left.

It was only moments later that a deep-maroon-colored brougham drawn by two fine Yorkshire coach horses pulled up in front of the house. They were driven by a handsomely dressed driver. Lady Dunaway had arrived. She waved happily from within the coach. "Dr. Gladstone," she called as I slipped on my jacket and went to greet her. "Come, come," she continued. "I'm much too excited to stop for tea. Let us go to the museum."

I stepped up into the brougham.

As I looked at Lady Dunaway I was struck anew by her presence. I was touched by the wistful happiness in her face. It was obvious she did not experience happiness very often. I fancied she had once been a spirited woman. One could see it in the way she held herself, a certain cast of the eyes. Her brow had long since hardened, but an ember still glimmered through. There was something else about her. It took me several moments, but then I objectified it. She effused a rare, even a profound determination. I did not know her well. I knew her not at all, but I could see it there, the hard core of an incredible will. The plaid cape and ulster and the two-peaked Sherlock Holmes cap took on new meaning for me. Her encounter with Niccolo had transformed her. The ridicule she had suffered had been the final straw, and her markedly masculine attire was an emblem of her rebirth. As in our first meeting she fondled the locket around her neck. It was not a nervous habit, but reverent, as if the trinket had some special value for her.

"Aren't you a little warm?" I asked, gesturing at her heavy garments.

"I'm not a healthy woman," she returned. "I catch a chill easily if I don't protect myself."

After several seconds of silence I continued. "This is a very nice brougham."

She shrugged. "It's Lucien's. Before I left, I went into his bedroom and took a good deal of money from his wall safe."

I raised an eyebrow. "That's illegal, you know."

She remained unaffected. "I'm sure he doesn't even know I know the combination. I'm afraid I stole the brougham as well. I hired the driver in Plymouth."

She opened the sliding panel of glass. "Oh, Ferguson, do you think you could go a little out of your way and pass through Regent's Park?"

He nodded.

"I so love Regent's Park," she said distantly. "And such a sunny day it is."

I smiled tolerantly. I was not overly fond of London in the summer. One had to endure the stench of the horse droppings and the swarms of flies that accompanied them. There was also the choking sulphurous fumes from the steam engines of the Underground Railway.

It took us twenty minutes to reach the rows of Georgian
homes circling the park. We rolled past armies of dark-
uniformed nannies pushing perambulators, and a cavalcade
of casually dressed men and women carrying brass-knobbed
walking sticks and parasols. I wondered how long it had
been since Lady Dunaway had been in London. She gazed at
everything as if she had once loved the city.

When we reached the British Museum we descended the
brougham and I escorted my new friend to the courtyard
where the statue stood. It looked much different in the
light of day. We approached from the back. It wasn't until
I walked in front of the marble figure that I saw.

Lady Dunaway squinted through her glasses. "I
thought you said the hand was broken off."

"Obviously they must have repaired it," I said, looking
at the monument with its outstretched appendage once
again intact.

"Yes," she murmured slowly. She meditated upon the
matter for a moment. "Shall we find someone who works
here?"

Before I could answer she strode off toward a large man
with broad shoulders and blond hair who was polishing a
bronze plaque on a nearby piece.

"Excuse me," Lady Dunaway said.

The man looked up. He had an elfish face and faint
blond eyebrows. "Yes, miss?"

"Are you in charge here?"

"Sometimes I is."

"Do you know about that work over there?" She pointed
at the Alexandrian scholar.

"Yes, miss."

"Well, I could have sworn it was missing a hand the last
time I was here."

"It was, miss."

"See, there I told you," she said, nudging me in the ribs.
"When did they repair it?"

"Just three days ago. Uncivil business. Broken by
vandals."

"Indeed. I suppose they had to construct an entire new
hand?"

He grinned. "That one is the strange part, that is. I

guess whoever broke it got guilty 'cause we got the hand by post about a week ago."

I felt a surge of excitement, but Lady Dunaway remained calm.

"What a nasty group of fellows. Do you think they got cold feet?"

"You can say that again, miss. Not English." He snorted and began to swagger a little.

Again she remained reserved. "Not English?"

"No, miss. It was the French. You know how the French are. Those blighters, they come over here and look down their weird little noses at everything."

"Did you catch them?"

"Oh, I say not. They're too cowardly for that."

"And how do you know it was the French?"

"Because of the address," he said matter-of-factly.

"What was the address?"

"Oh, I can't tell you that, miss. That's confidential museum business."

"I see. Thank you very much then."

After going through a labyrinth of intermediaries and stately marble corridors we finally were directed to the office of one Dr. Dalyrymple. We knocked for an undue length of time. Finally a young man no more than nineteen or twenty admitted us. Without saying a word he motioned at a little man napping behind a desk. The little man had ruffled gray hair.

He awoke with a start. "Hmmm, yes. May I help you?" He slipped on his pince-nez and squinted at us.

Lady Dunaway walked bravely up to his desk. "Yes. We're from Redgewood University. I'm Dr. Dunaway and this is Dr. Gladstone."

"Indeed," the little man greeted. "I'm Dr. Dalyrymple."

My courageous comrade continued. "We're interested in the statue of the Alexandrian scholar in the courtyard. Do you know anything about it?"

"Yes, it's from the Arch of Constantine."

"We read that on the plaque." She placed her gloved hands firmly upon his desk. "But do you know anything about the exact person it depicts?"

"No, I'm afraid that's lost in the mist of antiquity."

"Do you know anything about the scar on the back of the hand?"

Dr. Dalyrymple raised an eyebrow. "How did you know about that?"

Lady Dunaway was momentarily rendered agog. She turned toward me.

"We had an opportunity to examine the original in Rome," I offered quickly.

"That would be a good trick, considering the original is several hundred feet off the ground."

"We were part of an expedition sent to scale the arch for purposes of measurement."

"When?"

"During the summer of last year."

"How come I've never heard of this expedition?"

"It was sponsored in the States."

"Oh..." Dr. Dalyrymple finally assented, and I breathed a silent sigh of relief.

"So what can I do for you, anyway?"

"We wonder if you know anything about the scar?" I repeated.

He stood from his desk and took in a long breath. "Well... as you probably know from Jahn's *Ueber den Aberglauben des bösen Blicks,* there are many such hands with scars upon them to be found in antiquity. Indeed, we have several Etruscan and Roman examples here in the museum itself."

"And all of them have scars?"

"Well, not necessarily scars. Some of them have various fingers purposefully broken off, and inscriptions. We believe they are amulets for protecting against the evil eye."

"And is the hand on the Alexandrian scholar an amulet?"

He thought for a moment. "Nooo, I don't think so. You see, many of the amulets have other figures upon them. Snake tattoos and scales, frogs and scarabs. And, of course, there's the whip of Osiris or *courbash* of modern Egypt. The hand of the Alexandrian scholar has none of these." He paced across the room. "There's always the *mons* Jovis, the hand of the god, to consider as well. But it must have the face of a little divinity worn upon it like a ring, the Serapis, the Jupiter Serapis. The hand of the Alexandrian scholar has no Serapis either." Again he paced. "But then there's the Mano Pantea." He glanced distractedly off into space. "No, no, the Mano Pantea always has an eagle on it. And it's usually Hittite, not Roman."

"Do you have any explanation for the scar upon the hand?" I asked in exasperation.

"None whatsoever."

Lady Dunaway glared. "Then tell us this, Dr. Dalyrymple: Who recovered the hand after its recent mishap?"

"It was sent in anonymously."

"From where?"

"There was..." He looked at her sharply. "Wait a minute. Why do you want to know that?"

"Because Dr. Gladstone here is doing a paper on the sociological aspects of vandalism, and he would like the information for his research."

"Very well," he gave in, and went scampering to his files. Within moments he returned with a sheet of brown wrapping paper with several canceled French stamps upon it. He placed it on the desk and we both stepped forward excitedly. "I'm afraid there was no return address," he murmured. "But there's a postmark."

Several of the round inked circles were indistinct, but one was legible. In it were three words: Île Saint-Louis.

"The Île Saint-Louis is one of the two islands in the middle of the Seine, you know ... Notre Dame is on the other. The islands are the most ancient part of the city—"

"Yes, I know," Lady Dunaway began crisply, but then she mellowed. She smiled sadly at the little man. "Yes, thank you very much."

Outside in the hall she gripped my arm. "We must leave for Paris."

I sighed once again. "We still don't have an address. There are quite a few streets on the Île Saint-Louis, and many, many houses. Are we to search every one?"

"We must use our minds!" she reprimanded. "Surely a household of vampires stands out in a neighborhood. Oh, of course, they keep their identity carefully hidden, but they must be viewed as eccentric neighbors, to say the least. We will listen for stories, rumors, and suspicions.

Possibly someone has seen something strange, noticed a
certain household whose lights burn all night. Or heard
the most beautiful piano playing in a house where no
playing was heard before. We must go to Paris."

"What about Niccolo's warning?"

"What about it? We are not pawns. If we find ourselves
being swept into any games, we always have our free will.
We can leave. We must be careful and intelligent and we
will solve their puzzle. Surely you would do anything to
find your child?"

I stood gazing at the strange, tall, and handsome
woman with her spectacles and queer costume. She held
herself unperturbedly, but I could tell she was filled with
worry. Her hands were clenched at her sides. It was her
final hope. It wasn't that I was not willing to risk
everything for Camille. The wound was still open. I
simply wanted to consider all possibilities before making
a rash decision. The core of profound will rippled through
the woman.

"Will you go, Dr. Gladstone? Will you help me search
the Île Saint-Louis? Or shall I go alone?"

After several seconds of reticence I answered. "Yes, I'll
go."

When we reached the slick maroon-colored brougham
Lady Dunaway stopped. She examined the carriage
briefly and drifted into a reverie. "I'll have to sell it, I
guess."

"The brougham?"

"Yes. I have plenty of money, enough to last me for the
rest of my life. But this carriage"—she sadly stroked the
finish—"I can't take it back, you know. In fact, that's why
I must go to Paris. Lucien will be outraged at the loss of
his carriage and a handful of his precious money. If he
ever got his hands on me he would kill me. I can never go
back."

XIII

It was an understatement to say my decision was a relief to Lady Dunaway. She had obviously placed all of her hopes on my agreeing to cooperate, as if it were the single most important issue of her life. She touchingly reminisced about Ambrose, telling how frightened he was of mirrors, and unconcerned by heights. Her affection was so poignant I could almost feel the presence of the child. She insisted we leave for France that very night. With much diplomacy I convinced her that that was out of the question. There were too many arrangements to be made. I had to put to order my duties at Redgewood. There was my research to consider. Lady Dunaway still insisted I pack that afternoon—as a covenant of my intention to accompany her. There was such a look of faith in her eyes I found it impossible to refuse her.

After I had fulfilled that request she went with me to my laboratory. It was there I discovered what I could well have guessed. Lady Dunaway's unnurtured thirst for knowledge fully matched her determination. Those few women who had visited my laboratory in the past—other than Ursula, of course—had always recoiled with feminine delicacy from the experimental vermin, and the surgical horror. Lady Dunaway greeted the array of tinctures and glass as a marvelous world of mystery. She lacked information, her schooling in chemistry no doubt having been restricted to the mixing of watercolors at most. She made up for her lack of facts with an insatiable fascination. She fired a battery of questions at me, and hungrily absorbed my every word. How easy it must have been for Niccolo to pull her in as he had pulled me in. I wondered if there was some meaning in our mutual hunger for knowledge; if it was more than just the idiots savants who had entangled us with the vampire.

Much to my interest, after I finished showing her my most prized endeavor, the rabbit in the glass cupola, her

expression became grave. She turned to me sternly. "Dr.
Gladstone, I don't think you realize the potential effect
your discovery may have upon the world."

"I guess I haven't had time to realize it with the events
of the past several weeks."

"Well, you should realize it. I can well imagine, a virus
that will always prove deadly must be an astounding
scientific discovery, but it is also infinitely terrifying.
Have you fully considered what you have in your
keeping?"

"You are right, but I don't have the time now."

"You don't have the time to do anything, but you
certainly can consider what precautions you must take
for dealing with this discovery in the future."

I looked at her inquiringly.

Her mind seemed to be racing. "For example, when you
reveal it to your colleagues and to the scientific world,
what use will they see in your work?" From the tremor of
her expression a sudden realization apparently hit her
and she looked at me beckoningly. "You seem to me a good
man, but I have known men like Lucien. Might they not
see your virus as a weapon? Don't you see? There are so
many conflicts, so many wars. Surely our military will see
how advantageous it would be to release such a virus in
the homeland of a political enemy."

"That would be foolhardy. There is no guarantee that
the virus would remain within political borders."

"Exactly!" she said excitedly. "But don't you see? More
foolhardy atrocities than that have been committed in the
past." A hint of experience moved through her eyes. "And
many more are to come. If England were attacked by the
Prussians, or the Germans, with absolutely no hope of
victory, do you think some proper and stiff-upper-lipped
British general would think twice about releasing that
virus on the world before he would allow the black-booted
soldiers to rape his wife and his daughter?"

"I wouldn't dream of allowing my discovery to be put to
such purposes."

"What if it weren't your choice? What if Her Majesty
demanded it? Would you deny her?"

"I don't know."

"And after you've revealed the possibility of creating a

virus that completely lacks antigenicity, how long will it be until others duplicate your discovery?"

"Really, Lady Dunaway, it's impossible to say. Why are you so concerned?"

Again her face fell sadly. "Because I know the world, and I think you do too."

"What would you suggest I do with *Camillus influenzae* while we are gone?"

Her lips moved hesitantly. "Destroy it. Never breathe a word of it to anyone again."

It was the first time I had been disappointed in Lady Dunaway. I was moved by her words. I sensed in her a sincere concern, but it went against my every grain even to ponder destroying what I had worked so hard for.

"I could never do that," I said.

The tension in her brow eased as she gazed at me sadly. "No, you are too much the scientist, the searcher, aren't you? You would light a candle to explore a darkened room, never considering that the room might be filled with bales of cotton soaked in kerosene." She looked at the most recently infected rabbit resting peacefully in the glass enclosure. "I'm sorry, I shouldn't preach to you so much. Who is going to take care of injecting the rabbits while you are gone?"

It was a question that had caused me great concern. *Camillus influenzae* could only exist *in vitro*, or in a culture dish for a few days, and then only under the most exacting conditions. To perpetuate the virus it was necessary to keep injecting new rabbits. Modesty aside, if there was one thing I knew, it was the potential scientific magnitude of my discovery. Outside of my family there was nothing more important to me than my research. I am sorry to say, but in my innermost thoughts I realized trusting *Camillus influenzae* to one of my colleagues—in the publish-or-perish world of academia—was like entrusting steak tartare to a jackal. What would I do with the virus?

There was a sound at the door of the laboratory and we both turned to see Ursula coming in.

"Your trunks—" she began, but then quieted when she saw Lady Dunaway for the first time.

"This is my older daughter, Ursula," I introduced,

motioning toward the door. "Lady Dunaway," I said, nodding at my incongruous friend.

"Charmed, I'm sure," Lady Dunaway said politely.

To my surprise Ursula curtsied. "May I ask what this is all about?"

"Lady Dunaway has also had an encounter with the vampire," I explained.

Her eyes widened as she once again examined Lady Dunaway. "Where?"

"In Cornwall," Lady Dunaway broke in.

"Do you know where they are, where they live?"

"No, but—"

"When did you last see them?"

Lady Dunaway coughed, a little ruffled. "Please, dear, calm down and I will tell you." She proceeded to explain the entire story. When she had finished, something disturbing penetrated Ursula's breathless fascination.

Lady Dunaway's face became a little reserved. I fancied she understood Ursula's change in mood all too well.

"So you knew Niccolo?" said Ursula.

"Yes. I might guess you knew him also, didn't you, dear?"

"You guess correctly."

"Yes," Lady Dunaway continued. "Such a captivating young man. One cannot blame you for falling under his spell. Everyone does."

"Where are you going?" Ursula said, glancing one last time at Lady Dunaway before she once again turned toward me.

I told her about the stone hand and the postmark from Paris.

"So you're going there! Father, you must let me come. Please, you don't know how much it would mean to me." A thought shot through her expression. "Who's going to look after your work?" She looked at the cupola and then back at me.

How could I ask her? After everything that had happened, how could I expect her to take care of the injections? It was difficult, but I had to. Ursula was the only one with both the skill and the integrity to tend to the laboratory. I could trust no one else.

"I'm looking for Camille, not Niccolo," I said.

"But you must let me go with you. I might be able to help."

I looked at her imploringly. "You will be able to help me more if you stay here, Ursula. I'm sorry to ask you this. I wouldn't if it weren't so absolutely necessary."

Ursula tilted her head back and her nostrils flared as if she were about to stamp with fury. Her dark eyes met mine, first filled with anger and then, much to my surprise, she seemed to find something in my gaze that warmed her. She was still raging with disappointment, but she relented. Her shoulders slumped a little. All the blood rushed from her face, making her complexion chalky against her deep red hair.

"When are you leaving?"

"Tomorrow, early evening," I replied sadly.

"Do you know how long you will be gone?"

"A week or two, I suspect."

"You mustn't be too upset, dear," Lady Dunaway soothed. "You will be helping more than you might imagine."

"I know," Ursula sighed as she looked at me. Her voice was mechanical.

That evening I telegraphed Paris and made reservations for us at the Hotel Madeleine on the Île Saint-Louis. I finished packing my toiletries and tried to do as much work in the laboratory as possible before I left. The next day I finished the necessary preparations for my departure at Redgewood. It was much to my displeasure that as I was leaving I collided head-on with Cletus.

"Hello, John," he grunted cynically. He was sitting on a bench beneath one of two stone lions flanking the front entrance of Redgewood. He clutched a periodical in his hands. Majestic plane trees lined the length of the walk and the summer sun shone down warmly.

"Taking a break?" I retorted.

"Just thinking," he returned. "I hear you are going to Paris. For a holiday?"

"Yes, to get away from it all."

"The London police are still without any leads?"

"None."

"Ursula's quite disturbed you're not allowing her to go with you?"

"How do you know that?" I asked quickly.

"I saw her this morning. She came over to my office here at Redgewood." He calmly lit a cigarette as he watched my reaction out of the corner of his eye.

"Now, listen, Cletus, I don't like you having anything to do with my daughter. You know that. What's your interest in her, anyway? Why, after all that has happened between us, do you still insist on being interested in me and my life?"

"Oh, John," he snorted, "you don't have to worry. I'm too old to be any threat to Ursula."

"Then why?"

He snorted again. "I'm simply counseling her a little. She's considering going into medicine. In fact, she say's that's why you won't let her accompany you on this little holiday. She says you're having her take care of some very important 'in process' experiments you're conducting at home. Are you onto something, John?"

"Nothing," I stated simply and he gazed at me with his usual suspicion. "What about you?"

After all those years of secrecy I finally realized Cletus was involved in no grand projects. He never published. He only pretended. His enigmatic research remained enigmatic. His reputation for scholarship was based on intimidation. He was a hollow man.

"Oh, nothing ... nothing. I mean, at least, nothing in the scientific realm."

I regarded him blankly, refusing to grab at his bait.

"I have discovered something I think bears a little thought. I know you think I'm batty connecting Mr. Cavalanti with Chiswick's death, but in light of this kidnapping and all, it's just set me to thinking."

"About what?" I asked before I could stop myself. Why should I care what Dr. Cletus Hardwicke had to say?

"About Chiswick's paranoia. I'm still certain that somehow it's all involved." He puffed slowly on his cigarette. "In any case, I've been asking around, writing letters to colleagues at different universities and such. I've discovered a few things."

"Like what?" I said, becoming slightly more interested.

"Well, a friend of mine at University College in Liverpool says that about seven years ago exactly the same thing happened to a physician engaged in research there. He announced to the trustees of the college that he had made a discovery that would 'make history,' no less. Then, instead of carrying through with his announcement, he began having the most terrible rows with his wife."

"Is that so uncommon?"

"It was in his case. According to my friend they had a model marriage, at least until the physician *changed*."

"Changed?"

"Became obsessively paranoid. He locked the poor woman out of the house and suddenly insisted upon keeping his papers in a safe-deposit box. The trustees prodded him for his discovery. He snapped and destroyed all of his research and equipment and went over the deep end."

"Committed suicide?"

"No, committed to an asylum outside of Liverpool."

I refused to allow myself to be convinced. "And this happened seven years ago?"

He nodded.

"Cletus ... every single day there must be some physician somewhere going crazy. What's to connect your friend in Liverpool with Chiswick besides your imagination?"

"A feeling in my bones. Besides, that isn't all." He opened up the periodical he had been holding and held it so that I could just barely make out the print. "A friend of mine at Oxford says that recently an engineer there named M. W. Radner published an article here in the *Aerology Quarterly* alleging that he had made a major breakthrough in dirigible design. He says that his proposed dirigible would be faster, more maneuverable, and could carry more weight than any airship hitherto conceived. I don't pretend to understand the mathematical hodgepodge he spews forth in this article, but engineers who are in a position to judge say that he let out just enough to be impressive. My friend at Oxford says that Radner's dirigible could change the world."

I tilted my head so as better to see the article Cletus held in his hand.

"Radner announced that he was going to reveal his plan at an aerology convention just last month. Unfortunately, Radner's no longer speaking to anyone. He remains locked up in his office at Oxford and has purchased a chimpanzee to taste all of his food before he eats it to make sure it isn't poisoned. Tch, tch," Cletus clucked. "I guess a chimpanzee's metabolism is closer to a human's than a dog or cat."

"So perhaps he has professional enemies. Or perhaps he stole the idea from someone else, and now he's afraid of retribution."

"Perhaps," Cletus said, glancing down at the article and pretending to contemplate it.

"You still haven't convinced me," I ended. "All I know is if there's one person in this world I don't trust, it's you, Cletus."

The little man looked taken aback.

"And I'll thank you to leave the counseling of my daughter to me from now on."

"Our teas will have to be social, I guess," he sneered.

My temper rose, but I restrained myself. "As a gentleman I must ask you to stay away from my daughter."

For the first time he lost his smirk and regarded me with acerbity. "Or else?"

"Or else I will forsake my honor and expose you to the world for what you are."

When early evening came the maroon-colored brougham once again pulled up outside our house on Bond Street and Lady Dunaway stepped out. Cook was waiting with me at the front door, but Ursula had bid me a reserved *au revoir*, and had retired to her room. I was dressed in my black evening waistcoat with my gold watch chain hanging elegantly from pocket to pocket, wearing a bowler hat, and carrying a brass-knobbed walking stick. I had even doused myself liberally with Pinaud's Lilac Vegetal, a habit I hadn't indulged since my wife, Camille, had died. My luggage consisted of a large traveling trunk, two carpetbags, and a hatbox.

"Good evening," Lady Dunaway greeted happily, still dressed in her familiar ulster, cape, and two-peaked cap. She carried a small leather gripsack in her hand, and a silver sovereign-and-half-sovereign case. "So this is what you're taking?" she said, pointing with her long, gloved finger.

"Yes."

"This is my luggage," she said, holding up the single leather gripsack. "I'll get Ferguson to load your trunks."

Cook sobbed endearingly.

After everything was loaded we took our seats in the carriage. "We must bid my lovely brougham good-bye," Lady Dunaway murmured wistfully as we waited for the driver to climb onto his perch. "I've already sold it, and Ferguson will take it to its new owners as soon as he's dropped us off."

I smiled consolingly as the carriage started up.

As I waved to Cook I looked up at the dark bricks of the house; at the wooden portico of the door and the window above it, surrounded by a low parapet of wrought iron. The last remnant of late-afternoon sun shone brightly upon the façade, but still it seemed unusually brooding and somber. I noticed there was more ivy than I had recalled spanning its walls, weaving around window frames, and biting into the very cornice of the brick. As the old Victorian terrace house receded into the distance, there, behind a frame of tendrils and green leaves, and half-hidden by the panes of the oriel window, I saw Ursula watching.

XIV

It was twilight by the time we reached Dover, and I wondered if the Neapolitan hearse was still sitting, silent and empty, in the storage lot. Or whether young Inspector Inglethorpe had had it confiscated, to be sold, a macabre surprise, at some police auction. It had been such a warm day that there was steam rising from the water, and in the waning light there was something Stygian about the scene, like a Doré engraving of Virgil leading Dante on his raft. We crossed the Channel in the good ship *Strait of Dover*. Our accommodations were sumptuous, our cabin being of red plush with tasseled fringes on all the windows and sliding glass doors, and equipped with a shiny brass samovar. We first set foot on French soil at Dunkerque. I spoke French very well for an Englishman, having grown up with a number of French *au pair* girls in the house. I had visited France once before, with my father. I found myself oddly inspirited by this second visit, as if it were really my first. The train ride from Dunkerque took the longest, and it was in the early morning that we arrived at the Gare du Nord in Paris.

The city was breathtaking. The sun had not yet risen over the horizon, and yet, already the sky was aglow, a deep and refulgent orange. It seemed more like the vermilion of sunset than morning, the rich, oily hue of Seville oranges. On the horizon and cloaked in this golden mist were the spires of ancient churches, and the delicate ink lines of trees. In front of this was a panorama of blue-tiled roofs, crumbling stucco, and leaden cupolas. Everything was covered with the patina of corroded copper, and the grimy wash of a thousand rain gutters. Behind us gleamed the dirty white basilica of Sacré Coeur, and ahead, in the very middle of the fairy kingdom, loomed the most impressive sight of all, a silhouette that had not been there the last time I had visited Paris—an awesome fairy spire.

"So that is the work of that clever engineer we've been hearing so much about," whispered Lady Dunaway, "that Monsieur Eiffel."

I scarcely heard her, for I was much too busy contemplating what was before us. Hidden behind that somnolent postcard were all the bistros and mirror salons, sad ladies sipping absinthe, dandies and manifesto writers, intellectuals and *clochards* that comprised the mystique of the city. Something inside me told me I was looking at history, in some sense, in some form. This was the Paris of Baudelaire and Renoir, of the Symbolists, the mystics, and the Decadent artists. I wondered if somewhere out there, in some unknown flat, slumbered my little Camille.

Ignoring my silence, Lady Dunaway hailed a cab, and we were soon clattering down the Rue du Faubourg. When we reached the quai the sunlight shimmered like molten bronze upon the Seine, and we could see the smoky hulk of Notre-Dame with Saint-Chapelle beside it. Several tugs churned sluggishly by the two sleeping islands, and already fishermen and tramps lined the bank. So these two islands were the oldest part of Paris, already settled when the Romans invaded Gaul. *"Numéro quarante-sept* Quai d'Anjou," I told the driver as we turned onto the spidery steel bridge that led to the Île Saint-Louis.

The Hotel Madeleine was a modest four-storied stucco building, ivy-clad and lined with trellises of espalier fruit trees and vines. It wasn't as palatial as some of the other hotels on the island—the Hotel Lambert or the seventeenth-century Hotel de Lausun down the street—but it was fashionable and served an upper-class clientele. It also overlooked the quai and provided a clear view of the tree-lined Left Bank on the opposite side of the Seine.

As I stood gazing out the window of my room I wondered which of the hundreds of houses and flats that cluttered the Île Saint-Louis might contain a household of vampires. Who had sent the stone hand back to the British Museum? Was there a community of Niccolo's kind on this speck of land in the middle of the river in the very heart of Paris? Or had Niccolo and Lodovico merely stopped here on their way somewhere else? Question after question spun through my brain as I slipped beneath the flowered Jacquard coverlet of my modest oak bed and fell asleep.

Later that afternoon Lady Dunaway and I went over everything we knew about the vampire that might help us in our search. We pondered the fact that they never ate and never needed medical doctors, but these insights seemed futile. How could one determine which of several hundred households was not buying groceries or visiting physicians? We considered going to the census bureau to investigate the mysterious *Daysa*, and explore the possibility of his or her having a son, but we resolved that this was ineffectual as well. Not only were there too many *Daysas* in the city to check on, but also the irregular rules of French names made the number of possible spellings endless. Were we looking for Monsieur or Madame *Daysat, Deizad,* or *Dessat*? There were too many possibilities.

At last we resolved that the idiosyncrasy of the vampire that would be the most readily apparent was the hours they kept. That evening we began our search. Lady Dunaway kept notes in a small book of red Morocco leather. Beginning at midnight we meticulously strolled down every street of the tiny Île Saint-Louis, carefully noting every house whose lights were burning. It took us an hour and a half to complete the exercise. We repeated the search at three in the morning, and once again at half past five, scarcely an hour before dawn. All those houses whose lights had been turned off in one of the ensuing surveys were marked off our list. After our third and last walk we had a total of thirty-seven homes whose lights had been on all night.

"It's no use," I told Lady Dunaway as we sat in a little all-night café and watched the sun rise once again over the Seine. "Everyone in Paris stays up all night."

"But everyone can't stay up all night every night," she said, opening the little red book and surveying the names.

"Don't be too sure. Throughout most of his career Balzac drank thirty cups of coffee every evening and worked an average of eighteen hours."

"Surely the Balzacs in this city must be in the minority."

"As I say, don't be too sure."

"But we must continue. Surely if we go out again tonight we will eliminate a few addresses."

I sighed and began to massage my ankle. "Again tonight! And what if we cross off half a dozen names? Are we going to go out again tomorrow night, and the next night as well? My legs are not going to hold out for too many evenings. I'm afraid this method is much too strenuous."

She rested her head in her hand and sighed as the waiter brought us two very welcome cups of *café noir*.

"You're right," Lady Dunaway said dejectedly. "But we can't just give up. What are we going to do?"

We both sat thinking, and it was only after absentmindedly downing half of my steaming coffee that I realized I had severely burned my mouth. Balzac be damned, I thought to myself.

Suddenly Lady Dunaway squinted her eyes behind her thick glasses and I realized she had thought of something. "I've got it!" she said, sitting up and then leaning closer to me.

I shoved my coffee away and listened.

"We are working on the premise that the vampire is a completely nocturnal creature, correct?"

"Yes."

"So what we have to do is find those houses whose lights burn all night every night, correct?"

"Yes!"

"The problem is that it's too much work to discover those houses by looking for them ourselves. So what is the answer?"

I raised an eyebrow.

"Gaz..." she said in her most svelte and languorous voice.

"Gaz?"

"Why didn't we think of that before? Surely a household that is awake all night every night uses their gas jets more than anyone else, more *gaz*. We just go to the Services en Commun and get a list of the private residences that use an abnormal quantity of *gaz* every month."

I was about to congratulate Lady Dunaway, but she had already snapped the little red book shut and was off.

At the Services en Commun she once again utilized the lack of timidity and the ability to think on her feet that she had demonstrated at the British Museum. It was through bribery that we obtained a list of the several hundred abnormal *gaz* consumers in the city and chose the twenty most extravagant of those to begin our search. To our dismay, none of them were on the Île Saint-Louis.

As we traveled around the city it was easy to eliminate most of the extravagant *gaz* consumers. Quite a few of the "abnormal" private residences were immense seventeenth- and eighteenth-century homes. We didn't exclude the possibility (indeed, probability) that beings who were several centuries old might have accrued great wealth, but there were other reasons to mark such households off our list. The foremost reason was that our cab driver, a very knowledgeable chap, was familiar with the vast majority of those residences, and could tell us about their owners. Usually they were remnants of royalty or political figures, well known throughout Paris, and not known for their exclusively nocturnal habits. However, there were a few residences that our driver could not identify, and those we eliminated by another method. Using figures provided by the Services en Commun we were able to determine how much *gaz* a household of the size in question should use through normal consumption, and thus leave them off our list as well. By late afternoon we had narrowed the possibilities down to four households. The first two of these we crossed off because when we knocked at their doors, their owners answered, albeit in their evening robes, but squinting and grumbling in the full of the afternoon sun, nonetheless.

It was at the second-to-the-last residence that we had some luck. Lady Dunaway knocked at the door.

It opened slowly.

"Oui?" answered a tall and emaciated butler with an ivory complexion and sunken eyes.

"Is Madame de Beauseant at home?" asked Lady Dunaway.

"Madame sleeps during the day," he replied and began to shut the door.

Lady Dunaway planted her foot firmly across the

threshold. "Wait, I am one of Madame de Beauseant's relatives. Could you tell me when I could visit her?"

The butler looked highly skeptical. "Madame de Beauseant hasn't mentioned any relatives."

"Yes, but she'll want to see me," Lady Dunaway returned.

"Madame de Beauseant never receives guests," the butler returned and once again struggled to close the door.

Lady Dunaway stood firm. "Not even if the guests have information that is crucial to Madame de Beauseant's safety?" she asked.

Suddenly the butler became frightened and agitated. "What do you know?" he asked, gripping her arm with his skeletal hand.

"That is between Madame de Beauseant and me alone. Now will you arrange a meeting between us?"

"I'll see what I can do," he said when suddenly a police carriage pulled up behind our cab and several policemen rushed up the steps. The butler violently pushed Lady Dunaway back, slamming the door, and her plaid cape and ulster billowed out as she fell backward into my arms. Ignoring us, the policemen broke down the door and within several minutes, amid screams and curses, they dragged a very fat woman with intense red hair and a burgeoning cleavage, dressed haphazardly in night clothing and evening coat, into the street.

"Voilà le collier!" she screeched as she reached into her cleavage and flung a sparkling diamond necklace in the face of one of the policemen. *"Voilà le collier!"* She fell heavily upon the pavement and tried to crawl away but one of the officers grabbed her small white foot, and amid a flurry of arms and legs she was loaded into the police wagon.

"Merci, en tout cas," the butler said, shrugging as he propped the broken door back up in its frame.

Lady Dunaway straightened herself and frowned as she squinted at the sun. *"Elle n'était pas vampire,"* she murmured.

The last address on the list was a large gray stone house on the Avenue Victor Hugo with oriental wrought-iron grates in the windows, pink granite keystones, and a number of short and luxuriant lime trees in front of it. The lime trees were in full blossom and rained down their white fluff like snow, an incongruous sight in the balmy June afternoon.

"You handle this one," Lady Dunaway said as we stepped down from the carriage.

I gingerly lifted the knocker, a large ring in the mouth of a brass Ming lion, and waited.

Nothing.

I knocked again and finally a short, plump maid with rosy cheeks answered the door. Her eyes were brown and her dark brown hair was drawn back in a chignon. She was in uniform and wore a fine ivory comb in her hair and a white silk scarf around her neck.

"*Monsieur?*" she said, looking quite shocked and surprised.

"Is Madame Villehardouin at home?" I asked.

"No, *monsieur.* May I ask who calls?"

"My name is Gladstone, Dr. Gladstone. Could you tell me when you are expecting your mistress home?"

"Later this evening, *monsieur.* Do you have business with Madame Villehardouin?"

"Yes, you might say that. I'm looking for my daughter, a little blind girl named Camille. You might have seen her yourself. She plays piano?"

"You would have to ask Madame, *monsieur.*"

"Ahh, yes . . . would it be possible to come in and wait?"

"I'm afraid not. I'm just on my way out to do the dinner shopping."

"Very well. Perhaps we'll wait a while out here then."

"As you wish, *monsieur,*" she said, closing the door.

"Well, what do you think?" I asked Lady Dunaway as we walked down the steps.

"I don't know," she said, biting her lip nervously and staring at the house.

"She *is* going shopping for dinner."

"*She's* obviously mortal. The servants must eat, you know."

"Well, the maid seemed very cool and collected, but I have to admit, something about her bothered me."

"I agree," Lady Dunaway said. "Shall we wait in the carriage a little bit?"

I looked at her inquisitively.

"She told us she's about to go shopping. Let's call her bluff," she said.

We had sat in the cab for about fifteen minutes when the young woman, wrapped in a light black shawl, came out of the door carrying a wire vegetable basket. She completely ignored our presence as she strolled briskly down the avenue. "Let's follow," Lady Dunaway suggested as we paid the cab driver.

We walked a safe distance behind her, trying to keep enough people between us so that she wouldn't notice we were trailing her. She strolled from vegetable stand to vegetable stand, casually examining the produce.

"What is this telling us?" I asked Lady Dunaway as we stood behind a vendor.

"Sshhh," she hushed quietly. She looked around until she spotted several young boys playing in the street. As we watched one of them, a boy with short black hair and an oversized sweater sneaked up to one of the vendors and slipped a pear in his pocket. The old shopkeeper never saw a thing.

Lady Dunaway stole up behind the boy and placed a gloved hand firmly on his shoulder. He jerked and tried to run, but she held on. "My little *monsieur*," she said, "would you like to make ten francs?"

He looked at her with wide and amazed eyes. *"Oui, madame."*

She withdrew several coins from her pocket. "Then you see that young woman over there in the black shawl and wearing a white silk scarf around her neck?"

"Oui."

"Do you think you could steal her scarf?"

He looked at the scarf. "It is fastened with a stickpin?"

"Yes."

"Oh, it would be easy, *madame*." He clutched greedily at the coins.

"No, no," Lady Dunaway returned. "You get half now and half after you have succeeded."

The boy slipped five of the francs into his pocket and nodded excitedly as he melted into the crowd. He moved with the swiftness of a cat, past the shopkeepers and old women, and finally up behind the maid. His hand darted out, the scarf flashed through the air, and he was gone. The woman gave a slight cry, but then quickly composed herself.

The young boy slipped up behind Lady Dunaway and exchanged the scarf for his coins. "Here," she said, holding the cloth out. "Now go be a gentleman and return that young woman's scarf."

I accepted the square of silk and made my way through the crowd. I tapped the young woman on the shoulder and she turned around. As she stood there I noticed she was breathing heavily and looked a little anxious, even frightened. And then I noticed the discoloration on her neck. The smooth white flesh was bruised and a little swollen, not unlike the touch of an overly passionate lover. On either side of the elongated swelling were two festered holes, very red and scabbed with darkened blood.

The young woman glared at me as she snatched her scarf back and quickly strode off.

I excitedly returned to Lady Dunaway. "Did you see? Did you see her neck?"

"Yes, I saw," she said, happily clenching my hands in hers. "We have found the vampire."

"So what do we do now?"

"I think the first thing we should do is watch our Madame Villehardouin's home tonight and see if she goes anywhere."

"You think that's better than insisting she see us?"

"Yes, we should see if she leads us to other households of vampire before we scare her away. It increases our chances."

I agreed and that evening we passed the night sitting in a little square a safe distance down the street, watching the gray and pink stone house through opera glasses. It was a Friday night and the Avenue Victor Hugo was crowded with many hansoms and one-horse cabriolets. Occasionally I was eyed suspiciously by ladies of the evening, who wondered if I were a prospective client. Lady Dunaway regarded them coldly. From a little bistro down the street came the smell of *café noir*, and every once in a while a waft of cheap perfume and black cigarettes.

The lights in the gray and pink stone house were put on at sunset and continued to burn brightly all the while we

watched. At one o'clock in the morning the thoroughfare
was still going strong. It wasn't until three o'clock that
the crowd began to fade. I was yawning a great deal by
then, and getting very tired of sitting on park benches,
pacing, and holding the tiny hard lenses of the opera
glasses against my eyes.

"Look!" Lady Dunaway whispered at last as a young
man in livery brought a black hansom drawn by two gray
horses out of the mews beside the house. He tied them
loosely to the herma and then stood at the side of the door,
waiting.

The door opened.

For a moment it was impossible to see who the driver
was talking to. He nodded several times, and returned to
the mews, and at last the figure of a woman came into
sight. Even though she was standing several hundred feet
from us I could see her features clearly through the opera
glasses. To my slight surprise she was an Oriental, of
medium height, and wearing a long black pelerine or
hooded cape. My first impression was that she was a
mature woman, in her late forties. Her delicate, rounded
face was starkly white; her lips, small but full, were
quiescent, like the lips of a porcelain mask. Her petal eyes
were scarcely more than slits. Two cherrywood combs kept
her hair drawn tightly from her temples, allowing a few
locks to fall about her ears in a manner that suggested
erotic disarray.

I say she was mature because her visage possessed the
linear definition and stunning dignity that can only be
wrought by advancing years. However, as I gazed at her,
her face changed, seemed to flicker in my mind, and I
began to perceive another face. It was a youthful face, the
countenance of a young girl scarcely more than a child.
None of the woman's features actually seemed to have
changed. All the dignity and linear definition were still
there. But the youthful presence faded in like a ghost,
exuded a glow, a sensuality, silent but heaving, like the
breath of lovers. It was an injustice to say she was
beautiful, for she was a caliber above most beautiful
women. A sublimity of human perfection born only once
every hundred years. Standing in the surreal snow of the

lime trees she seemed unreal—ink-brushed, like an ancient watercolor, a Lady of the Willow World.

She stood very motionless on the steps, listening.

"Do you think she's a vampire?" I blurted out half under my breath. Lady Dunaway tried to hush me, but it was too late. The Oriental woman turned and looked in our direction. I felt a chill—it was too uncanny for her to hear at such a great distance. Her gaze cut quickly through the sparse crowd and came to rest on the opera glasses in my hand. She squinted, scrutinizing my face, and then Lady Dunaway's, before the woman stepped up into the driver's seat and cracked the whip at the horses.

Lady Dunaway turned about madly to hail a cab and we were off. Our adversary had gotten quite a lead on us, and it wasn't until we reached the square, and paused before the Arc de Triomphe that we spotted the black hansom with the gray horses in the distance. "Catch her and I'll double the fare!" I screamed at the squat little driver.

"Pardon, mes amis," he said apologetically to his horses as he snapped them soundly and we ripped through the city.

We chased the carriage down avenue after avenue. In the dim glow of the paraffin lamps it was miraculous that we were able to keep an eye on her at all. It was the sound that usually tipped us off—down narrow streets and busy boulevards—the clatter of frenzied carriage wheels upon the cobbles. We lost sight of her for several minutes as we rode by the river. Then we saw her, crossing one of the most beautiful bridges in Paris, the Pont Alexandre, with its gold-plated ornaments and stylish lanterns. The hood of her carriage had snapped down and the black cape swept out in a flurry behind her. The wheels screamed against the stone as she crossed the summit of the hill beyond the bridge. Then there was silence.

We crossed the bridge, but it was too late. She was gone. In desperation we rolled slowly down the quai. It was to no avail. It was as if she had been swallowed up magically by the night. There was no sound. No movement. Nothing but the bridges of Paris and the Seine shimmering darkly in the moonlight.

"No!" Lady Dunaway cried as she clenched her hands together. "Don't stop. Continue on to the Île Saint-Louis."

When we reached the little island we once again took up our slow and anxious search. After about twenty minutes we spotted a hansom with its hood down in front of one of the grand old homes on the Rue de l'Île. There were, however, no gray horses.

"Do you think this is it?" I gasped.

"I don't know," Lady Dunaway returned. "It looks like the carriage, but how can one be sure?"

The house itself was a sprawling gray stone giant with high-peaked, blue-tiled roofs. Its numerous wings were set at right angles to one another and seemingly enclosed the tops of archways and small courtyards. The windows of the rambling edifice were long, narrow, and heavily grated. A rusting system of rain gutters snaked over the entire structure, and I noticed there were gargoyles lining the cornices, strange gargoyles that looked like large squirrels or rodents, only possessing the beaks of birds or puffins, sitting on their haunches. Only the little round window above the door was lit. A small alley next to the house revealed a possible entrance to stables.

"The horses might be in there," Lady Dunaway said, pointing at the alley.

We stepped down from the cab and bid the driver good night. We approached the house. Beneath the knocker on the large oak door was a brass placard. On it and illuminated by the glow from the streetlamps was the name of the house's proprietor—one des Esseintes.

"No wonder it is not on our list," Lady Dunaway murmured. "Only the entrance light is burning."

I could scarcely contain my excitement.

"Don't you see?" I continued. "It isn't *Daysa's son,* or *Desat's son.* It's *des Esseintes.*"

XV

At last she saw the name as well, and an electricity swept through us. "Well, what do we do now?" I asked.

"Can't you guess?"

"No more waiting. I can't take it."

"I don't think we'll have to wait long."

"Surely they've seen us arrive."

"Nonsense. Our Madame Villehardouin is certain she lost us over the bridge. The residents of this house do not know that we found the postmark from the Île Saint-Louis. They have no reason to suspect we would search this tiny island for her black hansom."

"What makes you so certain they'll be leaving?"

"A feeling. An intuition. And besides, we've frightened them. We've discovered Madame Villehardouin, and I don't think they'll just sit still about it."

Anxious and reluctant, I once again agreed to hide like a common criminal in a dark alcove of a building down the street. To my delight we had been there only a few minutes when the large and imposing door of the house opened and out came the Oriental young woman. Behind her followed another figure, also a woman, and then a man. In the darkness it was impossible to make out any of their features. I was determined not to make a sound this time and I held my breath.

The man vanished into the mews and brought out the Oriental woman's two gray horses and hooked them up to her hansom. She got back in the driver's seat. Then he brought out another carriage, and the two remaining figures got in. Both carriages drove off.

"Where do you think they're going?" I asked.

"To escort Mademoiselle Villehardouin home?" Lady Dunaway offered.

"How long do you think that will take?"

"At least forty minutes. That should give us plenty of

time to go into the house." She stared at my undisturbed
face in the moonlight.

I said nothing.

"Aren't you going to argue with me?" she asked.

"Our children might be in there," I returned. "Now that
they know we are on to them we must move fast before it
is too late."

We walked up to the immense oak door. Much to my
amazement, Lady Dunaway removed an L-shaped tool
from her ulster and inserted it in the keyhole. The lock
began to rattle. As I shifted my weight nervously I
marveled once again at my companion. I imagined her
sitting on the rocky promontories of Cornwall and
thinking of her child. The mere possession of the felonious
little pick indicated she had thought long and hard about
what she might have to do to recover her little Ambrose. I
wondered how many locks she had practiced upon in her
own home. I did not know. One thing I did know was that
Lady Dunaway would not have ceased in her impressive
studies until she was certain no common lock would stand
between her and her son. I looked at the little pick
glinting in the streetlight. The lock opened. She cast me
one final anticipatory glance as she pushed the door open.

Inside was a large and very high-ceilinged foyer. The
walls were of a dark and elaborately embossed brocade,
and several candelabra shone faintly. It was also cluttered
with a cacophony of furniture and strange objects: gilt
and bronze rococo trimmed chests and bookcases, large
glass globes containing wax flowers, bullrushes and
stuffed birds, a black harmonium (played at untold
weddings and funerals?), barometers and crucifixes,
seashells and medieval icons. At the back of the foyer was
a sinuous tower of carved rosewood, an art nouveau
sculpture of a staircase, swirling up the balcony overhead.

The house was moldy with the odor of decay. There was
a dampness in it, a heaviness. It was the stuffiness of
rooms never ventilated. Oddly enough, there was
seemingly the smell of uncounted meals that had been
cooked in the house, the stink of the kitchen and the
scullery. These mixed with another smell, a faint miasma
of strange and fragrant scents; and all these ghosts
bombarded the senses in a silent and choking confusion.

A number of closed doors led off of the foyer, both at the ground level and from the balcony overhead. As we stood there listening the house was still, almost cavernously silent. Then we heard the crying.

Lady Dunaway turned to me, her eyes wide and breathless.

It came from deep within the massive house, distant and plaintive. It was not sobbing or tearful crying. It was a short, piercing wail, repeated over and over. There was something weak and futile about the sound, not quite human. It was like the whine of an animal caught helplessly in the steel jaws of a trap, and it sent a terrified chill to our very marrow.

Madly and without thinking we both charged up the swirling staircase and in the direction of the cry. From the second floor we could see many doors surrounding the balcony, and two other staircases led even farther up into the house. The wail repeated.

"Up there!" I gasped as I led Lady Dunaway down the hall and up another set of stairs. We followed the sound up through the dark labyrinth, past walls covered with strange gimcrack and huge portraits covered with sheets, and finally to a narrow and twisted staircase apparently leading to one of the turret rooms. The wallpaper here was wet and peeling and the wooden steps were half rotted from the dampness. Once again we heard the short cry.

"He's up there," Lady Dunaway said in a hush. Her eyes were glassy and I could see she was half insane with fear and horror. She quickly bolted for the steps, but I held her arm.

"Let me go first," I said.

"No, I'm coming with you."

We carefully made our way up the rotting steps, and the lines in Lady Dunaway's forehead deepened as I turned the brass knob in its collar. The hinges creaked as I pushed into the room.

The crying stopped the moment we opened the door. Everything was black. Something rustled in the darkness.

"Ambrose?" Lady Dunaway called.

No one answered.

I fumbled in my pocket until I found a match and

struck it against the wall. A faint circle of light illuminated the room. From what we could see it was sparsely furnished. The floor was polished black, as if it had been paced many times. A soiled mattress sat in a corner, bare and with its ticking ripped, and the white, fibrous stuffing spilling out. Across the room sat a plain wooden table, and a strange pair of leather gloves. There was something else in the room. There was a hideous stench, like the smell in the den of an animal.

I held the match higher so we could see more when suddenly something moved through the darkness. There was a rushing of air, and the piteous cry sounded once again. Something flailed and hit us, but lightly, strangely, a jerky, feathery something. I quickly lit another match and then we saw. There on the floor was a bird, a falcon. There was a leather hood tied around its small head, securely covering its eyes, and yet, still it had seemed to know our exact position in the room. It tilted its head, listening.

"It can hear us," I said, and instantly the falcon turned in our direction. Even though blinded it waited for another sound, a final coordinate of our position so it could attack once again.

I quickly pulled Lady Dunaway out of the room and shut the door. There was a thrashing of wings against the wood.

"Oh," she cried and buried her face in my arm, as much out of disappointment as of fear. Suddenly the decayed wood gave a little and we both fell to the bottom of the steps with a thud. At the same instant it seemed that there was the sound of a door opening or shutting.

"Did you hear that?" she whispered.

We both listened. At first there didn't seem to be anything. Then, at last, there was the discernible sound of footsteps.

"This house is so big," I said under my breath, "someone could come in, hang up their coat, and wander about through the rooms before we'd hear them up here."

"Or come out of a room on one of the other floors."

Something clicked, the distant ring of metal striking wood.

"We've got to get out of here," she said, looking at me.

We made our way down a set of stairs and saw the rosewood balcony at one end of the hall. Someone was definitely walking on the first floor. "We must hide," I said as I pulled my partner back and the footsteps stopped abruptly. In horror I remembered Madame Villehardouin hearing me at such an incredible distance. What inhuman ears twitched now; what head tilted up, and with undreamed-of senses determined our exact location in the house?

With all the stealth we could muster we inched down the hall away from the rosewood balcony. In the faint light I discovered a door that was slightly ajar and we slipped in silently. To my surprise, the windows were not boarded, as in the turret room, and there was moonlight seeping in. In the meager glow we could see it was a playroom of sorts. Ornate circus ornaments, music boxes, and wooden toys lined the walls. The floor was also cluttered with many objects—puppets and balls and several eighteenth-century French carousel horses. By the window was an immense dollhouse.

We quickly crossed over to the dollhouse and I examined it. The back façade was open like a pair of shutters, and we crouched behind the thin layer of tiny rooms.

For a while we did not hear the walking.

Then there came a strange sound, as of a man mumbling in monotone. The footsteps continued. We heard the distinctive creak of the rosewood staircase. The mumbling became louder.

Lady Dunaway gripped my hand.

Down the hall he came, slow and measured, pausing now and then at other doors. Through all of this the man's voice continued the mumbling. Words finally formed in the low grumble, and I could hardly believe my ears.

"Ad coenam agni providi," came the chant, *"et stolis albis candidi."*

It was Latin, a religious chant, something about the Lamb in white garments, about Christ.

The door to the playroom swung open.

Through one of the miniature windows of the dollhouse and divided by so many minuscule panes I saw the silhouette of a robed figure. In his hands he held a censer on a long chain, and it gave out wispy fingers of incense.

The figure walked into the room and continued to swing the censer. He paused, scarcely inches from the tiny window, and turned around. Suddenly he dropped down, and a thin face filled the window like a giant's.

"Tiens," purred a voice in French. "You don't look like mice." The man stood once agair and stepped back. "They're in here!" he called.

We stood up.

My first impulse was to run, but the appearance of our discoverer was so genial and unintimidating I was put strangely at ease. In the dim light for the oil lamps in the hall I could see he was tall and thin and wearing the simple brown robes of a monk. He had a drawn and bony, even birdlike face, with a prominent beaked nose, pale blue eyes, and monkishly cropped brown hair. His ears were rather large, his arms lanky and fingers long and slender, and still there was a dandyish elegance about him. Even in robes and carrying a heavy censer he stood like a fine gentleman. As for his age, he seemed to be in his early thirties. His face was youthful. His skin was satin smooth and white, without age spots or veins, but there was something very old about his eyes. They were not sunken like the statue of Lodovico, but there was something penetrating in them, an uncanny steadiness of gaze.

"Yes," he said in his forceful but pleasant voice, "I have the white-blue eye of my Gallic ancestors, their narrow skull, and their clumsiness in fighting. I find my clothes as barbarous as theirs. Only I don't butter my hair."

And then he chuckled, a private joke.

"Who are you and what are you doing in my house?"

"I'm Dr. Gladstone and this is Lady Dunaway," I introduced ludicrously, feeling somewhat like a polite burglar.

"And what makes you think your children are here?"

"We heard the falcon," I replied quickly. "We thought it was the cry of a child."

The ears pricked and the intense blue eyes leveled upon the rapid pulse of my temples.

Suddenly a swarm of people carrying candles scurried down the hall and crowded outside the door. I recognized one of them as the other woman who had accompanied the tall and monkish man when he had seen Madame Villehardouin home. Now, in these closer quarters, I could examine her more closely. She was a brown-haired Slavic woman, short and with a stocky frame. Her face was the face of a peasant, plain and round, with unusually wide and limpid gray eyes. Her hands were clenched. She swayed just a little within the folds of her simple brown dress, as if she were as frightened as we were by the encounter. Her skin was strangely soft and sagging, and yet she was not fat. At certain joints and contours of her body her large bones seemed about to push and jut through her very skin, and still, the way the flesh hung on her chin and arms suggested great weight. It suddenly struck me that at one time she had been a very heavy woman, but the mass was all gone now, drawn away by her supernatural condition. It was difficult to decipher how many centuries were hidden in her eyes. They were much too empty and frightened, like the eyes of a shell-shocked soldier. I wondered what had reduced her to such a shy fawn of a woman.

Behind her gathered a bevy of people in night clothing nervously holding their candles and whispering among themselves; a straw-haired young girl with a waxen complexion; another young woman, homely, with a short and rounded figure; several teenage boys and a young boy about seven or eight; a tall and lanky man with hunched shoulders, and apparently his plump, blond-haired wife; and a tall, thin, middle-aged woman with long, straight brown hair. Only the lanky gentleman was dressed—in the livery of a butler.

The most distinctive feature of the adults and older children were the things they wore on their necks. The women and girls all wore wide velvet chokers fastened with brooches and cameos. The man and older boys all wore white handkerchiefs. The middle-aged woman with long, straight brown hair, however, wore a contraption of bandages and gauze around her neck, apparently holding a poultice against a fresh wound. A streak of dark, dried blood trickled down from the poultice and flaked across her pale and freckled breast. She reached nervously to try to conceal the wound.

I quickly looked away, but it was clear to our discoverer

that I had seen it. In a panic I grabbed Lady Dunaway's
hand and rushed toward the window. With lightning
swiftness the thin hands of the monk reached out and
clamped on my shoulders like steel vises. My entire body
snapped from the force as he spun me about and stood me
up like some toy soldier. I was terrified and stunned.

"So you speak English," he said, unperturbed. He
nodded at the butler, and the elderly gentleman searched
us quickly for weapons. "That is much to your credit," the
vampire said when they found nothing. He nodded to the
man again and he slipped quietly out the door. The
vampire turned once again toward us. "Don't be afraid.
I'm not going to hurt you. And please don't waste my time
by panicking or lying. You're the ones who snatched the
scarf from the neck of Madame Villehardouin's maid, and
then chased Madame all over the city, aren't you? You
gave her quite a scare."

He glanced once again at the rate of the pulse in my
temples.

I didn't answer.

"And now you've seen my own servants." He smiled,
eccentrically, benignly, as if he were not at all disturbed
by our blundering in. "Won't you accompany me to my
study so we can sort this all out?"

I was shocked by how amiable he was, and once again I
wanted to ask the question I had first asked Niccolo: *Are
we in danger?* I looked at the face of the man who had just
manipulated me with the strength of three men, but I was
unable to read our situation in his expression. As it was,
the monk had one of those countenances into which any
sentiment could be read. It was impossible to tell whether
his smirk was gentle or sinister. The distracted twinkle of
his eyes might just as easily have belonged to a fool as it
could to a "brain of the first order." I was even suspicious
of his clothing. Were they the garments of a humble
personality, or were they another ruse, a seduction?

"Well?" he urged.

I wanted to run, but the inhuman muscles flexed. We
were like mice in the hands of the Gallic gentleman. We
were completely at his mercy. I looked at Lady Dunaway,
and to my surprise I saw she was not afraid, but more
spellbound by what was happening. I, too, was hypnotized

by certain aspects of our capture, by the incredible strength and acute senses of these beings, by the metabolisms that could produce such effects. All the curiosity I had felt with Niccolo came surging back, all the questions that had gone through my mind since he left. Did our captor know anything about the whereabouts of Camille and Ambrose? Did he know Lodovico? If not, what did he do? What secrets did he possess? And how ancient were he and the strange Slavic woman?

"Are we in danger?" I blurted out.

"Only if you put yourself in danger. You will have complete control over that matter."

I frowned, not quite knowing what he meant. It was a moot point. "Lead on," I said.

"*Très bien*," he returned, smiling. "Then everyone else to bed." He motioned at the human servants. He quickly scanned their faces until he located the blond-haired girl with the waxen complexion. "Except for you, Geneviève. Go fetch us all some tea."

The wispy creature in a nightgown swept off as the Slavic woman lifted a candelabrum high above her head, and the three of us—our host, Lady Dunaway, and myself—followed her down the hall in the opposite direction of the rosewood staircase. The monk walked beside us, watching us, and to my surprise I noticed that his walk possessed the same subtle but unusual rhythm I had first noticed in Niccolo. I had attributed Mr. Cavalanti's gait to the injury of his legs, but the Gallic gentleman moved with a similar graceful and faintly alien syncopation. It was like the walk of very tall animals, of giraffes and okapis. It was such a subtle carriage and movement I was not at all surprised Lady Dunaway had not observed it in the Italian. I glanced ahead and noticed that the Slavic woman walked with a hint of the gait as well.

We went up another set of stairs and down still another hall until we came to a door. The monk pushed it open. The room was large and had a spacious window and balcony overlooking the tops of other houses, with Notre-Dame brooding in the distance. Notre-Dame somehow exemplified the mood of the entire view from that window. The sleeping city. The silence. Stars glistened faintly in

the black sky, and the muggy summer air rustled through
the room. The monk entered and began to light
candles.

In the increasing light various features of the room
became visible. It was long and wide, with plain stone
walls and floor. Niches sheltered rosaries and icons, and a
meditation mat rested before the window. The right-hand
portion of the chamber was considerably less austere.
There were Art Nouveau bookcases brimming with
hundreds of volumes, a conference table of ebonized wood
and inlaid with painted panels of swans, a huge convex
mirror, gold brocade and tasseled tapestries, wooden
chairs, and an ebony desk. Sitting on the conference table
was a most curious object. It was made of carved cherry
and looked like an empty picture frame standing upright
on a three-legged stand. It was not unlike the type of
frame one normally saw embroidery or needlework
samplers displayed in. On closer examination I realized it
contained a beautiful and complex spiderweb, diaphanous
and unprotected by glass or backsheet.

There was more to the room, much more. In an alcove
was an incredibly crafted Louis XV tulipwood and
marquetry *coffre à écrire* with two Chinese porcelain
herons sitting on top of it. On the floor was a finely woven
Persian kilim, and dozens of neatly framed pieces of
artwork cluttered every square inch of wall space. They
were all drawings, prints, and paintings by French artists
of the day—a profusion of Moreaus and Redons, Puvis de
Chavanneses, Bresdins, and Carrières, along with works
of lesser artists, Boldini, Delville, Desboutin, and Osbert.
I also noticed stacks upon stacks of notes and letters on
what I assumed to be our host's cluttered desk—a
clockwork planetarium, a dragon candelabrum, racks of
test tubes, bottles, apothecaries, and flasks with candles
sooting their bottoms. Notes also cascaded out of every
nook and pigeonhole in the room, above and between the
books, in stacks and bundles against the walls, and out of
the partially opened drawers of the desk and *coffre à
écrire,* some of them written on fresh yellow paper, and
some dark with mold and age.

It was the room of a most eclectic personality.

"I suppose introductions are in order," our host finally

murmured. He pointed at the Slavic woman. "This is Ilga." He lit a final candle. "... and I am des Esseintes."

He motioned for us to take seats around the conference table. "May I see your papers, please?"

Lady Dunaway and I looked at each other. We were helpless to do anything but comply. We handed him our papers. He thumbed through them slowly, examining the visa markings with the greatest of care. He even held the pages up to the candlelight and scrutinized the watermark. "They seem legitimate."

"I assure you they are," I said.

"There is one final test." He stood and went over to his ebony desk, scanning the racks of test tubes until he discovered one dusty with age. Next he procured a scalpel from one of the cluttered drawers. He cut a small scrap of paper from each of the passports and placed them into respective flasks. Finally, he poured a little of the reagent from the dusty test tube into each flask and began heating one over the candle. Within about a minute it began to bubble and turned a deep Prussian blue. He looked at me and smiled. "Your passport is legitimate."

"I told you it was," I said, a little ruffled.

He gazed emotionlessly at Lady Dunaway and began to heat the second flask. We waited. At last bubbles began to form. It, too, turned deep blue. He smiled and nodded at my companion.

With that last gesture the elderly butler returned with the falcon perched on his gloved hand. It no longer wore its hood, and it kept its dark eyes trained upon us.

"Dr. Gladstone and Lady Dunaway," he introduced politely.

The butler and his falcon remained standing by the door. He gave an ever-so-slight bow as a trace of amusement crossed his lips. "This is Grelot," des Esseintes said, pointing at the man. "...'little bell.'" Again the butler smiled, not the least abashed by the demeaning name. The vampire returned to the table. "May I ask how you discovered Madame Villehardouin's house?"

"Through the Services en Commun," Lady Dunaway returned. "Because of the amount of gas she uses."

Des Esseintes smiled. "I've always told her to use candles. They're so much more difficult to trace. I place small orders with several different shops every month, no large quantities, and under assumed names." He paused. "And I've also designed the house so that most of the windows facing outward are always dark. That way no one can tell what hours I keep."

"You are an extremely cautious individual," I remarked.

"I have to be. One little slip and all is lost. By the way, Monsieur le Docteur, according to your visa markings you have not been out of the country for twenty years. You never travel?"

"No."

"May I ask why?"

"My work is my world."

"A man after my own heart," he said, and his smile seemed just the faintest hint more sincere. He turned to my companion. "Lady Dunaway, your papers were issued but a few months ago. However, they indicate you possessed previous papers and lost them. May I ask how you lost them?"

"My son inadvertently destroyed them," she said without faltering, and I noticed des Esseintes watch the pulse in her temples as she replied. "Why?" she countered.

"Because this loss seems suspiciously convenient to me. Perhaps you are covering up where you have been."

"Why would I do that?"

"Perhaps your travels would reveal too much about yourself. *Par exemple,* we know that a lot of vampire hunting has been taking place in certain cities. If more than a chance number of these cities showed up in your visa markings it would be most telling. *Enfin,* your papers have just been renewed, and I am left wondering. Are you a vampire hunter?" Again his gaze focused on her temples.

"Certainly not," she snapped. "It was the vampire who first hunted us."

"I think you are telling the truth, but you do not mind if I make one final check." Before we could reply he turned to the wide-eyed Slavic woman. "Lady Hespeth Constantina Dunaway," he read from her papers. "Born December 21, 1854, in Plymouth, England. Husband, Lord Lucien Dunaway. Is there any record of previous involvement?"

"No," Ilga replied simply.

"Family occupations?"

"Military and financial. A great-uncle in academics."

Our host's interests were piqued. "What sort of academics?"

"Sir William Limmeridge, born August 7, 1812, in Plymouth, England, D. Ph. in Indian history, and D. Lit. in ancient Hindu texts."

I might have been mistaken, but our host seemed a little relieved. Lady Dunaway's eyes were wide with incredulity.

"Ilga has a perfect memory," the monkish vampire explained. "I've had her commit all available social and scientific registers to those incredible gray cells of hers."

"May I ask if you were particularly interested in Ilga's reference to academics?" I interrupted.

He turned to me calmly. "Yes, I was. I am a scientist myself. I have many involvements with the scientific world, and I am extremely suspicious. Now let me ask you. You say it was the vampire who first hunted you. Would you please elaborate upon that?"

She related the entire story of our children, and when she mentioned the name Lodovico I thought I detected Grelot raising an eyebrow. After she finished des Esseintes took a long and measured breath.

"I'm afraid I know nothing of your children."

"Do you know the name Lodovico?" I asked.

He glanced slowly at the butler and back at us. "There is not a vampire alive who has not heard the name Lodovico."

The butler expelled his breath, almost as if relieved.

The monk's expression suddenly crumpled into sympathy. "Gentle lambs, I cannot lie to you. I guess there is no harm in telling. I knew Lodovico once."

Grelot straightened angrily, causing the spiderweb to twitch. Ilga reached out and steadied it. "Why do you tell them anything?" the human exclaimed.

"You have already told them with your eyebrows," des Esseintes murmured.

"You do not have to elaborate."

"It is harmless information."

"The less they know the better."

"They already know too much," he said and smiled sadly at me. "As I say, my involvements with Lodovico were in the past. I can shed no light on his present activities." He smiled oddly at Lady Dunaway. "I have no idea why he might be collecting idiots savants." And then he chuckled. "Forgive me, forgive me, it is not that I don't understand the emotions of your situation. It is just that such a flair for the macabre is after my own heart."

"Wait a second," Lady Dunaway broke in. "We know Lodovico was here." She turned to me. "The stone hand. The postmark." She explained the story.

Des Esseintes sat upright and seemed a little disturbed. "Lodovico . . . on the Île Saint-Louis?" He looked once again at the butler and shrugged his shoulders. He turned to Lady Dunaway. "If what you say is correct, Lodovico must have been here. It is not unusual that he would not contact me. We have not seen each other for a very long time."

"Old friends don't keep in touch?" I chided, remembering Niccolo's lies.

"As I say, it has been a *very* long time." He pushed away from the table and walked over to the darkness of the window. The light of the candles flickered over his beaked nose. He regarded me sternly. "Do you have any idea how much time my life covers, how many vampire I have known over the years, Monsieur le Docteur?" He shuddered. "I am over a thousand years old. I was born the month Charlemagne was defeated by the Basques. I became a vampire the year the rose was first introduced to Europe. I took my monastic vows the year Charlemagne died." He gestured at the window. "And still it was over three centuries before they would even begin building Notre-Dame." When he said the name of the ancient church I was struck by the quaver of emotion in his voice. I hadn't hitherto noticed it, but it was rare for any true emotion to surface in the mechanical lilt of his speech. But the words "Notre-Dame" he gave a special, almost passionate valence. "So you see, Docteur, when I say I knew Lodovico a *very* long time ago, what I am telling you is that he is as relevant to my present life as your great-great-grandfather is to yours." With that he drifted into a

THE DELICATE DEPENDENCY   183

silent meditation upon the chiaroscuro cathedral in the distance.

His words shook the very foundations of my scientific understandings of the world. It had been easier, somehow, to comprehend Niccolo's age. Niccolo had always been a magical creature to me, and there was the painting. But now here was a young man, younger than I, a normal-looking man nearly twice the age of Leonardo's angel. A monk older than Notre-Dame itself. A man whose flesh was resilient and unwrinkled who might have known Charlemagne. Part of me could not accept it. What was it then? A ruse? My own insanity? No, he was here before us, like the statue of Lodovico. He was real, another signpost to the staggering scope and meaning of the vampire. I looked at Lady Dunaway and saw that she was just as filled with distrustful wonder. In contemplating this I was struck by one of his remarks.

"Did you say you became a vampire before you took your monastic vows?"

"Yes."

"Wasn't that very dangerous, being a vampire and entering the Church?"

"My good Docteur, the Church was filled with vampire."

I was shocked, but I tried not to reveal it in my expression.

"You seem surprised at that," he said.

"It's a little ironic in view of the myth that vampire are supposed to be repelled by the cross."

"But not so strange, *monsieur,* if you think about it. The Middle Ages, the Dark Ages, were not darker for anyone more than they were for us. There was no learning, only savagery. Everywhere there was danger, the atrocities of the feudal states, superstition, and violence. We are im-mortals. We had interests and goals as different from medieval humans as yours today are from them. The safest place for us was in the monasteries and the convents, secluded in the forests and the mountains. There we were allowed to be completely reclusive and apart from the world. We had our libraries and our artworks."

An unpropitious twinkle crept into his blue-white eyes. "But come now, my good Docteur, haven't you ever

wondered why the Catholic Church is so prepossessed with
drinking blood?" He basked in the uneasiness his remark
created in us. "Let me choose something at random," he
continued, "the Vesper Hymn for the Festival of Easter.
Ad coenam agni provídi et stolis albis candidi—The Lamb
invites us to His meal, in white garments, radiant and
pure. *Cuius corpus sanctissimum in ara crucis torridum
cruore eius roseo gustando vivímus deo*—He offers us His
most holy body, sacrificed on the altar of the Cross, He
gives us His blood to drink, and we live in God." He
chortled.

The butler shifted his weight impatiently.

"Enough talk of me," des Esseintes assented. "I know
nothing of your children or Lodovico. The real issue at
hand is what to do with you."

"And what will you do with us?" I demanded.

"I don't know," des Esseintes said, throwing up his
hands. "You have no idea what a problem you present to
me. You may rest assured, it is out of the question to kill
you. I take after my brethren. There's been so much
killing. I cannot bring myself to harm even an insect.
Neither can I let you go. You know too much. I am forced
to keep you here."

I stood up quickly from the table, but in an instant the
falcon swooped across the room and perched upon the
chair. It emitted its machinelike cry as it looked first at
me and then back at des Esseintes. I noticed there were
deep notches where it dug its sharp talons into the wood.
It had perched upon the chair many times in the past. The
human butler leered.

"My fine old house," des Esseintes rambled on, oblivious
to my outburst, "my beloved home. You have no idea how
many years I've resided within these thick stone walls.
No, no, for my own safety I must keep you here."

"For the rest of our lives?" I asked breathlessly.

"I just don't know," he said with what seemed to be
honest compassion.

Again Grelot shifted his weight.

"Alas, but now the necessity of survival demands I tell
you something it is not altogether pleasant for me to tell.
Whatever you do, you must not try to escape, for the
falcon wouldn't like that. I must also tell you that we feed

the falcon fetid meat. Imagine those sharp talons ripping apart a rabbit that's been dead for several days. You being a *docteur* I don't have to tell you what the merest scratch from those unsanitary talons would do to you."

I looked at the bird and the grinning butler.

"I must now give you a demonstration I had hoped I would never have to give." He motioned for Ilga to step forward and she timidly obliged. Her eyes appeared even a little more frightened.

"We call Ilga *la machine,*" des Esseintes said, hugging her affectionately. "Let me show you." He dropped his arm from her shoulders and stepped back. "There's a brain teaser that Bhaskara composed in the year A.D. 1150. He recorded it in his great work, *Lilivati.* It goes thus: The square root of half the number of bees in a swarm has flown out upon a jessamine bush; eight ninths of the whole swarm has remained behind; one female bee flies about a male that is buzzing within the lotus flower into which he was allured in the night by its sweet odor, but is now imprisoned in it. What is the number of bees?"

Des Esseintes looked at me. "Tell me, Docteur, do you know the number of bees?"

"I could figure it out if I had paper."

"Ahh, but does the number come floating up in your mind instantaneously? With Ilga it does." He turned to the woman. "What is the number of bees, Ilga?"

"Seventy-two," she said without hesitation.

"Good, good, you see, with Ilga algebraic problems are second nature. Now let's try another. A twenty-decimeter ladder is leaning against a wall. The foot begins to slide away from the wall at three decimeters per second. How fast is the top of the ladder moving down the wall when the foot is ten decimeters from the wall?"

Once again he stared intimidatingly at me.

"I don't know, I—"

"Ilga?"

"Three decimeters per second," she said glibly.

"Oh, I see," I interrupted. "It's a trick question. The number is the same as the rate the ladder begins to slide away from the wall."

"Oh, no," Ilga returned. "It's just a coincidence that the two numbers are the same. The rates of change are related in the differential equation formed by—"

"It's all right, Ilga," des Esseintes intervened.

She lowered her head diffidently.

"You see, Ilga had a complete understanding of calculus before there was even a word for it. There are no mathematical puzzles to Ilga. There are no parameters to her thoughts when it comes to numbers." He gently placed a sheet of black paper beneath the cherrywood frame containing the spider web, and shoved it in front of me on the table. Then he withdrew a small porcelain bowl filled with soot and a fine white feather from the *coffre à écrire,* and handed them to me. "You will notice that the spider web is composed of hundreds of four-sided sections of decreasing size. With as much delicacy as you can summon I want you to dip the feather in the soot and mark about a dozen sides of any of those sections."

I glanced at him questioningly, and then at the silky web, and then I gingerly began to spot random strands with soot. The lacy cartwheel trembled.

When I finished, des Esseintes placed the bowl and feather back in the cabinet, and then handed a piece of chalk to Ilga. She stood from her seat and made a few deft strokes with the chalk, arcs and wavy lines, enclosing an area about six inches long. Then she stepped back.

Des Esseintes smiled. "Ilga can do more than solve brain teasers. Her mathematical genius allows her to see the world with an acuity few of us can comprehend. She's like a calculating machine. Her mind instantly perceives a situation, and then the probabilities of all of its outcomes, the fall of the dominoes. She can glance at the position of the pieces and instantly tell you who will win a chess game. She can study a king and his people and tell you how and when he will reach his demise."

He took a tiny pair of scissors from his pocket and began to snip each strand of the spider web I had marked with soot. As they were cut, one by one the web began to droop. At last it came tumbling down, and to my amazement it exactly filled the chalk outline Ilga had made on the paper.

"*La machine* understands the web. *La machine* knows

the future to the extent that it can be predicted." Des Esseintes turned to the Slavic woman. "Ilga, what do you advise I do with our two intruders?"

Her eyes flickered nervously. "You have no choice. For your own safety you must never let them leave this house."

I stiffened involuntarily and the falcon tensed.

Monsieur des Esseintes raised a single finger. "There's one other thing." He turned again to the woman. "Ilga, you know this house better than anybody. You know that there are forty-four windows on the first floor; five turrets, and four balconies, which are close to nearby buildings. You know the thickness of the stone, and the strength of the grates, and you also know the abilities and vulnerabilities of the falcon. If Dr. Gladstone and Lady Dunaway were to try to escape, what chance would they have of succeeding?"

Again her eyes flickered nervously. "Oh, no chance at all."

"And if they did try?"

"They would surely be killed by the falcon," she said as she shyly looked down at her feet.

Des Esseintes looked at us one last time as he finished the vapors of his tea. "Dawn is approaching and I must retire. Grelot will show you to your quarters." He turned to leave.

"And may I ask you one last thing?"

He looked at me.

"How did you find us when we were hiding in the playroom?"

He grinned jovially. "I smelled your cologne, your Lilac Vegetal."

XVI

Des Esseintes nodded good night as he left the study, and Ilga accompanied him. Grelot gestured at the door. Down the rosewood staircase he took us, and down other stairs, stone stairs. The air became cooler in these dark passages, and damp. The falcon followed behind, leaping from step to step like an awkward midget. It seemed to have a sentience, an awareness of us more humanlike than birdlike. We reached a sprawling fourteenth-century wine cellar, and Grelot lit torches. Some of the walls were of huge gray blocks, and seemed to form part of the foundation of the house. The floor was of slate. To my surprise, there were many towering racks of casks and bottles of wine. Beyond the gray foundation the walls were composed of an ocher-colored brick layed in rows with arches and larger bricks and keystones. They shimmered like wet clay, worn smooth by condensation. These walls seemed to be part of a more ancient subterranean structure. The ceilings were vaulted and everywhere dark corridors were sealed at the end with sturdy oak doors.

The man led us through a low tunnel where we both had to duck, and finally kicked aside a sturdy oak door with his booted foot. As soon as we stepped inside I noticed that the air seemed drier, and even warmer. Grelot lit another torch and I could see we were in a moderately sized vaulted chamber of the same yellow brick with two heavily barred cells forming one side of the room and divided from each other by a wall. Each cell was a lushly furnished bedroom with much carved wood, red velvet, and gold. Both possessed many exquisite rococo clocks, paintings, and statues, and an impressive red velvet canopied bed. Indeed, the apartments were so lavishly equipped, only the wall of bars betrayed the fact that they were deep in the moldy cellar of the house. I took it as an ill omen that none of the clocks possessed any hands.

In the middle of the vaulted chamber and facing both
the cells was a post with an arm across it, like a wooden
letter "T," about four feet high. The falcon hopped up on
the post.

With a set of keys Grelot opened each cell and lit the
fire in the fireplace. Then he motioned for us to enter.

"May I ask why it is not damp or musty here?" I said as
I reluctantly entered the cell.

"Des Esseintes designed it. Heating tunnels beneath
the floor," he grunted.

He locked me in and I pressed my face up against the
bars. The space between them was too narrow to allow me
to get my head through, but I could hear him locking
Lady Dunaway in beside me.

"Grelot," I called, "will you tell me how long we will be
kept in here?"

"No."

"Why not?"

He scuffed over in front of me. "It is none of your
business," he snapped. "The falcon will watch you and
after I leave I advise you to keep your hands off the bars if
you value your fingers."

His eye twitched as he left the room.

I turned around and momentarily admired the room.
For prison quarters one could not complain. There were
many richly bound books and I even noticed a decanter of
brandy and a thermidor of pipe tobacco.

"Lady Dunaway?" I called. I drew close to the bars, but
I noticed the falcon tilted forward and prepared to attack.
I stepped safely back.

"Oh, my goodness," her voice echoed from the adjoining
cell. "There's wood in here for the fireplace."

"You don't think we were expected, do you?"

"Oh, no," she answered quickly. "From the look of the
cobwebs the wood's been here quite some time."

"Well, what do you think of him?"

I heard her sit heavily upon her bed. "What do *you* think
of him?"

"I don't know. I'm awed by him. In some ways I
understand his position, but what can I think of someone
who holds us against our will?"

"Yes," she said slowly. "It is the children who are

important. We must persuade Monsieur des Esseintes to
let us go."

"Do you think that will be possible?"

"I don't know. I think . . . I hope Monsieur des Esseintes
is humane. But I just don't know. He's obviously very
worried about our illegal entry into his domain, but he did
go out of his way to assure us several times that we would
not be hurt."

I looked at the falcon.

"I want to trust him," she continued, "but—" Her voice
ended abruptly.

"But what?" I asked.

"But we must remember Niccolo's warning."

"You think Monsieur des Esseintes has lied to us?"

"I don't want to think he has. He seemed honestly
surprised by our mention of Lodovico, but we can never
know."

I agreed with Lady Dunaway's sobering words. In near
exhaustion I slowly began to undress as I slipped beneath
the heavy velvet bedcovers. I looked one last time at the
falcon.

I don't know how many hours I lay in the canopied bed
before I became aware of a lulling echo in the distance. It
was an even, harmonious sound. A rushing. It took a
number of seconds for my consciousness to sift out that it
was the babble of water. I quietly got out of bed and
padded around the room. Didn't that infernal bird ever
sleep? I thought to myself as the beryl eyes continued to
scan my every move.

I paused here and there to listen, and was finally able to
determine that the water sound was coming from behind
the far wall of the bedchamber. I wondered if it was the
sound of the Seine, or the whispering of the murky Paris
sewers. With my ear up against the paneled wall I
suddenly became aware of the sound of walking, and even
the barest fragment of what might have been a human
voice.

Then quite abruptly, the babbling was punctuated by
the low, heavy splash of an object entering the water.

"Lady Dunaway!" I called, wanting her opinion of the
noise.

There was no answer.

I turned around and said her name even louder. There was still no answer.

That was curious, I thought. Had she quickly fallen so deeply asleep that she could not hear me? Or was there a possibility that something had happened to her, someone had quietly stolen her away? I dismissed the thought as my imagination running rampant, but it took quite some time before I drifted into an uneasy sleep.

I awoke in a cold sweat only to hear a familiar and comforting rattle. I sat up to see Geneviève coming past the oak door with a tea cart laden with a most exquisite breakfast. Her red hair was plaited and wound around her ears like horns, and she wore a simple black velvet dress with white lace trim. Once again an elegant black choker and cameo concealed her neck.

"Good morning," I greeted, and she glanced at me with surprise. I smiled but she quickly resumed her timid silence. I noticed her complexion was almost tallow, and a faint web of bluish veins spread out beneath her transparent skin.

"Do you ever talk?"

"When I have something to say, *monsieur*."

She began shoving silver platters beneath the bars, and I slipped on an elaborate brocade robe I found hanging beside the bed. I placed the platters on a small reading table in the center of the room and began to stoke the fire.

"Do you know when des Esseintes intends to come for us today?"

"Come for you, *monsieur?*" She seemed puzzled.

"Surely he doesn't intend to keep us locked up here all day?"

"I don't know, *monsieur*."

She moved the cart out of sight and began to serve Lady Dunaway. To my relief I heard a stirring next to my apartment.

It hadn't crossed my mind that des Esseintes would leave us in our cells, but Geneviève's bewilderment struck a note of worry into my heart. The worry was momentarily eclipsed by awe when I lifted the silver lids. Before me was a breakfast of splendid dimensions: figs garnished with prosciutto and tiny boiled eggs; cruets of *fino* sherry, and *crème* sherry with salted almonds; *galette* potatoes with carefully arranged sprigs of parsley; croissants and French breads; cheeses, marmalades, and preserves.

"Do you know what kind of eggs these are?" I called to my companion.

There was a moment of silence. "Why, no, I don't. I don't believe I have any eggs," Lady Dunaway replied. "Oh, my goodness!" she exclaimed. "Now how was des Esseintes to know that I love toasted muffins?"

"He couldn't," I replied, doubting if even des Esseintes's perceptive abilities were that acute. "It must have been a lucky guess."

"Do you have codfish?" she asked.

"No. Do you have figs garnished with prosciutto?"

"No," she returned. "We must have been served different breakfasts."

I nodded, about to say something, but then I realized that the knowledge we had been served different breakfasts was far from being a significant fact. I looked at Geneviève and noticed she was waiting quietly for us to finish so she could remove our dishes.

"How often does des Esseintes have need of these cells?" I asked between sips of *crème* sherry.

At first she looked at me as if she were not going to answer, but then she obviously realized the harmlessness of the information. "This is the first time since I've lived here that he's used them," she said.

"Do you know when they were last used?"

Again she grew nervous. Her eyes darted back and forth between the two cells. "A long time ago, during the Revolution, two young men broke into the house. They were Royalists. One of them was my great-great uncle."

"How long have you lived with des Esseintes?" I continued.

"I have always lived with Monsieur des Esseintes."

"And your parents?"

"They were born here as well."

I became aware of a tremor of pride in her face.

"We can trace our ancestors back many generations. I serve Monsieur des Esseintes as my grandmother and great-grandmother served him."

"Don't you ever have any desire to escape?"

She became confused. "Monsieur des Esseintes does not keep us prisoner. We are free to go about as we wish. I spend a lot of my time going for long walks. I like the *Marché aux Oiseaux* on the Île de la Cité. Do you know what that is? I go there every Sunday."

"The 'Market of the Birds'?" I translated loosely, but the young woman's English was minimal.

"Oiseaux," she repeated and pointed at the falcon.

I nodded to show her I understood the word.

"Every Sunday from morning to afternoon they hold a street fair and the vendors sell birds, all manner of birds, cage after cage of doves and finches, canaries and mynahs. They also sell funny dogs, and monkeys."

"Does it amuse you to see things in cages?" I asked, peering at the bars of my cell.

"Oh, no," she returned. "It makes me very sad. In fact, des Esseintes gives me spending money just so I can buy a few birds every weekend and let them go. I go up to the top of Notre-Dame and let them go."

I felt a pang of sympathy for the insipid young girl.

"How nice," I heard Lady Dunaway murmur between bites of her melba toast.

I carefully opened one of the tiny eggs—quail eggs, from what I could tell—and began to eat it. "You worship Monsieur des Esseintes, don't you?"

"Oh, no," she said quickly, recoiling almost as if in fear. "Monsieur des Esseintes tells us not to worship him because . . ." She knitted her brow, trying to remember the words. *"Demon est . . . Deus . . . inversus.* Yes, that's it. *Demon est Deus inversus.* God is the devil backward." She was most pleased with herself for remembering so properly.

The words struck me as sinister. "What do you think that means?" I asked Lady Dunaway.

She did not immediately answer, but I heard her stand up from her breakfast table as if she had been particularly struck by the remark. *"Demon est Deus inversus,"* I heard her repeat.

"Does that mean anything to you?"

"I'm not sure, but I would guess it's something to the effect that in great adoration there is all the potential for great hatred."

Geneviève began to nod. *"Oui, madame,* that is it. Monsieur des Esseintes tells us only to accept, never to adore. He says that one man's evil is another man's good." She seemed a little swept away by this and began blinking rapidly. She anxiously eyed my dishes to see if I was done.

"I have another question."

Geneviève folded her hands and shyly regarded her feet.

"Does it hurt when they bite you?"

"Oh, no," she offered suddenly and then calmed herself. "No, it is very pleasant. First Monsieur des Esseintes gives us the pipe to smoke and then he plays the harmonium. There are the most wonderful dreams . . . and dizziness. He has an ointment that makes us feel no pain."

"What sort of music does he play?" I heard Lady Dunaway ask with macabre delight.

"He does not play music," Geneviève said cryptically. She became stiffer still, worried that she was saying too much. She approached the cell. "Are you finished, Docteur?"

"Yes, but I still have several questions."

"I think you should ask Monsieur des Esseintes."

"When will I see him again?"

"I don't know, Docteur." She gathered up the dishes. The falcon ruffled its wings as she left the room.

We occupied the rest of the afternoon by talking, and I found my esteem of Lady Dunaway growing. Her courage was unbelievable. Whereas any normal woman would have paced her cell with worry, my indomitable companion simply sat rocking. From the sound of her scribbling it was apparent she was taking notes about the situation, writing down every possible iota of information that might later prove helpful or valuable. Geneviève did not come again. Our other two meals were brought in by Grelot. By what I assumed to be only an hour or two before dawn I was in a near panic. What if Monsieur des Esseintes intended merely to lock us up and forget about us? I could tell my companion was growing worried as well, but by and large she still maintained her composure, yes, even better than I.

In his last visit Grelot brought us a sleeping draught, but both Lady Dunaway and I judiciously refused to touch it. Once again I lay awake in the canopied bed listening to the constant running of the water. I drifted in and out of sleep as in a fever, and I have no idea how many hours passed when I became aware of a movement in my room. I sat up quickly and listened.

For a moment there was silence, but then, in the constant glow of the torches, I spotted a large rat standing on its hind legs and sniffing at the reading table where I had taken my meals. The falcon, of course, had seen it long before and had frozen into a stare. "Good God!" I cried, throwing a copy of *Le Comte de Monte-Cristo* at the creature. The book clattered against the chair, but the rat did not appear to be intimidated. It turned away from the table, content that there were no remains, and ambled bravely toward the bed. I lifted a candlestick up from the night table, preparing to bludgeon the little monster if it came any closer.

The falcon remained motionless.

At length I spied the uneaten remains of a biscuit, also on the night table, and I gently tossed it outside the bars. The rat immediately waddled toward the scrap, but just as it reached the barrier it paused. It sniffed, looking at me suspiciously, and then back at the food. It contemplated the situation. And then finally it passed beyond the safety of the cell.

Like the branch of a young sapling being pulled back and released, the falcon pounced. The rat squealed piteously. The little neck snapped within the beak. The long tail quivered in a final convulsion.

At the same instant I thought I heard another sound, a disruption in the water similar to the splash I had heard the night before. I rushed over to the opposite wall and listened. This time it was unmistakable, the sound of human, or vampire, voices and the agitated lapping of the water. I heard a hideous rending of flesh as the falcon started to eat its filthy prey.

"Lady Dunaway!" I shouted.

She did not stir.

"Lady Dunaway!"

Still no reply. I ran to the bars and called as loudly as I could. The falcon attacked and narrowly missed my fingers. Was it possible she was so deeply asleep? Had someone come in and taken her, and if so, where?

At last the falcon finished its meal. The sounds subsided into the distant rushing. I lit all the torches and candles in my room and sat up for hours listening for some faint indication that Lady Dunaway was still in the cell beside me, or to hear the sound of someone bringing her back. If she had been taken away I reasoned that it must have been through a passage other than the cell door. The sound of the metal bars being opened and closed would surely have roused me from my sleep. I have no idea how long I sat in that timeless, quiet world. Finally, I went back to the bed and fell into a leaden sleep.

XVII

I awoke groggy and confused about my whereabouts. It took me several vigorous blinks to orient myself. When I finally pieced the world together out of the blur, I saw a well-dressed gentleman standing like a dandy in the middle of the room with his foot upon the chair.

"You did not like *Le Comte de Monte-Cristo*, Docteur Gladstone?" said a familiar voice as the man stared at the fallen book. To my surprise it was des Esseintes.

I sat up in bed.

"You sleep very late," he said, walking over to my side. "It is well past midnight. Get up. Get dressed."

"You've changed considerably," I said, eyeing his attire. He was fastidiously dressed in a black pinstriped suit with a white silk shirt, and a resplendent white orchid on his lapel. His fingers were covered with scintillant opals, as was his stickpin, and he boasted an expensive gilt cane. He was the complete antithesis of the monkish figure; the heir apparent of the loftiest aristocracy.

"I've already run an errand," he explained, gesturing at the suit. "I only wear the monk's robe when I'm being the monk."

"An errand?"

He chuckled as he swept around the bed, his eyes never losing me in their focus. "Oh, it's not what you think. I don't go out digging up graves or playing ghoul. I had a few papers to sign."

Again I was puzzled.

"Well, I do have business holdings. I have to have an income, you know."

"May I ask what businesses you own?"

"Of course not."

"Why?"

"Because the only other person besides myself who knows my business holdings is Ilga. It's safer that way."

"What about your solicitors?"

"What about them?"

"Are they human?"

"Most of them."

I pondered the remark. "And do the human ones know your business holdings?"

"Of course they do...but they do not know I am a vampire."

This surprised me once again. "Well, how do you manage that?"

"It is really very easy," he said, polishing his cane, "for two very simple reasons. First, solicitors and men of business care very little who it is they are taking their money from. I could be a murderer or a political maniac and they would not ask questions. In their way of thinking there is no good money or bad money. And second, if you are very rich you can get away with being as quaint as you want. As far as my solicitors and business managers know, I am an obsessive recluse. When I am with them, I pretend to hate going out. I also pretend to be morbidly afraid of the germs of human contact." Again he laughed. "Indeed, if you ever learn of an extremely wealthy person who seems to be a terrified hermit and never goes out, you might ponder the possibility that he is not an eccentric, but merely clever, a being of a higher order—"

"Oh, so you're a being of a higher order?"

"Most definitely, Monsieur le Docteur. Did you think I would be modest? Come now, you must accept my apology for leaving you in here so long. Unfortunately, a very urgent matter arose that took up most of my time these last few nights. I wouldn't normally be so cruel as to leave you locked up. As soon as you've finished dressing we must have a more leisurely chat, both you and Lady Dunaway."

"Lady Dunaway," I said abruptly as I remembered the incident of the night before. "Is she all right?"

"Are you all right, my dear?" des Esseintes called.

"I'll be all right in a minute," grumbled Lady Dunaway's voice as she obviously aroused from a deep sleep.

"Come now," des Esseintes prodded. "I told you to get dressed."

I heard her sniff again followed by the distinct sound of the brush going through her hair.

"What are we going to chat about?"

"About you. For instance, I don't even know what kind of a doctor you are."

"I'm a virologist."

"You're a virologist—see, I've learned something already. We have many things to chat about . . . about your future. Since our first encounter I've had time to think about a lot of things. I'm so isolated, so attached to my own perspective. I've been myself for so long, I don't immediately grasp how you might be viewing all of this. Well, I've had time to put myself in your shoes and I've realized how confused and frightened you must be. Especially after I was so insidious the other evening, talking about the falcon and all. I'm not really such a bad fellow. I thought if we had a more leisurely conversation you might be put more at ease."

"And will we still be kept prisoners?"

"We will talk about that also."

At last Lady Dunaway appeared, dazed but carefully groomed and still wearing her ulster, only minus the hat. I scrutinized her closely. It *was* Lady Dunaway, not an imposter. She didn't seem changed in any significant moods or aspects. There were no markings upon her neck. "Good morning," she greeted.

"Ah, yes," des Esseintes returned. "Shall we leave these dreary surroundings?"

We both nodded and followed as he led us past the falcon. It hopped down behind us. When we reached the first floor I saw that the house was a hubbub of activity. The women were all busy cleaning the foyer. They were dressed simply in black and magenta dresses trimmed in white lace. The older boys were polishing the glass globes containing the bullrushes as the youngest boy replaced candles. Grelot supervised everything.

Des Esseintes paused to point out some detail that needed polishing, and I took advantage of the distraction to move closer to Lady Dunaway. "Didn't you hear me last night?" I whispered.

She looked at me surreptitiously. "What?"

"Two nights in a row now I've heard voices and a

movement in the water and I've called out to you. But you don't answer."

She pursed her brow. "Do you call loudly?"

"Yes, last night there was a rat in my room and I fairly screamed."

"That's impossible. I heard nothing."

Des Esseintes pointed at an icon high on the wall that needed straightening and the young boy clambered up to fix it.

Lady Dunaway went on in a hush, "I'm a very light sleeper and I didn't hear a thing. Are you sure you weren't dreaming?"

"Of course not, I'm positive I—" I began, but des Esseintes once again turned to us. He made a gesture to follow him. Instead of going up the rosewood staircase he led us down a corridor to the left of the lavender foyer. This was lined with various alabaster statues of women. Some of them were life-sized nudes and others, busts and partial heads. All of them were done in a style that more closely resembled faces and body parts trying to break through sheets of wet gauze than statues. It took me a minute to realize they were of a single person, a woman, and in the midst of the frozen throng my eyes finally came to rest on a portrait.

Once again it was the same thirtyish lady, a frail wisp of a woman with meek brown eyes and spinsterly drawn hair. There was something a little different about the painting. In the statues she moved, lounged, danced. Occasionally there was anguish in the stone likenesses, but it was the anguish of a being struggling to be born, to free itself from the marble. It was the painting that revealed a deep melancholy. In front of the painting was a table, an altar of sorts, on which were assembled several simple but elegant long-stemmed vases. Each contained a purple orchid.

"Will you wait here please," des Esseintes murmured. He went to the opposite side of the corridor and unlocked a cupboard. Inside was a camera on a tall black tripod with a hood and flashboard.

"What are you going to do?" I asked.

"Take your photograph."

"Why?"

"For my scrapbook."

"That's a fine to-do. You keep a scrapbook of all of your human prisoners? How many of these pleasant forget-me-nots have you amassed?"

He carefully positioned the tripod and then looked up at us. "You amuse me, Monsieur le Docteur. I was joking about the scrapbook. I am taking your pictures as a precaution. There may come a time when I need such photographs."

"I don't understand."

"Smile."

"What possible need could you have—"

The magnesium powder went off in a burst of white light. Des Esseintes came out from under the hood. "Very nice. I think I captured Lady Dunaway's trenchant beauty perfectly."

Lady Dunaway blushed.

The vampire withdrew the photographic plate and handed it to Grelot, who had appeared with a silver tray. He carried it away officiously. Des Esseintes gathered the photographic paraphernalia together and once again locked it in the cupboard. He motioned us on.

At last he paused in front of one of the doors and pushed it open. Inside was an explosion of deep turquoise and gold, a simple and stunningly symmetrical Art Nouveau sitting room. It was in the Japanese style with wainscoted walls, upper walls painted with blue and gilt peacocks, and a black-lacquered fan-vaulted ceiling. There were carpets and pillows on the floor, a low table, a hookah, and a number of potted palms.

"The room was designed by Thomas Jeckyll, perhaps you've heard of him?" des Esseintes boasted as I caught a glimpse of the falcon watching us from outside the doorway. "The peacocks were painted by the American painter, J. McNeill Whistler."

I once again admired the rich and exquisite room as the Frenchman motioned for us to sit upon the pillows. When I glanced at the hookah I remembered Geneviève telling us how des Esseintes always had them smoke before he suckled them. Des Esseintes seemed not unlike a Chinese camprador on his opium mat. I experienced a flush of alarm.

"What is the matter?" our host asked. He gazed at me

for a second and then his face lit knowingly. "Oh, yes, yes . . . you're probably wondering how I know something is the matter. I forgot, I must explain things to you. I'm so used to being around my own kind." He removed what appeared to be a small ivory snuff box from the inside pocket of his jacket. "There's a quiver in the air. I have seen the quiver for so long that I forgot you cannot see it. It's similar to what you might see if you stared at a splay of frost on a window through a magnifying glass—a delicate cross-hatching that's so transparent it takes most vampire many lifetimes before it suddenly pops into their vision and they wonder why they ignored it for so long. We are like magnets in a box of needles; when we walk, we affect the quiver. Even our emotions—like the tinge of alarm you just felt—changes the pattern in the frost."

He took a dried crimson substance from the snuff box and placed it in the hookah as a second flicker of realization went across his face. "Ohh, Geneviève's been telling you about our personal habits. You needn't worry. This is not a feeding. But it was only a tinge, wasn't it? You're not really afraid of me, are you?"

"No," I said, "I'm not afraid of you in an emotional sense. Neither do I trust you. What are you putting into the hookah?"

"It's substance I create myself from orchids. You must have guessed my hobby is orchids."

He lit the hookah and inhaled. A very subtle but pleasant smell, not unlike the scent of camomile cigarettes, filled the air. "It's really quite enjoyable. Would you like to try it?"

"What does it do to one?"

"I couldn't begin to tell you. All I can tell you is that it is enjoyable to me."

"No, thank you," I returned. "I would never take anything into my lungs that I had not studied completely."

"I admire your caution," he said, nodding. He turned to Lady Dunaway. "And you?"

She blinked, a little shocked that a gentleman would offer such an indiscretion to a lady. Her eyes played back and forth between us for a moment. She demurred politely.

"Funny..." he said wistfully. "I rather thought you would." He smiled faintly at my compatriot. "I know your name, but would you recite it for me?"

She looked at him curiously. "Lady Hespeth Dunaway," she repeated.

"Hespeth..." He allowed the sound to roll slowly over his tongue as he took another puff. "That's a very old name. Did you know that?"

She nodded, still not quite following what he was saying.

"That's another thing you're probably not aware of. Names are often much more transient creatures than you realize. For example, there are many young men named Paul and Marc today, but these names may not last forever. They may die, just as Childeric and Pepin have died. Even my beloved Paris has not always been called Paris. I first knew the city as *Lutèce*. For centuries and centuries, since the time of Caesar, it was *Lutèce*. And then, under the reign of Clovis, it became *Paris*. It was named after the *Parisii*, the first tribal community to settle on these two tiny islands. These islands are very old, you know. In any case, I like your name. Hespeth. That is what I shall call you if you would allow me to."

Lady Dunaway melted into a smile. I could tell she was endeared by the gesture.

Des Esseintes turned once again toward me. "I have not forgotten that you said you don't trust me. I think that is wise on your part. May I ask, is there any particular reason you don't trust me?"

I was surprised by the question. "Isn't it obvious? Because Niccolo deceived me and took my daughter."

"So for you there is wisdom in mistrust?"

"Yes."

"I am glad to hear you say that because you may more readily understand my own position. I have thought about it a great deal and I am forced to the conclusion that I must also mistrust you. I'm afraid you and Hespeth must remain my prisoners for an indefinite length of time—"

I'm sure our shock registered in the quiver. "What about our children?" Lady Dunaway asked frantically.

"Indefinite?" I retorted. "How long is indefinite?" I was incensed, but I contained my temper. "Oh, how long do we mortals live, anyway?" I asked mockingly. "A mere sixty years? It will be like keeping a pet, a bird locked up for a while, won't it?"

"I was hoping we could deal with this without such hard feelings—"

"You're talking about the rest of our lives."

"Monsieur le Docteur," he said placidly, "how many times must I remind you that it was you who broke into my home. I did not invite you. I did not ask for this situation." He took another healthy puff from the hookah and sank back against the pillows. A faint smile crossed his face as he closed his eyes pleasurably and twitched once or twice. "What was it the caterpillar said in *Alice in Wonderland*? Take a bite from one side and you grow. Take a bite from the other side and you . . . get small?"

I found his enigmatic sense of humor flippant and irritating.

"Come, come," he continued, "I think you are only looking at the bad side of the matter. You forget what an opportunity you have in meeting a creature such as myself. You must remember, I am even much older than this vampire you speak of, this Niccolo. Think about it. I am as ancient to him as he was to you. That makes me a different creature entirely. Why, you haven't the faintest glimmer of the fantastical things swirling about in this narrow skull." He fanned his slender hands. "Oh . . . the things I could teach you; the stories I could tell. I've lived the lives of dozens of men. I've moved through a world that is alien and dazzling to you. I could even make you enjoy staying here. I could hypnotize you with my words."

I greeted this remark with mixed emotions. He was quite correct. I yearned more than anything to probe the vastness of his memories, but I also prickled at the thought of abandoning my pursuit. I felt compelled to speak. "My good Monsieur des Esseintes, I'm sure you could tell me much, but I can inform you with utter conviction, nothing will ever make me give up my search for my daughter."

Instead of replying he merely gave another odd smile and pulled a tasseled cord. In moments Geneviève brought in a tray of cordial glasses and a bottle of Crème de Cassis. As she poured the syrupy reddish-purple liquid I noticed she was glancing at me out of the corner of her eye. As soon as I detected this she quickly turned away and left the room.

Lady Dunaway and I watched our host.

"Come now, isn't there anything you'd like to ask me? Isn't there something about the vampire you would like to know?"

A myriad of questions suddenly swept through my mind: the nature of their condition, the extent of their knowledge. In the kaleidoscope of my curiosity I once again saw a flash of lightning, a stone hand, the sunken eyes of the Alexandrian scribe. "Yes," I said. "Tell us about Lodovico."

A hesitant excitement spread over Lady Dunaway's face. Her eyes widened fatuously behind the thick lenses of her spectacles.

"Ahhh, Lodovico. I knew I could draw you into a story. That is why I had the cordial brought in." He took another rapturous inhalation from the hookah and blew the smoke out in a billowy cloud. The glassiness of his eyes increased. "I will tell you how I first learned of Lodovico. It was in the Middle Ages. To begin, I must tell you how I became a vampire." His eyes flashed. "I know you won't mind." He nestled deeper into his pillow.

"It was very long ago . . . oh, so *very* long ago. As I have told you, I was born during the time of Charlemagne, and what a different world it was. Believe it or not, I was a simple man. My beginnings were very simple. I grew up in the beautiful valley of the Rhone River. My parents were freemen, but rented land from a wealthy baron who owned vineyards. We helped grow the grapes for the Burgundy the baron produced, a very good Burgundy, heady and sumptuous red. Even as a child I was fascinated with the process, with the growing of the grapes, the way the tendrils curled up the runners. The flowers. The buzzing of the bees, everywhere, over everything. I had a mind for such things.

"When I was a young man I took over my parents' portion of the work. I married. I had children. I was still fascinated with the bees and I began to observe and

understand their role in the vineyards. My mind
burgeoned with ideas, and it wasn't long before I was
experimenting with the little insects, causing them selec-
tively to pollinate various varieties of grapes. I did many
incredible things, things that had never been seen before.
I controlled the plants. I modified their growth and
output, influenced their very chemistry, much like the
baron controlled us. Only with passion. You see, I am of
the opinion that plants are our dearest friends. I also
believe they are the greatest little research laboratories
in the world. If you have a rapport with them, know how
to coax and pamper them, you can get them to do
anything.

"Within a few years I doubled the quality of the baron's
wine and tripled his production. Word of my achievements
spread throughout the valley and the provinces and soon
other landowners were coming to visit me to learn of my
methods."

Des Esseintes's voice became softer.

"Alas, the baron did not like this. He forbade me to
reveal any of my secrets, but, alas, I did not like that. You
see, at that time I felt the wisdom of nature was for all to
share. I was angered and bitter. I continued to tell anyone
who asked, knowing full well that the wrath of the baron
would be severe."

Des Esseintes took a final puff on the hookah and
pushed it away. With this I noticed there was something
visibly different about his face. His eyes were unusually
shiny and a veritable hum of energy seemed to come from
the tranquil visage. He leaned forward and poured us
each another drink.

"What happened?" I asked. "Did the baron do anything?"

He shook his head. "No, he wasn't able to."

"Did you do something to stop him?"

"No. You see, civilization was even more primitive then
than it is now. Pillaging was very much in vogue. Before
the baron discovered my insobriety a roving horde of
Magyars swept through the valley. They stormed the
baronial castle. They burned down the houses and
trampled the vineyards. I survived in a cellar, hiding
behind a huge vat of wine for three days as they drank

and reveled. Finally they were run out by a detachment of mounted knights loyal to the barony." He smiled, an oddly dissociated smile, devoid of any emotion. "The baron was killed."

For a few moments both Lady Dunaway and I shifted in our pillows.

"What happened to your wife, your children?" she finally asked.

"They were killed as well," des Esseintes said bloodlessly.

Lady Dunaway regarded him with horror.

"Oh, please don't judge me harshly just because I do not seem bereft. That is another thing you must realize about me. Just because I don't seem to express emotion does not mean I am not feeling it, Hespeth, my dear. I simply deal with emotions in ways that are very different and very alien to the ways you have been taught to deal with them.

"To continue, late one evening just a few days after the mounted knights, a small group of monks arrived at my door. They were very kindly monks. They said they had heard of my work. They soothed me and told me what I had not yet articulated—that I was vastly different from the great mass of humanity; that I was a glimmer of consciousness, of genius, amid the dark and lurking beasts of my species. I offered them Burgundy, but they did not drink it. Instead, they only sniffed its bouquet.

"One of the monks also had a treasure, a grape without seeds, and they told me if I would visit their order they might share their secrets with me. They would teach me their alchemy. Dazzled by the proposition, I agreed to accompany them. However, they refused to travel by day. They said that it was safer in the darkness. At night one could smell the campfires of the roving Magyars and Norsemen, and thus avoid them. Also, these monks, Columban by order, said that due to the darkness of their monastery, they had developed the ability to see at night fully as well as I could see in the day.

"So we traveled. Before dawn approached we took refuge in caves, and finally we made our way to the monastery, high in the Vosges Mountains. I was amazed by the monastery. It was even more fortified than a castle. The style of living was much different from what I was accustomed to. Pigs and fowl did not have the run of the house, and beds were elevated with feather mattresses. My first few evenings there were very strange. They were already performing some experiments with plants, with sweet peas, but they never tended them during the day. They only worked in the garden at night by the light of torches, and oftentimes as I meditated in my cell I heard the sound of secret passages and chanting.

"One evening while I was praying to a statue of the Virgin in the chapel of the monastery a small group of the brothers came to me. I wondered why the Virgin smiled so oddly; what malformation of her teeth could account for the peculiar curling of her upper lip. They told me many incredible things. They told me they were very learned alchemists, and that they possessed a number of magical secrets. One of these was the secret of immortality. They told me that I had been invited to join their order, and if I accepted, I too would be made deathless."

Des Esseintes tilted his head back. "Memory of what happened next is misty. You see, I was given a drowsy syrup. The votive candles burned. The hooded figures closed in about me. I remember seeing an icon of the Passion. A gentle and brotherly kiss upon the neck. I was moved, deeply and spiritually moved... and strangely feverish. There was more of the drowsy syrup. I woke up the next evening with quite a hangover. It was several weeks before I noticed my teeth were changing."

At the mention of the drowsy syrup I began to notice that the peacock walls had acquired a familiar gleam. I had just finished my second drink, and I was beginning to feel the effects of the alcohol. I wanted to ask about Lodovico, but another question came into my mind: "Was it the bite on the neck that turned you into a vampire? Is that what transforms you?"

"Oh, no, it is a little more complicated than that. Otherwise Geneviève and all the servants would be vampires. I discovered later that in my delirium I had been given a transfusion of one of my comrade's blood. They had matched our types previously and performed the task with a leather flask and a hypodermic needle fashioned out of a fishbone. The only time that one is lucky enough to become a vampire from a mere bite is if the vampire has an open sore in his mouth."

"From that it would follow that vampirism is a disease?"

"I am pleased that you would articulate that, Monsieur le Docteur. It is nice that even though you are a human being, you have the interests of a physician—a virologist, as you say. You are quite correct in your observation. Vampirism has some of the aspects of a contagion, not unlike syphilis. But if it is a contagion, it's a very strange one. No bacterium has ever been isolated as its cause. The common belief is that it is viral, but if it is, it is even a very strange virus. It has been discovered that the transfusion must be made with great speed, for the virulent blood only retains its ability to transform for a brief flicker of a second once it has been separated from a living body. It's as if the virus needs to be close to the energy of the human metabolism to stay alive. We may thank the gods for that. Otherwise vampirism might have spread through Europe as the bubonic plague did—through the bites of fleas and rats. All the craven beasts of humanity would have been made immortal. Can you imagine a nineteenth-century Europe still swarming with Mongolians and Crusaders? What a hideous problem 'rampant immortality' would pose for humanity. As it was, before the secret of transference was discovered, our procreation was haphazard and extremely sporadic."

"And when was the secret discovered?"

"I'm afraid I cannot tell you."

"Why not?"

"I can't even tell you that. Suffice it to say that when I entered the monastery of the Vosges, the vampire already had a recorded history that dwarfed human records. Of course, we weren't always called the vampire. Indeed, it was the roving bands of Magyars who began to spread that terminology, *vampyr* being a Magyar word. We were known by many names, depending upon which aspect of our character we were recognized by. Those who knew us from our dark side called us the *lamia* or *lamya*, from the ancient Greek term for vampire, *lamiae*. We're mentioned in the first English translation of the Bible, *Lamentations* 4:3, circa A. D. 1382, as 'The cruel beestis cleped (or called) *lamya...* ' Oddly enough, in the King James version someone has changed all of the references to the *lamya* to 'sea monsters.' " He gave a strange little smirk.

"Among ourselves we were neither the vampire nor the *lamya.*"

"What were you?" Lady Dunaway asked, shifting excitedly in her pillow.

"Can't you guess? You have heard the term before. Swirling amid the myths and legends of the Middle Ages there have always been rumors of a secret society of intellectuals, a society who possessed knowledge far beyond the human culture, who were immortal, great alchemists and philosophers, who secretly pulled the strings of history. And who were we? What is the name by which we knew ourselves? ... the illuminati." He recited the term with another grand flourish of smoke from the hookah. "Yes ... *we* were the illuminati."

With an obdurate sense of good manners des Esseintes once again filled our liqueur glasses with Crème de Cassis. As he turned around to set the decanter behind him I noticed Lady Dunaway clandestinely emptying her drink in the water tray of one of the palms. Obviously she was feeling as uncomfortable as I was under the increasing influence of the alcohol.

"I must warn you not to confuse the vampire illuminati with the various human organizations that subsequently stole the term. Many secret societies sprouted up and tried to mimic us. History is littered with their names— the Masons, the Freemasons, the Knights Templar, the Rosicrucians, the Dionysiac Architects, and the Society of the Unknown Men. Although a number of these organizations were originally formed by vampires, the names were copied and corrupted by a host of imposters. In sixteenth-century Spain there was a group of mortal heretics who called themselves 'the illuminati,' as did an obscure human sect in seventeenth-century France during the reign of Louis XIII. None of these were the true illuminati as the monks in the Vosges were."

"But if the vampire kept their identities hidden, how did such human organizations learn about you to copy you?" Lady Dunaway inquired.

"We kept our secrets hidden, but *we* were not so hidden.

You can still find accounts of these things in the old
records. I was out for a stroll one evening a few weeks ago
when I came upon some bookstalls still open in the park
next to the Bibliothèque Nationale. I discovered a book
written about thirty years ago by a native Parisian, a
man named Eliphas Levi. He called the book *Histoire de la
Magie*. In it he quoted several medieval chroniclers on
their accounts of a thirteenth-century French monk
named Jechiele who possessed 'a dazzling lamp that
lighted itself.' It was a lamp without oil or wick, and
Jechiele sometimes put it in his window at night, much to
the fascination of his mortal contemporaries. Although
he was accredited at the court of King Louis IX and even
served as an adviser, Jechiele never revealed the secret of
his lamp.

"According to his chroniclers Jechiele also possessed a
very special device for discouraging unwanted visitors
who knocked at his door. He 'touched a nail driven into the
wall of his study, and a crackling, bluish spark
immediately leapt forth. Woe to anyone who touched the
iron knocker at that moment: He would bend double,
howling as if the earth were about to swallow him up, and
then he would run away as fast as his legs could carry
him.' In this way, by the terror he aroused, Jechiele saw to
it that he was left in peace. I was amused by my discovery
of the account, for I knew Jechiele. He was a vampire, as
we all were. We kept our pointed teeth and culinary habits
hidden, but all of Europe knew of the illuminati. We were
not so hidden then as we are today. Medieval humans were
much easier to intimidate and control. There were many
advantages in putting on a sort of show with our
knowledge."

"What other secrets did the vampire possess?" I asked.

"Oh, many things. For example, the vampire of the
Vosges possessed an advanced knowledge of horticulture.
In a time when the tools of justice were the caldron of
burning oil, and the wheel, and barnyard animals were
brought to trial for witchcraft, they were grafting
different species of plants together, and creating plant
mutations. You may be more intrigued by their other
avenue of research, and that was automata. Fully five
centuries before the clock of Strasbourg, there were

vampires at the monastery who could build mechanical
clocks with dozens of moving figures. They also possessed
a diminutive mechanical horse that whinnied, stamped,
and reared up in a manner exactly as if a real horse had
been shrunk to such size. Perhaps most magical of all
they possessed a clockwork bee of gold and jewels that
crept on flowers and even flew around the room."

"Were all of these things kept secret from the mortal
world?"

"Yes."

"When you worked for the baron, you believed
knowledge was for all to share. You even risked your life.
Why did you choose to keep these things secret?"

"You misunderstand me, Monsieur le Docteur. You see,
they were kept from most of the vampire as well. When I
entered the monastery of the Vosges I learned there was a
very rigid hierarchy of secrecy among my new brethren. It
was not unlike an ancient mystery institution. One had to
pass through various levels of initiation. Puzzles were
unfolded slowly, and oh, what puzzles there were.

"Par exemple, I discovered of all the monks at the
monastery, few were over three centuries old and most
hovered around two. None of these younger vampire knew
why this was so. The older vampire, the *abbés* of the
monastery, kept secret council and seemed to know much
more about the 'grand design behind it all.' It was
generally recognized there was a vast and complex
organization behind our kind; that somehow populations
of vampire communicated all over Europe. Emissaries
were even venturing into the Orient. And yet, we younger
vampire did not know how this communication was going
on. It was rare that visitors ever passed to or from our
monastery, save for the mortal members of the Church
bringing letters from the human powers, and exchanging
common manuscripts. When we had such mortal visitors
we were instructed to leave our research and go through
the actions of more normal Church functions. We chanted.
We copied liturgies. We read the mundane and religious
manuscripts. Nonetheless, being so high in the mountains, visitors were rare. We were as isolated and aloof
from the world as the stars. And still, the *abbés* told us
what was happening among the Lombards and the

Britons. They informed us of advancements made in the lesser alchemies, and occasionally brought compliments on our own discoveries from that mysterious network.

"It was at this time that I heard of the Unknown Men. It was an expression I heard often. On one occasion one of the *abbés* gathered us together and announced simply, 'One of the Unknown Men has been slain.' On another occasion was the decree, 'An Unknown Man has been revealed.' It did no good to inquire further on these cryptic remarks, for the *abbés* would say nothing, and otherwise a general ignorance prevailed. Were the Unknown Men leaders? Were they older vampire? Or special vampire, changed or mutated in some unique way? Were there many of them? Were there few? Were the *abbés* Unknown Men? Were there any among us? No one seemed to know, and all possible rumors and theories circulated on the matter. Throughout all of this, one name became a whispered legend, an enigma, a mystery. It was mentioned as often as the Unknown Men, although no one knew why, or what their connection was. That was the name Lodovico."

XVIII

With this des Esseintes suddenly jumped up from his pillows and announced, "Let's go look at the orchids!"

Lady Dunaway and I looked at each other.

"Is that all you're going to say?" I gasped.

"Aren't you going to tell us more?" Lady Dunaway exclaimed.

"Perhaps, Hespeth—*mon petit chou*. But right now my state of mind demands more resplendent surroundings."

Once again, "Hespeth—my little dear" and I looked at each other. It was difficult to imagine more resplendent surroundings than the turquoise-and-gilt sitting room. Des Esseintes looked at my empty glass and filled it. I looked at this, my fourth goblet of Crème de Cassis, and felt a momentary horror. I was very drunk. The horror passed quickly, for I was once again drawn to the codeine luminescence of the room. Everything now seemed to glow with a subdued and yet powerful light, like the drone of a distant turbine—the black-lacquered dados, the satin outline of the pillows. Amid this, the thin gentleman seemed even more charged, eyes glazed as a dervish, and yet imperturbably placid. He moved gracefully across the room, and once again I became acutely aware of how completely alien his movement and gestures were. There was a striking absence of any human gesticulation. No stroking of the brow. No nervous play of hands. As it was, he held his long hands limply, but in a manner unlike any gentleman or dandy I had ever seen. He was not unlike a praying mantis. I flushed at experiencing such a bizarre perception. I looked again at the deep purple liquid, wondering if I had been drugged.

"No, you weren't," des Esseintes anticipated, apparently "sensing the quiver."

He hit a secret button, and one of the painted panels hissed out of sight revealing two narrow, mist-covered glass doors. He flung them wide and we were enveloped in

a gush of humid air. It was warm and ponderously
fragrant, and at last I realized the source of the strange
scents that had bombarded me when I had first entered
the house of des Esseintes. Inside was a greenhouse, a
large and lush greenhouse, overflowing with orchids.
They covered trellises and cedar arbors, and climbed to
the very top of the enclosure. Everywhere one looked one
was confronted with the living, fleshy wall. Orchids of
every possible shape and color. Some were heavy and full;
others, unimaginably fragile. They were illuminated by a
series of torches situated around the perimeter of the
transparent enclosure. Through the glass towered the
walls of the bleak and mammoth house, and beyond, the
obsidian night. Against this infinite blackness and
imbued with the light of the fires, the orchids were
overwhelmingly beautiful. Impossibly, it was even more
resplendent than the peacock sitting room.

Des Esseintes crackled, raised to a euphoria by the
environment, the muggy, sweet-scented air, the almost
suffocating beauty.

As I took in the details of the greenhouse I grew even
more astonished by the variety of the flowers. At first
they hit one's senses in a single mass explosion, like a
field of tulips, or a rolling meadow of white crosses on the
graves of anonymous soldiers. Then a multitude of
differences began to reveal themselves in the masses. The
orchids started to take on the identity of other creatures
and objects. Here I fancied a cluster of red-hot pokers;
there, a flock of flying blue swans. Indeed, the experience
was disconcerting. My imagination suddenly suggested
these were more than orchids, that they were telepathical-
ly reflecting some unconscious part of me. The hidden
images I saw in the blossoms became stranger. Here, the
head of a monstrous and deformed child popped in and
out, there an obscene and hunchbacked dwarf bulging
with lavender veins. In my altered state the foliage shone
with a kind of glassy, jadelike radiance.

I was so preoccupied with the orchids I was a little
stunned when the details of the greenhouse itself
suddenly loomed into my consciousness. It was as if the
greenhouse also had a presence, was jealous of my
fascination with the flowers. I was compelled to examine

it as well. For the first time I noticed there were many doors surrounding its perimeter. It was alive with the hiss of steam. It might have been a salon of the Grand Palais were it not in such a state of dilapidation. All of the glass panels were intact, but waxy with grime and condensation. The paint on the intricate white framework was peeling and rust-stained. It was like the conservatory of an abandoned old home, overgrown with gnarled figs and mosses. A hollow in a deep, dark forest. The matted hiding place of a deer.

I found it strange that a man, or vampire, of des Esseintes's wealth would allow such a garden to sink to overgrown ruin.

Suddenly I spotted the white face of a stoop-shouldered humanlike form standing behind one of the arbors. Like everything else, I expected it to fade into the camouflage of the flowers. I was quite surprised when it remained real. This confusion flickered through me for but a few milliseconds before the world rearranged itself and I saw that it was only Ilga.

Des Esseintes turned abruptly in my direction. "You just affected the quiver, Monsieur le Docteur. Is there some reason for your uneasiness?"

"I think cautiousness is, perhaps, a better word, Monsieur des Esseintes," I said in defense.

"Step forward, Ilga," des Esseintes beckoned. Hands clasped quietly behind her, she obeyed. He turned once again toward me. "You know, orchids are most curious flowers. Do you know anything about orchids? You should, considering the orchid mania that is now sweeping England. Orchids can be found all over the world, from the steamy treetops of the Venezuelan jungles to the misty valleys of the Himalayas." He turned to the shadow woman. "How many varieties of orchids are there, Ilga?"

"As of May there were 16,235 varieties occurring naturally, and an estimated 32,000 hybrids," she averred.

He smiled at us. "So you can see, with so large a population it should come as no surprise that orchids can be found that mimic virtually everything in our life—butterflies and miniature men, lizards and doves. I come in here frequently to meditate upon the orchids. One can see anything in them. Do you agree, Hespeth?"

She shrugged in oblivious wonder and gazed around at the flowers. Something about her expression told me she was not experiencing what I was experiencing.

"And you, Monsieur le Docteur?"

"Whatever you say, Monsieur des Esseintes. My mind is still bothered by something else."

"What is that?"

"Who were the Unknown Men? What else did you learn of Lodovico?"

"Oh, yes . . . Lodovico. You must be patient, Monsieur le Docteur. You do not realize how much time I waited before I knew more than just the magic of his name. It was in my hundred-ninety-second year that I gained my first direct knowledge of Lodovico. I remember the date distinctly because it was the same year a tremor of excitement swept through the vampire cloisters and monasteries. It was announced that many things were transpiring. 'An Unknown Man was in the Baghdad Caliphate,' and a vampire named Gerbert, a monk of St. Gerard d'Aurillac, had been named master of the schools at Rheims. This was quite an achievement. The human members of the Church did not know there were vampire in their midst, but they did know certain of their members were party to secret societies. They were constantly on watch to keep any individuals who trafficked with the hidden forces of alchemy from power. If Gerbert had been named master of the schools at Rheims, it either meant he had succeeded in concealing his identity, or, unbeknownst to us, there was another of our kind even higher up in the hierarchy of power. In any case, it was at this time that I became aware of the fact that I was beginning to walk differently. It was a moonlit night as I strolled beside a placid little lake. There was a line of us out collecting plant life, and in our reflections I noticed we each possessed a most subtle and abnormal gait. I mentioned this to the *abbés* and they were very excited I had noticed this distinction between mortal and vampire. They encouraged me to study it, but would say no more. At length, word came from an ancient set of lips that Lodovico was pleased. Pleased that I had noticed I walked differently? At my own minute changes? Lodovico? That elusive and almost mythic figure taking

an interest in what I considered my most obscure
discovery? I pleaded with the *abbés* to tell me why he
found this so commendable, but they steadfastly refused."

"Did they tell you any other secrets?" I asked.

"What other secrets?"

"The secret of transference and Jechiele's lamp?"

He remained impassive, but for some reason I suspected
the question bothered him.

"No," he finally confessed. "I was no longer ignorant of
the things you mention."

"And you still did not share them with the mortal
world? Why?" I demanded. "Why did you allow mankind
to remain in the Dark Ages? Why did you hide the
hypodermic needle while millions died of the plague?"

"Always the virologist," he said distantly. "So dedicated.
So removed. There were many reasons; some you would
not understand. I will give you one. What do you think the
age that ultimately perpetrated the Inquisition would
have used the hypodermic needle for? Deforming unborn
children? Injecting boiling oil beneath the skin? One
thing is certain. They would not have used it in medicine.
As one of the most 'learned' humans of the time, the
twelfth-century 'scholar,' St. Bernard of Clairvaux, put it,
'. . . to buy drugs, to consult physicians, to take medicines
befits not religion and is contrary to purity.' He turned
and suddenly scrutinized a yellow blossom. "Oh, an
aphid!" he gasped, lifting the small white speck from the
flower. Instead of crushing it beneath his slender fingers
he dropped it into the bloom itself to be drowned by the
nectar.

A wave of both wonder and repulsion swept through me.
Such a sense of power poured out of the ancient
gentleman. He seemed filled with such tranquillity. And
yet, while discussing the gravest of matters, he could
become preoccupied with an aphid. All the fury I had first
felt upon discovering Niccolo's healing agent came back.
The alcohol pounded dizzily in my temples. I could take it
no longer.

"You're unholy," I said. "You say you have a reverence
for life, but you coolly allowed millions to die."

Lady Dunaway's eyes widened in shock at my outburst,
as des Esseintes's shoulders tightened. He turned upon

me in a manner suggestive of a blind and utter rage. I
shrunk back, expecting to see blood-reddened eyes and
bared fangs. But once again I was jolted to see the all-
encompassing serenity of his expression.

"I must remind you one more time: Please do not judge
me harshly if I do not seem bereft. As I've explained, I'm
very different from you. I experience my emotions in ways
you can never hope to equal. I also don't display them as
readily and unconsciously as you do. You may perceive me
as cold and insidious on the surface, but, believe me, you
haven't the faintest inkling of what's going on in this
narrow skull.

"I also must set you straight on another matter,
Monsieur le Docteur. You seem to be under the opinion
that we, the vampire, the illuminati, kept all of our
knowledge from the mortal world, and this is not true. We
only kept those discoveries that we deemed dangerous.
There are many other things for which you owe us more of
a debt than you can possibly imagine. Let me give you an
example. Keep in mind it is but one example. One
example out of more than I could begin to convey.

"This vampire named Gerbert that I have mentioned
did not strive to become master of the schools at Rheims
for mere egotistical achievement. He had higher intentions for his appointment. Through the normal human
channels of the Church we heard more and more about the
fame of this Gerbert. Letters from the Pope himself
announced that Gerbert had become abbot of Bobbio. He
was moving in high circles of power then. He was the
confidant and adviser of Emperor Otto II of Germany. At
this point something happened, of which even I am not
sure. The Church trembled. Something had cast Gerbert's
'nature' into doubt. The mortals seemed to realize
intuitively they had been fooled. There were accusations
of alchemy and darker things, but it was too late. Otto II
died, and at the age of sixteen Otto III became the boy
King of Germany. The vampire's influence on the boy was
profound, and in the year A.D. 999, the youngster monarch
named Gerbert Pope."

I gave a start. "A vampire Pope!"

"Yes."

"I don't believe it."

"Who cares?"

I drew back, slightly embarrassed. Once again I became aware of the unnatural presence of the orchids. I almost fancied they were chuckling, like a bunch of peeping fairies. I knew this couldn't be. I knew it had to be the effects of the alcohol, but my uneasiness increased.

"In any case, Monsieur le Docteur, your own books and records relate how strange this Gerbert d'Aurillac was. Everything I tell you can be found in your own accounts of history. As for my story, this Gerbert, or Pope Sylvester II, as he then became called, made the world quite different for both mortal and vampire. In the year A.D. 1000 he crowned Stephen I King of Hungary and persuaded him to organize the Magyars according to the lines of German feudalism. With the countryside freed of those barbarians, vampire were able to travel from cloister to cloister with greater safety. With the assistance of Sylvester's puppet king we flocked to Hungary, built many monasteries and villages, and even shared some techniques of agriculture with the mortal population. So you can see we did not keep all of our knowledge from the populace. It was we who transformed Hungary from barbarism to civilization. It is ironic that in the eighteenth century Hungary paid us back by instigating the greatest vampire hunt the world has known.

"Now, don't raise any eyebrows. As I say, everything I tell you can be found in your own chronicles. Sylvester II traveled to Spain to visit some very learned Hindu alchemists—vampire, of course—living in exile there, and brought back many wonders. One of the wonders he brought back was an automaton, a bronze head that would answer YES or NO to questions put to it concerning politics and Christianity. Sylvester II also brought back something else."

Des Esseintes released a rope and caused a basket of orchids to lower swiftly in front of us. The blossoms were full, not unlike irises, and bloodred. "These are known as *Miltonia liberte*," he announced. "If you look closely you will notice that each bloom has a carefully formed Arabic numeral on its lip, printed in white."

Lady Dunaway and I examined them, and, indeed each one did possess a perfectly printed Arabic numeral.

"I don't paint them on. They're hybrids, taught to grow that way. That is another thing Sylvester II brought from the Hindu vampire."

"Orchids?"

"No, no, our current system of numbers. Before Sylvester's time all of Europe used Roman numerals. Those, of course, were clumsy and difficult to perform arithmetic operations with." He turned to Ilga. "When did the Arabs adopt the Hindu system of numbering?"

"In A.D. 775," she answered, like a clockwork creature herself.

"Thank you, Ilga," he said and turned back to us. "In the year A.D. 775 the Arabs took the Indian numerals 1 through 9 from the Hindu and in the year A.D. 1000 Sylvester gave them to the world. He also produced a simplified abacus with instructions for its use, and wrote at length on the methods of multiplication and division. In astronomy he spoke of the roundness of the earth and taught of the movements of the planets with a set of spheres.

"I could go on and on about the knowledge Sylvester gave to the world. He was one of the greatest collectors of books the Dark Ages knew. He revealed the steam engine, the lightning rod, and the first clock driven by weights. But did the mortal world have the vision to see what Sylvester was giving them? Once again it is the same old story. No one cared that the clepsydra would be replaced by the mechanical clock, that the earth was round, or that lightning was an avoidable disaster. In the year A.D. 1003 Sylvester II, monk of St. Gerard d'Aurillac, and Pope of all the Holy Roman Empire, underwent a 'philosophical death.' A coffin weighted down with stones was placed in his grave, and he returned to the anonymity of our world."

Des Esseintes shrugged as he raised the basket of flowers with the Arabic numerals on them back to the ceiling. He turned around to examine another blossom, and in a single sideways glance from those sharp blue eyes I saw something I had not seen before in the eyes of the gentleman monk. He was amiable on the surface, but for a moment his warmth was mechanical. His smile seemed disturbingly unrelated to the feeling he was giving off, not unlike the smile of madness. It was as if he were spending only a small portion of his thoughts in dealing with us while the vast majority of his concerns were very far away.

He looked again in our direction. "Forgive me for drifting off. You may not realize it, but it is not so easy for me to communicate with you over long periods of time. I'm used to speaking with ... well ... my own kind. Before we end would you like to hear one final reminiscence about Lodovico?"

He scarcely even had to notice the nodding of our heads.

"It is in reference to one further discovery of mine, similar to my observation of our alien perambulation. On occasions of mortal visitors to our monastery, as I pretended to pour over the mundane liturgical manuscripts, often my eye was bothered by clumsy wordings and cryptic references. For a long while these merely disturbed my vision, and I did not understand them. Until one evening I noticed something in the scrollwork of a common Gospel book. I blinked once or twice. I could hardly believe what I was seeing. There in the gold and purple filigree was a detailed diagram of the microscopic anatomy of a sweet clover—a diagram I myself had done some years earlier. To be sure, it was disguised and unlabeled, but, undeniably, in the filiate decoration were all the vascular bundles and nectaries of the plant. I turned the pages and discerned more hidden shapes. In the haloes of saints were microscopic studies of pollen; in the heavenly cosmologies, the schematics of cells.

"Exuberant, I took my discovery to the *abbés*, but they remained as immutable as ever. It struck me that they were probably fully aware of these hidden illustrations. But why weren't we novices told? What else lay hidden in the strange and clumsy writings; what further codes and ciphers? Was this how the patriarchs communicated with other monasteries? As always, my older brethren remained moot to my every question. Neither smile nor twitch of eyebrow revealed they knew more than they were saying. They simply encouraged me to study the matter further. It was a number of months later that the adjudication came once more: 'Lodovico was pleased.'

"*Pleased*, I thought? Pleased, and still no guiding

hand? Pleased, and still nothing was pointed out? I was left by myself with the enigma? At length, I discovered a few of the other brothers had also noticed these things in the manuscripts, but once again it was the same story: Secrecy prevailed."

He sighed. "Now, my dear friends, the need is pressing. I am used to communicating with my own kind. It is most fatiguing for me to restructure my language in a way that you will understand. I must be alone with my orchids, to meditate. Our visit must come to an end."

"But what happened . . . did you ever find out about Lodovico and the Unknown Men?"

"Oh, yes."

"You're not going to tell us?"

"At a future date all will be revealed. There is plenty of time." He smiled.

So that was his tactic, I thought. To control us with curiosity. The *Scheherazade* technique. I was maddened, but he had us. He had us completely. He was too powerful physically to overcome, like a jaguar or jungle cat.

As he gently began to shuffle us out I noticed once again the peculiarity of his movements. I could no longer contain my curiosity. "Why does the vampire walk differently?" I asked.

"Why does a child walk differently from an adult?" he countered. "Each age has its vocabulary of movements. How often have you noticed that a young girl no longer walks like a girl, but a woman? Look at a very tiny and very old woman. Does it not seem incongruous that a being with the stature of a child walks with such maturity? If you observe them closely you will notice that a twenty-year-old man moves differently than a thirty-year-old man. Little do most mortals realize, but there is a silent and complex language of gestures and walks. These continue to change distinctively with each stage of human development. They cease, of course, with death. However, if one does not die, they continue to evolve. Just as a mineral contains the predestined lattice of a crystal and each rose unfolds anew, so each vampire contains the components of a constantly unfolding language of movement. It is quite natural that you may see my walk as strange. You are observing the gait of a thousand-year-old man."

When he had finished I realized that I had been deeply moved by what he had said. More than ever I realized we could not underestimate our host. We were dealing with a being who was far removed from anyone we had ever before encountered. Once again he tried to escort us out, but I resisted. "I have a final question," I said.

He looked at me with surprise, as if vaguely startled I dare go against his immediate desires.

"Yes?" he said sibilantly.

I glanced at my companion before I continued. "Well, for two consecutive nights I've called to Lady Dunaway, and although she says she is a light sleeper, she has not heard me. I'm certain I've called to her. Why hasn't she heard me? Have you drugged her and taken her away?"

Lady Dunaway turned toward Monsieur des Esseintes with obvious concern.

"Oh, yes, I overheard you whispering in the foyer. Silly of you to think I could not hear. No, Monsieur le Docteur, I can tell you with absolute honesty that I do not ferret good Hespeth away every night. If it's true she is a light sleeper and you are positive you were not dreaming, I can provide only one answer to your puzzle."

"What is that?"

He reached into a wall of foliage and withdrew what looked like a cluster of leaves covered with shiny blue wasps. "They're flowers," he explained. *"Ophrys speculum.* They grow in the Mediterranean. Not only do they resemble wasps, but also they emit the same odor as the female of the species they mimic. That way when the male tries to mate with the flower he picks up pollen masses, and unwittingly fertilizes the next flower he comes in contact with. Seduction by proxy." He chuckled.

"I don't understand. How does that answer my question?"

"Well," he said, holding up his fingers and counting off the points of his argument, "if Hespeth is a light sleeper, and if you are certain you are not dreaming, something else entirely must be going on, something that has not even crossed your mind. Perhaps while you sleep your

room is not next to Hespeth's. Perhaps the rooms of this
old house move about at night. One thing is certain: You
are in the same position as the wasp. You are confronting
a reality you do not have the powers of conceptualization
to understand. The only explanations you have come up
with are incorrect, and you have not figured out the
proper solution."

He allowed the foliage to snap back into its hiding
place.

"Please," he ended, "now I must be left alone." He
stopped to busy himself with one final blossom before he
showed us out, and I once again became aware of the
hissing of the steam and the stifling fragrances of the all-
pervading greenhouse. Another wave of images swept
through the flowers. Was it just the alcohol, I thought?
Was it some sort of shock from all the information des
Esseintes had spewed forth, or was there some chance I
had been drugged? Again I discerned a movement in the
periphery of my vision, but I did not turn in its direction. I
was certain it would simply pop out of existence, as all the
other hallucinatory movements had done. To my alarm
the movement did not vanish. There was a chink of gravel,
a rushing sound coming toward me, like a creature
making its pounce. In terror I pivoted around, expecting
to see that the flowers had, indeed, come to life and were
closing in upon me.

To my relief I saw that it was only Ilga. Some unknown
agent had activated her, and she brushed by me, face
blank and arms limp as a sleepwalker's. Des Esseintes
readily discerned the alarm in my expression. For many
seconds he held his blue eyes upon me, smiling, knowing,
as if the vastness of his experience allowed him to see
every facet of my soul laid bare. At last he spoke.
"Meditate upon this question, Monsieur le Docteur. Think
about it for a long time and answer it only to yourself." He
twirled a blossom between his fingers as he stared at me
out of the corner of his eye. "Are you sure you have not
seen something in the flowers?"

XIX

With that last remark des Esseintes escorted us back past the double glass doors and into the peacock sitting room, where, inexplicably, Grelot was waiting for us. I was a little surprised to see the falcon still standing in the hallway. I wondered why it had not followed us into the orchid conservatory. "Take care of my friends," our captor ended as he vanished once again into the hissing and the steam. Grelot grunted and cocked his head toward the door.

When we reached our cells we discovered Grelot had made a trip to the Hotel Madeleine, and all of our possessions had been transferred to our plush but limited quarters. It was more than Lady Dunaway could take, as if the presence of our luggage gave a more ominous note of permanency to our situation. She gave a cry and started to fall backward. I rushed and caught her as the falcon thrashed dangerously close. I did not want her to lose hope. I needed her. For the first time I realized the extent of the strength I myself had derived from her own unusual fortitude and courage. As I caught her I became acutely aware of her body. To my relief it was warm. Perhaps it was the gauzy influence of the liqueur I had drunk, but the mere pressure of her form, even of her very bones pressing through the svelte contour of her clothing, comforted me. Was that all? No, there is an ineffable something that comes from a woman. I felt it then, from this strange, beautiful creature in my arms. As I have said, she was large for a woman, but she seemed almost weightless.

Grelot angrily intervened and helped her into her cell. After he had left I heard her voice close to the intervening partition.

"Dr. Gladstone?"

"Yes, Lady Dunaway?"

"Please, I'm so frightened. Are you sure you called as loudly as you could last night?"

I did not want to frighten her. I hesitated, imagining her dark and panic-stricken eyes behind the incongruous lenses. "I'm afraid I did," I said softly.

There was silence. I imagined her standing motionless as she fearfully contemplated my remark. It was rare to sense such a helplessness in her—she who had risked everything, who had crossed half of England and half of France to find her child.

"What do you think is going on?" she finally gasped.

What did it all mean, des Esseintes's cabalistic talk of orchids and rooms moving about? "I do not know."

"We must escape. We have to keep looking for our children."

"Yes," I agreed. "Somehow, in some way we must find a way out of here."

There was the sound of pacing, as if she had turned and walked to the center of her cell. The steps returned.

"Dr. Gladstone?"

"Yes, Lady Dunaway?"

"We are friends, aren't we."

It was not a question. It was a statement. It embodied all of our impotence and frustration, and yet it reached through the very bars themselves and soothed.

"Yes," I returned, "we are friends."

Her steps returned to the center of her cell and I heard her sit down on her bed. I stood at the bars for many more minutes. When I finally turned toward my own quarters I suddenly spied a letter Grelot must have retrieved from the Hotel Madeleine sitting on top of my trunk. It was from Ursula, dear Ursula. What would she think when I did not reply? How was my work? My laboratory? I opened it and found but a brief inquiry. *How was I and what was my progress?* She did not even inquire about Lady Dunaway. I opened the thermidor of tobacco and filled my pipe.

The night passed without incident. The falcon watched. Geneviève brought us another splendid breakfast. By afternoon I had already emotionally prepared myself for being locked up for several days when Grelot appeared in the cellar doorway.

"Monsieur des Esseintes has requested I inform you, tonight one of you will be granted the freedom of the house."

"One of us?" I asked.

"The falcon cannot guard both of you."

"The freedom of the house?" I heard Lady Dunaway question.

"You will be allowed to wander around as you wish," the butler said contemptuously. "There are some rooms you are not allowed in but the falcon will let you know which rooms. Of course, the falcon will not let you leave the house."

"Well, if only one of us can go, why don't you go," I called to my companion.

"Oh, no, Dr. Gladstone, you are too kind, but I insist you go."

"Oh, no, I couldn't."

"No, no, I insist."

"But if I go—"

Grelot scuffed his foot. "So it's you, Monsieur le Docteur?"

He jingled the large ring of keys and approached the bars. The cell door opened with a creak. The falcon jumped off its perch the moment I stepped into the anteroom. As we left I glanced back and saw her sitting in front of the fireplace with one hand under a shawl on her lap. She was reading a book. "Do have fun and remember what we discussed," she bid happily.

When we reached the lavender foyer I noticed that the bustle of the human maids and cleaning boys had moved down into the corridor of the statues. Grelot lit a candelabrum, handed it to me, and started to walk briskly away.

"Wait," I called. "Aren't you going to watch me?"

"Monsieur des Esseintes says you can walk around with only the falcon as your guard tonight. He gives you that measure of trust."

With that he sauntered swiftly up the rosewood staircase.

Infernal creature, I thought as I glanced down at the

little beast. Nictitating membranes flicked quickly over
its dark copper eyes. *So I was free to wander around the
house.* Was it mere kindness or did the vampire have other
motives in this unusual liberty? I glanced longingly at
the front door, and back at the bird. I still fancied it
possessed the sentience of more than just a falcon. I
decided to test my freedom.

I took a step toward the door.

The bird did nothing.

I took another step.

Still nothing.

At last when I lifted my foot to step within about three
feet of the heavy latch . . . calmly . . . silently, the falcon
haunched its shoulders, readying its attack. From the
tension of its muscles and the sudden prickle of the
feathers about its neck I could tell that my slightest
movement would spur it into action. I looked at the
meathook edge of the talons. I very gingerly moved away
from the door. I admired the bullrushes and stuffed birds
and ran my fingers across the black harmonium before I
made my way up the circular staircase.

As always, the falcon hobbled behind me, hopping
ludicrously up each step like a court dwarf. On occasion it
gave a flap or two with its broad wings to propel it, but it
never really took to the air. Aside from my shadow, I was
like a child on Christmas morning wandering about the
house. On impulse I made a motion to move toward one of
the thin and narrow outside windows. I had become so
disoriented keeping such odd hours and being locked up. I
wanted to see Paris to reassure myself that it was still
there.

Again the falcon acted. It casually jumped upon the
sill. It blinked at me. It ruffled its feathers. It was as if it
were daring me to make a further move. At first I thought
this was odd. The window was heavily grated. I could not
escape. Then I remembered des Esseintes's remarks about
keeping the windows dark so no one would notice his
nocturnal habits. It was true: All of the rooms were
separated from the outer walls of the house by hallways.
Thus, any windows they possessed faced inward to one of
the various courtyards of the house. Even when the rooms
were being used it enabled the gentleman monk to keep

the hallways and outer façade dark. Was it possible the falcon was keeping me from flashing a light in the window? Could it possibly be so well trained?

Undeniably, it was guarding the window.

I felt a chill. What was I up against in this bird?

I moved farther into the darkness of the house, and heard the tap tap of its talons following me on the slate floor. Although it was dark I noticed the vast labyrinth of rooms seemed to be quite empty. Grelot had vanished and the rest of the servants were apparently cleaning the downstairs corridor. I opened each door cautiously, but with a youthful anticipation, as if opening a gift, to marvel at the room beyond. First I returned to the playroom where Lady Dunaway and I had hidden. I wanted to examine the toys more carefully, the puppets, the circus ornaments, the eighteenth-century French carousel horses. Some of the music boxes seemed very old and I wondered if any of them had been made by the monks of the Vosges. I took a particular liking to a tiny nightingale in a miniature cage. I touched it and was entranced to see it tinkle into life. The song it sang varied little from the songs of other music-box birds, but its repertoire of movements was impressive. It lifted its feet. It moved its wings. It blinked. It preened.

When the song was finished it even tilted its little head and seemed to gaze at me sadly with its lifeless glass eyes. The falcon tilted its head curiously at the captive bird. So you are not infallible, I thought. You do not realize that this is a clockwork creature. The discovery made me feel slightly more at ease about my adversary.

It was then, in the midst of this reverie, that I noticed something most significant about the playroom. From the corners of the floor to the corners of the dollhouse, everything was immaculate. This room was used, I thought to myself, but used by whom? An unseen child in the house? Camille or Ambrose?

I moved on with a new hope, searching for some further clue. After all, the house was massive. Our children could be under our very noses and we might never know.

In one wing of the second floor I discovered the quarters of the human servants. Their furnishings were meager and they displayed but the simplest array of possessions:

here a scenic French postcard tacked tastelessly on the
wall; there a shawl of Flanders lace. In what I presumed
to be Geneviève's room I saw shelf upon shelf of empty
wicker and wire birdcages. I gave a grim smile, amused by
the pathetic irony of it all.

In other wings I discovered the more sumptuous rooms
of Monsieur des Esseintes, and here I stood in awe. So this
was the inner sanctum of a vampire. All of my notions
about his breed, of castles and dark belfries were
banished, for the endless splay of rooms exuded life, more
life than is found in most mortal dwellings. To describe
the splendor of the rooms would take many books. Suffice
it to say, they were the palatial chambers of an extremely
wealthy nineteenth-century Parisian gentleman. Each
one was as incredible in its own way as the turquoise-and-
gilt sitting room. The first thing I noticed was the
openness of the spaces. Unlike Victorian interiors, one
room flowed into the next, and from the warm glow of
many lamps I discerned an airy maze of Arabian columns
and arches. There was also a magnificent richness of color
and texture: fine woods and Indian mattings, Japanese
papers and iridescent Tiffany glasses. Indeed, there was
an unusual accumulation of these Tiffany glasses with
their deep and flowing colors, slender vases and blown
glass orbs. My eye fell upon a Favrile paperweight on a
low table and for a moment I was lost in the swirls of
indigo and Prussian blue. Somehow the very spirit of the
rooms was distilled in these glasses.

All of this served to substantiate a theory I was
forming, that in some strange way des Esseintes needed
this richness. Everything suggested it: his use of drugs,
the incense, the orchids. He was not unlike an elderly
person who has salted his food until he can no longer taste
it. It was as if he had been jaded by the centuries into
needing greater texture and complexity in his surroundings.

As I strolled from room to room I realized it was like
being in a museum. As always, there was a clutter of
furniture, ornately carved tables and bureaus, Turkish
sofas, gossamer curtains, and stained-glass lamps. These
in themselves were impressive. What was truly unbelievable was the profusion of treasures large and small. My eye

never stopped taking in more details. Every inch of floor
and wall space housed an endless array of objects. An Art
Nouveau gramophone with a horn shaped like a blossom-
ing flower. A suit of armor. Scarabs. Postage stamps.
Snowstorms in glass globes. Hundreds of portraits and
miniature paintings. Doll's heads. Austrian crystals.
Shadow boxes filled with seashells. Ebony walking sticks.
A crystal unicorn. A twelfth-century ivory chess set.
Innumerable jeweled boxes, vases of peacock feathers,
porcelains, and ormolu clocks. It was not unlike the horde
of a noble ancestry, like the endless memorabilia one finds
in an old English manor house—save that there were no
family trees, crests, or coats of arms. It was the collection
of a single personality, and for all its clutter it possessed
an odd homogeneity.

In the throng of objects I began to discern that des
Esseintes had, indeed, come from simple origins. Some of
his accumulations were not unlike the treasures of any
country adolescent gifted with a desire for knowledge.
Hidden within the displays of butterflies and rocks was
the suggestion of a young boy who searched the meadows.
Concealed within the motif of birds, the peacock feathers,
and the porcelain herons was the intimation of a mind
that had spent hours watching the marshes and the sky.

What memories objects contain, I thought. I recalled
how but a brief glimpse of the pianoforte conjured up
Camille. I wondered how magnified this experience must
be for des Esseintes. For a moment I imagined him
wandering through these rooms, tall and gaunt and
draped in a flowing silk robe. How easy it must be for him
to become lost here, to stop and fondle his panoramic
memories. How disorienting and isolating immortality
must be, and how strong he must be to weather it.

Reluctantly I moved on, still possessed with the hope of
finding a further clue that there might be a child in the
house. I went up another flight of steps, to the third floor,
and came to the door of des Esseintes's study. Just as my
hand was about to reach the brass knob the falcon ruffled.
So I was not allowed in there. I cautiously withdrew my
hand. I hated the bird. I hated it with a growing passion.
When I reached the next door I watched it closely to make
sure this was allowed. It regarded me for all the world as if

it thought I was a fool. My hand touched the knob. The
door opened.

I had to hold the candelabrum high in here, for it was
quite dark. On the opposite wall was a single grated
window from which one could see the opposing wing of the
house, somber and traversed with balconies and ivy. When
I finally looked around I was a little surprised to see it
was another study, just as eclectic and cluttered as the
first. It was different in that it was musty and cool. It
obviously was not used very often. I was struck by the fact
there was a marked absence of any contemporary objects.
Everything was antique.

I went to the next room, and the next. And each one was
a study, a little older, a little more forgotten than the one
previous, but each as packed with books and papers. In
some it was even evident what branch of knowledge the
vampire had been pursuing when he had used it. One
contained a profusion of charts of the heavens, yellowed
and molded, a dusty telescope, an antique planetarium.
Another was filled with cages, many empty cages, and the
mounted skeletons of a myriad of small mammals. Still,
even in these older studies one subject remained beloved
above all others. Not a single alcove was without its racks
of abandoned growing trays, mounted leaves, and charts
of plant filaments and seeds. That was the thread. Many
branches were explored, but that was the first and
continuing love. I marveled at the scholar who did not die
at the end of his field of research, but moved on to the
next, and the next. What creature, indeed, would a Galileo
mutate into? A Linnaeus?

Oddly, I felt a sudden overwhelming kinship with this
being, even an envy. In a meditation, I moved toward the
courtyard window, and saw the orchid conservatory far
below, nestled like a jewel amid the surrounding wings of
the house. To my surprise I could see the tiny form of des
Esseintes working among the flowers. He was once again
dressed as the monk and Ilga stood a few paces away. It
was difficult to tell but des Esseintes seemed to be
performing some sort of experiment. In his hand he held a
clutch of papers and every few moments or so he would
walk over to Ilga and apparently read something. When
he finished, Ilga would murmur some dictum, which des

Esseintes would furiously scribble down and then return to his work. It was easy to see why he had referred to the pathetic creature as *la machine*.

I was drawn to him because of the world he had been allowed to carve out for himself. When I worked it was always against time. When I pored over my papers it was with the hope that I might make that one cherished medical discovery before I died, but he, he had miraculously been picked out of the river of seekers and placed in an infinite world. I was jealous of his freedom. I felt kinship for his devouring mind, but I was still frightened by him. For all of his human characteristics, he was not human. There was no telling how nearly a dozen centuries had changed him; what really lay hidden behind his tranquil and mechanical smile.

At length I moved on, and in the last study I entered, a very old study, I noticed a distinct path had been traced through the dust on the carpet. The air was also not as stale, but fresher, as if the room had been opened quite recently. I followed the path across the room and to a wall of books. Madly I began to scan the volumes. What book did he come here repeatedly to get? What page did he turn to and why?

They were very old books, handbound and crumbling with illegible gilt titles. I held the candelabrum steady in one hand as I moved my finger across the bindings, leaving a distinct line in the dust. At last, on the bottom shelf I came to a row of volumes on which I left no line. They were not dusty. The gilt on these was also newer and more legible. Hands trembling with excitement, I withdrew the final volume and gazed at its cover. On it was written the words, *Histoire de ma vie,* or *A History of My Life: The Memoires of Childeric, Pepin, Brother C.L.R., Frederiche von Ulrich, Baron de Bourbon, Comte de Saint-Vallier, Jean-Francois Auguste des Esseintes.*

No, it couldn't be. I stood back to admire the collection. These ninety volumes, the memoires of the gentleman monk? Were these names all people he had posed as? I remembered his referring to the names Childeric and Pepin as being "dead." I shook my head in disbelief. Ninety volumes? It seemed inconceivable, and yet the memoires of Casanova filled ten. Why not ninety volumes for the

memoires of a vampire, an entire case of books to record the
experiences of a Methuselah genius?

Excitedly I flung the cover open with my thumb.
Instantly, a flurry of wings knocked the book from my
hand. I screamed. The candelabrum fell to the floor. In a
frenzy I jumped back, trying to avoid further entangle-
ment with the bird, but it was too late. To my horror one of
its talons had snagged in my vest, and its wings thrashed
violently in my face. Somehow I managed to grasp the
garment at the shoulders and struggled to pull it away
from my flesh. Anything to keep the deadly talons from
scratching me. Finally, with the full of my strength I was
able to rip the vest out at the seams, and I flung it, bird
and all, to the floor.

The candle flames sputtered and emptied wax in a dark
puddle on the carpet. I set the candelabrum aright and
quickly unbuttoned my shirt to search for scratches. To
my great relief I remained unscathed. I was badly shaken,
and my hands were trembling uncontrollably. I took
several deep breaths trying to steady myself as I gazed at
the bird. It flopped jerkily about on the floor until it had
freed itself from the vest, and then it, too, seemed to
compose itself. It ruffled the feathers about its nape. It
lifted one of its talons and carefully examined it. And
then the golden eyes returned my gaze . . .
blinking . . . watching.

I longingly eyed the last volume of des Esseintes's
memoires as I picked up the candelabrum and began
pacing backward to the door.

The bird took to wing.

Again I cried out, shielding my eyes with my free arm
as I broke and ran into the hall. I felt a rush of air beside
my head as the falcon swept past. It glided down the hall a
ways before it swooped up and lit on the cornice of the
paneling near the ceiling. After it turned around it glared
down at me and screeched threateningly.

What manner of beast was this? What uncanny
training had ingrained in it which books I was allowed to
touch and which I was not? I was no longer merely
bothered by the bird. I was on the verge of a blind panic.
For my own mental well-being I had to get away from it.

I turned and walked briskly down the hall.

Behind me I heard a familiar gush of air as talons once again lightly touched the carpet.

I struggled to settle my thoughts.

As I walked on I noticed the hallway was in an increasing state of decay. What had once been a splendid corridor was damp with the redolence of mildew. Further on, the walls were peeling, and in the fringe of dust lining the baseboard scurried beetles and centipedes. I was just about to turn back when suddenly I noticed the twisted stairs leading to the turret where Lady Dunaway and I had first encountered the falcon.

The bird ambled by me and took a perch upon the bottom step.

So we're in your territory, I thought. When you're not being guard this is where they keep you.

In the mist of my memory I recalled seeing the ticking of a mattress in the room. For the first time I reflected on this. Why would there be a bed in the room of the falcon? I glanced up the narrow passage at the closed door.

I don't know why I looked at the door for so long. In particular, I looked at the keyhole of the rusted latch. As I stood there holding the candelabrum high, I got the sensation someone was staring back. I shivered a little. Could there be someone in the room calmly watching me through the keyhole? For a moment the thought crossed my mind that Camille might be in the room. I dismissed it. Even des Esseintes could not be insidious enough to keep a child in such a hellish place. For a change, I looked at the falcon and felt a quiver of relief in knowing the bird was not about to let me investigate.

As I turned to leave, once again I imagined I felt eyes... eyes burning into my neck, my back. Indeed, the presence was so powerful I quickened my pace. At the opposite end of the crumbling hallway I discovered a door that was slightly ajar and nudged it open. When I thrust the candelabrum into the darkness I gasped to see that it was another lavish room, a magnificent baroque salon, only different from all the others, for it was completely enshrouded in dust and cobwebs. It was haunting, more haunting than anything I had yet encountered in the house of des Esseintes, for in no other part of the house had I sensed such a presence of another era, a different age. Every rococo swirl, every gilt seashell corner and delicate Louis XIV chair was draped in the spidery gauze of time. The lines of the room had all but vanished beneath the gossamer and womblike pall.

As I scuffed through the carpet, gray with an inch of dust, I noticed a multitude of vermin had long since overtaken this forgotten room. Wood bugs crept in every cranny, and mice padded along the moldings. The falcon displayed an obvious but fleeting interest in the rodents. It was too well trained to take the full of its attentions from me.

In a beautiful decanter, long since marked by the sedimentary evaporation of its wine, a solitary beetle tried unsuccessfully to scale the glass. Above a pink marble fireplace at the opposite end of the chamber a portrait caught my eye. I crossed over to it and held the candles high to obtain a better look. Through the patina of dust and mildew it was difficult to make out at first. It was a woman, a rather thin and dispirited woman dressed in farthingales and puffed sleeves. At last, behind the powdered wig and beauty spot I discerned it was the same woman whose image I'd seen in the gallery of the statues.

As I turned to move on I noticed the falcon had cocked its head and was closely watching the door. I looked in the same direction expecting to see a mouse. There was no mouse.

In the hallway a floorboard creaked.

I squinted at the darkness. The door was cracked about a foot and a half. Beyond, the corridor was black as pitch. It was impossible to make out anything in the murk, but once again I was overwhelmed by the feeling I was being watched. Intuitively, I was convinced someone or something was standing in the darkness ... waiting for me to come to them. I looked madly about the room.

To my relief there was a door next to a painted cabinet. I turned the porcelain knob in its collar and slipped through.

At first what lay beyond seemed to be a cavern of vast and empty space, and it took me a moment to realize it was an enormous ballroom. I had entered onto a third-floor balcony. In front of me an elaborate tier of marble stairs circled in two directions to the floor below. Like the previous room, the ballroom was from a different age, frescoed and veiled by spiders. I wondered how many generations had passed since grand ladies had walked these floors, perhaps ladies of the court. In the tenuous light of the candelabrum I could see the floor was covered with a multitude of dusty and webbed crates.

Suddenly something sliced by me, and as I turned I saw it was the falcon. It held its wings perfectly still as it glided weightlessly over the balcony and dipped into the gloom. It drifted away from me with an awe-inspiring grace, wings still eerily motionless, until it alighted on a vast chandelier suspended in the distance. A thousand glass pendants tinkled as the chandelier began to swing and sent a fairy fall of dust slowly to the floor below.

And then the falcon turned to watch.

I prickled. There was a movement in the room behind me. Whatever it was had come in from the hallway. I turned around. Once again there was only darkness, but the presence was undeniable. It was hidden, but it was looking at me, looking right into my very eyes. Only there was a difference this time. It no longer stood silent. There was a rushing. Something brushed against a chair. It was coming for me.

I stumbled backward, somehow dropping the candelabrum, as I frantically descended the stairs. When I reached the floor I dashed between a gap in the crates and penetrated deep within the labyrinth before I paused. Then I listened. Over the pounding of my heart and my muffled breath there was nothing, save for a slow squeaking sound, like a door being moved back and forth on a rusted hinge. I looked upward and saw it was the gentle swaying of the chandelier high over the crates.

The falcon flapped its wings to keep its balance.

In the moonlight from the upper windows I could also see the way the falcon tilted its head. From its vantage I saw it look down at the crates, at a location hidden from my eyes. And then I saw it look at me. It repeated the process. Obviously, it saw both the hunter and the hunted. It was a macabre feeling, to be watched by an animal spectator. From the angle of its scrutiny I determined where my pursuer was. It was nearing the foot of the steps. I cursed the bird. If my unseen foe possessed any intelligence at all it could easily use the same method to locate me. There was no place to hide.

The bird's gaze followed something to the edge of the crates.

It was no use. I was trapped if I remained. I slithered on through the maze. With horror I watched as the feathered demon surveyed the progression of the game. I moved. It moved. It was slowly closing. I raced to reach the opposite edge of the crates. When I finally broke into a long and narrow clearing against the far wall I noticed from the falcon's gaze that my pursuer had also reached the clearing, only a short distance away. I could still see nothing, but there were many planks and immense picture frames covered with draperies against the wall. Whatever it was . . . it could be hiding anywhere.

My impulse was to keep running, but something tugged within me. Why had it stopped? Why did it wait now that it was so close? Again fear demanded I move on, but my rational mind objected. What was the use in running? It seemed to know this house much better than I. It could overtake me anytime it wanted to. Was it the hunt it was enjoying? Did it simply want to continue the chase?

My anger overcame me.

"Come out!" I cried. "Come out and get it over with."

For a few moments . . . *nothing*.

I waited.

And then calmly, almost magically, a figure stepped out from behind a folding screen about ten feet away. In the bluish light I saw it was a handsome and swarthy boy, possibly Arabic. He was tall and lithe with high leather boots, tight breeches, and a whorl of dark hair behind the lacings of his tunic. He had a large nose, but not overly large, a prominent jaw, and a full black mustache, incongruous against so youthful a face. His lips were expressionless; his eyes, black and expansive. He was magnetic, even lustful, a dark satyr of a boy, but there was also a discordance in his presence.

In the half-light I imagined those youthful eyes held the knowing glint of great age.

"How old are you?" I asked impulsively.

"I don't know," he replied. His voice was gentle, disturbingly gentle.

"When were you born?"

"I'm not sure. About five hundred years after the Hejira."

"Who are you? Why, were you chasing me?"

"My name is Hatim, garrulous old man. I was chasing you for fun."

"Do you often terrify people for fun?"

"Why?"

He took a step forward and I stepped back. White teeth gleamed into a smile.

"Because they enjoy it."

"Well, I certainly did not enjoy it."

He placed his hands casually behind his back as he shrugged, and something about his movement jarred me. For lack of a better word it seemed familiar. He began to pace forward.

I continued to step back. I was not about to let him close the distance between us.

He stopped.

"What are you doing in des Esseintes's house?" I asked.

"I live here."

This startled me. "I did not know anyone else lived here."

"The house has many secrets."

"Why have I never seen you before?"

"You are unobservant. I've seen you. I've watched both you and that woman as you've slept."

"Are there any children here?"

"Just the servants'."

"Are they allowed to use the playroom?"

"No."

"Who uses the playroom?"

"Des Esseintes."

I was taken aback. Nothing in the young man's expression indicated he was lying. He loosened his shoulders, rolling them about in their sockets as a fighter might before he steps into the ring, and again I experienced a sort of *déjà vu*. Why did his movements seem so familiar? I wondered if he beheld the gamut of my emotions as easily as the elder vampire. "Hatim," I asked, "can you see the quiver?"

"No." He seemed vaguely irritated by this.

"Why not?"

"That is just the way it is."

"Why can Monsieur des Esseintes see the quiver?"

"He is very old. He has gone through many changes."

"You are almost as old."

"You are a very garrulous old man." He slowly tilted his head back, keeping his black eyes leveled upon me at all times, and revealed his fangs. He sedately toyed with one of the canines as a gentleman might toy with his mustache. It was obvious he was trying to cause me consternation.

"I'm sorry if I seem overly inquisitive, but I do have another question."

He made no comment.

"What do you do for Monsieur des Esseintes? Why are you here?"

He broke into another leering smile. "You do not know? Haven't you guessed?" He clenched his fist and extended his arm out beside him. Within seconds ... gracefully ... effortlessly ... the falcon drifted down from its perch and lit upon his wrist. I noticed the boy was wearing the same leather glove I had first seen in the turret room.

As I looked at the two together for the first time I realized how similar the boy's eyes were to the falcon's. His gaze was unflinching, vacuously intent on its prey. He had clearly surrendered himself to the calculation of his instincts. I felt the discordance of his presence the strongest when his vision was upon me. A nail on a blackboard. The scream of the falcon behind those liquid eyes. It was with an eerie recognition that I realized the stillness of his stance was the stillness of the falcon. The slow pivot of his neck, the movement of the falcon.

"You are the bird's keeper, aren't you?"

He nodded. "Falconry used to be the most noble of professions. The duke of Burgundy ransomed his son by sending twelve white hawks to his captor, Sultan Bajazet. There was a time when the office of grand falconer of France was one of the highest and best paid in the kingdom."

I continued to look into his eyes. He seemed more a nature spirit than a boy.

"Is the falcon a vampire?"

"No."

"Each time a falcon dies, you train a new one?"

"Yes."

"How many falcons have you trained for des Esseintes?"

"Dozens."

"For what use?"

"For protection. To help him in his work."

"His orchids?"

He grinned. "No, the work. The work."

"What work?"

"The work he receives so many letters about. The work he reads half a dozen newspapers every day for. It's what they all work for. It's why they send me out every night."

"What is the work?" I demanded.

He shook his head. "Such a talkative old man." He gave a nod to the falcon and it sailed to the floor at my feet. "I must go now. You should ask Monsieur des Esseintes that question." He grinned one last time. "Oh . . . yes . . . as you seem to have suspected, in our game this evening you were quite correct. I could have taken you whenever I wanted."

With that he snapped a button off his trouser pocket and threw it forcefully at my feet. I looked in the direction of the sound for but a second, bewildered at the purpose of such a distraction. When I looked up again the young man was gone. Without a sound. Without a trace. The long and narrow clearing was quite empty.

XX

After the events of that evening something very strange happened, something that my most calculating instincts could have never foreseen or understood. Lady Dunaway began to change. I first noticed it when I was returned to my cell. I recited in detail my explorations of the house, my frightening encounter with Hatim, the falcon trainer, and his mention of "the work" of the vampire. At first I thought it was my imagination. Between us there had always been an excited sharing, but she absorbed my description of the house with a strange sort of listlessness, even disinterest.

As the days passed her change in attitude grew more pronounced. She no longer wanted to discuss things with me. She lapsed into lengthy and inscrutable silences. Sometimes, if I interrupted these she would snap at me angrily. At other times she was oddly regretful. It was as if an iron door had suddenly and inexplicably closed between us, and if I even mentioned her changing moods, she would furiously deny them. The intensity of her denials, the breaking of her deep voice from the cell beyond, only indicated to me that she was well aware of her change. I was at an utter loss. She was a completely different person from the woman who had so recently and passionately confirmed our friendship. What could have happened? Had the pressure of our situation caused her to give up? I did not think so. Although she irritatedly shunned any discussion of Ambrose or escape, all of her mettle still rippled behind her voice. Nothing could have caused me greater torment. Even in our bleakest hour I had kept my courage because she had inspired me. There had been two of us. Now I was alone.

I racked my brain trying to figure out what might have caused the change. One other possibility suggested itself, that Lady Dunaway had been turned into a vampire. After hours of anguished thought I found this possibility unsatisfactory. Everything I had thus learned about the

vampire indicated that the bestowal of their condition
was a very rare gift indeed. Niccolo had been changed for
his unearthly beauty, des Esseintes for his voracious
intellect, and Ilga for her computing facilities. Exempla-
ry though Lady Dunaway was above the multitude of
Victorian women, she simply was not a likely candidate.
Furthermore, if she had been changed, why wouldn't she
simply tell me? It did not explain the reason for her
almost guilty secrecy.

I was completely baffled, and yet my intuitions told me
a puzzle had been carefully and deliberately laid in my
lap. I could not help but think that Lady Dunaway's
disappearances had something to do with her change.
From des Esseintes's remarks about the orchids and the
rooms shifting places at night I was convinced he knew
what was going on. He was purposefully baiting me, but
why? To what end?

My bewilderment and concern were only deepened by
an event two evenings later. On my breakfast tray was a
silver salver containing a letter and two telegrams from
Ursula. The telegrams were sealed and showed no obvious
signs of tampering. Similarly, the letter was fastened
with sealing wax impressed with Ursula's signet, but
when I picked at it with my thumbnail it popped off with
suspicious ease. A closer examination revealed that it had
previously been carefully removed and then resealed with
paper mucilage. They were addressed to the Hotel
Madeleine. The letter read:

Father:

I understand you are probably consumed in your
search for your Camille. Perhaps my first letter was
premature. Perhaps I am overanxious to expect some
word before the end of a fortnight.

In any case, if it is within your magnanimity, could
you inform me of your progress? I am engaged in a
little search of my own. Browsing through old
newspapers.

Cook sends love.

Warmest regards,
Your other daughter, Ursula

I shook my head sadly at the sarcasm of her letter; her reference to *my* Camille. If she only knew my situation. *Cook sends love. Browsing through old newspapers?* What was it she was looking for? Had she thought of some further historical reference to Niccolo or Lodovico?

I opened the first of the telegrams:

> Good Doctor Gladstone . . . might one beseech you to wire me no later than this very afternoon . . . it is most important. . . . Mistress Gladstone of the rabbits.

And the second telegram sent but a day later:

> Are you there? . . . One begins to worry. . . . If you have not wired me by morning I shall notify the Préfecture de Police.

And when had that morning passed? Yesterday? The day before? How I wished I could sort out the nights. It was ironic that the Préfecture de Police was but ten minutes away on the Île de la Cité. At this very moment the authorities were probably scouring the city, completely unaware that I was sequestered so nearby.

Why was it so important for me to get in touch with Ursula? Was it merely to quell her growing anxieties, or was there some deeper meaning?

It was an evening later that Grelot brought me word des Esseintes wished to see me. Out of lifelong habit I stared at the clock without hands, and silently reprimanded myself. Was it dusk already? If it was, we were barely into twilight, for I was as tired as if it were the wee hours of the morning. Lady Dunaway was still asleep.

"She'll stay here," Grelot said. He added no explanation. We left without waking her.

When we reached the foyer we turned right and passed through a small parlor. From the parlor we entered the orchid conservatory through still another of the multitude of doors encircling it. We discovered des Esseintes sitting in one of two peacock-backed rattan chairs, and wearing a jeweler's glass in his eye. He was in the process of measuring one of his orchids with a pair of calipers. He was dressed in a black velvet smoking jacket,

most unsuitable attire for a greenhouse, and the jacket
was beaded with moisture. He looked up and smiled.

"*Bonjour*, Monsieur le Docteur." He picked up a brass
kettle from a small table beside him. "Aniseed tea?" As
usual he thrust a cup in my hand as his eyes instructed
me to take a seat. He dismissed the butler.

"Once again accept my amends for neglecting you for
so long. I cannot impress upon you the complexity of my
affairs. How long did I leave you in there this time?"

"Almost a week," I said without emotion.

"One of those evenings you had the freedom of the
house?"

I nodded.

"Did you enjoy it?"

"I was bloody near killed."

He did not flinch. "How so?"

"How so?" I repeated. "First I was attacked by that
murderous bird, and then I was hunted like some wild
beast by your young Arabian friend, Hatim."

"*Mais bien sûr*, Hatim. I'm sorry about Hatim. You must
forgive him. He's a mischievous sort, and by the way, he's
Persian, not Arabian." Without explanation he said,
"Here, look at this." From his velvet smoking jacket he
withdrew the photograph he had taken of Lady Dunaway
and me outside the peacock sitting room. The vacant and
astonished expressions on our faces were still further
nightmarish reminders of our helplessness.

I thrust the photograph back at him, angry that he
should interrupt our conversation so flippantly. "I don't
care what he is, but he's not mischievous. He's malevolent."

As usual des Esseintes maintained an air of deadly
calm. "If you only knew him as I know him, you might
understand a little more. When I first encountered Hatim
he was the grand falconer of the Malik Shah at
Naishápúr. He was the most renowned falconer in all of
Persia. He displayed such a rapport with his falcons that
it was said they shared a common soul." The Frenchman
casually glanced at the air around my head, and I realized
he was observing the quiver. "You could tell, couldn't
you?"

"Tell what?"

"That Hatim and his falcon vibrate to the pulse of a single heart, a common soul?"

"I sensed in them a more than normal similarity."

"There is hope for you yet, Monsieur le Docteur," he said, staring intently into my eyes. "You are not entirely blind to the more subtle worlds." He lifted the tea to his nose, and his nostrils flared. "Malevolent or not, Hatim can get the falcon to do things no one else can. You can see why I turned him into a vampire. I don't think I would have survived the Middle Ages without him."

"I think you would have."

He smiled his empty, frightening smile. "You did not have to live through the reign of a monarch known as Charles the Simple."

I did not share his sense of humor. "We are playing a game of chess, aren't we?"

He remained implacable.

"Can we eliminate this game?"

"Be my guest, Monsieur le Docteur."

"I know you have done something to Lady Dunaway. I do not know why she could not answer when I called to her, but she has changed. You know why she has changed, and you have hinted at it with your obscure ramblings about orchids. What do you want from me? What is going on?"

"I do not know."

"I think you do."

"Perhaps I do, but I said I don't."

My temper rose. "Hatim told me to ask you about the work of the vampire. He said it is the work you are all interested in. He said it is the reason you keep a constant vigilance on the newspapers. Pray tell, Monsieur des Esseintes, what is the work of the vampire and how does it involve us and our children?"

"I told you I know nothing of your children."

"I don't believe you."

"That is your choice."

"What is the work?"

He answered in the flash of a second, coldly and calculatedly, "I cannot tell you."

I was outraged. *"Why?"*

"Because there are things you do not understand, would

not understand. There are some realizations that cannot
be conveyed. They must be felt. Internally. You are being
told things all the time that you pay little or no attention
to."

I felt the blood surge up in my temples. "I can't take it
any longer. I can't remain locked up in that cell!"

"There, there," he soothed. "Would it help if we went out
for the evening? Would you like to go on a carriage ride?"

I looked in his face. There was no emotion behind his
words. It was merely an appeasement.

"I could tell you another story. I could tell you more
about Lodovico."

I was still furious, but the mere mention of the name
had a magic that reached down and gripped something
deep within me. It was the first time I realized how much
control it exerted. I tried to fight it. In the privacy of my
thoughts I rationalized and told myself that every tidbit
of information I might gather on the mysterious and
mythic vampire might offer some key to the solution of
the puzzle, but I knew this was an equivocation. Whether
I enjoyed admitting it or not, the name of the Alexandrian scribe had an irresistible hold upon me. My
captivation was evident.

His blue eyes flashed. He knew he had me. He burst
through the door. Outside, once again, I discovered that
the falcon had not entered the orchid conservatory, but
remained just beyond the door. In the foyer des Esseintes
exchanged his smoking jacket for his evening coat and
cane, and then gripped me lightly by the arm. "This way,"
he directed. We went back through the parlor, and
through a glassed corridor leading to the stables beyond.
To my delight the vampire gentleman directed the falcon
to remain behind.

The stables themselves were large and housed no less
than five elegant coaches as well as eight fine Hackney
stallions. As I might have suspected, one of the human
servants, a fourteen-year-old boy dressed in livery, already
awaited our arrival.

Much to my interest, the moment we entered the green
atmosphere of the stables all eight of the stallions began
to pull uneasily at their fetters. The boy in livery began to
lead two of the horses by their reins to the center of the

stable where we stood waiting. The closer they drew to my
companion the more they protested. Their flanks rippled.
They stamped their hooves. They began to arc their
massive heads so violently I feared they might jerk free
from the poor boy. Des Esseintes gripped the reins and
began to close the slack. The Hackneys flared their
nostrils as they pulled their heads sideways and stared
with wide and empty terror at the tall gentleman. I do not
know exactly what he did next. With a single deft
movement he brought his hand down alongside one of the
horses' necks. It gentled. He repeated the process with the
other.

"Horses have such easily disturbed spirits," he sniffed.

He led me to the coach, a spacious black hansom. "Do
you notice anything different?"

I looked at the cab. I did not notice anything different.

"The finish," he continued. "It's not shiny, like most
coaches. I've had it constructed of a special material that
reflects no light. It's more difficult to see in the dim
shimmer of the streetlamps. It takes better to shadows.
It's the same with the wheels." He kicked them. "You
see ... soundless against the stone."

He opened the carriage door.

Inside I was not at all surprised to discover the same
eccentric use of wealth that permeated des Esseintes's
entire world. The black leather seats were ornately
buttoned. The front of the enclosed cab was equipped with
a small teak shelf containing a library of pocket-sized
books bound in turtle-shell leather. Other insets boasted a
decanter with goblets, a small collapsible writing desk,
and a rack of various inks, blotters, papers, and envelopes.
An inlaid ship's telescope descended from a pivot in the
ceiling.

"Be completely aware of the fact, Monsieur le Docteur,"
des Esseintes said as he shut the door, "I am well versed in
many ancient arts, and I can render you unconscious with
but the most delicate application of pressure. If you make
the slightest attempt to escape or tell anyone of your
situation I will not hesitate to use any measure to stop
you."

We drove out of the stables.

The street was lined with the familiar paraffin lamps of

Paris. The buildings towered protectively. As des
Esseintes had foretold, the hansom wheels were abnormally silent against the granite. We moved down the
evening street as though in a dream. Even the clip-clop of
the horses was absent, silenced by some unknown means.

"Where are we going?"

"Who knows?"

"And Lodovico? What were you going to tell me about
Lodovico?"

"In due time," he parried.

I was about to ask another question when my companion placed a finger to my lip. I did not like the sensation.
His finger was cool to the touch. A little cadaverous.

"Look around you," he quieted. "This is *Paris.*"

I looked around. The summery evening air wafted
through the windows of the carriage as we moved. There
was life. It was exhilarating to be out of the house, to be
in the legendary city. I had forgotten what it was like, as
if I had been in a delirium for days and days. On the street
corner an accordionist played.

I looked at des Esseintes. He sat back leisurely in the
black cushions dapperly balancing his slender white
hands upon the gilt knob of his cane. I was somewhat
surprised to see a deep and honest affection in his eyes as
he gazed out of the window. It was unusual for any
emotion to gleam past the Cheshire cat façade. "I love this
city," he said passionately. "I love it as I love few other
human achievements. It is eternal." He turned in my
direction. "For me Paris is not just in the nineteenth
century. It is a montage of all ages. Every corner and
crumbling wall holds a memory. When I look at the square
before the Tuileries I cannot help but see it filled with a
ballet for fifteen thousand people given by Louis XIV to
celebrate the birth of the Dauphin. And when I look at the
Champs-Élysées, who are there but mourners, mourners
on that bitter-cold December morning when Napoleon's
funeral coach rolled by. I was there when they lit the
Opéra with the electric arc light. I have seen Sarah
Bernhardt. This city is my lover, my oldest and dearest
friend."

We crossed the bridge and I noticed it was sparsely
scattered with carriages and one-horse cabriolets. I

looked at the skyline of the Left Bank and wondered what it was like to remember when each building had appeared in the river of time. Indeed, what a vision he was privy to. I felt another pang of envy for the insights immortality must have opened for him.

"So you want to know more of Lodovico," he said at length. "You recall in my last account of him I was still a monk at the monastery of the Vosges. I had known of Lodovico only from his mythic reputation, but through the medium of the *abbés* I had received word of his approval of a discovery of mine, the discovery that the knowledge of the vampire was hidden in code and cipher in the common Gospel books. I have told you to be patient. You will appreciate it was more than two centuries after the 'death' of Sylvester II before I actually came face to face with the master, Lodovico. To be sure, much had passed. I had traversed the world. I had learned more than ten men, but still the identity and purpose of the Unknown Men was a mystery to me. I knew virtually nothing about the internal organization of the vampire culture.

"I must tell you what France was like in the twelfth century. Like most things, it covered a spectrum from one extreme to the other. On the dark side, it was the age of the Crusades, and all of Europe was united under the cause of the Holy War. It was the good fortune of the vampire of the Vosges that the war took place in the East. Nonetheless, it was a foreboding indication of the powers of history we were confronted with.

"On a more positive side, it was during these two centuries that French medieval civilization reached its zenith. Religions mingled in urbane amity. Great cathedrals rose from the ground. Women were imperiously beautiful and morals were loose. It was also the age of the troubadours. Do you know who the troubadours were? They were vagabond musicians. For a century and a half they scoured France singing and spreading ideas.

"The troubadours were odd characters. Many of them were wealthy, and yet they were homeless wanderers. They have been described as the most courteous men in the world, but advocated deception in love. They were proponents of lyric poetry, licentiousness, and paganism. They definitely were not proponents of the Church. Indeed, they were often anticlerical to the extreme.

"It thus came as some surprise in the middle of a blossom-laden spring when a troubadour arrived at the monastery. It was even more puzzling when the *abbés* took an unusual interest in this troubadour, and welcomed him into their secret chambers. I saw him briefly as he passed through the courtyard about an hour after sunset. He was richly dressed, like a noble, with a large hat trimmed in gold embroidery, and wore many costly furs. Strangely enough, he was on foot, like a common country juggler, and he carried his ancient violin or vielle nonchalantly under his arm.

"I caught but a glimpse of his countenance as he passed out of sight. His gleaming white face had a puckish quality to it. It was a mixture of foolishness and infinite wisdom. There was something most disarming about his smirk, his twinkling eyes."

We passed the Asian dome of a street urinal or *pissoir* encrusted with cabaret posters.

"Good idea—those," des Essientes interrupted. "There was a time when the sewers ran through the streets."

He turned to me. "Well, as you might imagine the first thing I did was see if the troubadour was a vampire. I reached out with my senses. I determined the heat of that gleaming face; the beat of the heart. To my surprise, his body temperature was the normal 37 degrees Centigrade, or 98.6 degrees Fahrenheit, of a mortal, as opposed to the cool 20 degrees Centigrade, or 68 degrees Fahrenheit, of one of our kind. His heartbeat was around 78. A vampire's beats a slow and healthy 35.

"I did not see much of the troubadour the first evening of his stay, but in the next couple of evenings I noticed him more and more. At first I thought these meetings were chance, but in time I resolved he was watching me. As I paced the windy parapets meditating on the deep purple mountains I would see him gazing from the tower. As I worked in my garden in the moonlight I would spy him on the balcony. He was not at all timid whenever I caught him at this. but would simply nod and continue that unsettling smile.

"Look," my companion interrupted himself and wafted a hand at the window.

I saw that the carriage had circled west, and was now passing through Montmartre, that idyllic part of Paris with its quaint houses and hidden gardens.

"Just as day has a transition period into night, a twilight, so it is with the people of the streets," he explained. "It is only an hour after sunset. If you are observant you'll notice a distinct transition in their ebb and flow, an almost precise moment when the twilight people vanish, and that strange breed, the creatures of the Paris night, first begin to appear."

I peered out the front window of the hansom at the street before us. In a narrow doorway a concierge sat in her loose blouse peeling vegetables. Next to a thick retaining wall shored up by balks of timber strolled a group of women in heavy carpet slippers and carrying baskets in their arms. In another doorway sat a girl trimming her bonnet; the girl was pale and exhausted from the heat. They seemed oddly oblivious to our presence, as if the silence of our carriage and horses made us unseen.

"In any case," des Esseintes went on, "I was not frightened by the troubadour. What could a mortal do to me? I was perplexed. Why was he so special that the *abbés* would take him in? Why was he so interested in me?

"He had been there fully a fortnight when I finally heard him beneath my window. The words of his song came clearly to my ears:

> *'Summer is a-coming in,*
> *Loudly sing cuckoo!*
> *Groweth seed and bloweth mead.*
> *And blossoms the woodland now:*
> *Sing cuckoo!'*

"I looked out into the courtyard. There he stood playing his vielle and looking up at me:

> *'Ewe bleateth after lamb,*
> *Loweth after calf the cow;*
> *Bullock leapeth, buck turns off;*
> *Merry sing cuckoo!'*

"At first I thought he was singing for his own enjoyment. When I glanced down at him he just happened to be looking up. But when I turned to walk away from the window, the intonation of his voice made it obvious he was trying to communicate something to me.

> *'Cuckoo, cuckoo, well singest thou*
> *cuckoo?'*

"I looked at him again. He continued to smile and play. Who was this minstrel, this fool with such a knowing grin? He tossed me a final glance as he turned with vielle and arched bow in hand and started to leave the courtyard. It was a moonlit night and I could clearly see him kick the huge wooden doors aside as he left the enclosure.

"I could take the mystery no longer and was compelled to follow. When I had crossed the courtyard and reached the gate I could see him halfway down the hill. He was still fiddling that fey and whimsical song as he danced like an elf in the moonlight. Not that I wish to convey the size of an elf. In actuality he was quite tall for a man of that time, fully reaching 1.82 meters.

"Through the wooded valley he led me, through the katydids and the lacewings, the damp spring mists and the dewy ferns. When he reached the meadow and turned about merrily on the hill I could see only his silhouette against the starry sky. He was perhaps fifty meters away. I monitored him closely. There was no rapid change in his heartbeat to indicate he was tense and might be planning some secret attack. His body heat mirrored what might be expected of a mortal exerting such energy, even a little less than normal. His breathing was long and full. It was obvious he was completely relaxed, even ecstatic in his Pied Piper dance.

"We reached a rock promontory that extended out from the cliffs. Beyond were the cool gray and blue ripples of the distant mountains, and below a drop of a hundred meters. It wasn't until he reached the very precipice that that man of flourish and wide gilt hat, that Fool of the Tarot deck, turned his eyes and froze them upon me with an almost demonic intensity.

'Cease thou not, never now;
Sing cuckoo now, sing cuckoo,
Sing cuckoo, sing cuckoo, now!'

"He cried out the words, and with that he began to play upon the vielle even more madly than before. I watched in amazement as his hands moved faster and faster. The music changed. It was no longer pastoral and gay. Tones twisted and screeched. It was not just the dissonance of a clumsy player, but an expanding spectrum of strange and grinding vibrations that had a peculiar effect upon my vampire ear. I felt a shiver of electricity shoot down my spine. Here a muscle twitched. There a tingle.

"What was this sorcery of music that cut to such a visceral level of my being? I could not run or move. I was drained of all muscle strength as the vibrations shimmered through me like heat discolorations upon forged iron. It was as if a strange force, a genie of sound, had swept through my body, and was coursing along each nerve and tendon... searching... changing. It moved with pattern and intelligence, guided by the skilled hands of a master magician. And then it stopped.

"I slumped forward a little, as if released from another's grip. The troubadour lowered his vielle and bow and strode quickly forward. He gazed at me penetratingly. 'Do you see?'

"'See what?'

"'Look around,' he commanded, gesturing at the forest and the meadow behind us.

"'Do you *see*? Can you *see*?'

"'I—' I stammered and shrugged.

"With that he became completely agitated, and before I knew what had happened he had drawn his hand back and smacked me firmly, just above the center of my eyes and in the middle of my forehead.

"I must tell you that it is not easy to strike a vampire. No matter how unexpectedly, if you ever tried to hit me, before your fist reached the halfway point of its swing, my hand would be firmly around your wrist deflecting the force. This should give you some indication of the incredible deftness of the troubadour's blow.

"I cannot tell you what a profound effect that blow to

my forehead had upon me. It was as if I fell backward in slow motion, and broke through a mirror. There was a crystalline tinkle as shards of platinum light glistered about me and I imagined I was slowly plummeting to a placid moonlit lake far below. As I recovered from that vertigo, I immediately noticed everything had changed. The woods, the meadow, even the very air had acquired a faint but undeniable luminescence. It was as if the cataracts had fallen from my eyes. Yes. I possessed over five hundred years of wisdom and experience, and the cataracts had just fallen from my eyes. It was an overwhelming sensation, and yet oddly familiar. It was as if some part of me had always seen the luminescence. It had always been close and I had merely forgotten, like a memory hovering just below the threshold of one's consciousness. It was the first time I completely experienced the *quiver*.

"The troubadour stepped back, pleased at the childlike wonder he saw in my face. I turned, slowly taking in the details of my new world. I ran down through the meadow. I pity you that you do not see the *quiver*, for oh, what a wondrous world it was. As I trudged through the waves of millet and timothy all the night insects hidden in the grass glowed like fairies and took to the air in a sheet of sparks. Vast luminous undulations moved through the very meadow itself, like wind through the grasses, or the shadow of clouds. I could see the circulation of the fluids through the leaves of the trees. I discerned the very movement of the stars. When I dropped to my knees beside a forest pond my vision plummeted through the microcosm of the water and I saw the microscopic protozoa as if they were immense glowing beings. I could see their rippling hairlike cilia and the cytoplasm flowing ghostly blue among the granules of their organs.

"Through all of this the troubadour followed me and slowly I became aware of something else. There was heat rising off his body. I didn't notice it at first, but at length I realized he was becoming cooler. His heart was slowing down. The throbbing filled my eardrums, dwindling more and more until it reached a familiar rhythm. He continued to smile, but the twinkle shifted in his eyes, and at last I saw the true depth of those impermeable orbs, the tomblike hush of inconceivable age.

"Like a stone dropped off a cliff... those eyes.

"'So you are a vampire after all,' I said.

"He nodded.

"'Then who are you?'

"'Lodovico....' he said."

Des Esseintes paused for breath.

Even though I was attending most carefully to his words, for some inexplicable reason my eye was drawn to the carriage window. To my surprise, all of the twilight people had vanished. On the street corner stood a lone figure, a woman, eyes painted with kohl, fat and red-haired, with a powdered face, black satin blouse, and red scarf. Her painted eyes blinked. Her hair and blouse fluttered, not unlike plumage as she proudly stood the wind, this first creature of the night.

"I asked him how he had done it."

I continued to gaze out the window as des Esseintes spoke.

"He shrugged."

The woman looked in our direction.

"I asked him what he wanted."

We drew closer.

"'You,' he said."

We rolled slowly by the woman, as if on a strange carousel. For a fleeting instant, as her face was closest to the carriage window, she stared right into my eyes. She blinked again and I saw the iridescence of her sedate and heavy lids, like fly's wings, heavy with antimony.

I turned quickly to my companion. "You? What did he want with you?"

"To tell me something."

"And what was that?"

"To tell me there were more things in the world to *see* than I had ever imagined. To help me enter a new realm of perception."

"What else did he tell you?"

"He told me the Unknown Men were engaged in a very special work. He said someday I might help in that work, but I would have to prove myself."

"How would you prove yourself?"

"He would not say. All he would tell me was that the
time had come for me to leave the monastery of the
Vosges permanently. He said I was to move to Paris and
there further instruction would be given. When I asked
what sort of instruction, he said to look for a flower. The
true flower. The *veri floris*. Then he recited an ancient
poem. He told me, 'Under the figure of the true flower
that the pure root produced, the loving devotion of our
clergy has made a mystical flower constructing an
allegorical meaning beyond ordinary usage from the
nature of a flower.'"

"What does that mean? What is the true flower?"

Des Esseintes smiled as he tapped on the window and
gave the boy in livery a nod. "I will show you."

The hansom turned south and we headed back toward
the Seine.

"So that is when I first came to Paris, at the very height
of the Middle Ages. Surprisingly, the flavor and soul of
Paris have not changed all that much, lo these many
years. Oh, the skyline has altered. The city has spread and
grown, but it is still magnificent. It is still dirty. And it is
still a mecca for many learned men and women. In 1331
Petrarch described it as 'a great basket in which are
collected the rarest fruits of every country.' You have no
idea just how true those words are."

My gentleman companion lapsed into silence as we sped
on.

It was well into the night now. Stars twinkled overhead.
We passed little parks and small-waisted women standing
with their lovers in the shadows, and still we moved with
the hush of a ghostly Black Maria. We crossed the bridge
leading to the Île de la Cité. We rolled by the huge
eighteenth-century complex of administrative buildings,
and an occasional *agent* until at last the Gothic outline of
Notre-Dame loomed across a spacious square, flanked by
leather-green trees. The horses slowed before the ancient
cathedral.

"Closer," des Esseintes directed.

We crossed the square until at last we stood before the
spireless towers of the West Façade.

"Let us get out," he directed.

He opened my door and I stepped down onto the

pavement. Again it was an odd sensation to be standing upon solid ground and in the open air. My captor slipped out behind me and placed a white hand upon my shoulder. He allowed the other to drift up toward the somber and majestic giant.

"Behold the true flower," he said with a reverent calm.

I looked up at the profusion of Gothic ornament, the towers, the innumerable angels and saints, the stone quatrefoils. The granite shimmered blue-gray in the moonlight. Unavoidably my vision was drawn to the elaborate cartwheel of tracery in the great rose window. A rose. A great stained-glass flower.

"The *veris floris*," I whispered in realization.

I recalled Lodovico's poem. "Under the figure of the true flower that the pure root produced..." Under the flower. I looked beneath the rose window at the three sets of massive iron doors.

"Very good, Monsieur le Docteur," des Esseintes complimented. "You are quite correct. It *is* the doors. I am sure you do not see what I see when I gaze at those doors."

I looked at the magnificently ornamented portals. I turned back to the vampire questioningly.

"Do you know who built the doors of Notre-Dame?" he asked.

I shrugged my shoulders.

My ancient friend smiled. "If you look it up in your history books you'll discover a demon is matter-of-factly given the credit." He threw his head back and laughed. "A demon! A demon named Biscornet!" He spun about, oddly amused by it all. "And it is true, *mon ami,* if you examine the doors you'll discover they are incredible achievements. In all their ironwork it is impossible to perceive any break in continuity, any trace of brazing or welding. This complete lack of seams indicates each door was formed from a single sheet of iron. I suppose that is partly why the humans of the Middle Ages assumed Biscornet was a demon. They knew their human ironworkers were incapable of such an achievement. In their minds, only the fires of hell could have forged such doors.

"But it was no demon. It was the vampire who created those doors."

It should have shocked me, the fact that the doors of one

of the most famous churches in Christendom were built by
creatures from our darkest mythology, creatures fully as
strange as the gargoyles above our heads, but I was
becoming numbed to the incredibility of des Esseintes's
world. "So vampires built the doors."

"The doors and much of the church itself. My good
Docteur, you owe it to yourself to do a little historical
investigation. Often when the mortal architects of the
Middle Ages were unable to finish their projects, *others*
were called in, *others* who possessed knowledge far
surpassing their human contemporaries. More often than
not, your venerable old records list them as demons, as in
the case of Biscornet. All over France are bridges
attributed to these demons—the bridges of Beaugency,
Pont de l'Arche, Vielle-Brioude, and Pont de Valentré, to
name a few. There are 'devil's bridges' all over England
and Spain as well, and the Teufelsbrücke in Germany are
exceedingly numerous. That is why the secret group of
others first became known as stonemasons and freemasons, for they were the builders of the impossible monuments."

"And all built by vampire?"

"To varying extents."

"So what do you *see* when you gaze at the doors of
Notre-Dame?"

"What do I *see?* I'll tell you. After Lodovico vanished
into the night and I moved to Paris, I searched the
evening streets. And finally, when I discovered the great
rose window and looked beneath it I saw all the secrets of
the vampire revealed before me. You see, just as the elder
vampire had hidden knowledge in code and cipher in the
common Gospel books, so they had hidden great secrets in
the hieroglyphics of those doors. Indeed, the entire
history of the vampire is concealed in the iron and
stonework of Notre-Dame. Do not grow anxious if you see
nothing in the symbols, Monsieur le Docteur. You see, it
takes a brain of a different order to perceive the hidden
language of the doors. Not even all of the vampire possess
this faculty." He turned to me. "That is what I must
communicate to you. As the bumblebee perceives the
ultraviolet, as the migrating bird navigates by the stars
even when it is cloudy, I move through a different world.

It is more than just perception. I think differently. The very symbolic functionings of my brain have altered. I can immediately see meaning in patterns your brain can only understand as random. I may look human, but I am a separate species entirely. Just as the moth can never fully share the logic of the swallow, there are certain things I cannot convey to you."

His eyes drifted back to the ancient structure, scanning the bell turrets and the winged monsters. "I know nothing of the spiritual. I don't pretend to, but I do know one thing about the brain. There is evolution. There is change. If there is an afterlife, perhaps the same thing happens to you after you die. Perhaps we change because we do not die. All I know is that I have transformed. I was fortunate. It took me only five hundred years to mutate, to shed the last vestige of my humanity. That is why the *abbés* could not tell me certain things. They were waiting for my brain to be able to understand them. Lodovico saw I was changing. He assisted, but it was as I stood before the portals of Notre-Dame that I truly understood what it meant to *see*. To be illuminated. An *illuminatus*."

Once again I regarded the complex and foliate decoration of the doors. Was I so blind? Were we mortals so piteously inadequate beside creatures such as des Esseintes? Try as I might, I could discern nothing in the symmetrical decorations that even faintly resembled a secret language. When I turned to des Esseintes, however, he appeared to be experiencing a distinct restlessness. He held himself with composure, but something feverish shone in his face. I was taken aback. It was the most emotion I had felt emanating from him since he had crackled with energy in our first encounter in the orchid conservatory. I looked again at the dark portals and still saw nothing. The trees flanking the church rustled.

"What do you see in the doors?" I beseeched the tall and pallid gentleman.

"What do I see?" he asked as he continued to gaze at the iron monoliths with a wandering and vacant air. He took a slow step forward. "Oh, so many things. I see the most incredible and carefully guarded alchemical secrets of the vampire. And more, I read my destiny. I perceive my purpose, my role in the work of the vampire."

"And what is that?"

"To survive, Monsieur le Docteur. To preserve our culture and our learning."

"But never to share that learning?"

He turned on me as if in a rage, but again his face was calm. "You are wrong. Have I given you that impression? We shared our knowledge. As I have said before, you owe us more of a debt than you have ever realized. When I arrived in Paris in the twelfth century there were already many special vampire living here. Like me they had been drawn and changed by the lodestone of the doors. All of this had been planned long ago by the Unknown Men and recorded here for us. We formed a center of learning for mortal and vampire alike. At night we met in the cloisters of this old church and held classes. As the years passed the number of our students grew. Within time it was known all over Europe that Notre-Dame was the haunt of alchemists. That is where you get your expression *sub rosa* or 'under the rose,' referring to a meeting held in secret. It was the school of Notre-Dame that ultimately became the University of Paris."

"It was the vampire who taught at the school of Notre-Dame?"

"Yes."

"Why hasn't history recorded the names of the vampire teachers?"

"We kept our identities hidden, but really, Monsieur le Docteur, you know us by our students. Look at the names of those men who were pupils at the school of Notre-Dame, such distinguished intellectuals as Abelard, Albertus Magnus, John of Salisbury, Siger of Brabant, Roger Bacon, Thomas Aquinas, Bonaventura, Duns Scotus, William of Occam—nearly the entire history of philosophy from 1100 to 1400."

"You were the teachers of these great men?"

"I and my brethren."

"What did you teach them?" I asked as a warm wind suddenly caught us up in a little devil's eddy. Des Esseintes paused before answering as the trees enclosing the cathedral continued to whisper. He folded his arms and frowned. "I will tell you, but I fear we must start back. It is a little too hot out here for my blood."

He returned to the hansom ahead of me.

For a moment I was swept with an impulse to run. I feared it would be my last chance to escape for quite some time, and yet I was torn. Something held me back.

Des Esseintes slowly turned around, arms still clasped. "You are doing well, Monsieur le Docteur," he said with an utter calm. "Don't ruin it now."

I succumbed and followed him to the carriage.

"I do feel like walking," he continued. "It is a short distance back to the house. Would you like to stroll?"

I nodded.

"You may return ahead of us," he said to the boy in livery. "We've decided to walk." The boy nodded and the horses pulled silently into the night, leaving us alone in the square. The vampire beckoned and I quickened my pace to catch up with him.

"You ask me what we taught our students. We taught them many things. As you might expect, we taught them how to make automata. You remember Sylvester II possessed a bronze mechanical head that could answer YES and NO questions. It is no coincidence that your history books record the Franciscan friar and sorcerer, Roger Bacon, also possessed such a head. So did the famous alchemist-philosopher, Albertus Magnus. Unfortunately for posterity, his more famous student Thomas Aquinas thought the device was diabolical and destroyed it after Albertus died."

"And these clockwork heads would actually answer questions?"

"Yes."

"I can't believe it," I said. "I'm sorry. I can believe in many things—hypodermic syringes and horticultural advances—but I find it difficult to believe even the vampire of the Middle Ages could create such a mechanical being."

We rounded the back of the cathedral.

"Alas, but you do not recognize one thing, Monsieur le Docteur, one thing that you will find very difficult to comprehend. The twelfth century was quite different from today, different in a most special way. You see, the entire world believed in magic, and this affected things. It altered the world we perceived, everyone perceived,

mortal and vampire alike. You will not be able to accept
this, but it altered the very laws of physics. Magic was a
little more real." He suddenly fanned his hands in the
darkness. "But I do not want to discuss this. We are
opening a hornet's nest if we do."

I was enraptured. A thousand questions waited in line,
but I suddenly realized he was drawing me in again. With
his web of words he had made me so completely forget my
anger, Lady Dunaway, Hatim's taunting remarks. "So
that is all that you read in the doors, to teach, to be the
beneficient fathers." I shook my head slowly. "I may be
sadly limited in my powers of comprehension, but I do
have some wits about me. I know that you are keeping
things from me. There is more to the work of the vampire
than you are letting on. I saw it in the eyes of that demon
boy. It is not just the pursuit of knowledge. There is more,
isn't there?"

He turned to me as we entered the footbridge of the Île
Saint-Louis. I stared deep into his pale, cold eyes. "Yes,"
he said simply.

"What is the work of the vampire, will you tell me?" We
continued to face one another. I could glean no hint of
what he was thinking from his expression. His face was
blank. How I wished to penetrate beyond those slow-
blinking lids, wrest secrets from that skull. I was helpless.
He knew it. I knew it. A ricochet of energy passed back
and forth between our eyes as my frustration mounted.

"No," he said.

I was infuriated. I'm sure he felt it, felt the air turn icy
with the pins of the quiver. It did not matter. He slowly
resumed his forward gaze. The warm wind traced through
the chestnuts on the tree-lined street. It was an odd
sensation walking beside him, this partner with a
thousand-year-old mind. I could not run. I was trapped.
Nothing had changed. If anything, the things he had told
me created even more fear in my mind. I had always
viewed the vampire as the interloper, but if they were so
interwoven in our history, if they were responsible for
many of our ancient churches and monuments, how must
they view themselves? They were not homeless ghouls or
wanderers. They communicated with one another in ways
we could not fathom. What sense of possession must they

feel for this world, and how must they view us mere scurrying mortals?

Monsieur des Esseintes's intense self-possession betrayed him. There was no doubt that he viewed this world as his. What was most disturbing of all was that they were here, they moved among us, and no one knew. I looked around me. There were carriages gathered around the stately hotels, and not a few strollers on the residential streets. I looked at their faces. None of them had the faintest inkling that the gentleman accompanying me was not human. He could have walked right up to any one of them and asked the time. How often had I walked by vampire in the past, how often do we all walk by them completely unaware that the gentleman just a few feet away has senses that make ours look aboriginal, that the lady shopping a short distance from us is smugly aware that she is not human? What other manner of creature had assumed a comely shape and moved freely down our evening streets?

My footsteps set into a cadence with his own as we continued through the oblivious passersby. What did he experience as he strolled through this bustle of human life? A constant barrage of heartbeats like the resonance of so many drums? A dozen varying rhythms of breath amplified as through a deaf horn? I was so immersed in my thoughts I almost didn't notice the figure of a woman moving through the sparse crowd. She approached on the opposite side of the street. Her dress was a plain brown cloak and hood, and she had a determined, forward lean in her stride.

I recognized her walk, something about her form, immediately. As if guided by a hidden power she looked up and her face became visible beyond the crescent shadow of her hood. It was Ursula. She had come to Paris.

I tried to conceal my shock, but as calm as I remained outwardly, there was no keeping my emotions from des Esseintes. He turned to me at once. "Is anything the matter?"

In the flash of a second I had transferred my gaze to a gentleman on our side of the street and then to another— all the time trying to maintain my previous anger as a smokescreen. I prayed that Ursula would have the presence of mind to look away as well, to continue to walk on, but I dared not look in her direction to see what her reaction was.

It seemed to work. Out of the corner of my eye I saw my companion scan the street. Could even the vampire sort out the noise of so many heartbeats and discover the one significant rhythm in the crowd? He looked back at me, tried to peer a little closer into my soul, and I luxuriated in another wave of anger. I ran through my mind everything he had said that had frustrated me. I tried to focus on anything and everything except the unexpected appearance of Ursula. With every ounce of self-control I possessed I upheld my brooding composure and glowered at des Esseintes. I did not answer, hoping he would be fooled by my reticence.

Impossibly, he seemed to dismiss the occurrence. I resumed my forward glare. Of course, he was so adept at controlling his façade it was impossible to determine what was going on behind his blue eyes. And yet, every intuition in my body told me my subterfuge had been successful. I was certain he had not noticed my recognition of Ursula. I was elated. So he was not infallible. So even des Esseintes had his limits. I, a blind and stupid mortal, had performed a brief but unseen sleight of hand. It gave me new hope, and yet I dared not even ponder the victory for fear of arousing des Esseintes's suspicions.

At length we arrived at the familiar street, and des Esseintes withdrew his keys. He opened the large oak door and allowed me to pass before him. Inside, the lavender foyer was quiet. The sinuous rosewood staircase stood empty and it was apparent that all of the human servants were sleeping or busy elsewhere. Perhaps it was exposure to the vampire that gave me a heightened awareness of my senses. Whatever it was, I was swept with the second surprise of the evening. The air still possessed a tinge of mold. It was filled with the smell of the scullery, and the always present heaviness of the orchids. Even so, I discerned several new smells, smells that had not been there before. A lingering aroma of various colognes and tobacco. The house had been filled with people.

"Who has been here?" I asked.

"Friends," des Esseintes said without batting an eye.

The intruding scents were perhaps as obvious to him as photographs.

"What friends?"

"Vampire friends. There are more than a few of us in Paris, you know. They use my house as a meeting place. They've wanted to remain unseen until we knew a little more about what to expect from you."

"I don't suppose it would do me any good to inquire what their meetings are about?"

"No good at all."

"As I thought."

"You are catching on, Monsieur le Docteur," he said, smiling as he replaced his jacket and cane.

"More than you imagine," I returned.

Of course, he would not give me the pleasure of seeing him raise an eyebrow, but I was confident I had struck a note of curiosity within him.

It was only in the privacy of my room that I allowed myself to experience my full surprise at seeing Ursula. Lady Dunaway was not in. Grelot had informed me that it was her turn to be given the freedom of the house, and I was worried about her. God protect her from that falcon and that terrible boy. I wondered what Ursula had done after she found me. She was an intelligent young woman. Certainly she had assessed the situation and understood I was in trouble. I also thanked God she had walked on without rushing into the very midst of des Esseintes's realm of power. But afterward, had she followed us? Had she watched from a safe distance until she spotted the house and even now was contacting the agents of the Sûreté? I paced my cell excitedly with this new hope. What would happen to des Esseintes? I did not want to expose or hurt him, but I would also do anything to continue my search for Camille. I was suddenly jolted by the possibility that he would ferret Lady Dunaway and me away so that the authorities would find nothing. Des Esseintes had survived a very long time in the human world. Surely, he had had encounters with the authorities before. No doubt he had a countermove for every situation that might intrude upon his territory. And yet I dared not allow myself to consider it. I could only wait.

XXI

It was in my hands now. My mind was heavy with one
desire, to discover at any cost what had caused Lady
Dunaway's alienation from me. I did not see her until the
next evening, when Grelot came and woke us up. To my
surprise, he announced we would both be given the
freedom of the house. We were to be separated. He was to
guard my companion. I, by virtue of some hideous whimsy,
was once again left in the care of the vampire familiar,
the falcon. As we made our way to the first floor I tried to
get Lady Dunaway's attention, but she was clearly
reluctant to look in my eyes. She seemed numbed, as if
she had been drugged. When she finally did look for one
fleeting second her expression revealed the same vapid
regret. I surreptitiously scanned her throat for bite
marks. In my reading I remembered the vampire sometimes bit behind the ear. Her raven-black hair was drawn
tightly behind her head and I got a clear view of her
chalky skin. There were no visible markings. We reached
the foyer. I watched as Grelot led Lady Dunaway off to
some other part of the immense old home.

I found some solace in the fact that this freedom seemed
to indicate I was correct. Des Esseintes had been
completely unaware of our brush with Ursula. What could
she be doing? I thought. At any moment I expected to
hear some disturbance, a chief inspector at our door. What
would the falcon do then? I tried to calm my anticipation,
but resolved to remain within close vicinity of the foyer. I
strolled once again into the corridor of the statutes. The
falcon followed.

I had made no error. The sad, sweet subject of these
marbles was the same woman in farthingales in the
forgotten baroque salon. The altar of purple orchids in
front of the portrait in oils was carefully maintained. In
light of the obvious longevity of the mysterious woman I
examined the portrait more closely. The face was young,

and yet the eyes held a wide and limpid wisdom. The dress was simple, clearly at least a generation or two after farthingales. It was difficult to perceive the exact era to which it belonged. The surface of the painting was crosshatched with a fine matrix of cracks. The portrait was at least a good sixty or seventy years old.

From the foyer I heard the knocker rap clamorously against the front door. I swung around and the speed of my movement alarmed the falcon. It leaped in front of me. In the distance I could see the tall, middle-aged woman with brown hair crossing the foyer to answer it. I took a step forward, but the falcon made a purposeful attempt to herd me backward. I could hear the door open, and voices. I looked at the falcon. A pin feather had caught beside its nostril and it moved back and forth as it breathed and glared at me.

"Monsieur!" the woman called. There came the familiar creaking of the rosewood staircase as des Esseintes descended.

The falcon blinked.

I took a chance. I began to walk forward. The falcon flapped its pinions threateningly, but it did not screech. It did not dare. Whoever was at the door would hear it. It hopped backward, flapping its wings again. I continued my slow pace. By the sound of the footsteps whoever it was had entered the foyer. Des Esseintes came into sight and looked at me with alarm. It was too late. I stepped into sight.

It was no police officer. It was a man in a black short-coated suit and cloak. In his hand he held a letter. He handed it to des Esseintes, who, after his initial surprise at seeing me, seemed completely unconcerned by my intrusion. He was much more concerned with the letter. The man nodded politely, casting me a cold glance. On his neck I noticed a fine white cambric handkerchief of the type worn by all of the male servants of the vampire. He turned and left. The middle-aged woman with brown hair closed the door and latched it.

Des Esseintes read the letter and pondered its contents for a few moments. Then he looked at me. "Monsieur le Docteur, you have two daughters, do you not?"

"Yes, how did you know that?"

"My work is of great concern to me. Your breaking and entering my home affected that concern. For my own well-being I had some investigations made on you and your family."

I felt a chill and noticed his eyes moved to the space around my head. He returned his inspection to me. "Do you know where your older daughter is now?"

My heart sank. Had he discovered? Again his sight traced the outline of the quiver. "At our home in London," I returned.

He deliberated for a moment. "I think you are lying, Monsieur le Docteur."

I lurched forward, pretending surprise. "That is where I left her. Where is she now?"

He folded the letter in two. "I do not know. I only know that she has not been seen at your house in London for five days." Again he observed the quiver. "You do not find it so surprising that she is no longer there?"

"Why do you make such a remark?"

"You felt a pang of emotion as soon as I brought up the subject of your older daughter."

"Is that so unusual?"

He stared at me for another few moments. "Perhaps not, but you did not seem so surprised when I told you she was no longer there."

"That is because I feared as much." I sighed and drooped my shoulders. "My daughter, Ursula, is very defiant. She did not want to be left in London. After hearing no word from me she no doubt set off on her own."

Des Esseintes grew increasingly contemplative. "She knows you came to the Île Saint-Louis, but we are not sure if she has definitely left London."

Ignoring the falcon, I took a step forward. "You've been having my house watched?"

He said nothing, but turned to go back upstairs. I followed. "Tell me. She is my daughter. I have a right to be concerned."

He ascended the rosewood staircase.

When we reached his current study he hesitated, surveying the conference table of ebonized wood and the *coffre à écrire* with the two Chinese porcelain herons sitting on top of it. He turned around and looked at me pointedly. "Very well, you may enter."

I followed him in and the falcon hobbled behind.

Nothing much had changed. Through the window Notre-Dame was still visible above the sleeping rooftops of the Île Saint-Louis. Candles flickered throughout the room, but the candles beneath the flasks and alembics on his desk were not lit. It was not alchemy that occupied Monsieur des Esseintes this evening. Spread everywhere were newspapers, current newspapers, from the major cities of half the world: *The Illustrated London News, L'Osservatore Romano, Le Figaro, Neue Freie Presse, The Times, La Stampa*, the *Asahi Shimbun*. Mixed among these were current issues of a startling range of scientific journals: *Nature, L'Ami des Sciences, Abriss der Logistik*, the *Quarterly Journal of Metaliferous Ores, Gerontologia, Almanach der Österreichischen Akademie der Wissenschaften, Medico-Surgical Essays, Nauka I Tehnika za Mladezhta, Revue des Deux Mondes*, and on and on. Each paper and periodical was open and filled with clips and bookmarks and scribblings. On the ebony table I spied a large ledger in which he apparently indexed and annotated his voluminous reading. I hated him and I did not hate him. How could I not admire such an omnivorous intellect, so cultivated a mind?

I was still deeply worried. "Why have you had my house watched?"

He ran his fingers through his thin brown hair as he scanned his work. He seemed not to hear. He lifted a monograph delivered to the Cambridge Scientific Club and appeared to absorb it in a single plummeting glance. "I am an extremely cautious individual. That is how I have survived for so long."

"If my daughter comes to Paris I beg of you to leave her be."

In one of the newspapers he spotted something that piqued his interest. His white finger shot down and marked the spot as he scrutinized another paper. "The matter is in her hands, Monsieur le Docteur," he murmured. "Let us pray she is not as clever as you and does not meddle in my affairs."

I wanted to say more, but I knew it was to no avail. The

wind rustled the curtains, and the medieval icons danced gold in the candlelight. I looked down at the falcon and turned to leave.

"Monsieur le Docteur," he called behind me. I turned and saw he was looking up at me. His finger still marked the place of intrigue in the newspaper.

"Yes."

"I wanted to let you know. This coming week I am giving a party. You and Hespeth are both invited. First, I'm going to give a banquet, a grand banquet, and then I'm going to perform. You will get to meet some interesting individuals."

I was maddened. I could no longer take it. At every twist and turn I was being toyed with like a child. I knew that des Esseintes would not answer my questions. When I left the study I instantly became aware of the same eerie sensation that someone was watching me. I turned. I did not see anyone at the end of the corridor, but I did hear something. In the hushed silence of the huge old house there was breathing. I would not be intimidated. I strode to the end of the corridor expecting to come face to face with the Persian boy, but when I rounded the corridor there was nothing. I knew it had not been my imagination. There had been someone there.

I spent the rest of the evening on the first floor, anxious, but increasingly pessimistic about my chances for rescue. Perhaps Ursula had been afraid to follow and had not seen where my captor had led me. I did not know. Several times as I paced the foyer I heard creakings above me, and once, in the darkness above the rosewood staircase, I fancied I caught a glimpse of a dark face watching me. What an odd beast that boy was. I almost found myself believing he did have a supernatural rapport with the falcon, but then I dismissed it. It occurred to me that of the vampire I had known, only Monsieur des Esseintes seemed to have flourished and fulfilled an enviable destiny. Niccolo came the closest to the gentleman monk, but Niccolo possessed a deep melancholy the latter visibly lacked. Ilga was a mere shell of a being. Hatim was an afreet, a demon of the Muslim underworld, more an animal than a creature of intellect. I recalled the filthy cagelike room, the discor-

dance behind those liquid eyes. Thus I consoled myself
that evening, cataloguing what I knew about their
species, indexing my own information in my own primitive way, and wondering what type of creatures would
attend the auspicious banquet.

We were returned to our cells by Grelot during the last
waning hours of darkness. After I had sat at the reading
table for some time I called out. "Lady Dunaway?"

There came the clack of an embroidery hoop, the squeak
of her rocker. "Yes."

"I entreat you one last time. You know you have
changed. I see it in your eyes. We were once friends."

She pretended to be surprised, but it was only pretense.
"We are still friends." A thimble clicked against a needle.

I was exasperated. "I will ask you again: Why have you
changed?"

The rocker stopped. There was a meditative silence, and
then it slowly started up again. "I have not changed," she
croaked unconvincingly.

If her remark had been designed to throw me into bewilderment it would not have worked more effectively. I was
utterly despondent. What was I not seeing? I had not felt
so helpless since my marriage with Camille, my beloved
Camille, but even then, the impotence I had felt had been
different. I had had some control over the situation. It had
been my tyranny. I was to blame. But now I was as
powerless to affect this thing between Lady Hespeth
Dunaway and me as I was to remove the bars of our cells.
Something nebulous divided us. It swirled around me just
beyond my reach. I felt deadened, unfeeling.

It was long after I had drifted asleep that I was
awakened by a voice.

"Father."

I opened my eyes. The embers of the fire cast a dim glow
over the plush furnishings of the room. Could it be?

It came again.

"Father?"

I quickly jumped out of bed and raced to the opposite
wall. Beyond the surface of books was the familiar sound
of water rushing. The babble was suddenly interrupted by

a hollow popping sound like a stone falling into a very deep well.

"Ursula!" I shouted.

"Father?" came back the muffled reply.

I emptied the books off the shelf and looked quickly around the room until I spotted the chimney of one of two hurricane lamps sitting on the plinths of the mantelpiece. I retrieved the glass tube and placed it against the back of the emptied shelf to amplify the sound.

"Ursula, I'm here. You've found me!"

I heard another sound, and then she cursed. "Oh, dear . . . oh, how awful."

"What is it?"

"I'm in the sewer, you know."

"How did you find me?"

"Just a minute, until I get closer."

There were a few more muttered curses. In other circumstances I would have corrected her language. Then her voice became quite distinct, as if she were on the opposite side of the wall.

"There used to be an opening here. Can you hear me? Yes, it's been bricked over."

"Yes," I called excitedly. "I hear you clearly!" There were no words to describe the elation I felt. I wanted to reach through the stone itself and hug her dearly. A curious guilt swept through me. I could think of no great instant when I had done Ursula an overt wrong, but I still felt guilt. "Oh, Ursula, you have no idea how good it is to hear your voice."

There were a few seconds of silence. Maybe she was shocked to hear it. Then she spoke. "You have now idea how good it is to hear your voice, Father."

"Ursula, I'm sorry I did not tell you about Niccolo. I only kept it from you to protect you."

"Protect me from what?"

"From being afraid, I guess."

"Were you afraid of him, Father?"

I thought back to that original moment with brandy snifters before the fire in the study, when he had first revealed his luminous world to me. If I had been afraid it was a captivating fear. It had plummeted down to a strata of emotion seldom tapped in mundane life. For all of my disparagements, I would still give the vampire that.

"I would not have been afraid. I am your daughter, Father," she said through the stone.

"How did you find me, Ursula?"

"I'm still not sure where you are."

"In des Esseintes's house, of course. You mean you didn't know?"

"No, I followed them."

"Them?"

"Yes, there's a boat here."

"A boat?"

"Yes, here in the sewers. A flatboat. I suppose that's how they travel."

"They?"

"Yes. *Oh*, let me start at the beginning. Naturally, I followed you the other night. I don't think your Monsieur des Esseintes even knew it."

"No."

"I came to the house I suppose you're in now. However, that is not how I came to be here. You see, I've registered under an assumed name in the Hotel Madeleine. It took several evenings, but finally an Arabian gentleman came to pick up your mail. He's very handsome. Some of the young women at the hotel know him. They're all quite taken with his presence."

"Hatim!" I recognized. "Is he young? Does he . . . does he resemble a falcon?"

"A falcon? I never thought of it. He's rather slender, and he has eyes like large black pearls. Yes, I guess you could say he resembles a falcon."

"That's Hatim," I said. "And he's Persian, not Arabian."

"Whatever he is, he's a vampire. He only shows up after nightfall. I brushed against him the other evening and felt the coolness of his flesh. I think he thought I was just another one of those swooning young women. He smiled. That's how I managed to trace him here."

"What do you mean?"

"The first evening he came to the hotel when I tried to follow him he evaded me. I don't think he knew I was following him. It's just a precaution he takes. I don't know how he does it, but one moment I was following him down the street, and the next moment he vanished. He's like a cat. He looks over his shoulder. He slips through the fingers of the night like quicksilver. The next evening I hid in the street, but again it was without success. I . . . I just don't know," she murmured through the wall. "I never see him fade away, but he does something. One moment there are footsteps. The next moment there is nothing."

"How did you trace him here?"

"There's a chambermaid at the hotel who's desperately fond of him. There's a look in a woman's eyes when . . . well, you know, when she's given herself. The chambermaid possessed such a look for that dark young gentleman, that vampire. I made discreet inquiries as to her address, and the third evening instead of waiting outside the hotel I passed the evening watching the chambermaid's house in Montmartre. My suspicions were correct. Two hours past midnight a figure appeared. I could not see his features, but he scaled the ivy-encrusted wall with such facility I knew it was he. His very fingers and toes seemed to grip the edges of the stone. The window opened. He melted into the darkness."

I might have been mistaken, but I thought I detected a hint of excitement in Ursula's voice. "When he left you followed him here?"

"I followed him, but he did not come here."

"Didn't you think that was dangerous?"

"He was not as vigilant when he left the chambermaid's house as when he left the hotel. They're so smug. They're so sure no one could possibly second-guess them. No, he did not come directly here. In fact, he prowled around for several hours. He did not seem interested in anyone. He was restless, possessed. He stopped in the Moulin Rouge. He appeared to be well known there. No one noticed he did not drink. Finally, he went to another house."

"On the Avenue Victor Hugo?"

"No, here on the Île Saint-Louis. It's only a block or two away. It's really very clever. I waited until the full of the afternoon sun, and then I went into the house. It was completely empty. There were no furnishings. It was quite clear that the cellar was well traveled, and when I descended the stairs I discovered a door leading into the sewers. That's how I came here. I followed the path on the ledge and now I discover there is a flatboat here."

"Of course," I said. "Des Esseintes does not want Hatim coming to and fro from this house so he has him go through the other. A rabbit always has two holes."

"Exactly. And do you know what else? Hatim is not the only one I've seen coming and going from the other house. Why, the very night I saw you walking with that tall gentleman I saw a group of half a dozen people vanish into the house. I daresay if I'd been able to follow all of them I would know where half the vampire of Paris live. As it was, I only followed Hatim."

"And where did he go?"

"It's curious," she said. "He went to a house at 24 Rue de la Glacière, on the very edge of Paris."

"What is so curious about that?"

"He didn't go in. He merely went from window to window, furtively looking in. Then he took a rock and soundly broke the latch off the door."

"Then what?"

"He ran away. There was no purpose to his action, save as a malicious prank. The people investigated the sound and were very frightened. They were human. I do not know why he did that, but I cannot help feeling something is going on at that house."

"What did you say the address was?"

"It is 24 Rue de la Glacière."

"I must admit, Ursula," I commended through the wall, "you are a most resourceful young woman. I cannot tell you how impressed I am. But Ursula, you must tell me. Who is tending the laboratory?"

"You needn't worry about that, Father. The laboratory is quite all right."

I had been so bound up in the world of the vampire I had all but forgotten my work. "But Ursula, the rabbits—"

"As I said, you needn't worry. The rabbits are in quite capable hands."

I grew more alarmed. "Whose hands?"

"Why, Dr. Hardwicke's, of course."

"Dr. Hardwicke's!" I dropped the lamp chimney and it shattered against the floor. How could she? My worst enemy. There was no telling what that little monster would do. One thing was certain: After our last encounter he would exult at the opportunity of returning my rancor. "Ursula, don't you know how terrible this is?"

"But Father—"

"That is the most blindly irresponsible thing you have ever done."

"And was I supposed to leave you here alone?"

"I—" I shook my head and tried to calm myself. "With my life's work in Cletus's hands my escape is imperative. Are there any doors out there leading into the cellar?"

"Yes, but—"

I turned and saw the falcon flapping its wings as its eyes reflected the deep amber light of the torches. It was like a stone idol whose sockets had come alive. Volcanic.

"But the falcon," I gasped.

"No, the door is locked. It's massive. It would take an army, but—"

"But what?"

"But why do you want to escape?"

The words hit me like a hammer against brass.

"Why? Ursula, what do you mean?"

"I guess it's stupid of me. I mean, you brought Niccolo into our house. You were his friend. I guess I thought you'd found your world, where you wanted to be. It never crossed my mind that you'd want to leave it. I was envious. I came here to join you."

I was stupefied. How could she see things so different-ly? How could I have fostered such a daughter? I stepped backward, and one of the shards of broken glass cut neatly into my toe. It sliced deep into a little cap of skin, like the cap of a mushroom, and it was several seconds before dark, warm blood filled the gash.

"Have you gone mad?" I screamed. "I'm being held here against my will. Camille is still out there somewhere. You must help us escape."

"There's no way."

"Get the police!"

"I cannot."

"Ursula, you must!"

"I cannot!" she cried. "I cannot! I cannot! You don't understand me. I wired and told you I was doing a little research of my own. Obviously, everything I've done has been wrong so I won't bother to tell you what I discovered. I'm sorry I'm such an idiot."

I heard her footsteps echo in the hollow beyond. "Ursula!" I shouted, but it was to no avail.

In anger I hobbled over to the table and grabbed a handkerchief to wrap around my toe. It did not hurt yet. There was just the electric tingle of shock. It would be another half hour before the gash began to throb.

"Lady Dunaway!" I bellowed at the top of my lungs. The sound thundered out of my throat, guttural, and resonated throughout the cellars. I rushed to the bars and repeated the blast of fury and emotion.

There was no reply.

XXII

My position was critical. I did not know what Ursula would do. I did not care. There was no telling what Cletus might be up to. He was a hollow, soulless man, driven by acrimony and self-pity. At the very least he might concoct a paper on *Camillus influenzae* and present it to the university as his own work. Of even graver concern was another thought, a notion I scarcely dared to entertain. What might he do when he realized the full import of the virus I had created? What would a man who loathed his fellow men, a creature of cunning and contempt, do with a disease that lacked all antigenicity?

I did not know where Lady Dunaway was. It was clear she was not in the room adjoining mine. Whatever the case, I could no longer trust her. I would not tell her of Ursula's visit. I was angered with Ursula, but I still did not want des Esseintes finding out about her. I was alone. I had one aim: to escape at all costs.

I was haunted by a number of thoughts. The goings-on at 24 Rue de la Glacière intrigued me. Was there a purpose to Hatim's prank above and beyond his innate maliciousness? And what had Ursula discovered? It occurred to me that it could be any of a gamut of possibilities. Somehow I still felt it concerned Niccolo or Lodovico. Possibly she had uncovered Lodovico's present-day identity. Maybe he was even an historical personage, a famous politician or artist.

We were given the freedom of the house every evening preceding the promised banquet. After nightfall Grelot released us. He always guarded Lady Dunaway in one wing of the house while I was sent with the falcon to the other. I was even allowed to take my meals in one of the upper rooms, alone, of course. When I did see Lady Dunaway we were cordial, but distant. It was queer how

285

our relationship could change so drastically with so little
said between us.

I shunned the third floor for fear of running into
Hatim. I spent most of my time on the second and first
floors. I seldom saw des Esseintes and when I did it was at
a distance. Whenever he was not "out conducting
business" for what grew more and more to look like quite
a vast financial empire, he balanced his time locked in his
study or working in the orchid conservatory. It was not
uncommon to see him from the upper floors tinkering
with an array of glass tubing and boiling flasks. Ilga was
forever at his side.

Several times messengers knocked at the door in the
middle of the Paris night, sometimes more than once
during the evening. Des Esseintes always read the wires
with interest and then slipped them into his breast
pocket, vanishing once again into his study. Often, when I
was returned to my cell, I heard the muffled sounds of
voices and unknown personages arriving in the flatboat.
It was evident that the house of Monsieur des Esseintes
was the center of mysterious activity. I never saw the
secret visitors, but more than once I spied a pair of gloves
left behind, an umbrella, or smelled des Esseintes's
hookah, and a feminine Eau de Cologne.

I spent my freedom in the house examining and re-
examining every point of possible escape. The windows
were out of the question. They were heavily grated and
the falcon would not let me within three feet of them. The
front door seemed likely, but again, I was not allowed near
it by the falcon. The cellars also seemed to be vulnerable
points. I recalled the doorway leading to the sewers
mentioned by Ursula, but several problems remained.
First, where was the key to the door kept? I did not
possess Lady Dunaway's skill at picking locks, and time
was too precious to risk making an attempt. Second, the
main doorway leading to the cellars was delicately
balanced upon its hinges so that if I did get through it a
second before the falcon, it would still provide no obstacle
to the bird. Every possible avenue was reduced to a single
factor, this small dappled creature, a few scant pounds of
muscle and talon. I was never without the falcon. Any
plan of escape must first include some way of dispatching

this bird. I still could conceive of nothing. I could not risk fighting it hand to hand. The slightest scratch would be my demise. I had no access to any medicaments with which I might drug the beast. I was stymied.

Not unlike Hatim I took restlessly to retracing my steps, searching, desperately hoping there was something I had overlooked. It was on one of these perambulations that I discovered a further secret about Lady Dunaway. It had become my habit to walk as quietly as possible, wishing to keep my activity concealed. I was creeping by the playroom when I heard her muffled voice. The door was closed.

She was humming softly, accompanied by the counterpoint of the music box. *"Ahhh, my little one ... my little one. Your needs are so few."*

Who could she be talking to? The playroom? 'My little one'? And then it dawned on me. What one thing could have caused her to betray me—a woman of principles and courage, a woman who had forsaken her home and reputation, crossed half of Europe? What was precious to her above all else? Visions of toys kept free from dust and little Ambrose's wonderful knots swept through my mind. I tried the knob. It was locked. Lady Dunaway's voice stopped. There was a sliding sound.

"What's going on in there?" I called.

The falcon ruffled.

At last my former compatriot opened the door. She was breathing rapidly. I looked past her, but the room was empty.

"What do you want?" she demanded angrily.

"Who were you in there with?"

"No one." She tossed a glance at the mechanical bird still tinkling plaintively on the shelf. "I was talking to the music box."

I could not believe she would openly lie to me. "There was no one else?"

"No," she said. I knew she was lying. I saw it in her eyes when they hesitantly passed mine. I saw something else. I saw relief, relief that I had finally discovered her secret. She turned and walked away.

I was too stunned to say anything else.

I knew she had not been talking to the little mechanical bird. There had been someone else in the room, someone who had left through a secret passage. That was why she was content to remain des Esseintes's prisoner. That was how he had gained control over her. Perhaps she left at night to soothe him, to calm his weeping. Little Ambrose was here! But where was Camille? Why did they keep this from me?

I could no longer contain my rage for Monsieur des Esseintes. It was clear that he had lied about the whereabouts of at least one of our children. For unknown reasons he had divided Lady Dunaway and me. It might have been simply to isolate us, to inhibit our plotting together to escape, but the fact remained: The vampire had a purposeful interest in idiots savants. They had abducted them for some reason. I did not know where Camille was, but somehow I knew her condition was a key or cornerstone to the puzzle.

As the evening of the party approached, the house exploded in a beehive of activity. Inexplicably, the servants began preparing a magnificent feast. On several occasions I saw Grelot and one of the boys bring in crates of fresh vegetables, fish, poultry, and even a suckling pig. Expectedly, des Esseintes delighted in the mystery of all of this and his standard retort became, "Wait and see! Wait and see!"

I knew it was the evening of the party when I awoke to find a fine black dress-suit draped over the end of my bed. The only thing missing was a silk topper, but prisoners being kept inside have no need of toppers, I supposed.

"Lady Dunaway," I said calmly, more out of curiosity than a need to communicate. There was no sound of movement. Grelot had come to release her before I awoke.

I wandered through the lower rooms of the house until I discovered Monsieur des Esseintes. *"Bonjour,* Monsieur le Docteur,"* he greeted simply. His attire surprised me a little. I had expected something more extravagant: ruffled cuffs and a profusion of jewelry. As it was, his dress was contemporary, an elegant but conservative black silk suit, much like one would see on any gentleman in the cabarets of Paris. A simple diamond stickpin and cuff links were the only hints of his wealth. He adjusted one of the cuff links as he examined my own attire.

"As I suspected. Your suit fits perfectly."

"Yes. Did you measure me while I slept?"

"I have a tailor's eye. Are you limping, Docteur?"

"I stepped on a piece of broken glass. When are the guests arriving?"

"Soon, very soon. Impatient?"

"Rather. It will be the first time I've seen a large number of 'your kind' in one gathering."

"At least the first time you were aware the gathering was 'our kind,' *non?*"

He glanced at a clock high on the wall of the foyer. It was a quarter past eleven. *"Je m'excuse,* Docteur. I have a few last-minute preparations." He finished ascending the stairs and vanished toward the back of the house.

I remained in the foyer. I peered into one of the glass globes and for the first time I noticed one of the stuffed birds was a falcon. Its glass eyes were perfectly reproduced and made me shiver. "That will happen to you someday," I said to my unwanted companion.

At length Grelot appeared in white gloves and tails. His clothing set a silly edge to his eternally disgruntled air. He looked straight out of the burlesque. He tried uneasily to ignore my presence. On occasion during the first few minutes of our wait carriages pulled close to the house, but none of them stopped. At eleven-thirty sharp came the first sound of wheels coming to a halt. There was the sound of voices. A carriage door opening and closing. Footsteps. The knocker rapped against the wood.

With no small amount of flourish Grelot opened the door.

In the distance stood a shining black hansom pulled by two slender roan mares. On the step stood a most pleasant-looking young gentleman in a black pinstripe suit and a fashionable straw hat with a black ribbon around it. His hands were in his trouser pockets.

"Allô," he said politely.

Grelot took his hat.

I was struck by the unpretentiousness of his dress, simple but refined. I extended my hand, but he politely declined.

"You must be *le Docteur.* My name is Fernande."

As he stepped across the threshold I examined his features. In appearance there was really very little to indicate he was different from any young gentleman one might see picnicking on la Grande Jatte. His hair was red and slicked back with brilliantine; his eyebrows, very red and quizzical. Of course, he had that flash of the eyes particular to the vampire, but it was not noticeable unless one were looking for it. His skin was very white and youthful, with an ever-so-slight iridescent quality to it, like mother-of-pearl. He could pass for early twenties.

"When were you born?" I asked before I realized the utter impropriety of the question.

He stared at me blankly for a moment. "August 2."

I became a little embarrassed, not knowing what to say.

At last recognition shone in his face. "You mean the year, *non?*" He tossed his head back and gave a gentle laugh. *"Mais oui,* the incredibility of the year. In the early 1370s, as far as I can determine. A year after the invention of the steel crossbow." He drew back and went through the pantomime of firing one, and then gave another gentle laugh. "Do not ask the ladies that, *monsieur.* They would take offense."

I was mortified. How could I have allowed my curiosity to cause me to blurt out such an insolent question? As he walked by, although he was several inches from me I felt a gentle but distinct prickle of something unseen, much as if someone had gently drawn hosiery charged with static across my arm. I gave a start, but the young man did not seem overly aware of his influence.

No sooner had he advanced into the foyer than another carriage pulled up. Out of this stepped two people, a man and a woman. The woman was most fashionable, with a small-waisted, black crepe dress. Around her neck was a voluminous bow of white silk, which fell down over her bosom. She balanced a very-wide-brimmed, black-ribboned hat with poise. Her eyes were sable and her features, petite. The man wore a black suit with a thin black tie. He sported an auburn goatee.

Again I was impressed by the unassuming stylishness of their appearance.

They introduced themselves by their first names alone.

The man's was Nicolas. The woman's was Perrenelle.
They too moved in their own glow of invisible energy.

In no time at all carriage after carriage pulled up until
the street was filled with them. I don't know what I had
expected: a barrage of ancient *grande dames*, powdered
wigs, and medieval raiments? Whatever it was, I found
myself repeatedly startled by the youthfulness and
simplicity of the continuing arrivals. This was no
ghoulish masquerade, this gathering of the vampire. It
was a congregation as festive and everyday as if the
clientele of the *Moulin de la Galette* had been transported
here intact. It was a parade of gay bonnets, striped pink-
and-blue dresses, ruffled blouses, black suits, and black-
ribboned straw hats—as intoxicating and careless as if
they had been plucked out of a Renoir. Only a lack of
pinkness in their cheeks perhaps betrayed their nature to
a discerning observer, a haunting porcelain sheen framing
haunting eyes.

It is difficult to describe their attitude toward me. It
was not snobbish. Aside from an overall unwillingness to
shake my hand, they were all most genial. Still, there was
an unexpressed something. Little cliques and gatherings
formed in the foyer. As their numbers grew the electrical
atmosphere of their presence became intense. It was not
unlike the pall of ozone, as if a bolt of lightning had
struck within the room.

I was most disquieted by this. I had always tried to
understand vampirism as a pathological condition, a
disease. The vast majority of my observations as well as
my firmly rooted scientific positivism supported such a
precept. Even des Esseintes's ability to see the quiver I
could construe as physiological. I, too, pretend to know
nothing of the spiritual, but I do know there are many
perceptual operations we know little or nothing about. It
is easy for me to imagine that his abnormal powers of
perception, and even the alleged mutation of his thinking
processes were hitherto unknown, but quite natural
phenomena; purely physiochemical functions of those
miracles we know as the retina and the human cerebrum.
But this electrical presence was not so easily explained.
What was it? Why was it there? As I stood gazing at the
crowd, a curious thing occurred. Three different vampire

spread out across the room; all loudly snapped their
thumbnails in rapid succession, but apparently utterly
independent of one another.

I heard a voice behind me and turned. The first thing
that caught my eye was the fiery splay of Fernande's red
hair against the lavender walls of the foyer.

Beyond, Monsieur des Esseintes descended the
rosewood staircase.

It was a quarter to twelve and about two dozen vampire
had arrived. Des Esseintes made his salutations, and the
guests began to filter through the house. For the
gathering Grelot had lit scores of additional candelabra,
and although they provided more light, the increase in
sources of illumination multiplied the number of shadows.
Each youthful profile, each movement of the hands cast a
dozen silhouettes about the walls and ceilings of the
grand old home.

The atmosphere did not allay my uneasiness. I strolled
into the parlor and noticed Ilga standing next to one of
the doors of the orchid conservatory. She was silent as
always. For the first time I realized that even among the
vampire she was a freak. Her flesh hung unnaturally. Her
eyes held none of their age or sparkle.

At midnight a final coach drove up, unexpectedly. I
heard a murmur of voices and returned to the foyer to
investigate. Grelot opened the door. There in the entrance
was a dream, a shimmering vision of a woman in a black
and silver striped dress. I recognized the quiescent lips,
the petal eyes at once. It was Madame Villehardouin. On
her hands she wore white gloves. On her wrists, gold
bracelets. The portion of her bodice covering her breasts
was of a white translucent cloth and over this, an endless
cascade of pearls. Her hair was up and fastened with a
flower. In the midpoint of her décolletage was another
bloom. She clutched a glittering gold mesh purse.

Again I was swept with the fog of her beauty.
Unearthly, a caliber above all mortal beauty. As I have
said, even though she appeared to be in her forties, there
was a tremulousness in her, an emotion brought close to
the surface. Beneath the gauze of her dress I was
intensely aware of her breath rushing in and out. And yet,

when she moved her head, the line of her neck, the ripple of her amber flesh was like a tigress.

"Does anyone come to greet me?" she said.

"Naturellement," des Esseintes returned, proffering his hand.

She slowly crossed the room to accept it.

"My invitation seems to have been lost in the mail," she said ambiguously. "I do hope it is not an absolute requirement."

Des Esseintes smiled and shrugged. He led her toward the parlor. The other guests seemed abnormally attentive. It was odd. Something was going on. Had des Esseintes purposefully not sent her an invitation? Was she chiding him? Why would he want to snub a member of his own species, let alone such a singular creature?

I followed them.

Much to my interest, when Ilga caught a glimpse of the Oriental, a trifle of emotion actually filled Ilga's face. Actually, it was more than a trifle. It was a look of heartfelt dread. Des Esseintes rushed to her comfort, and took the poor thing by the shoulder into the foyer. Madame Villehardouin withdrew a small Chinese pocket spittoon from her purse and proceeded to use it—delicately, but vulgarly.

Now, why was that? I caught her eye and I could tell she recognized me. But of course. She was simply using the faculties of her breed. I recalled her scanning both Lady Dunaway's and my face like some photographic machine the first time she had seen us. There was a hint of knowing in her glance. She walked by me. Uncontrollably, I held my breath like some retiring schoolboy. She was so spectacularly beautiful. As she passed I felt the palpitation of my heart. But there was one thing I did not feel: the electrical atmosphere that these other vampire possessed. I turned and watched her stroll through the crowd. Why should she alone lack the drone of energy I had first sensed in des Esseintes in the orchid conservatory, and I now perceived so strongly in his brethren?

I felt the flesh on the back of my neck crawl from an ionized presence. I turned to see Fernande standing behind me.

"What is it?" I inquired. "Wasn't Madame Villehardouin invited to the party?"

"I suspect not."

"Why?"

"Because she's a rogue. She wanders free from the herd."

"Is that why she frightens Ilga?"

"Not exactly. Do you know about Ilga?"

I shook my head.

"There was a time when Ilga was a happy, normal young woman. She was a *professeur*, a teacher of mathematics. It is said her dream was to found a university in Kiev. She was in Kiev when it was sacked by the Mongols. She was one of the unfortunate ones who survived. You may understand that better when you are aware that witnesses after the fact say that for kilometers around, the countryside was dotted with skulls. Monsieur des Esseintes found her being taken care of in a nunnery. Her soul was gone. All that was left was machine. He preserved her for his own purposes."

"Was Madame Villehardouin one of the invaders? Is that why Ilga shuns her?"

Fernande tossed his head back and laughed. "Madame Villehardouin—part of the Mongol invasion! No, Madame Villehardouin was quite some distance removed from the slaughter. She was a creature of silk and ermine, a concubine of the Emperor. It is not Madame Villehardouin that Ilga shuns. It is the epicanthic fold of her eyes."

Beyond the flicker of candles I saw the subject of our conversation drift gracefully into the darkness of the adjacent hall. Fernande's words had kindled an interest in me, but what was even more intriguing was the discovery that she did not emanate the enigmatic energy. I turned to follow, but as I stepped into the crowd the same mysterious thing occurred. Independent of one and other, several of the people in the parlor loudly snapped their thumbnails.

From nowhere, Perrenelle, a deathly beauty in her black crepe, appeared in front of me. Her sable eyes glistened.

"I've been meaning to ask you something, Monsieur le Docteur."

I glanced at her impatiently as Madame Villehardouin drew farther away. "Yes?"

"Are you married?"

Her question took me quite by surprise. I looked at the young Parisian woman and noticed what I thought was an honest interest in her eyes. Did I say 'young'? How many centuries had this pale creature seen? "Why do you ask?" I inquired.

"Because we must seem rather callous to you. We've taken you prisoner. We intend to keep you in captivity for the rest of your mortal life, and yet we laugh and carry on around you like you're an ignored child. Do you have someone who misses you? Are you married?"

"No," I said. "My wife passed away a few years back." I was touched by her sentiment.

"*Je me le regrette.* Is there anyone else? A family?"

How extraordinarily concerned, I thought. But then something struck me as being not quite right. "Yes, I have two daughters," I said, trying to figure out what it was. "I miss them very much, and I'd do anything to see them."

She shook her head disconsolately. Something about her reminded me of someone else. She continued: "It is an unfortunate world we live in. You have no idea how desolate I am over the necessity of your captivity. But fate has chosen to put two intelligent species upon this earth, the mortal and the vampire, and it is the inexorable distance between us that makes our actions necessary."

I wanted to believe her, but then I remembered. Many years before, when I had been an interne, I had encountered a middle-aged gentleman at a medical institution I was visiting for purposes of study. He reported to me at length about his incredible adventures in Ceylon, and all the while he spoke I had been troubled. It was only as he neared the end of his tale that I realized he had little or no awareness of my presence. In fact, he was a mental patient, and everything he had said had been a lie. I suddenly realized that Perrenelle possessed the same subtle detachment from what she was saying. It was a perfunctory condolence. In truth, the complex machinations of her thoughts were a thousand miles away from the words she was speaking.

"Please forgive us if we seem ignorant of your plight.

We are so different. They say we are the undead, and it is true. Our mortal sensitivities became obsolete long ago. After so many years the human in us has died."

I looked in her eyes. I admired the whiteness of her skin, her fragile features. "Tell me, Perrenelle, if the human in you dies, does love endure?"

She looked at me for several moments, but did not answer. She turned and stared at the man with the auburn goatee. For some reason her deliberation caused my heart to stop. I realized her answer meant more to me than I would have previously suspected. The rustling of her dress, her transcendent air only added to my suspense.

"Yes," she finally said and I experienced a flush of relief. "But it is different. We are different. We have changed."

I sadly gazed at her one last time before I excused myself and drew away. I wandered down the corridor searching for Madame Villehardouin. I caught a glimpse of her as she rounded an immense Chinese vase, but when I reached it she was nowhere to be seen. Around the corner and out of sight I caught a fragment of conversation.

"*Mademoiselle,* does Savin continue?"

"No, a pinch of cardamom."

"It was not ruined, was it?"

"Silk."

"Only to taste."

"He fell and ripped his suit."

I turned the corner and rushed headlong into the gilt-and-turquoise sitting room only to see Grelot arriving with a silver tray and two steaming cups of coffee. A gentleman with a Hapsburg mustache took a pinch of cardamom, sprinkled it in one of the cups, and handed it to the woman he had been talking to. Both regarded me blankly. The same clicking of thumbnails passed quickly through the room.

I grew apprehensive. What did it mean? Their conversation was nonsensical. It followed no direct line of reasoning, yet there was a hint of convoluted sense to it. I suddenly remembered des Esseintes's remark about restructuring his language in a way that we could comprehend. In a flash of wonder I understood. They had hammered it into me. Their thinking processes were different. The syntactical logic of their language had permuted, gone beyond our plodding and linear communications. I surveyed the crowd of half a dozen vampire standing in the room. In all of my experience I had never known des Esseintes to reveal a hint of nervousness. He was as placid and immutable as the Sphinx. As I scrutinized the figures before me, however, I detected a host of minute fidgetings and movements. Here a finger flexed. There a cheek twitched. I also noticed that the vampire in the room were exceedingly observant of all of this. Eyes moved languidly from movement to movement. Thumbnails clicked. It dawned on me that they were signaling one another. I have heard it said that the ancient Incas possessed a language of knotted strings. More and more I realized I had to consider the vampire a separate culture—indeed, a separate and distinct civilization existing hidden and within our own. Why wouldn't they have developed a language just as alien and unique? The incalculable generations of their camaraderie alone would have created such a language. They knew each other like actors who had spent a lifetime on the stage together. I suspected the complexity of communication conveyed in their glances, in their most subtle gestures, was greater and more rapid than most mortal conversations.

As I moved through the room I realized they might be discussing anything, the price of attar of roses, or the fate of my own life, and I would have no inkling of it. I was an exile among most peculiar foreigners. I could understand the words, but not the language.

As I entered the room the conversation shifted into a decidedly different gear. It became more narrative and understandable to me, but something about it still suggested it was a code of some manner and possessed a second veil of meaning.

"I discovered a curiosity shop the other day," said a young woman with a camellia corsage. "I wished to purchase a gift, a stereopticon, to give to a woman. She lay in her deathbed, you see, and I wished to raise her spirits. I met her in the darkness and placed the magic lantern in her hands. It spun ... *chatoyant* ... emitting changeable

rays like the eyes of a cat in the dark. It tinged her
eyelids, and molded the lineaments of her hands."

At exactly the same moment, two people at opposite
ends of the room lightly scuffed their feet.

A woman standing opposite the first continued the
patter. I circled the room looking for Madame Villehardouin. I was forming a theory about her as well, and if I
was correct I suspected she, if anyone, might provide the
key to my escape. I did not see her in the room. I turned to
leave, ignoring the allegorical conversation of the two
young women, when my ear suddenly selected a meaning-
ful fragment from the prattle. "—*Rue de la Glacière.*"

I spun about.

The two women stood against the wall. The gentleman
with the Hapsburg mustache had joined them. Intrepidly,
I approached the group. "Excuse me for interrupting so
rudely, but did you just mention the Rue de la Glacière?"

"*Oui.*"

"I only venture to say something because that street
above all others means something to me. It's a very
special little street, don't you think?"

"All streets are special, Docteur," she returned calmly.

"Ah, yes, but I still maintain the Rue de la Glacière is
special above all others."

"*Chacun à son goût,*" she said politely and nodded her
head. I noticed her glance at the palpitation of the
heartbeat in my temple.

"You do not see the 'quiver,' do you, *mademoiselle?*" I
said.

"*Non,*" she returned, reassessing my eyes.

I gave a courteous bow and walked away. I was about to
continue to the next room when Grelot appeared and
announced dinner.

Like the finest of genteel crowds, the guests moved in a
slow and ceremonious wave toward what I presumed to be
the dining room. I had not seen the dining room before. It
had always been packed with human servants, and I had
not wanted to burst into the middle of them. Now, as I
passed through the tall amboina wood doors, I saw it for
the first time. I need not describe its opulence in detail,
save that it was a masterpiece of fine woods and
marquetry. The two most prominent features of the room

were the great chandelier of deer antlers over the table, and the carved falcon heads on the arms of each of the numerous walnut chairs.

As we entered I heard Fernande mutter, "The buffet once belonged to Louis XV."

I looked at the buffet and saw that it was, indeed, worthy of the possession of a king. Furthermore, it was covered with a kingly array of food. That was rich, I thought, glancing at the canines of a young woman tilted back in laughter.

I was still searching the guests for Madame Villehardouin when Lady Dunaway appeared in the doorway. I had forgotten about her. To my surprise she wore a low-cut black evening gown. It was the first time I had seen her broad white shoulders and long neck. Once again I marveled at how she carried her large and awkward frame with such an exotic beauty. Her black hair was done up atop her head and elegantly accented her broad face. The only flaw remained her glasses, ever present, and she wore long black gloves. The regretful smile had faded from her face. Now she was only watchful and distant.

At last Madame Villehardouin appeared and Grelot begrudgingly set a place for her.

And then he began to serve the food.

The table was set in a magnificent explosion of silver and crystal. Wine was poured. Platters were served. But not a morsel was eaten. Instead, they only sniffed it, luxuriating in the vapors like some fairy aristocracy congealed for a make-believe party in the material world. Forks lifted. Goblets clinked.

And what a feast it was. Roman-style suckling pig with pine nuts. Truffles and cognac-perfumed duck. Escargot à la Bourguignone, black breads, and cheeses. Consommé with marrow and purée of chestnuts with Bordelaise sauce.

I ate, but I was so luridly fascinated with the macabre spectacle going on around me I merely picked at the food. I was no longer cognizant of the secret communications going on between the vampire, but I did not doubt for a moment that they were there. I suspected each chink of silver. I looked for other meanings in every glance. I was enveloped with a feeling of utter loneliness and isolation.

In my low spirits I became painfully aware of something
else. In some ways I considered myself the oldest member
at the table. My face had started to crease. My hair was
graying. I looked at my hands. They were not old yet, but
they were different from all the others around me. In
them was the shadow of what they would become. Time
had begun to sculpt.

I surveyed the crowd.

These were not old people. They were children, strange
young children with sloe and scintillant eyes, toasting
and inhaling life. Château Hautbrion flowed like blood.
Oranges in Grand Marnier syrup passed before me.
Pastries with buttercream mousseline. Rum mousse and
candied violets.

Across the table I saw Lady Dunaway sitting silent. She
nibbled listlessly on a sliver of duck. Her hand brushed
against the locket around her neck. Every ounce of her
attention was upon me. She was a very special woman.
Even against the vampire she fared admirably, a creature
of rare determination and voracious instincts. Perhaps
she had been manipulated by des Esseintes. Perhaps I
could understand, but the fact remained, we had come
into this together. We had fought and worked together,
and she had betrayed me. Our eyes met for one brief
second. I could take it no longer. I stood and left the room.

In the foyer I heard footsteps. I looked up and saw
Hatim standing on the balcony, his eyes trained on
something in the shadows. There was a fascination in his
gaze, much like the falcon's when it spied a rat in the
cellar. More footsteps, but not Hatim's. He was stalking
someone.

Whoever it was vanished before I saw him. The Persian
boy followed. I made my way up the rosewood staircase.
The falcon followed behind. I looked in the direction I had
last seen the hunter and his quarry. At the end of the
corridor I heard a woman gasp. It was an odd exhalation,
ambiguous as to whether it had been caused by pleasure
or fear.

By the time I reached the end of the hall they had
already gone farther into the warren of ancient rooms. I
heard someone stumble. The footsteps quickened. There
was another slight cry. I scaled the second set of stairs

two at a time, and this caused quite a bit of frenzy in my feathered foe. It obviously did not like me moving so frenetically. I reached the damp and mildewed hallway in time to hear the creaking of the steps leading to the turret room. There was another series of faint and rapid exclamations. Was it a playful panic? Was the woman in trouble? I reached the steps of the turret room.

The door clicked shut.

I lifted a foot to ascend the stair when I caught the brazen eye of the falcon. There was a thud, as of someone sitting or being thrown upon the filthy mattress.

For a few moments I was frozen, wondering who the woman was. What was happening? It was useless to feel the rage of helplessness. The ancient boards creaked. There was movement in the room. A gasp. Movement. With a shudder I recalled the wretched smell of the little chamber.

I heard a sound behind me.

I turned to see Madame Villehardouin standing in the shadows just a few feet away.

"Are you really in so much curiosity?" she asked.

"What is happening up there?"

A warm wind wafted through the house and fluttered the rotting curtains as she stepped forward. She appeared gilded in the flickering light of the ormolu candelabrum. Her pearls rustled languorously over her bodice. Her teeth shone white, as white as her necklace.

"Of what concern is it to you?"

I blushed. I had never been so discourteous in my life. A gentleman had no place doing and saying the things I found myself doing and saying. On the other hand, my every uncivil inquiry might prove vital to my survival. How preposterous my mannerly existence was in the face of the unknown.

A faint suspiration rose from the room.

"You have heard of the incubus?" she said. "The male spirit or devil who seduces women?" She tossed a glance at the door above. "Just because we are of such low blood pressure does not mean certain bodily functions do not work."

"You mean Hatim's . . . well, his more gentlemanly operations are intact?"

"How delicate!" she chortled. She spun impishly about, throwing her head back and closing her eyes in wicked amusement. "How vedy, vedy proper!" Her movement caused a tempest of dust to stir from the walls and swirl through the candlelight. It was a disarming juxtaposition, the vibrancy of her beauty against the deteriorating house.

"Accounts of the incubus invariably refer to their uncommonly low body temperature. Have you ever wondered why? *C'est la mer à boire. Chacun à sa marotte.* Go and witness for yourself!"

She stepped in front of the falcon as she nodded me on. I climbed the rotting stairs carefully. I peered through the crack in the door at the decrepit little room. It had not changed. It was still malodorous. The floor was worn black from endless pacing. My vision passed over the sparse furnishings, the table, the falconer's glove. I could not see the mattress for the angle.

"The archives of the Parliament of Paris in 1616 recorded the testimony of a twenty-three-year-old woman who had been seduced by one of those wanderers of the night," Madame Villehardouin called from below.

I leaned far over the railing until at last I saw the ticking of the mattress and the shadows rippling over Hatim's naked torso. His breeches were loose and his brown and muscled loins moved rhythmically.

" '. . . she knew the devil once,' " the Oriental woman continued. Her breath was sibilant.

Beneath the Persian was a woman, her face severed by darkness. He moved a brown hand slowly up her rib cage, kneaded the large pink aureole of her white breast.

" '. . . and his member was like that of a horse, cold as ice and ejected ice-cold semen.' "

A pearl of saliva dripped slowly to her neck as he moved with sinister precision.

" '. . . and on his withdrawing it burned her as if it had been on fire.' "

I am ashamed to say I was frozen in my voyeurism. It was the same immobility I had felt at the eggshell window of my youth. Who was the woman, I thought? With terrifying grace he sunk his fangs into her jugular. She shot up, wracked by the draining kiss as she wound

her arms around his dark shoulders and enveloped him in
the tangle of her hair.

For a moment I thought the hair looked familiar. The
hands. The image wavered in my mind. No, it couldn't be.

"Ursula!" I cried.

Madame Villehardouin tried to stop me, but I burst into
the room. Hatim dropped the woman and lurched back,
blood frothing at his lips. His eyes were aflame with the
same obsidian gleam of the falcon's.

"Ursula!" I repeated, but it was then that I saw. It was
not Ursula. It was Geneviève. Her eyes were red and
glassy. Only the faintest hint of awareness shot out of
them, a furtive, half-present modesty.

I quickly retreated.

Within moments, in the darkness, I heard Madame
Villehardouin's slippers padding in the rotted carpet.
There was a hush of breath near me.

"Who is this Ursula?"

I turned and gazed into the petal eyes. They were
darkly intent upon my answer.

"My daughter," I said simply.

She accepted the information, and something told me
her cerebral machinery, a mind centuries old, was quickly
mulling it over, processing it behind the sublime and
probing eyes. "I see," she said with a knowing edge to her
reply. She looked at me with an odd mixture of distance
and sympathy.

All of these things—her reception at the party, her
searching eyes, her uncharacteristic hint of sympathy—
convinced me my theory was correct. Madame Villehardouin, like Niccolo, had been changed to a vampire
because of her phenomenal beauty. Even Hatim had been
changed because of a talent, not because of genius. This
was the dividing line. She was an outcast because she was
not privy to their secret language. I had suffered just a
fragment of the resulting alienation only minutes before
in the gathering below. What sort of melancholy or
spiritual devastation would such segregation cause over
the centuries? To be alone from humanity, to be a
vampire, was one thing. But then to be alone again. I
began to understand the depth of Niccolo's sadness and
Hatim's abandon to his instincts. She had not changed as

the other vampire had. She had not shed the last vestige
of her humanity. Therein lay a hope.

My eye traced over the bridge of her nose, her
cheekbone. "May I venture to tell you how exquisitely
beautiful you are," I said. I had hoped the compliment
might soften her, but it had exactly the opposite effect.
Her pupils narrowed.

"I was a concubine of the Kublai Khan," she said
without feeling. "Just as he collected leopards and roe
bucks and sent hordes of elephants over all his territories
to bring back the most grand and immense trees for his
gardens, so he collected beautiful women. We were rated
in carats, like gold. Every feature had its measure, one
carat for shape of face, another for sweetness of breath.
He imported five hundred of them a year, from Ungut, in
Tartary. For many years I was one of his more favored."

She ended abruptly. I wanted to ask her to continue, but
I did not want to offend her. My heart was pounding.
"May I inquire as to what happened next?"

She turned to me slowly, the gauze of her bodice
whispered over her shoulders. I realized she came from an
age and culture of even more rigid protocol than my own.
There was a time when even the most trifling breach of
social etiquette made in her presence might have resulted
in a flogging. A trace of contempt passed through her
expression as if she were considering putting an end to
further questions, but then she looked at me with the
same remote pity.

"I died," she said unadornedly.

Again I noticed the ambiguity of her age. There was
something both youthful and timeworn in her.

"My last human memory is of touching my hard, dry
lips. I was taken in a pestilence. I drifted into darkness."

"How is it that you are here to tell me these things?"

"I am here because an astrologer of the court also
favored my countenance, a vampire. In China the dead
were not immediately buried. They were kept in their
coffins in the stables, often for many months, until the
astrologers fixed upon a favorable day for their interment.
In the delirium of my fever the astrologer infected me. My
first vampire memory is of the coffin opening and seeing
the face of the astrologer framed by the stars."

She emitted a long exhalation and I gazed at her rising breast behind the veil of her dress. There was no trace of pestilence, of chancre or open sore. Her flesh was as healthy, as smooth and golden as a fallow deer.

"So you were changed because of your beauty."

"Yes."

"Is that why you are an outcast?"

She turned to me and glowered.

"*Madame*, I most humbly beg your pardon—"

She shook her head, anger brimming in her eyes. "The times . . . the times," she said. She looked past me and lapsed into a deep reflection. "I once met an artist here in a café. He was a very disturbed man. His name was Edvard. He said there were three types of women, only three: the virgin, the widow, and the whore. He could not desire without feeling it was evil. He was afraid of women. He thought their hair was embued with life. He feared it would entwine and smother him."

I was at a loss as to why she was telling me this.

She looked back at me. "Why did you come to my house? Why did you chase me all over Paris?"

I told her the entire story, of Camille and Lodovico, and she raised her eyebrow. When I finished she spoke.

"You see, they are up to something."

"You do not know what?"

She became scornful. "They do not tell me anything. But I do know they are very busy these days. There are vampire all over Paris, stealing about and mingling with the unsuspecting. They are playing a strange game. I do not know what the game is, but I do know one thing: If Lodovico was here on the Île Saint-Louis, des Esseintes knew about it. Des Esseintes knows everything that goes on in this city. There is no stone he does not have eyes under."

I had already realized it was true, but her confirmation still had its effect upon me. It had happened again. Like Niccolo, des Esseintes had lied from the beginning. He, too, was working for Lodovico. He had used Ambrose to gain control of Lady Dunaway. He most assuredly knew where Camille was. And where was Camille? Something in my heart told me she was not in this old house.

A breeze once again fluttered the candle flames and the

flower in Madame Villehardouin's ebony hair. Once again
the visage of a young girl, ardent and nubile, appeared
like a specter in the mature lines of the face. The advent
of the apparition caused her to take another deep breath.

"What do you think of des Esseintes?" I ventured to
ask.

The eyes darted sadly. "What can I think? I despise
him."

It was as I had thought. Here was my chance, my one
opportunity. "Madame Villehardouin," I entreated, "if you
have any notion of how I must feel here, if you have ever
loved as I love my daughters, would you help me escape?"

She was struck dumb with horror and surprise. The
youthful presence instantly faded. "Oh, no, *monsieur*, I
cannot do that," she said, shaking her head as the full
extent of her dread slowly shone in her face. "I dare not."

"Madame, with all submission I beg of you."

She shrunk back, still shaking her head. She gently
lifted her skirts and turned to leave. "Daintily, daintily, I
retire," she said, saturnine and deranged, "with a footfall
so light not even the moth is disturbed." Her dress scraped
against the rotted carpet as she quickly rushed away.

There was one thought in my mind, one thought alone.
I turned in the opposite direction and rushed down the
hallway. I descended the first set of stairs, the falcon
flapping and hopping behind me. When I reached the
rosewood staircase I discovered the party had moved into
the foyer and were lounging about on chairs and pillows,
passing the hookah. Their eyes were glassy, and a cloud of
blue smoke hovered in the room. Monsieur des Esseintes
was seated at the black harmonium. Around him were
strewn orchids.

He looked up.

"Monsieur le Docteur, you are just in time. I'm going to
play now."

I noticed Fernande smiling.

"I did not know you were musical," I said.

"It is not music, exactly," des Esseintes returned. "You
see, I've disconnected the pipes. A different fragrance of
orchid has been placed in each bellows. When I play, sound
does not come out, but smells!"

He adjusted the harmonium.

"How like the vampire the orchid is," he said, holding a bloom aloft. "They are called parasites, and yet they do not kill their host." He placed the bloom in a receptacle attached to one of the pipes. "They can live in darkness. They would wither in the hot sun." He sealed another bloom. "They are rare and delicate creatures, and they grow in hidden places."

I noticed Lady Dunaway sitting next to the glass globe containing the bullrushes. To her left the young gentleman with the Hapsburg mustache finished with the hookah and passed it to her. To my horror she accepted it. She inhaled deeply and then gazed at me. She was not sheepish, but blank. Changed.

Des Esseintes posed his white hands over the keyboard. He began to play.

Silence.

A chorus of admiration rose from the throng as the first smell swelled in the room. His long fingers danced over the keys in haunting silence. He brought them crashing down in empty cadenzas and graceful imaginary arpeggios as fragrance after fragrance filled the room. *Cattleya. Cymbidium. Lepanthes.* A dream garden. A phantasmagoric fugue of scent.

They were lost, lost in their own world.

I was not a part of it. I was awed by its foreign splendor, as I might be awed by the world of the shark, or the deep-sea fishes, but I could never survive in it. I looked at des Esseintes. He had lied with such ease. At least Niccolo had felt some anguish, but des Esseintes had woven a tapestry of deception with callous and unflinching facility. How could I ever feel safe again? He had assured me I would not be hurt, but how did I know that was not just another deception? Nothing could surprise me. Anything could happen next. I had to escape.

I left the foyer and wandered into the corridor of the statues, searching still another time for something I had overlooked. The falcon watched me closely. I burst into the turquoise sitting room and madly scanned the black-lacquered fan-vaulted ceiling, the wainscoted walls. I spun about and gave a slight gasp when I noticed *la machine* standing motionless in the corner.

"Ilga," I burst, "is it true? Will I die if I attempt to leave this house?"

"Oh, yes."

"Then it is impossible for me ever to escape?"

Her pale gray eyes fluttered. "Oh, no."

I was stunned. "What do you mean?"

"You would die if you attempted it on your own. But you could escape if you had help."

She rattled off the words mechanically. Not a speck of emotion played in her face.

I trembled. "Ilga," I asked falteringly, "would you help me? Would you tell me how I might escape?"

"Why, yes," she said with perhaps just the tiniest bit of surprise.

I checked the hall to make sure no one was within earshot, and then I returned to the timid creature. She explained in detail how I might make my escape, noting to the second precisely how much time I would have for each of my actions. She finished and lapsed back into her vapid, dreamy state.

"Ilga," I prodded, "if I do this, des Esseintes will not be able to stop me?"

She looked vaguely worried. "If you do everything correctly. As I have said, time is the crucial element. You must not waste a second, or all is lost."

I looked down into her eyes. There was only a fleeting and bleary awareness in them. "Ilga, I have one other question."

She made no reaction.

"Do you know where my daughter, Camille, is?"

"In Italy."

"Where in Italy?"

"I do not know."

"Do you know why they have taken her?"

"No."

I looked toward the door. I had to hurry. I did not want anyone to see me speaking with her. I grasped her cold, lifeless hand within my own. "Thank you, Ilga."

I ran over everything in my mind as I returned to the foyer. Des Esseintes was still seated at the black harmonium, crooking his arms and swaying like a spider over its web. His head fell back weightlessly. His eyes were closed in ecstasy. The vaporous tracings of the hookah hung low over the room. Each face smiled, eyes closed. Even Lady Dunaway was enchanted by the spell.

I had a decision to make. Would I take her with me?

I no longer trusted her. I had no idea what concessions she had made to the vampire, but my sense of English honor ran too deeply. I could not abandon her. It would be the ultimate act of cowardice and dishonor. I crept behind the crowd and placed a hand upon her shoulder. I was somewhat relieved to feel the warmth of her flesh. Her head lolled back, eyes glassy. When she saw the expression on my face she took a grip upon herself. Her gaze became more serious. She followed me into the corridor of the statues.

"I'm leaving," I said.

"Now?" she demanded.

"I've asked Ilga. She's explained to me a way."

"What about the falcon?"

"Ilga has told me something about our little friend here. He doesn't like the orchid conservatory. He's afraid of it. He never goes in. If we enter through the sitting room and cross over to the parlor entrance to the cellar we will gain exactly three minutes, forty-seven seconds' lead on our little demon. Enough time for us to escape through the cellar and into the sewers."

"It's a trick. It won't work."

"I'll have to take that chance."

"They'll catch you in the sewers. You can't outrun them."

"I have a trick of my own up my sleeve. I believe it will work."

She was obviously very troubled. She glanced back anxiously in the direction of the foyer.

"Lady Dunaway," I said, gripping her arm, "I know about Ambrose."

Her eyes widened.

"I know they are using him to control you, but if you ever want to get away from here, have your child back on your own terms, we must leave."

"Then what?"

"The authorities."

Her temper flared. "No, you can't . . . we can't. The

vampire are not evil. I have spoken with des Esseintes at
length. He does not confide in me any more than he
confides in you, but I have observed him closely. I believe
he is a creature of ethics."

"*His* ethics."

"But he is not evil."

"He lied to me."

"He lets me see Ambrose. He has been kind to
Ambrose."

"If they are not evil, why have they taken our
children?"

"If you turn him in, what do you think it will gain for
you? The authorities laughed at me. Do you think they
will believe you?"

"At the very least we can use what we know of his
identity as ransom to get our children back."

She could not argue with that.

"I am leaving. Do you want to come with me?"

She looked upward. "What about him? We can't leave
without him."

"Where are they keeping him?"

"There are rooms inside the house, secret rooms. He is
locked in one of them."

"Do you have any notion how we would get him out
without arousing their attention?"

"We have to try. Surely you don't expect me to leave him
here."

"My good Lady Dunaway, I do not expect you to do
anything. I felt it was my moral obligation to ask you to
accompany me. We would have to leave Ambrose here. As I
have said, if you ever want your child back on your own
terms, I feel this is your only chance. Will you come with
me?"

I could see it in her eyes, thoughts of Lucien and her
barren life in Cornwall. She could not go back. Was it
possible that this had become her world, a dazzling and
alien treasure trove for a woman misplaced and unhappy
in her human existence? I braced myself for her refusal.
Her lip quivered hesitantly.

"Yes," she returned at length, and much to my surprise.
"I will go with you."

"Then it's now or never," I returned. "We must not give

the falcon any indication of what we are about to do until the very last second. As Ilga has explained, the moment it realizes we intend to enter the conservatory it will attack. If we get in and start to make our way across it will immediately go around through the house and try to head us off. We must move with speed and precision."

She nodded as we walked slowly toward the sitting room. The falcon followed dutifully. When we reached the chamber of turquoise and gilt we pretended to be examining the walls. Ilga still hovered in the corner, alabaster and mute. I glanced down at the falcon. It watched as it always watched, never tiring of its scrutiny. Always acute.

"The craftsmanship is superb," I said, allowing my finger to drag along the wainscoting. We took a step back and toward the secret panel concealing the French doors. I gestured at the black-lacquered ceiling, taking still a further step backward.

Nictitating membranes flicked.

I glanced at Lady Dunaway. She watched intently. Casually I made a motion as if I were merely leaning against the wall. In an instant my hand hit the secret button I had seen des Esseintes hit. One of the painted panels hissed out of sight, and as the pinions spread to fan the air we burst through the steam-covered doors.

The falcon gave a cry.

It was too late. It flapped helplessly beyond the threshold, oddly intimidated by des Esseintes's bejeweled and balmy garden. We were on our way. I looked back only once to make sure the bird was not following. Beyond that every second was too important to spend time watching as the feathered devil set off on its own course of interception. After making our way through the diminutive jungle we darted through the conservatory entrance into the parlor. Lady Dunaway fell.

"My ankle!"

"Let me see." I stooped beside her. She looked at me helplessly. I turned her white ankle around in my hand. She uttered a cry.

"It might be broken."

"Yes," she gasped halfheartedly.

I looked toward the door. "We must continue!"

"I don't know—"

I grasped her gloved hand and pulled her upward with the full of my strength. We limped toward the cellar entrance.

"I don't know!"

She leaned heavily upon my shoulder as I dragged her through the cellar doorway. I shut the door behind us, knowing it would do little good. It swung lightly on its hinges and there was nothing in sight with which to prop it shut. I struggled to help her down the steps. It was too much. She seemed helpless. "You're not trying!" I hissed. My fingers gripped deep into the flesh of her arm as I pushed her on. "I've seen you put your weight on that foot. It's not broken if you can do that. You must continue."

I harshly propelled her forward and she stumbled a few steps, but did not fall. She turned and glared at me with alarm. When we reached the cells I told her where Ilga had said to find the key, and sent her to the door leading to the sewers. I turned again, expecting them to discover us at any moment. I dashed into my cell to retrieve the necessary objects, a handkerchief, my papers and money clip, and my half-empty bottle of Lilac Vegetal.

As I turned to catch up with Lady Dunaway I was stunned to hear the flutter of wings, and see the demon's eyes glint amber as it alighted. We had taken too long. Lady Dunaway's fall had given it the few seconds it needed to catch up with us. I moved back.

It stepped forward into the light like a pompous little general. It strutted ludicrously, eyeing me with clear delight. I grabbed one of the torches from the wall, and the flame gave a windy sound as I brandished it at the bird. It hopped back, a hint of sudden concern in its glowing eyes. Its head swayed back and forth like a cobra's as it calculated my vulnerabilities.

"Dr. Gladstone!" Lady Dunaway called.

"Stay there, the falcon."

It hopped to one side and I swung around, keeping the torch between us. It continued to pitch back and forth in slow undulation as step by step it circled about me. I thrust the torch at it once again and it leaped back. A rasping screech came from the hook of darkness beneath the beak. It groused.

As I neared the exit it grew more frantic, spreading its pinions, and casting grotesque shadows against the wall. Suddenly, talons plummeted through the air and I batted the torch. The falcon flapped in an explosion of feathers and came at me again.

"Dr. Gladstone, please!" her voice echoed in the maze of tunnels beyond.

"Is there a boat, a flatboat?"

"Yes. Can't you please hurry? What is happening?"

The very instant I started to involve a portion of my mind in answering Lady Dunaway's questions the falcon perceived its chance and came at me again. This time I struck it soundly with the very brunt of the fire. There was a hideous crackling as it screamed and fell to the floor. The air filled with the stench of burned feathers. In a flash it was on its feet. A large area of its breast and neck were singed to its sickening gray flesh, but it was still intact. It was livid. The coppery irises of its eyes expanded and contracted in the changing light.

I moved.

I could almost feel it behind me. I swung savagely in the darkness and was wracked by the heavy thud of another impact. It gave a second iniquitous and riveting screech as I reached the entrance of the sewer and swung the door shut behind me. On the other side the falcon threw the whole of its weight desperately against the wood, and only my holding the planks kept the door from swinging open. It thrashed again.

"What do we do?" I heard my companion gasp. I turned to see her still garbed in evening gown and gloves and standing on the slimy edge of rock. A peeling and ancient flatboat rocked gently in the black and fetid waters of the Paris sewers. Beyond, as Ilga had described, stretched the openings of three dark passages. Water flowed through them like blood through an abattoir.

In the flatboat was a large squarish stone used as an anchor. Lady Dunaway brought it to me and I propped it solidly against the door. Again the falcon crashed against the wood, shrieking and floundering in rage.

Lady Dunaway started to get into the flatboat.

"No," I said. I opened the bottle of Lilac Vegetal and emptied a small portion of it upon the seat of the boat. I

wedged the torch upright in the prow and untied the raft.
Giving it a shove, I sent it drifting downstream in the
inky current. The flame illuminated the aged, vaulted
arches of the sewer as the boat swiftly swept into the
distance.

"No, we go this way," I directed, pointing upstream. I
motioned at the narrow parapet of ocher stone. I resealed
the bottle of Lilac Vegetal and washed it in the filthy
water.

"My foot is aching," Lady Dunaway complained.

"Why are you doing this? You must continue." She
glanced anxiously at the door. Was she having second
thoughts about leaving Ambrose? She reluctantly continued. We inched into the darkness.

I did not know how old the sewers of Paris were. Older
than London's. I recalled but a fragment of history about
Henry II renovating them, and that was before
Shakespeare was born. Without the torch it was difficult
passing. We had to feel our way along the clammy, slime-
encrusted walls. It was a necessary unpleasantness. We
paused to listen and could hear nothing but the babble of
the water and the ominous scurrying of the sewer vermin.
Here and there dark shafts twisted upward through the
vaulted tunnel and ended in the gratings of the gutters
sixteen and twenty feet above our heads. A faint light
shone enticingly through the slits.

Lady Dunaway slipped and nearly fell. "This damn
gown!" she cursed.

At last we came to a shaft through which snaked a
rusted ladder.

"Do you think you can make it?"

"Yes," she sighed, slowly starting the climb.

I followed.

I was duly impressed when her strong arms pushed
against the heavy metal plate and slid it adroitly upon the
bricks of the street. She clambered out.

When I finally stood beside her I saw, as Ilga had
predicted, that we were immediately before the footbridge
leading to the Île de la Cité. I looked around. Surely they
had discovered our absence by now. I only prayed that my
ruse with the Lilac Vegetal had worked and they were

following the wrong trail. If it had not worked we were lost. No carriages yet. We crossed the bridge.

I felt a strange rush of feeling as we made a wide path around Notre-Dame. Half a millennium ago, a gathering place of alchemists. A monument to the vampire filled with strange symbol and cipher. At one and the same time it represented an awesome and fascinating secret and the last vestige of my imprisonment.

Winded, we reached a battery of police wagons lining the street outside the Prefecture. Some were emptying new patrons and others were just pulling out. We slowed our pace and tried to look as casual and dignified as possible. In the darkness the spattering of sludge and filth upon our handsome clothing was somewhat invisible.

Lady Dunaway looked at me curiously as I ripped the handkerchief I had brought into shreds and surreptitiously tied one onto the back railing of one of the empty wagons. Next I dribbled a generous portion of the remaining cologne upon the remnant. I proceeded to do the same to the next wagon.

"You cannot do that," she said sternly.

"Why not?"

"We do not have the time."

"This is our only hope. You know as well as I do we will have no chance if they catch up with us."

"Hein? Que faites-vous?" exclaimed a voice as a figure in the familiar blue rounded cap and cape of the police rounded the corner.

"Admiring the horses, my good fellow," I said in my most chipper English.

His expression changed from anger to mere irritation. *"Vous êtes anglais. Quel un casse-pieds, vous anglais—"*

"Yes, yes, terrible pests, we English. But tell me, if we were attending a coronation would we wear teacups or armchairs?"

"I speak perfect English," the officer said to my surprise. "You are speaking absurdities."

"Most absurd, we English. Which way to the Champs-Élysées?"

He pointed his baton toward the river. "That way, *monsieur.*" He regarded the muddy bottom of Lady

Dunaway's gown with perplexity. He walked away shaking his head.

Lady Dunaway said nothing as I tied another shred to a wagon farther back and doused the shred with cologne. I paused in my work as a group of officers stepped into the first wagon and pulled onto the cobblestones. The shred of handkerchief wafted in the wind. I was about to do another when a sound caught our attention.

We turned.

In the distance along the avenue of paraffin lamps rolled a fashionable black coach drawn by Hackney stallions. My heart froze. "Up on the steps," I ordered as we passed between the police wagons and ascended. The coach approached slowly.

Are we safe, I thought? Surely they would not dare follow us into the Préfecture. The seconds ticked by slowly. I gazed at the hooves of the horses. They clopped loudly on the stone. Too loudly. The wagon glided by. The driver was oblivious. In the back a middle-aged gentleman, very drunk, laughed and rolled a doxy in his arms.

I breathed a sigh of relief. I looked at Lady Dunaway. She was not relieved, but worried. The evidence was too telling, her complaints about her ankle, her apprehensive glances. Either consciously or unconsciously she was trying to slow us down.

"Let's go into the station," I said.

Lady Dunaway frowned at me suspiciously. "You're not going to turn des Esseintes in?"

"No."

Still mistrustful, she followed.

I knew what I had to do. I knew that within hours after our escape des Esseintes would temporarily suspend "the work" of the vampire in every corner of the city. As Ilga had said, time was of the essence. I also knew that I had to move alone, and Lady Dunaway would never willingly submit to that. She was too strong-willed.

When we approached the bench the desk officer looked down at us wearily.

"Monsieur l'Agent," I began. "I discovered this poor creature trying to commit suicide. She was walking into the Seine, but I forcefully rescued her. Could you please see to it that she is protected from herself?"

Lady Dunaway turned upon me with such rage she was speechless. She swung about as if to run when her eyes came to rest on the four-barreled pocket pistols of the two approaching officers. She returned her gaze to me, her eyes filled with such venom I almost regretted my action. But she had betrayed me in her secrecy about Ambrose. At least my betrayal was for her own welfare.

"*Vraiment,*" said the desk officer as the agents led her away.

Once out of the Préfecture I was heartened to see that another one of the wagons tied with a scrap of handkerchief had pulled out of the station.

There were no cabs in sight so I proceeded on foot. They would be looking for two of us, two of us running, or a speeding hansom. They might ignore a solitary figure. I threw the remains of the bottle of Lilac Vegetal into the Seine as I messed my hair and ruffled up my dirty coat. I hunched over and ambled as much like one of the *clochards* as I could master as I crossed over to Quai Montebello and headed south.

Once a hansom sped by me, swiftly and silently. I paid it no heed, not wanting to arouse attention. I do not know if it carried my pursuers. As I neared the Sorbonne the streets became more active, filled with students out reveling and cluttering the cafés. It was on the Boulevard St. Michel that I recognized a carriage of the vampire. Sitting sedately in the back was the same man with a Hapsburg mustache and young woman I had seen at the party. I skulked quietly into a little bistro and watched from the window. I did not think they saw me.

The carriage stopped and they stepped casually to the street. Again I noticed how unobtrusively they melded with the other young people, just another couple in the crowd. Who would dare imagine they had walked these same streets with Thomas Aquinas or Becket?

With no particular sense of purpose they crossed.

I scanned the bar. It was thinning out. A woman in a black-and-lace-fringed dress stood behind the mirrored counter and only a few tables remained occupied. It would be difficult to hide. I glanced again at the street. They were approaching the door.

I made my way to the back exit.

As I neared the door a hand reached out and latched onto my arm.

"Pardon, monsieur..."

In terror I searched the young gentleman's face. Had he been at the party? His eyes were hazel, his beard black. Was there age in his eyes? They certainly sparkled. His cheeks were pale.

I laid my hand against the flesh of his arm and was swept with relief to feel that it was warm.

I pulled quickly away.

"His lace is untied," I heard him say incredulously behind me. *"Mon Dieu,* only his lace."

I burst into the narrow alley. It was time to run. Above the narrow warren of tenements I saw the stately dome of the Sorbonne. I kept to the alleys. I iontinued south. It was beneath a stone ledge closely flanked with a wrought-iron fence that I stumbled into a rubbish pail and sent it clattering down the bricks. The sound roused another presence. I heard movement, but I could not see what it was.

In a panic I stupidly tripped over still another pail and made my way toward the narrowest pass between the ledge and the fence. Something else also made its way.

It was tight, not meant for human passage.

There was a rushing of air.

I burst into a little square centered by a fountain. Behind me came the sound of wings. A shadow swooped above. I was too terrified to scream. I merely lurched forward, stumbling and trying to protect my head. It was then that I saw my pursuer.

Pigeons! A flock of pigeons disturbed by my clamor. They spread out over the fountain and alighted on the cornice of an opposite building. There was only the gentle sound of water splashing. Above that, silence. The square was empty.

The farther south I traveled the more secure I felt. They could not cover the entire city. It was some time before I reached the Rue de la Glacière. I strolled along the neat row of houses until I came to No. 24. It was a quaint little structure backed by arbors and a minuscule garden. The house was dark. In the garden was a tiny shed. I stepped over the fence and crept along the rows of convolvulus and poppies. I looked through the glass window of the shed. In the moonlight I made out a perimeter of counters covered with bell jars and scientific equipment. It was a makeshift laboratory. I moved to another window and discerned a desk, a shelf of books, and papers. It was difficult to focus, for a thick wire mesh had been placed over the window and played tricks with my eyes. I leaned against the door of the shed and my fingers brushed against something cool and metallic. I glanced down to see a row of no less than eight locks spanning the various latches of the door. Either there was something very important in that laboratory, or it was run by a very frightened person. Or both.

I flashed back to Chiswick ... Dr. Chiswick ... the grates over the windows, the paranoia of the locks. I tried to recall everything Cletus had told me in our last meeting. A doctor going mad in Liverpool. An airship capable of carrying tremendous cargoes. What was it they all had in common? Each one was a scientist. Each one had made a discovery. And what was the most sought-after thing of these cold-blooded creatures? Knowledge. But why had every one of them gone mad? Was it because the vampire was such a different order of being, prolonged interaction with them caused mere mortals to lose their minds? No ... that was not it. It was something much more deliberate. More sinister.

A twig snapped on the walk outside the house.

I turned to see that a light had come on in the little house. Someone was moving about. I stealthily slipped into the shadows beside the shed. The front door opened. In the faint and misty lamplight I saw a figure round the corner of the house. A woman. It was difficult making out her features. She seemed young, slight of frame. I caught a glimpse of her face as she passed by the light of the window. Yes ... she appeared frightened, but her brow was determined. She held her skirt up to pass through the dewy convolvulus and poppies. She paused in a clearing in the garden.

I heard her voice, but it was too low to determine what she was saying. She was speaking to someone. A large bush blocked my view. I wanted to move to get a better look. But dare I? Was she a vampire? Would she detect the slightest squeak of grass beneath my shoes?

Another voice sounded. A low murmur.

I had to see. I moved like a cat slowly leaning into a pounce. I scarcely breathed. The infinitesimal rustling of my shirt seemed thundering. It took an eternity before I gained a better vantage. At last, among the foliage of the bush I saw the woman and her companion standing in the garden. The moonlight shone full upon his face, that same innocent face.

Niccolo.

I knew at once what was happening. *Oh. . .* I did not know the purpose, the complete meaning of the design, but I knew what was transpiring there in that garden. That woman was being drawn into a mysterious world, allured by a guileless youth. And she was in danger of her life. Soon they would prey on her worries, riddle her with doubt and fear, until she destroyed this little shed. And herself. I recalled the words of the woman at des Esseintes's party: *I wished to purchase a gift, a stereopticon, to give to a woman. She lay in her death-bed . . . and I wished to raise her spirits. I met her in the darkness and placed the magic lantern in her hands.*

A game was being played. A cruel and enigmatic riddle of the Sphinx.

For what purpose?

A test?

An amusement?

The woman raised her voice. "But why . . . *why?*" I heard her gasp. To no avail. Niccolo melted into the night. I could not see her expression, but I knew it was wrought with concern. As she lifted her skirt to return to the house I stepped out of my hiding place.

"Mademoiselle?"

She turned quickly. She considered running.

I approached within a few feet of her.

"Monsieur?" Her voice faltered. She reached to a small silver cross around her neck.

"Mademoiselle, I do not know who you are. I do not know what that incredible young man has told you, or what you have hidden in this little shed. But I do know one thing."

Her frightened eyes searched my face.

"I'm not asking you to trust me. I'm asking you to trust no one. You are in great danger. You must choose no allies but yourself. That boy who was just here, that angelic boy. He can enchant you with his tales. Some of the things he says are true, but he spins a web of lies and manipulations. You must get away from here. Before it is too late, go somewhere for a few weeks where you and your work will be safe."

I could tell she was stunned by the urgency of my voice. She tightened the chain of the crucifix until it bit into her neck. She was wondering. Dare she believe me? Dare she accept? She trembled, her dark eyes madly trying to penetrate what lay hidden in my face. She turned quickly and rushed back into the house.

In fear for my own safety I swiftly made my retreat from Rue de la Glacière. I tpent the remainder of the evening huddled behind the rectory of an old church. It was scarcely twenty minutes after I had left the woman in the garden that I heard the pealing of the bells of Notre-Dame. Was it a coincidence? How deeply did the hierarchy of their power extend? Was the baleful tolling of the bells another cipher, an alarm meant for special ears?

I waited for dawn before I ventured out of my hiding place. As soon as the first haberdashery was open, with some of my remaining money I outfitted myself in a respectable suit and proceeded to the Préfecture. The desk clerks who had seen me the night before were off duty. I presented myself as Lady wunaway's physician and she was released in my care. I had already wired Cook to learn what name Ursula had registered under. Expectedly, Lady Dunaway was incandescent, and we fought like Kilkenny cats all the way to the Hotel Madeleine. When we reached the address the bell captain directed us to her room, and when the door opened we discovered Ursula standing beside a wickerwork portmanteau and a walking stick protruding from a sausage roll of tartan-plaid traveling rug.

Without a word spoken we raced toward one another and embraced. All of the anger I had felt seemed unimportant. It was a strange sensation feeling the solidity of her flesh and bones beneath my hands. It must have been quite some time since I had embraced her so, because for some reason I realized, as if for the first time, it was no longer the solidity of a young girl, but a woman. I thought back to the closeness we had once shared. I stepped away and looked at her.

She seemed older. Her red hair fell loosely over her shoulders, flowing and abundant, and caught the sunlight in a way that reminded me of her mother. I did not remember its being so wavy, but then again I was not in the habit of seeing it before she had done it up. I was impressed anew by her beauty. Her long neck, round face, and large eyes still possessed a determined and melancholy cast. Her dress, however, had undergone a further transformation. She now wore the full uniform of the New Woman, a bold denial of conservative female fashion. Her skirt was a dark blue with a bright red belt, and she wore a full blue-and-white-striped blouse with a tiny lace collar.

"Father," she finally said, "what are you doing with her?" She tossed an irreverent nod at my companion. Lady Dunaway, still in her muddied evening gown and an overcoat given to her at the Préfecture, stiffened and bristled.

"Why shouldn't I be with her?" I asked. "Not that we haven't had our differences. But we're still in this together." I noticed a copy of *The Continental Time Tables* resting on the bed. A grim thought passed through my mind. "Ursula, you weren't leaving while we were still prisoners?"

She appeared hurt, but not surprised by my remark. "No, Father." She picked up a letter resting on the portmanteau and handed it to me. "It's to the Sûreté de Police," she went on. "Inside I've explained to them all of the criminal details of the case and told them to contact Inspector Inglethorpe of Scotland ard for confirmation. I did not find it necessary to add that Monsieur des Esseintes was a vampire."

"But why the deliberation, Ursula? Why didn't you do this the first evening I saw you?"

Lady Dunaway's ears pricked.

"I've been living in a world of confusion. I had to think about everything."

I glanced again at the traveling paraphernalia. "And where are you going now?"

She was sad, but determined, even affectionately apologetic. "It's not what you think, Father, but I'm going to follow Niccolo. He booked passage this morning at the Gare de Lyon."

My heart sank. I had just regained her. I did not want to lose her.

"Niccolo!" Lady Dunaway cried. "What do you know of Niccolo?"

"Enough," Ursula said. "For two consecutive evenings now I've followed him after he's left a human household at 24 Rue de la Glacière. Last night I trailed him from there to the Gare de Lyon."

"Gare de Lyon?" I said. "Do you know where he's going?"

"Where does anyone go from the Gare de Lyon? To the Mediterranean. To Italy, I presume."

Lady Dunaway was lost in alarm. All of the blood had run out of her face. "What was he doing at 24 Rue de la Glacière?"

"I'm not quite sure," I returned. She was expecting a reply from Ursula, and Lady Dunaway turned to me in shock. Her mind seemed to be racing ahead, making other connections.

"I was also there last night, but I did not see Ursula. I went there after I placed you in safekeeping at the Préfecture. As for what Niccolo was doing, he was speaking with a young woman in the garden. I suspect he was playing a game of the mind, spinning Gordian knots. I wanted to warn her, but how does one warn against such a chimerical and undefined danger? The same way Niccolo admonished you. I told her to trust no one. Nothing is as it seems. I told her to get away from here."

"How did you know the address?" she demanded incredulously.

"Ursula visited me through the sewers."

She gripped my arm, and even through the glove her hand was clammy with shock. *"Why wasn't I told?"* she gasped. At first the intensity of her reaction surprised me, but then I realized. The occurrences at 24 Rue de la Glacière seemed to have unknown and fearful meaning for Lady Dunaway. What was her one vulnerability, the nerve that would invoke such a response from her? Her son. Had the meeting in the garden at 24 Rue de la Glacière somehow involved the safety of her son? Emotion raged in her face. "How could you interfere without confiding in me?"

How could she ask such a question? She commanded such a sense of utter vindication I nearly answered her. But I did not. I had other concerns.

"Ursula, why do you want to follow Niccolo? It's not because you want to be taken into the world of the vampire. Otherwise, why didn't you just present yourself at Monsieur des Esseintes's door?"

"Well?" Lady Dunaway repeated.

Ursula's expression fell a little.

"Believe me," I said, "my only concern has been and always will be your safety and well-being. Is there any chance that you might believe I'm honestly worried about you?"

Lady Dunaway's fingers dug deeper into my arm.

"Ursula, I don't want you to go."

Lady Dunaway flew into a rage. "Well!"

I turned to the older woman. I could not help but feel it was a little pathetic—we were both so deeply and desperately concerned for our children. "How can you ask that after what you have done? We had an agreement, you and I, but you abandoned it. Your only concern was your own child. Once you found out Ambrose was safe, you clung that one discovery to your bosom and allowed nothing else within your trust. You let des Esseintes use Ambrose to divide us. Don't you see how he manipulated you?"

"Oh, Father!" Ursula reproached.

I looked into the older woman's eyes one last time before I turned to my daughter. She held her weathered expression with nobility. I could not help having compassion for the depth and conviction of her instincts.

Ursula spoke. "Don't you know? It's what I wanted to tell you the night I visited you, but we argued instead. But surely you must know by now." She expelled her breath resentfully as the words blurted out of her lips. "There is no Ambrose."

XXIII

I looked at Lady Dunaway.

"Is this true?"

She remained mute, but the unflinching steadiness of her gaze told me her reply.

"How did you find this out?" I asked Ursula. The two women glared at each other.

"Through the papers, of course. One would think the kidnapping of the son of a British lord would receive as much attention in the press as the kidnapping of the daughter of a prominent physician. Imagine my surprise when I could find no mention of it. Imagine my further surprise when I discovered Lord Dunaway is listed as having no children in the Social Register."

I don't know what I felt at that moment. What a fool I had been. I had unquestioningly allowed a total stranger to become my closest confidante. I now had no idea what manner of creature, good or evil, lurked behind that most sincere and uncalculating face. "Who are you?" I said, stepping back, reading fearful new meaning in the large and powerful arms, the alien qualities of the woman. "What possible reason has caused you to deceive me as well? Are you working for Lodovico?"

Was she still another incredible and inhuman species of being—not vampire, but something quite as strange—an automaton, a further mental oddity working in alliance with the master race? Nothing could shock me. No possibility would be too unbelievable. A hint of movement passed beneath the ominous camouflage of the overcoat.

"Leberecht," she murmured cryptically as she wrung her hands together. "I must wire Leberecht." She paced anxiously toward the window as both Ursula and I stepped back, wondering what was going to happen next.

"Who are you?" I repeated.

"What's in a name?" she asked impassively. She demanded no absolution. She began to pace again and then stopped, looked at us, and glared. "I lied. Your daughter has done her research well. I really was talking to the music-box bird when you overheard me in the playroom. I purposefully did not quell your suspicions because I did not want you to know the truth—that there is no Ambrose. There never was."

She showed signs of resuming her pacing when she realized we were still aghast. "Oh, come now, Dr. Gladstone, is there any use in my telling the truth? I might ask the same question you inquired of your daughter. Is there any possibility that you could ever accept what I said?"

"Only if you give me the chance."

Without further argument she said: "Your daughter might also tell you that the Social Register lists Lord Dunaway's wife as Sarah. In truth, I have no idea what Lucien and Sarah's matrimonial life is like. As for myself, my real name is Hespeth von Neefe, M. D., D. Ph., D. Lit. I am a member of that disparaged and ridiculed breed, the vampire hunter."

She stood proudly after reciting the words, as one who had just revealed the Gospel to the pagans.

"How do I know you are telling the truth?"

She spied a fountain pen on the bureau, dipped it in ink, and scrawled across a piece of stationery: *Dr. Leberecht Weber, University of Vienna.* "You may ask Dr. Weber of my credentials."

"Who will vouch for Dr. Weber's credentials?"

"The University of Vienna as well as half of the academic world," she said indignantly. "He is a renowned philologist and folklorist. Naturally, the university knows nothing of his pursuit of the vampire."

Dr. von Neefe proceeded to draw a picture of what it meant to be a vampire hunter that was quite contrary to what I was prepared for. I had assumed that she and her colleagues carried stakes and hated Niccolo and his kind, but nothing was farther from the truth. The network of vampire hunters consisted largely of scholars and a few wealthy eccentrics. They knew the vampire existed. They studied their historical traces, and the actual rare meeting between mortal and vampire. Most of all, however, they were drawn to and enchanted by the vampire. The rabble may have viewed the vampire as loathsome and monstrous, but to the well-fed and intellectual upper classes their world was a glittering ultima Thule. They hunted the vampire because they envied them. They were drawn to them out of a sort of romantic vision, as any scholar might be drawn to his field of pursuit.

"Why didn't you tell me about yourself in the beginning?" I asked when she had finished.

"You wouldn't have taken me seriously. It was much more expedient to appeal to your emotions."

"Do you think I will take you seriously now?"

"I believe you will."

"Why?"

"Because you have been through a great deal. *We* have been through a great deal. The unbelievable has become a part of your everyday life. I think you are much more willing to believe me when I tell you I am deadly serious in my line of work. I think you can now understand what it means when I say I am haunted by Niccolo and Lodovico. You see, my uncle was a vampire hunter, as my grandfather before him. My grandfather actually met Niccolo briefly, in Vienna. My grandfather's crumbling diary describes in detail the same youthful and disarming face we know today. Look and see."

She withdrew the locket from around her neck and opened it to display a painted miniature and an engraving. The miniature was of a craggy and moonstruck old gentleman with ruffled white hair and porkchop sideburns. The engraving was in a style reminiscent of the old German masters. The subject was undeniably Niccolo.

"You see, I am on an ancestral spiritual quest. I am motivated by a desire perhaps even more deeply felt than your own."

"What of Niccolo's warning? Did you make that up?"

"No," she said distantly. "It is true it was not delivered to me, but I did not make it up. It was given to my grandfather one snowy evening in that city of the harpsichord and the waltz."

"What do you know of the vampire that I"—I looked at Ursula—"we don't know?"

The tension in the air had lessened. The haggard woman walked over to a chair before the window and sat down. "Very little, I think. Dr. Weber and I have scoured the genealogies of kings and the graves of a hundred famous men and women. We and our colleagues have discovered the names of a dozen or so suspect personalities. For example, there are some who believe the entity who was to become Sir Francis Bacon has appeared throughout history under a number of different identities. They cite evidence that his funeral in 1626 was a mock funeral and assert that he later appeared in Germany under the name of Johann Valentin Andreae. It is true engravings of Andreae and Sir Francis Bacon are uncannily similar, but who can say? The exact dates of births and deaths before the nineteenth century are limited to parish records, and even these are sketchy and difficult to track down."

She looked at me with uncertainty. "You recall des Esseintes spoke of the references in the first English translation of the Bible to the vampire or *lamya*. It was Sir Francis Bacon who edited the King James version of the Bible and changed all references of the vampire to 'sea monsters.'" She searched for the fountain pen once again and scribbled a note to herself. "I must wire that to Leberecht."

"What of the work of the vampire—what do you know about that?"

Her expression became very serious as she looked out the window and nervously wrung her hands together. "As I have said, it is very difficult to obtain information on them. We believe they have been among us at least since antiquity and probably before. We know that on occasion they have mingled with kings and even infiltrated the highest offices in the land, but we do not know the true extent of their involvement in our cultures, the amount of their influence, or their ultimate purpose."

"You must have some theories."

She turned to us again. "There are those who say they are tampering with history. I do not know. I do know one thing: Their abduction of your daughter was a most astonishing act. Under ordinary circumstances they prefer to remain behind the scenes and perform their deeds indirectly, by influence and trick. That they would act so boldly and directly is most unusual. It must be a very special time for the vampire. Something very urgent is at hand, a major turning point."

I recalled the similar remark of Madame Villehardouin, but I was befuddled. How on earth did my little Camille fit in? What possible consequence could my innocuous daughter have upon the matrix of history? I noticed that Dr. von Neefe had once again lapsed into her troubled meditation out the window. The trees on the Left Bank shone brightly in the sun, but it was not the scenery that disturbed her. It was something she was not telling us.

"Dr. von Neefe, you still have not offered your beliefs on why they are doing these things. Is there some malevolent purpose to it?"

She regarded us pointedly. "I do not know. That is why I was so reluctant to leave Monsieur des Esseintes's house. I felt I was getting closer to the truth. What that truth is I only wish I knew. There are some who believe there is a very definite evil close at hand, some danger. I"—she shook her head—"I just don't know. I don't believe there is. I don't want to believe. Dr. Weber has always proposed that the game of the mind is only an illusion, a side effect due to the vastly different rationale of our thinking and existence. He has done much research on encounters between widely dissimilar cultures—"

"That's preposterous. Niccolo's deception was no side effect. He lied and created confusion for a specific purpose. His meeting with the woman in the garden is also no side effect, and the fact that the woman is apparently a *professeur* at the Sorbonne is no coincidence. They have a very definite interest in scientists, and their intentions are most definitely evil. They are sowing confusion and their objective is to drive their victims mad."

A look of horror crossed her face. "How do you know that?"

I told her in detail about Dr. Chiswick, the engineer at Oxford, and the doctor in Liverpool. I told her all the other things that fit in as well, Madame Villehardouin's words and des Esseintes's meticulous scouring of a profusion of newspapers and scientific journals. I had not seen the

Aerology Quarterly among them, but I had no doubt that it
was there, that des Esseintes or Lodovico or some other of
their number had spied the article on dirigibles by M. W.
Radner and for unknown reasons sent out their minions
to begin the game.

Profound disappointment shone in both women's faces,
although Dr. von Neefe's expression had a stamp different
from Ursula's. In Dr. von Neefe's features was a subtle
indication she already knew or at least had considered
what I was saying. It was also obvious she did not want to
believe it. She shook her head slowly.

"Perhaps you are wrong. Your evidence is all very
circumstantial."

"I don't think you believe I am wrong."

She said nothing, but her grim countenance revealed
her answer. She turned again toward the window.

"Why were you sometimes absent from your cell when I
called to you?"

Without turning she replied, "There was a secret
entrance. Des Esseintes often sent for me."

"Why?"

"He is a creature of exceptional cunning. He met with
each of us separately to gain a free hand in dividing us,
setting us against one another."

"Did he know your real name or that you were a
vampire hunter?"

"No."

I was skeptical. "But certainly des Esseintes could have
looked you up in the Social Register just as Ursula did
and discovered that you were lying. Why on earth didn't
he?"

"Because of my passport," she answered simply. "As you
yourself have seen, my passport does list my fraudulent
identity. I have certain connections that enabled me to
obtain a forged passport printed on official paper and
with legitimate government seals. Because the passport
itself proved genuine Monsieur des Esseintes did not
question the information it contained."

Still another question surfaced in my mind. "But why
did you behave so strangely and refuse to speak with me
about your disappearances?"

"I was afraid. I remembered Niccolo's warning to my

grandfather"—she fingered the locket—"to trust no one. Des Esseintes used that to make me suspicious of you, to drive us apart."

Suddenly Ursula stepped forward. "I have a question: How did you know it was Niccolo who had kidnapped Camille? When you read about it in the newspapers how could you be so sure it was the vampire?" The acuity of her inquiry pleased me.

"Because of this," Lady Dunaway—or Dr. von Neefe—asserted and pounded her bosom with her fist. "There is something in my heart that guides me. I am compelled. It is my destiny. I think you may comprehend even more fully than your father the nature of this special obsession. We are seekers of a magical world, you and I. We are possessed by a mysterious and unknown force. All I can say is that, inexplicably, the moment I read about your little sister in the papers I knew with complete conviction it was the work of the vampire."

In her typically proud and aloof way Ursula prickled at the comparison between herself and the older woman. Dr. von Neefe noticed this, seemed disappointed by it, but took it in stride.

"I have another question," Ursula continued. She directed it to both of us. "What will Monsieur des Esseintes do about your escape?"

Dr. von Neefe answered. "About that I think we can both agree. For the sake of his survival alone he will be intent upon recapturing us. If your suspicions are correct, Dr. Gladstone, that the vampire are involved in some sort of vast design, they may be willing to risk everything to get us back."

"There is but one thing for me to do," I said.

"Yes," the older woman replied. "If your daughter is correct about Niccolo's booking passage at the Gare de Lyon, we must follow him."

"No," I said.

At this Dr. von Neefe's eyes widened in shock. "What do you mean?"

"I have discovered my life's work is in the hands of a man of no integrity. It is imperative I return to London."

An unreasonable rage returned to her face. "You can't be serious! You mustn't abandon this chance. If"—she faltered—"if you are correct about the vampire, somehow your daughter seems to be the crux. Surely you must realize Niccolo is leading us right to her."

"Of course, I realize it. Ilga herself told me Camille was somewhere in Italy."

"And your work is more important to you than your own daughter?"

"No!" I snapped angrily. "I have much greater concerns than my investment in my research or even my daughter. Do you remember what I told you about the virus I was working on? You yourself recognized how potentially dangerous it is. It is a strain of *influenzae* that completely lacks antigenicity. You are intelligent enough to know what would happen if it were ever released." I shook my head. "You do not know this man as I know him. I know it is the height of folly to return to London, to the very place they'll be looking for me, but if *Camillus influenzae* were to be handled improperly, more than just Camille's life may be in danger."

Dr. von Neefe stormed toward me. "But—" she sputtered. "You—" And then another change shot through her face. It was as if she suddenly realized the seriousness of the situation. With wrenching reluctance she said, "Very well, London. We will go to London first."

"We?"

"As you said yourself, Dr. Gladstone, we have had our differences, but we are still in this together. Won't you understand? Won't you forgive? We are still striving for a compatible goal, you and I. Given our ignorance of what dangers lie before us, isn't there still an advantage to our working together?"

Was there? A thousand little doubts flitted about my mind. I still harbored a great deal of resentment over what she had done, even mistrust.

"Very well. If you wish to accompany me, you may. I must warn you, however, you will not sway me from my decision."

With a resurgence of painful resignation she said, "Then I will accompany you." Again something in her winced. "But Niccolo . . ." she murmured. "We can't just let him slip away from us."

She turned to Ursula.

"You must follow him."

Ursula's eyes darted toward me for acceptance. In light of the peril of such an undertaking I writhed at the notion of letting her pursue this seraphim of a darker realm.

"Father, please," she begged. "All I've ever wanted was your approval. I understand the risks involved. I want to help."

"She has already proved herself to be extraordinarily resourceful and capable," Dr. von Neefe added. "I will put her in contact with Dr. Weber for advice and counsel. She will not be able to wire us while we are in transit, but she will be able to wire him at the university. For the sake of little Camille we cannot let this chance pass us by."

I looked again at Ursula standing before me in the garb of the New Woman. Expectedly, she still prickled at Dr. von Neefe's assistance. Ursula was such a proud creature, but the hope and need in her eyes struck me to my soul. I looked again at the portmanteau. It was unheard of to allow a female to undertake such a dangerous and responsible mission, let alone one's daughter. It went against everything I had been taught. In the whirlwind of my confusion I recalled a little boy who had stood before his father, longing, wishing with every fiber of his existence that insight would somehow transcend tradition.

"Very well," I consented.

We sent out for a couturier to outfit Dr. von Neefe. For her dress she was content with plain brown cotton. As for her outer garment, she was not happy until she had a tweed cloak and ulster. In the short time permitted we were unable to obtain a two-peaked cap. I was terribly angry with her, particularly in light of the gravity of our situation, although I discerned new significance in her Sherlock Holmesian attire. In view of her new identity as a vampire hunter, several other quirks of her character made more sense as well—her unladylike aggressiveness at the British Museum, her resourcefulness in seeking out the Services en Commun, her artful display of lock picking when we first broke into des Esseintes's house.

I was also struck by something else. I had underestimated the woman I had known as Lady Dunaway. I had seen certain unusual and admirable traits in her, but I had not foreseen the intellect or the full scope of the personality now before us. Indeed, the fact that she had been able to carry off such a masquerade so unwaveringly was a tribute to her ever surprising will. Although I did not tell her, these new insights into the woman I now knew as Dr. Hespeth von Neefe only increased my already marked esteem of her. I was still deeply chafed by her hoodwinking me, but another equally powerful emotion swelled within me. Although I tried to conceal it, and didn't even quite want to admit it to myself, I was intrigued and fascinated by her newly revealed line of work.

It was afternoon when we finally bid Ursula a tortured farewell and left the Hotel Madeleine. On the way to the Gare du Nord we stopped to wire Dr. Leberecht Weber at the University of Vienna. Dr. von Neefe was taken aback when I insisted on reading the message and address for myself. I was not going to take any chances. Considering the knavery she had perpetrated already, I thought such an action was completely justified. The address appeared to be legitimate and the message was an innocuous and brief account of our status as well as an introduction for Ursula. During the day when Niccolo was sleeping Ursula was to wire Dr. Weber from the resting point and wait for his counsel by return wire.

We had but one purpose in returning to London: to get *Camillus influenzae* away from Dr. Cletus Hardwicke. I did not know exactly how we were going to achieve this. I knew we could not waste time bringing in the authorities. Not only would this give Cletus time to formulate some plan of evasion, but it also would give the vampire more time and opportunity to intercept us. I had only one option: to take my old adversary by surprise and confront him myself. I did not know how I would retrieve my work. I only knew from the rage and hatred within me that I would succeed.

At last we reached the Gare du Nord and purchased one-way tickets to Dunkerque. Even though it was the middle of the sunny afternoon I was apprehensive. Dr. von Neefe's words kept passing through my mind. *For the sake of his survival alone he will be intent upon recapturing us.* I looked around at the crowded bookstalls and the waiting rooms. There was the typical rush and bustle. *If your suspicions are correct . . . that the vampire are involved in some sort of vast design, they may be willing to risk everything to get us back.*

We had no luggage. We went directly to the boarding line. There were perhaps twenty people ahead of us. It was the same at the other gates up and down the cast-iron supports of the roof. The queues were backed up and at the head of each line was a conductor punching tickets and two men in plain clothes checking papers. I looked at the station bar behind us. It had been gaslit and busy when we had first arrived in Paris. Now it was closed, but several conservatively dressed gentlemen still leaned against the counter. People were grumbling all around us. It was unusual for the queue to be moving so slowly.

I looked again at the two plainclothesmen at the head of each line, and back at Dr. von Neefe. She did not seem particularly worried about them. I snapped my fingers and motioned for a porter. "Could you please find out what is taking so long?" I said, producing a sizable bank note. His eyes twinkled at me knowingly. He strolled up to the gate and scuffed about with a perfect air of slovenly disinterest. It was obvious he was an old hand at it. He asked one of the men for a light and casually perused the papers he was holding. He engaged in a brief discussion and then walked away. Instead of coming directly back he assisted a lady with her luggage. I glanced at the men at the station bar. They were looking in the opposite direction.

At last the porter returned to me. "They're Agents de Sûreté, *monsieur*. They are looking for an Englishman. It is said he stole a vast fortune of jewels from a wealthy gentleman on the Île Saint-Louis." He winked at me shrewdly. "May I suggest, *monsieur*, that you go down the street and take the stagecoach to Chantilly. From there you can take the railway to the coast." I nodded and covertly pressed another bill into his hands. Thank God it was a day and age when porters had to help the passengers—or starve.

Dr. von Neefe made a pretense of ruffling through her cloak and forgetting something. I shrugged my shoulders with commiseration and we sedately turned to leave. In the flurry of the crowd no one paid any attention. We slowly made our way to the door. I turned one last time and looked at the men leaning against the counter of the station bar. Their eyes were still on the gates.

We walked through the exit into the street. I was about to squeeze Dr. von Neefe's hand when we walked face to face into Grelot. He was fashionably dressed in a dark frock-coated suit. His hair was pomaded. The falcon perched upon his arm.

"Bonjour, Monsieur le Docteur, were you going somewhere?" He lifted the hood from the falcon. A third of its body and the side of its face were singed and blistered. It ruffled what few remaining feathers it had left against the nauseating gray of its flesh. It leveled its enraged eyes upon me. It gave a low and guttural rasp of recognition.

"We were wondering which station we would intercept you at."

"What are you going to do?" Dr. von Neefe demanded.

"Nothing if you will slowly walk toward that waiting carriage." He nodded at des Esseintes's black hansom across the street. The same liveried boy sat in the driver's seat, waiting patiently for us.

"And if we don't?" I asked.

For the first time since I had known him "little bell" broke into a grin. "I will allow this falcon to make its reparations."

"I think not."

The smile was short-lived. "Do not tempt me, Docteur."

"Do not try to make me believe what is not true."

"What do you mean?"

"The station is crawling with police officers. I do not think you will make the falcon attack us in front of so many witnesses. Don't you realize you would be sent to the guillotine for that?"

It was obvious Grelot was not an intelligent man and had not considered that possibility. He was visibly shaken. He looked first in my eyes and then in Dr. von Neefe's. "You would not take the risk."

"Oh, wouldn't we?" I said, taking Dr. von Neefe's hand. She hesitated, but then turned.

"Stop!" Grelot called behind us as we slowly walked away.

I could feel it, feel the falcon's rabid eyes burning into my back. It gave another feverish and grating cry.

"I warn you for the last time: Stop!"

We continued to walk away, expecting at any second to hear the falcon take to the air. But it did not. When we had traveled a good distance down the street I turned to see Grelot standing and shifting his weight from foot to foot, speechless. When we reached the carriage stables there was already a stagecoach loading. The driver motioned for our luggage, but when I told him we had none he motioned for us to get in. Once seated on the fusty, straw-stuffed cushions inside I looked back at the station. Grelot had overcome his stupor and rushed inside. I did not have to be told why. He was frantically enlisting the aid of the Agents de Sûreté to track down the thieves who had "stolen" Monsieur des Esseintes's fortune in gems. I leaned out the window. "When is this coach due to leave?" I inquired.

"We're already ten minutes overdue, *monsieur*, but I've had instructions we're to delay for some old lady."

I looked back at the station. By now he had surely attracted the attention of the men at the station bar and was explaining the situation.

At last an elderly lady appeared in a mammoth hat with netting, hobbling and talking a mile a minute to her browbeaten maid. The lady motioned to her footman to take care of her trunks.

I looked again at the station. They still had not appeared.

The old dowager grunted and heaved, taking an impossible length of time to step up into the coach. Her spiritless maid assisted ineffectively from behind. At last, amid a ponderous flurry of knitting, penny dreadfuls, and boxes of bonbons she settled into the seat and forced her servant to position herself in the remaining crevice.

In the distance the plainclothesmen appeared in front of the station and madly looked around. Grelot broke into the street and pointed at the coach.

Oblivious, the driver cracked his whip at the horses and we started to roll away. The faint sound of whistles met our ears. I casually peered out the rear window and saw the plainclothesmen running and waving wildly for us to stop. We picked up speed. It was too late. For the moment they had lost us.

From Chantilly we took the train to Boulogne without incident, and I told Dr. von Neefe all of the intricacies of my past experiences with Hardwicke. It was while standing on the deck of the ferry and gazing at the dark and foggy waters that I began to realize something else about the woman beside me. I sensed her presence, sensed it reaching out toward me, but in the same stream of thought I sensed something else. There had been something very unintimidating about Lady Dunaway. She had exuded something comforting and frumpy, and that was no longer present in Dr. von Neefe. It had not occurred to me before, but there was a new edge to her character. There was something detached and even clinical about her and it frightened me a little.

It was on the train from Hastings that a startling thought occurred to me. The falcon was Monsieur des Esseintes's heavy artillery—his trump card, as it were. Since it was logical for him to assume I would be traveling south in pursuit of Camille, it would have made more sense for him to send Grelot with the falcon to the Gare de Lyon and send someone else to the Gare du Nord. However, he had sent Grelot and the falcon to the Gare du Nord. That seemed to indicate he knew there was something drawing me to London, something even more urgent than the pursuit of my daughter. Did he know about *Camillus influenzae* and Cletus's interference? Had he understood and anticipated my fear, a fear powerful enough to wrench me away even from little Camille? And if so, *how?* What was Monsieur des Esseintes's involvement in London?

We arrived at the station in the dead of the night. It was their time again. Monsieur des Esseintes had most certainly wired the vampire population of the city. There was no telling how many of them would be out looking for us.

We had to reach Bond Street without being spotted. It would be pure idiocy to approach the house from the front.

There was only one possibility. To most discerning eyes the garden enclosed by the terrace houses was completely sealed off from the street. However, between two of the houses flanking the rear of the garden there was a gap of three feet, which had been sealed off with rose trellises. My one hope was that they were unaware of this passage. Running parallel to Bond was Albemarle. If we took a circuitous route to Albemarle we might be able to make it through the rear entrance without being seen.

We approached Albemarle cautiously. There was no one. As stealthily as possible I pried back the trellises, scratching my hands painfully on the thorns. At every second we expected a voice to stop us. All was silent. We passed through the narrow passage and moved slowly into the garden. I looked at the chestnuts and the lilacs and the astrolabe resting solemnly in the starlight. The garden appeared empty. We stole softly through. I turned the latchkey in the back door and we slipped inside.

We found Cook wandering around in her flannel nightgown. She was pale and frightened and talking a mile a minute about people knocking at the door in the middle of the night and prowlers. In the midst of her dither she interjected something about rashers of bacon and breakfast, but food was the last thing on our minds. After calming her I rushed to my laboratory and discovered what I had so dreaded. I had known it was true, but seeing it with my own eyes still had its effect upon me. The glass cubicle was empty. The living rabbit containing *Camillus influenzae* was gone as well as all of my notes and research. Perhaps I had a bit of a mysterious and unknown force in my own heart, for something told me we could not waste a single second.

I burst into my bedchamber and experienced anew the darkness of the reptilian green walls, the looming presence of the seashell chair. In the second drawer of the bureau I found what I was looking for: two hundred pounds in cash I had kept there for emergencies.

I went downstairs to see Dr. von Neefe. She was peering through the curtains of the foyer. "There's a man out there," she said breathlessly.

"What did you expect?"

"I simply cannot believe it. It's a nightmare." She looked at me sharply. "You're going somewhere."

"I must."

"For God's sake, wait until daybreak."

"I cannot."

Cook looked back and forth at each of us worriedly. "Shall I call out the window for the constable?"

"No, I don't want to alarm them."

Cook burst into tears. "Is it the little one? Do they have the little one?"

"I'm going with you," Dr. von Neefe stated flatly.

"I think it would be better if you stay here."

"Certainly not. I've proven myself by now. I could be of help."

I wanted to refuse, but the urgency I saw in her eyes persuaded me. I reluctantly consented.

We slipped back through the garden and made our way to the stables. I bridled up the horses and mounted the brougham myself. If Dr. von Neefe still believed the vampire were incapable of evil, she was doubting it now, for I had never seen her so completely bloodless. Even the fear she had displayed when we had first hidden in des Esseintes's playroom did not match the look of dread now in her face.

"How are we going to get out of here?"

"We're going to drive by them."

"They will see us."

"They will not see you. You will be hiding in the brougham."

"What about you?"

"They have seen no one new enter the house. They will assume I am the driver out on an evening errand."

She remained unconvinced, but she had no choice. She climbed into the brougham and stooped down so as not to be seen. Her entire manner was dragging and hesitant, as if some part of her had guessed what was to happen next. And what was to happen? Why did we both seem to realize every second was crucial? I pulled my collar up around my neck and slipped on the driver's flannel cap resting on a nail in the stable. I opened the door. I drove the brougham out slowly so as not to arouse any undue attention. I stepped down from the seat and closed the stable door behind us.

As surreptitiously as possible I surveyed the gaslit street. There was a single black carriage parked some distance down and a lone figure leaned against it. He watched me casually. I got back up into the brougham and started up. To my dismay I heard Dr. von Neefe shifting about loudly in the back. I saw her peeking through the window, but as we drew near she slunk back down fearfully. The horses slowly clopped by the parked carriage. I did not look down at the gentleman standing beside it. Was he a vampire? Could he hear the rapid pounding of our hearts, or was he merely another human minion? He displayed no reaction as we passed slowly by. I held my breath as we continued. It had apparently rained earlier in the evening, for the streets were a quagmire of potholes and mud, and the brougham rocked gently. My heart sank when I heard the sound of carriage wheels slowly start behind us.

I dared not look back. After a prudent length of time I edged the brougham toward the curb lane. To my growing concern I heard the coach repeat the maneuver, slowly, portentously. Was he merely taking the precaution of following us, or had he recognized me? It did not matter. The game was afoot. I quickly turned a corner and cracked the horses into a trot. I continued my evasive actions and turned again. He was on to us now. I had only the slightest of leads and I had to make of it everything I could. I knew what I had to do. I cracked the horses again and we tore down the cobbles. The brougham bounced violently every time we hit one of the potholes and sent a spray of muddied water up over the sidewalks. By the time we reached the end of the street the driver was behind us again. Dr. von Neefe let out a cry as she rocked about in the back.

I stayed ahead of him, begging everything I could from the horses. When we passed Bolton Street I looked down it desperately. Was it there? I had taken a gamble. I had only caught a glimpse of the street as we had flown by. In my mind's eye I tried to pick out the details. The streetlights. The quiet houses. The carriages. I turned around. Our pursuer was just now passing Bolton and he, too, glanced down the street. He motioned savagely with his arm and pointed in our direction.

So I had been correct!

Within seconds a second black carriage flew out of Bolton and careened around the corner.

"In God's name!" Dr. von Neefe shrieked as she spotted the second carriage. "We are through! There is no stopping them now!"

I ignored her words. I spun the brougham around still another corner and sent the woman crashing into the side window. We were now headed toward the river.

For one last time I whipped the horses, and their hooves sent a spray of water up over the carriage. The two black coaches were scarcely a block behind now. Abruptly, I turned into Green Park, but instead of continuing on through, I jerked the horses off the road and behind a group of trees. In a flash I jumped down and placed a hand on each of the horses' muzzles to keep them from snorting. On the dimly lit road beyond, the two black carriages clopped briskly by.

As soon as they were out of sight I mounted the brougham again and pulled it back onto the road. I turned back in the direction from which we had come.

Dr. von Neefe pressed against the dividing window. "Have you lost your senses? What are you doing? Don't you realize they're going to come back looking for us?"

"They won't be back for a while," I said. "I was leading them toward the river, in the direction of Scotland Yard. They'll continue there looking for us."

"Why are you turning around?"

"Because Grelot and the falcon were waiting for us at the Gare du Nord, not the Gare de Lyon."

"So?"

"So Monsieur des Esseintes was more concerned about keeping us from returning to London than keeping us from following Niccolo. There is something going on here they did not want us to interfere in."

Dr. von Neefe sat back silently.

I don't know what I had expected when we turned onto Bolton Street. It certainly wasn't the picture of tranquillity that Dr. Cletus Hardwicke's narrow house presented in the distance. It stood black and silent. Its finials and gingerbread windows were quaintly inviting. From the expression on my companion's face her mind was racing. She gripped the handrest as we pulled before the somber house. Her eyes went immediately to the one troublesome aspect.

The front door was open. Silent.

"That shouldn't be," I said as I stepped down and rounded the side of the carriage.

"Don't go in!" she begged, clutching forcefully at my arm. I paused and once again peered into the tomblike darkness beyond the door. She drew me closer, and gazed deeply into my eyes. There was an unusual tenderness in her voice. "What if they are in there waiting for you?"

"I don't think they are."

"If you are correct, if there were only those carriages, don't you think they will be back as soon as they realize you have fooled them?"

"Yes, but we have a little time."

An emotion not normally present in the older woman's face suddenly flickered into existence. "Dr. Gladstone, I don't know what I would do if I lost you. Please, for my sake, don't go in."

Her plea struck an odd chord within me. To my surprise it tugged at my heart a little. I looked straight into her eyes, so entreating, so uncommonly vulnerable. My feelings fought among themselves until the stronger won out. "I must," I said as I pulled away and approached the front step.

"Hello?" I called when I reached the opening. The house was awesomely still. I stepped down upon the threshold and noticed the row of shiny new latches that had been installed upon the door. Six of them. Unbroken. Each carefully opened and no sign of tampering. The floor creaked.

"Cletus?"

Nothing . . .

I crept into the hall.

Inside, a fine wash of moonlight shone through the leaded windows and revealed a hint of the tumult within. Furniture had been hacked to bits and piled up beneath the windows. Remnants of stale meat and dirty clothing lay strewn about. Life had been nervous and prowling

within the house. Untold days of restlessness and fear
were written in these haphazard droppings. Mirrors had
been shattered as if the inhabitant could no longer bear to
look in them.

And where was the inhabitant?

I continued to the dining room. With each creaking step
I expected to hear some sound. A scraping. A rustling.
But there was nothing. I noticed the massive oak table
had been propped on its side and nailed against the door
leading to the garden. Stalagmite droppings of candles
trailing down its broken legs revealed still further signs
of a curious vigil. At last out of the all-encompassing
silence came an undisturbed voice.

"I've been waiting for you."

I looked up. Resting sideways and wedged awkwardly
between the stair railings was Cletus's gaunt countenance. His eyes still held a hint of their former intensity,
but their soul was gone. They no longer stared at me, but
through me. He remained reclining like some strange
puck. Like the house there was a disturbing serenity in
his gaze.

I did not have to be told what had transpired. All of
the windows were barricaded. There were six shiny new
latches on the door. Like Chiswick before him and the
woman at 24 Rue de la Glacière, Cletus had been the
victim of their game. Stratagems had been woven
around him with the same insurmountable conceit as
the gods of Olympus strewing illusions and chimeras in
the paths of the Argonauts. But why? Why had they
done it?

Then it struck me. What an imbecile I had been. What a
complete and utter fool. The game was not simply one of
their depraved vagaries, nor was it a test. It was a
carefully conceived criminal activity. The victims were all
scientists, but there was more. They—or we—were all
scientists who had discovered something, something the
vampire wanted. My focus had always been on little
Camille, on wondering why they would want an idiot
savant, but what if she were a diversion? What if they had
always been after something else?

"Cletus," I said firmly, "where is the virus?"

"Oh, yes," he chortled dazedly, not seeming to recognize

me. "That's what you want, isn't it? That's what you've wanted all along."

What was it Niccolo had said—*Yes, I would be most interested in seeing your work?*

I was numbed. The cogs tumbled once again. They had used Camille to lure me away. Why were they still keeping her? Why didn't they simply break into the house and steal the virus? For some reason this was out of the question. They infinitely preferred to play an elaborate charade. I presumed they had wanted me out of the picture because they saw Ursula as a more vulnerable victim, perhaps because of her enchantment with Niccolo. That meant that all the while I had been a prisoner in des Esseintes's house, he had known about it, known the villainy that had been intended for her. Anger boiled within me as I thought of the vampire with his orchids, so genteel, so frighteningly vacant of emotion. It was the ultimate irony that Cletus had intervened and taken possession of what they so fervently sought. He had unwittingly signed his own death sentence. He had become the victim of the game.

"Cletus?" I repeated.

For a moment the mist cleared. A hint of recognition trembled in his face. "Gladstone?"

"Cletus, why do they want the virus?"

His eyes were glazed. He toyed deliriously with the banister. "The virus?" Then the disquieting self-assurance returned. "Oh, no . . . you can't fool me. You think I'll believe it's you."

"It is I, Cletus."

He became uncertain. His expression revealed an inner struggle. "Gladstone?" He lifted himself up a little, gripping the banister tightly. "Gladstone, is that you?" He knitted his brow tightly as he peered down at me and attempted to make some sense of my face.

I stepped closer and he went rigid with fear. I quickly raised my hand to calm him, but he remained tense. "Cletus," I said again, "do you know why they want the virus so desperately?"

My different phrasing of the sentence seemed to cut through the fog of his confusion. He looked at me with piercing horror. "A dirigible capable of carrying vast

cargoes. A virus against which the human population
would have no defense." He suddenly shifted his gaze from
me to the gloom beyond. His face was expressionless. "It
would spread like any epidemic," he said with alarming
softness. "It wouldn't necessarily effect genocide. Certain
enclaves might survive. There is always the chance that it
might spontaneously mutate before razing the far corners
of the globe. But it would cripple and weaken as age
weakens the antelope before the hyena kills." He looked at
me again and cocked his head to one side with boyish
innocence. "What more perfect weapon for a species
whose specialized metabolisms provided such complete
immunity?"

He abruptly dropped his vision to the bottom molding of
the banister, as if the crack he was toying with were of
infinitely greater importance than the words he had just
spoken.

"Cletus, please tell me where the virus is."

He regarded me with childlike sadness. His eyes teared
as if he were about to cry. The same inner struggle
seethed within him. He was coming out of it. Somewhere
deep within his weathered skull he was summoning the
full force of his will to speak. A fearful recognition
flickered in his eyes. "Gladstone—" His head was
wrenched suddenly to one side as if possessed by a
demonic force. His deformed old frame was shaking as he
tightly clenched his teeth and struggled to watch me out
of the corners of his eyes.

His trembling ceased abruptly. For a few uncanny
moments he held the contorted position, and then slowly a
smile crept across his face. "Oh, no . . . ." he chuckled
throatily. "You can't fool me."

"Cletus!"

He stared at me vacantly for a moment.

In a single deft movement he kicked something and
there was a resonant gurgling sound as of a can
emptying. A liquid began to trickle down the banisters.
The smell of kerosene permeated the room. In an instant
he was up and bolted through the doorway behind him.

I tore up the stairs, stepping carefully over the
spreading puddle, and then froze. He stood in the
disheveled laboratory. The remains of what had been my

papers were scattered all around him. On the lab table were my shredded notebooks and a number of the Petrie dishes containing what I assumed to be the remaining cultures of *Camillus influenzae* in various stages of incubation. Also on the table was an empty glass cage and in the little man's arms was a black-and-white rabbit. It was familiarly lethargic.

Its heart beats so very fast, Niccolo had said.

What was he going to do?

Cletus smiled at me, depraved. "Is this what you want?"

"Cletus, you must not do this."

"Little bunny," he purred. "Do you want to pet my little bunny?"

I gaped in horror at the pathetic little man. Was this really the great Dr. Hardwicke, the wily and deceitful blackguard who had once so intimidated me, who had caused me so much grief? There was a time I had hated him. But now, seeing him reduced so totally and so heartlessly by creatures of greater cunning, I could feel only pity for him. I lunged forward to stop him.

In a flash he struck a match and threw it into the puddle of kerosene. Flames surged up, spreading, moving like the wind into the hall. I jumped back and shielded my eyes.

It was then I became aware of Dr. von Neefe.

"No, you mustn't!" she said and the thunder of her voice was deafening. But somehow, in some way, my life was being consumed. My work. My papers. Half crazed myself, I felt my legs begin to carry me into the room. Dr. von Neefe's voice faded into an indecipherable drone. It was as if I were trapped in a dream. I no longer possessed any volition. My legs moved. The heat was intense. My head lolled about scanning the table, my papers, a closed Petrie dish. My hand reached out. The glass of the Petrie dish seemed unreal. Rubbery. My legs moved.

Impossibly, I made it back into the corridor. I turned to see Cletus dancing in the flames, a cackling, twisted Rumpelstiltskin. The rabbit squealed as it slid weakly and piteously from his arms. In horror I watched as snake tongues licked his face, crackled away the thinning hair, and bubbled the yellowed skin. His eyes were wide and

crazed. His ecstatic hands quivered and blackened. Even
as he crumpled to the floor he laughed.

Outside in the street the gingerbread windows began to
glow like ovens, and fire bells rended the London night.
We nervously scanned the street. They were not back yet,
but they might reappear at any moment. For the moment
we had foiled them. The fact that Cletus still had both the
rabbit and the Petrie dish meant that they had not yet
been able to get the virus. They would be doubly angry at
us for intervening. We had not a second to lose. As we
crossed the street a feeling of such intensity descended
upon me I had to pause. It was unlike anything I had ever
felt before. It was a spiritual emptiness, as if for a
moment all the life and air had been sucked out of the
world and nothing was left but the cold stars and the
black and infinite void. I had never been clairvoyant, but
for a moment I felt that I had entered a timeless nether-
world, the dream time of the aborigines. Somehow I
sensed that a moment of awesome importance had just
passed. A sphere of destiny had somehow played itself out
and we were in that brief interim where for one mote of a
second there was nothing, nothing until the massive
forces and machineries of fate shifted into a new gear, and
all the air rushed back into the world. I glanced down at
the remains of a life, the Petrie dish. The smear of agar
contained a living colony of the virus. If properly
maintained it could survive a short time outside of the
laboratory. A very short time.

Once back in the carriage Dr. von Neefe started pelting
me with questions and I told her everything I had learned
from Cletus of the vampire and their intentions to
engineer the release of the virus.

"Is it true?" she cried.

"How can you doubt it?" I returned.

"It's just too incredible. I can't believe—"

"You must, damn it! You must! You have been laboring
under a romantic vision of the vampire. How much more
evidence do you require?"

Her face aglow in the lambent light, she at last seemed
to understand the import of the virus and a presage of
what might lie ahead. "You should have let it burn," she
said savagely.

I had just seen my oldest enemy burn to death. I was in no mind to accept criticism. I would have snarled something back had my thoughts not been reeling with the more urgent matters at hand—how to preserve the last living strains of the virus, and first and foremost, how to combat the vampire. If the virus was as important to them as I thought it was, there was no telling what they would do to get it back. We needed help, but I was at an utter loss as to how to persuade the authorities, let alone any national sovereignty, that there were creatures of a different blood among us and plotting our overthrow. Any normal institution would think we were raving lunatics. I feared even my closest colleagues would never believe such an incredible tale. We were alone and helpless.

There was only one human faction that might consider our case, one small minority who would not immediately dismiss the terrible plot we had uncovered: the mysterious network of the vampire hunters. We had to get in touch with Dr. Leberecht Weber and get him to mobilize what meager resources we had.

As for the virus, as long as it was safely in my hands there was one other matter that restrained me from seeking out a safe place to hide and maintain it. Again I could not leave it with a colleague because I feared the vampire would take him unaware. Further, I could not go into hiding with it myself because of the one other matter, and that was my little Camille. While Cletus had had the virus and there was danger of its being released upon the world I had been able to forsake her. But now that I had reclaimed it, my voracious desire to rescue her had returned. There are some who might consider my rash willingness to rush into the very lair of the enemy to be the height of folly, but to them I can only say that they have not experienced blind and selfless rage. Every second of captivity in the home of des Esseintes had only fomented my anger. Every trick and torturous manipulation of the vampire had only increased my desire to spare her even one more second in their grasp.

Dr. von Neefe did not dare argue with me.

When we reached Victoria Station we discovered it unusually busy for the hour. The street was dark. The

gaslamps shimmered, and yet out of the inky blackness
came a slow but steady stream of hansoms. Was there
some reason for it? Were the vampire here? We eyed the
crowd. Families gathered in front of the rambling wooden
Terminus building. A woman in gloves and an ornately
embroidered dress fluttered her fan. Children played, as
wide awake as if it were afternoon. A woman with a hat of
egret feathers stepped into the traffic and caused a cab to
swerve to one side. I wondered if it were the stifling heat
that caused so many upright Londoners to travel in the
dead of the night.

I drove on past the Terminus and parked the brougham
a block away. I took the precaution of hiring a porter to
purchase our tickets, and prepared a makeshift carrying
case for the Petrie dish from a canvas satchel in the
hansom.

"I will enter first," I told Dr. von Neefe. "If I do not
signal for you within ten minutes you must get out of
here. You must understand what danger we are in." I
looked at the virus, wondering if I should leave it with her.
I looked at her and for the first time since the shock of
seeing Cletus die in the flames, a hint of her former
strength returned. I decided against giving her the virus.
If the vampire did catch me I might be able to destroy it
before they could reach it.

"You're not going to leave me?" she gasped.

"Only until I go into the station. If I don't come back
out I want you to promise me you will try to get Camille
back. You must get Dr. Weber's help. Do you hear me?"

She straightened. "I hear you quite plainly." She
glanced toward the station. "They're in there, you know.
They won't have enlisted the police this time. You're on
your home ground. Your name is well known in London,
and no officer in his right mind would believe any charges
they might have brought against you. Besides, their
purpose in using the authorities in Paris was to keep you
from getting to the virus. Now that you have it, it is their
game alone. How do you propose to get through to the
trains?"

"I have to go in there. Perhaps they won't recognize me.
We would not have been recognized at the Gare du Nord if
it had not been for Grelot."

"What about the photographs?"

"Photographs?"

"The photographs des Esseintes took just before he showed us the orchid conservatory for the first time."

But of course. I had forgotten. What had he said? He was taking them simply as a precaution? No doubt he had already considered the necessity of such identification should we ever happen to escape. "Surely the photographs will not arrive until the morning post."

Almost tauntingly she said, "What makes you think he has not already distributed the photographs throughout the vampire population of Europe? If he had the forethought to take the photographs in the first place, why wouldn't he have posted them the very next morning?"

I did not know. I only knew that I had to cling to one hope. "Possibly he did," I retorted. "And possibly this very moment there are a hundred sets of eyes examining those very pictures, memorizing details that aren't even visible to our human eyes. But possibly, just possibly, Monsieur des Esseintes's gargantuan ego caused him to feel that the chances of our outwitting him were so small that the mere taking of the photographs was precaution enough."

She looked at the station worriedly and shook her head again. All of her anger and exasperation bubbled up in her face as she turned to me. "I told you," she said bitterly. "I warned you at the very beginning that you were blind and did not see what others would see." She looked sharply at the canvas satchel and then back at me. Her resentment melted and once again she took on a tenderness not normally present. It was a warmth, even a sensuousness, although this time there was something different about it, a hidden sorrow. Once again I was astonished to find it thrilling, and she was aware of this. If it had not happened so spontaneously, so passionately, I'm sure we would have both felt denuded by it. "You did not take my advice then. I will implore you one last time. Won't you please destroy the virus?"

I felt empty. "I cannot."

"Why?"

"Do you know what you are asking? You are a scientist

and a scholar. Don't you see that civilization would not
advance if we destroyed our discoveries?"

"Advance!" she laughed shrilly. "And how, pray tell,
does your saving that debased virus advance civilization?"

How could I explain to her everything the virus was to
me? It was my memorial to Camille, the result of five
years of anguish and hard work. "It is the principle that
concerns me here. It is principle that furthers civilization; not the virus. Don't you see? We cannot destroy
knowledge. I have come to question many things, but one
thing I cannot question, one truth I hold above all others
is that knowledge is good. To destroy the result of years of
work and study, to blot out a discovery would be
censorship of the most odious kind. To destroy the virus
would be to destroy the quintessence of myself. I cannot
do it."

After I finished speaking there was a ringing silence. It
was as if we had touched fingertips in the darkness,
speechless with expectation, only to recoil once again to
our own desolate islands. I, for the first time, realized the
virus *was* the quintessence of myself. She, for the first
time, realized how vast and immutable the emotions that
divided us were. In other women I might have expected
perplexity or denial, but not in her. Once again she
revealed her singular character, for she seemed to
understand. In fact, that was the source of her sorrow. She
had comprehended my answer all too well.

Suddenly I felt another rush of something black and
measureless. It was as if the same sixth sense were trying
to tell me that unseen forces were working around us, but
the message was indistinct. All I knew was that the
cantilevers of destiny had swung into place. I did not
know what that destiny was. I only knew that I was a part
of it, a part of some quivering web.

"Very well," she said, as if it were a decree. "Then we
have one hope, that we will not be recognized." She slipped
off the telltale cloak and ulster and left it in the
brougham. "We will go into the station separately. I will
go first."

I was about to say something when she slipped down
from the carriage. "We must stand together," she repeated

as she strode toward the station. I had no choice but to
follow. I held the satchel unobtrusively at my side. I
pretended not to know her and trailed a safe distance
behind. I was certain she observed me out of the corners of
her eyes. She remained quiet and dignified. We entered
the station.

Inside, the concourse was a hubbub of activity. Perhaps
it had been a long time since I had been in Victoria
Station at such a late hour. Perhaps it was the tension of
the situation, but again it seemed peculiarly crowded.
People milled everywhere, fashionable ladies and dowdy
matrons, slithering and struggling, a hodgepodge of
carpetbags, portmanteaus, and parrot-head umbrellas.
Near one end of the immense chamber and standing
behind several large palms was a delegation of Punjab
Indians in turbans. At the opposite end of the concourse
and framed by a waiting locomotive gathered several
hussars in their white dress uniforms and spiked and
tasseled white pith helmets. A hiss of steam pushed them
on. Metal clanked. Cylinders keened. It could be any one
of them.

With a pang I realized again that my world had
unalterably changed. A few months ago this would have
been the most harmless of sights, a crowd of people. Oh, it
might have held some secrets—a diplomat, an illicit
affair—but it was an artless backdrop, the middling
swarm. Now these were no longer my fellow beings. They
were out there. It was incredible, but it was true. There
moved among us creatures who were not quite human.
They had been out there my entire life. They had been out
there during my father's life, my grandfather's—walking,
smiling, mingling brazenly, and no one knew it. We were
utterly alone in our knowlege. If we tried to tell anyone
they would think we were mad. They were out there, and
now that I knew it I could never look at the evening crowd
again without wondering. Which face? Which smile
conceals the jackal teeth?

Were their eyes upon us now? I looked at the dusty
satchel swinging casually at the end of my arm. *Knuckles
too tight.* That was just the sort of thing they would be
looking for. I relaxed. They would also be looking for two
of us. I allowed Dr. von Neefe to draw still farther ahead.

The woman with the hat of egret feathers brushed by
us, now accompanied by a little girl in puffed sleeves
and a straw boater. I paused at a newsstand and
pretended to be interested in a notice. My head was
facing the paper, but my eyes gazed beyond. Across the
concourse the Punjabs had begun to edge toward the
pier. Was it they? The boarding whistle blew and I
glanced up to see that Dr. von Neefe had reached the
train.

I too made my way toward the platform.

In my casual efforts to maintain a lookout I bunglingly
walked right into one of the hussars.

"Sorry, sir," he said.

I nodded in apology. I searched his eyes suspiciously as I
walked quickly away. Gentle periwinkle eyes.

And then through the crowd I saw him, a massive
gentleman. Bowler hat. Patriarchal beard. Gold watch
chain and a panatela in an amber holder. So des Esseintes
had been scrupulous enough to post the photographs
weeks before. The massive gentleman's gaze was fierily
determined, even trancelike. He strode with incredible
speed and grace for his size, weightlessly, like a wraith
swiftly cutting through the crowd. He might have been
any arbiter of elegance were it not for the eeriness of his
gait.

Dr. von Neefe did not visibly glance at the fellow, but
her own increase in speed indicated she was aware of his
approach. She lifted her skirts and paced rapidly by the
waiting passenger cars. I too had reached the train and
hastened my step. Until we stepped up into the cars he
had no way of being certain we were taking this
particular train. I looked behind and saw he was closing
the remaining thirty feet between us. The final whistle
sounded. We continued moving along the pier as the
gentleman bore down upon us. I turned to see he had cut
the distance in half. The engine driver opened the valve to
clear the boiler, and every sound in the station was blotted
out by the rushing screech of escaping steam. The train
started to move.

His gaze remained unchanged. Dr. von Neefe stepped up
on the train. He was only a few steps behind me. It would
soon be too late. In an instant I leaped upon the

accelerating train and turned, expecting to see hands closing in upon me.

But the gentleman maintained his forward gait as we swiftly passed by him.

It was an odd reprieve. Was he truly unconcerned, just a peculiar gentleman in the crowd? Or had he simply maintained his demeanor, not wanting us to realize he had failed? Not knowing was even more psychologically devastating than if we had actually seen his fangs, or felt his icy grip upon our flesh, for we were forced into an unreasoning paranoia. We had to work from the premise that the portly gentleman had been a vampire, and they now knew which train we were on. It would be easy for them to wire ahead and have us intercepted at the next stop. We were not even sure that the man with the panatela had been a vampire, and still we had to dodge every suspicious stranger.

The leering and shining-white face of a passing conductor interrupted my thoughts. "Beware 'a card sharps on this train," he intoned.

What if they were on this train? What if the portly gentleman had been a decoy to keep us from seeing someone else who stepped upon the train farther down the platform? It was impossible to use my rail key to lock us in our compartment, for we were forced to share it with other people. I say other people, and yet I did not know. One was a woman furiously doing petit point, her hands moving like the spinnerets of a spider. The other was a gentleman sitting and reading a small religious tract. We sat down uneasily, I keeping my hands on the satchel containing the virus, and Dr. von Neefe keeping her eyes on our fellow passengers.

It was on the train that I began to entertain several troublesome thoughts. With all their superior knowledge and worldwide exchange of information, why did the vampire have to resort to stealing scientific discoveries? Was it that they lacked the human passion necessary to love investigation for its own sake and could not carry through with the boring mechanics of discovery itself? After all, des Esseintes was a great mind, but in the final analysis he was a dilettante. Or was it an even more basic component of their being? Just as they were incapable of producing their own blood, was it necessary for them to vampirize knowledge as well? The second thing that troubled me was the fact that they were bent upon destroying the human race. Didn't they need us, not only to feed upon, but also, given their inability to reproduce, to ultimately replenish their ranks? One possibility was that they felt their household servants would fulfill all of their requirements. Even more sobering was the possibility that they intended to establish farms, domesticating us, as it were, to supply all of their culinary and reproductive needs.

At the first stop outside of London we waited until all of the disembarking passengers had gotten off the train before we stepped down. We saw, or at least recognized, no one. Every stranger's glance filled us with dread. We changed for a train headed toward Portsmouth. It was out of our way, but we hoped that if we hadn't been followed we might be somewhat safer taking a more indirect route. Every landmark outside the speeding train was portentous: The moonlit fields, the sleeping villages, every black town and glowing furnace underlined the fact that we were in their time. At long last the first faint amethyst traces of dawn enshrouded the horizon. When we reached the ferry the sun was shining in full. For a while we were safe.

Or were we? I could not help feeling that we had gotten away too easily, that somehow the vampire knew our every move and were just biding their time, knowing full well that when the moment came they would act swiftly. Did they have a group of human followers who were assisting them? Considering the unassuming and dull-witted human servants we had encountered thus far, I thought it unlikely. The vampire, like the English with their dogs, seemed to prefer stupid and obedient servitors. However, I realized this notion was born of a desperate hope. If there was a human alliance after us as well, all was lost. There would be no hour of safety. The terrible truth was that we had to consider every contingency. I still could not dispel the awful feeling that through some unknown means they knew exactly where we were.

From the ferry we sent out a battery of wires. Several to Dr. Leberecht Weber elaborating upon the seriousness of

what was transpiring and begging for some news of
Ursula's safety and whereabouts. I bitterly regretted that
I had allowed Ursula to attempt such a thing, and was
ripped apart with worry. We instructed Dr. Weber to wire
his reply to the train station at Le Havre addressed to an
assumed name. We sent other wires to various colleagues
of Dr. Weber's and Dr. von Neefe's throughout Europe—all
members of the network of vampire hunters.

As I have said, the network consisted largely of scholars
and a few wealthy eccentrics. As such, they were little
more than a network of correspondents. It would be
exceedingly difficult to organize them into any effective
body. To begin, most of them held the view that Dr. von
Neefe had held, that the world of the vampire was a realm
of enchantment. It would be a task in itself to awaken in
them any awareness of the true dangers of the forces now
amassing. Second, even if we did succeed in obtaining
their support, there was little they could do. They were
ardent in their studies, but their jurisdiction was largely
academic. They had no real means of countering an
enemy from within.

All of these obstacles weighed down heavily upon both
our shoulders, but the weight was especially telling on Dr.
von Neef. She had spent her life scrutinizing the vampire
without recognizing what she must now understand to be
their true nature. I suspected she felt extreme guilt over
trying to inhibit our escape from des Esseintes's, and she
was now pouring all of her concentration into a desperate
attempt to amend her past blindnesses. She was certain
Dr. Weber would believe her, and with the aid of his
academic stature he might convince some of their other
colleagues. But most of her hope she put into a *società*
based at the Museo Gregoriano in Rome. The *società* was a
small organization of fanatics devoted to the opinion that
since time immemorial the vampire had been conspiring
to bring about the end of human civilization. Until now
they had been generally disdained by the rest of the
network as misguided zealots. Little was known of their
activity, save that there hung about them the same aura
that hung over many Italian secret societies, tales of
assassinations and secret handshakes. Such gossip had
been viewed as infamous and inconsequential until now.

The change in opinion wore grievously in Dr. von Neefe's countenance. The time of the *società* had come.

Throughout the morning we gave different porters a series of wires to send to the Museo Gregoriano. We entreated that all replies be wired to the Stazione Termini in Florence and left under a fraudulent name. If possible, it was our passionate hope that someone from the *società* might even meet us at the station and somehow assist us in our final attempt to find Camille. We offered a password that would enable both parties to identify each other with certainty.

When we reached Le Havre we found a number of wires from Dr. Weber waiting for us. Expectedly, they were tormented and confused, but through the terse fragments of the mode of communication we pieced a coherent picture. Ursula had followed Niccolo to Florence, where he had hired a carriage and vanished into the night. He had headed west, toward the seacoast. She had inquired at the stables where the carriage had been hired and discovered its destination was the tiny village of Massa Marittima.

Massa Marittima. The meaning of that information did not have to be explained to us. Somewhere near the village was Lodovico's villa, close enough to Florence that he could have trafficked with the Medici, but secluded enough within the rolling green hills of Tuscany that he could live out his centuries in privacy. It was from there that he was orchestrating everything. It was there that Niccolo had returned, and it was there that I knew we would find little Camille. In another wire Dr. Weber told us Ursula had proceeded to Massa Marittima and was making further investigations. Were there any wealthy *padrones* who were only seen at night? Had any of the major landowners acquired a reputation for being reclusive or eccentric?

In Dr. Weber's last wire he advised us that we had one hope. He offered the grim and reluctant suggestion that Dr. von Neefe had already anticipated, that we contact the dread *società* in Rome and beg for their assistance. From Le Havre we sent off two more wires, one requesting that Dr. Weber make Ursula remain in Massa Marittima until we reached her, and the other a reiteration of our plea to the *società* at the Museo Gregoriano. Again we requested the replies to these be made at the Stazione Termini in Florence.

Once aboard the train we locked ourselves in our compartment and tried to get some sleep.

It was high in the Pennine Alps that the train stopped unexpectedly. At first we thought it was fallen snow upon the tracks, but the conductor soon put that hope to rest. It was *politiques*. Several black sleighs had appeared in the mountain pass and some mysterious gentlemen were talking with the engine driver. We were speechless. I looked out the window to try to determine what was happening. It had been dark for several hours. A light snow was falling in the moonlight, and beyond, at the head of the black train, stood a number of dark figures speaking and gesturing with the engine driver. On our side of the train most of the passengers had opened their windows and were looking out. In the distance the figures turned and scanned the passenger cars. I did not have to be told what they were looking for. Could they spot our faces among the crowd? Did their inhuman senses reach out and discern which hearts had stopped?

I don't know what they said and did. Perhaps they simply bribed the engine driver. Perhaps they had somehow procured the necessary papers to intimidate him, but somehow they gained access to the train. As we watched in horror three of them boarded and the train lurched forward once again.

We were trapped. We could not leap from the train in the middle of the frozen mountains. We had no choice but to sit and wait for them to come to us. How had they found us? I looked at the map and saw that there were three probable train routes we might have taken without going hundreds of miles out of our way. Was it possible that they had watched each pass and stopped each train as it went through?

We heard voices coming from the front of our car. They were here. In French I heard the conductor tell them they had no authority. A reply, insidiously calm, told him they had no intention of bothering the passengers, but were simply making a few observations. There was a rustling of papers, and by bribe or intimidation they quieted the conductor. He shuffled off.

"Pretend to be sleeping," I whispered to Dr. von Neefe. The footsteps approached. She had no time to argue, but turned away from the door and pulled the traveling rug tightly around her. I dropped to the floor and inched toward the door, holding the canvas satchel firmly at my side. From the scuffing of the carpet it was apparent they were at the compartment directly adjacent to us. I looked at the windows of our compartment directly above me. The door was locked and the curtains were drawn, but as is the way with trains they never quite covered the panes. A figure loomed at the crack.

I held my breath.

From my vantage I had only a fragmentary and distorted image of our pursuer. In the dim light it was difficult to tell, but he seemed swarthy. Was it Hatim? One of the Punjabs? I could only see the black of his hair and the jet black of his Russian sable collar. Eyes inspected the room. Dr. von Neefe's breathing continued relaxedly as she pretended to be unaware of the intruder. From the shifting of his weight it seemed that he was about to continue on when something else piqued his senses. I felt a rush in my spine. Did he see the quiver? Was it disturbed, betraying my exact location in the room? He returned to the narrow crack between the curtains and the door frame. My lungs were about to burst. And then I realized. Even if he did not perceive the quiver he could sense my presence. Just as Niccolo had been able to hear the rabbit's pulse within the glass cupola, so this vampire could hear the beating of two hearts within the compartment.

The porcelain handle turned slowly in its collar.

On discovering it was fastened he paused. What was he going to do? My temples pounded. He might be able to hear my heart, but the constant rocking and droning of the train might make it difficult for him to discern where in the compartment I was hiding. Suddenly, more voices appeared in the car. The conductor had apparently returned with two of the green-liveried porters. I heard him tell the intruders in French that the *chef de train* wanted to speak with them in the conductor's car. The man standing before our compartment refused. The conductor grew annoyed and insisted.

I could stand it no longer. Uncontrollably, I expelled my breath. From the sudden silence beyond it was obvious every one had heard me gasp for air, including the vampire in the Russian sable. "Very well," he told the conductor. Two of them would go with him to see the *chef de train,* but one of them would remain behind. He made some pompous excuse about securities investigators and stolen property, but the conductor would hear none of it. His authority had been challenged and he was livid. What happened next I am not sure. One of the porters cried out. There was the sound of a scuffle.

"Through the window!" Dr. von Neefe cried as I leaped up from my hiding place.

There was the distinctive sound of a body crashing to the carpet. I recalled des Esseintes's mentioning that he was well versed in many ancient arts and could render one unconscious with the most delicate application of pressure, but there was no time to confirm my assumption. She flung the window open and at the same instant we could hear footsteps crashing toward the door of the compartment. It is said that people in a blind panic have been known to perform feats of impossible strength and dexterity, that men have lifted huge blocks of stone off their fellow workers, and it must be true, for the adrenaline coursing through our bodies enabled us to act without regard to danger of human limitation. Incredibly, she climbed out into the frozen rush of air and grasped something above the sash. She pulled herself upward. I heard the door being kicked effortlessly to bits as I followed. I slipped the canvas satchel inside my jacket. When I was out I saw that Dr. von Neefe had somehow managed to clamber to the top of the speeding train. The wind tore at us. She reached down to assist me up and as I slowly reached the sash I saw the remains of the door come slamming down inside the compartment. I saw a flash of black coming for me as I continued to pull myself up, and a deathly white hand in black sable reached madly for my dangling leg. I made it to the top just beyond the creature's reach.

It was a nightmare. They had to be desperate to be willing to act so boldly and without regard to the consequences of their insanity. The train sped on over a

ledge of mountain with a steep gorge beneath us
menacingly on our right. One of them was coming
through the window after us. Snow ripped by us in the
darkness as we heedfully made our way toward the back of
the treacherously rocking train. We finally reached a
smoking platform between two of the cars. I glanced back
and saw two of them hunched over like cats and following
in furious pursuit. They were less than a car's length
behind us. We dropped down to the smoking platform and
burst through the door to the next car.

The contrast from clawing through the dark and cold
and literally fighting for our lives to what we entered
next was galvanizing. Inside was a splendid Italianate
dining saloon. The tables were covered with fine linen and
were scintillant with silver and crystal. The walls were
richly paneled, and handsomely uniformed waiters scurried to and fro over the mock-Jacobean carpet. The dining
car was crowded and all eyes were upon us as we raced
through toward the next car. Before we had scarcely
reached the exit we heard the sound of the door at the
opposite end of the saloon being thrown open, and the
people in the car gasped at the force employed by our
pursuer. The third vampire had caught up with us.

Where was the *chef de train?* Surely word of the
disturbance had reached him and he would be here soon.
In desperation I pulled an opulently decked serving cart
from one of the stunned waiters and shoved it in the
vampire's path behind us. Another gasp rose from the
crowd as the diners nearest us knocked over tables and
chairs to get out of the way. We fled to the next car.

By now the other two vampire had reached the dining
saloon and were also right on our heels. We passed
through a second-class car, and then another, causing a
swarm of faces to gasp and turn. We ran in mindless fear
until we neared the end of the train and passed through a
luggage car. Where could we hide? No matter where we
paused, as soon as our pursuers caught up with us their
acute senses would be able to pinpoint our location.

Our commotion caused something else. Barking. Suddenly, the crowded luggage car was filled with the
barking of many dogs. In the blue moonlight coming in
from the icy landscape I saw cage after cage filled with

sleek canine forms. Greyhounds. Racing greyhounds on their way to Rome.

"Behind the cages!" Dr. von Neefe exclaimed. We scampered over one of the cages and dropped to the floor. The door to the luggage car slid open violently.

I understood her reasoning at once. Amid so many conflicting smells and heartbeats the senses of the vampire might be confused. We held ourselves close to the floor, as still as rocks, as three sets of footsteps entered the room. The dogs continued to bark.

Through the mesh of the cage I saw the bottom of a Russian sable coat sweep by. Then all three figures stopped and stood silently. The clicking of the points gently resounded from the tracks below. I noticed some of the dogs had stopped barking, and in the moonlight I could see that the greyhound in the cage adjacent to us was flaring its nostrils. It was taking in the myriad of scents that filled the car... sifting them... reading them. I did not have to see their faces to know the vampire beyond were doing the same.

Our ruse seemed to be working, for one of the vampire took a step to continue.

"No, listen," commanded the same voice.

A flickering of shadows passed quickly through the room. In the distance the whistle blew.

"There are two human heartbeats in this room," said the voice. There was a pause of several moments and then the other two padded toward the opposite end of the luggage car. They began to search among the trunks. Each scraping, each heavy thud meant they were drawing closer to our hiding place. It was inevitable that they would find us. There was no place to run.

"Dr. Gladstone," addressed the voice unexpectedly, "there is no escape. Why don't you make it easier on yourself and just come out?"

I remained silent.

The other two figures pulled out one of the cages just a few feet down from us and shuffled around behind it. The greyhound snarled savagely.

"We will not harm you," the voice murmured placidly. They moved one of the trunks next to us. It grazed the

bottom of my boot, but I dared not withdraw it. Dr. von
Neefe looked at me with horror.

"Very well, suit yourself."

White hands clamped down on either side of the cage
concealing us.

At the same moment there was the sound of voices from
the next car. The *chef de train* was coming. From the
seriousness of the disturbance there was no doubt he
would be armed and accompanied by numerous men. The
figure reaching for the cage concealing us hesitated.

"The door!" shrilled our adversary.

From the sound of his footsteps it was apparent that the
third vampire raced toward the sliding door dividing us
from our rescuers and braced himself against it. The door
rattled as those beyond tried to force it, but the strength
of the single vampire was more than equal match. There
was shouting and suddenly the splintering of wood as a
crowbar began to smash through the barrier.

The white hands gripping the cage concealing us
faltered.

The door gave way and the three vampire were forced to
flee. Amid the barking of the greyhounds and the
whistling of the wind and snow coming through the
broken door was the sound of a group of men charging by
in pursuit. And then the voices faded in the distance and
we were left alone.

About half an hour later we heard the sounds of the
men coming back through. From their conversation it was
apparent the vampire had eluded them. They, too, were
hiding somewhere on the train. No doubt they had
employed their superior strength and agility to slither
through some crevice or even creep like lemurs along the
very side of the speeding train. We dared not move for fear
of running into them. Because of the dangers we were
certain they would remain hidden until the train reached
the next stop. We traveled the remainder of our journey
cowering in the luggage car, accompanied only by the cold
and the sporadic howling of the hounds.

The temperature rose rapidly as we descended the
mountains. It was still dark when we reached Florence.
We knew that the vampire would be crawling over the

Stazione Termini, watching every disembarking passenger, and so we had one choice. As the train slowed down to a crawl and pulled into the station we leaped to the platform on the opposite side.

Had the *società* answered our plea? Was someone waiting for us inside the station? Regardless of the hazards, we had to go in. Again we traveled with a wide distance between us. We went into the station and I kept watch on the crowd while Dr. von Neefe went to the Information desk. From the rapid gesturing of her hands it was apparent there were no wires waiting for us from either Dr. Weber or the *società*. Why? Had something happened?

She glanced at me briefly, worriedly, as she left the Information desk and strolled toward the entrance. We had instructed the *società* to look for a woman standing by the entrance and stroking her earlobe. She remained there for several minutes performing the movement. No one came.

We searched the crowd nervously.

I had no idea what to think. Had the *società* simply disregarded our message? How could they? The seriousness of our cry for help could not have been misread. Or could it? Had the *società*, viewed as fanatical by the entire network of vampire hunters, in turn seen our telegrams as crank? Had they thought we were joking, making a mockery of their way of thinking?

Finally a man with grizzled black hair and beard, and wearing a disheveled raincoat, approached Dr. von Neefe. He glanced around tensely. It was obvious he was frightened. In accordance with our wire he murmured the secret password to her and in a flash they were both out the door.

I was about to follow when I noticed a man moving through the crowd with a Russian sable coat draped over his arm. I stepped back behind one of the pillars of the station. Within moments another man joined him and said something. Then the other man went back toward the train. I was certain it was they. I waited until the man with the sable coat was looking in the opposite direction, and then swiftly made my way toward the exit.

Under other circumstances I might have been enraptured by the dark streets of Florence. Memories came

flooding back. So this was where it all began, where a frail
and gentle youth first gazed into a pair of flashing eyes.
Where Leonardo struggled with his passions and where
Lorenzo, Il Magnifico, flourished his cape. At another
time I might have imagined hoofbeats echoing in these
streets, beneath the red-tiled domes and towers of the
palazzos, hoofbeats and laughter. But now the dark
streets of Florence seemed only threatening to me. At the
height of a Medici carnival the vampire had walked these
streets, and somewhere in the darkness they still walked.

I discovered Dr. von Neefe and the disheveled and
bearded man standing beneath the arches of an ancient
building down the street. The man's face moved into the
moonlight as I approached. He was pale and frightened.
His eyes were red. Dr. von Neefe nodded to let him know I
was to be trusted.

"Do you speak Italian?" she asked.

I shook my head.

"I speak very little." She turned to him and muttered
something. He shook his head sadly. They talked back and
forth in a tense and fragmentary manner. The emissary
from the infamous *società* was not what I had expected.
He had the kind of mournful eyes one expected from the
deeply religious. He might have been a scholar. But he
seemed most like an inmate from a mental asylum.

During the course of their exchange Dr. von Neefe
looked more and more alarmed. She clawed tightly at his
arm. The conversation continued for a few more minutes
and then finally she turned to me.

"He says the day is at hand," she said solemnly, almost
as if she were under the influence of some drug. "The
società has been disbanded by the vampire. I can't quite
make out what means they used. He says that its
members have been separated and all are in hiding. What
has been feared for so long is coming to pass. The vampire
are ready to act. The day is at hand."

I considered her words for several moments, unable to
say anything.

She continued her discussion. In her hesitant dialogue I
heard her mention the name of Dr. Weber. The disheveled
man shook his head sadly. He spoke several words
hesitantly and somberly. Dr. von Neefe's eyes widened in

disbelief. She grasped his arm again. Then she repeated
the words, drew her head back, and uttered a heartrend-
ing cry. She collapsed and I caught her in my arms.

"What is it?" I demanded.

Her lips trembled. "*Leberecht.* The vampire have
murdered him. The police say he was pushed in front of a
train by a madman, but it was the vampire."

I could not believe it. "What of Ursula? Does he know
anything about Ursula?"

Dr. von Neefe used every ounce of her will to compose
herself. She struggled to stand, but as she turned toward
the man we saw that his eyes were on the station in the
distance. I too looked and saw that the vampire carrying
the Russian sable coat had come out of the Terminus and
was speaking to someone in an antique black *calèche.*

"*Dios me libre,*" gasped the disheveled man and
instantly the vampire's eyes sliced through the night. He
had spotted us.

We broke into a run.

A cab pulled out of the darkness ahead of us and I
hailed it. There was the sound of footsteps on the cobbles
behind us. When we reached the cab I flung open the door
but the very moment I had stepped inside I saw that it
was already occupied by a young woman. She gazed at me
with wide, dark eyes. She was very beautiful and very
frail. She wore a graceful hat of osprey feathers, and her
collar and cuffs were frilled and tight around her delicate
ivory hands. She leaned forward as if to inquire what was
going on when suddenly one of her hands sprang forward
and clamped around my wrist like a steel vise.

I screamed and tried to pull away, but the cold white
hand held me with a preternatural strength. The woman
gazed at me with the fascination of a serpent who was
about to encoil her prey. Her eyes were obsidian,
hypnotizing. She opened her delicate mouth and brandished her fangs. From nowhere the man from the *società*
brought a piece of wood crashing down upon the small
wrist. The fingers released me immediately as she let out
a bloodcurdling scream of pain.

The horses of the carriage reared as we stumbled back
and made our way around them. The vampire with the
Russian sable coat was almost upon us. In the distance we

spotted another cab. I prayed that this one was empty. Dr.
von Neefe reached it first and opened the door fearfully.
There was no one inside. She jumped in and offered her
hand to me.

"Fretta!" cried the man from the *società* to the driver,
hastening him on. He looked confusedly at the scene
before him. *"Fretta!"* the man screamed again.

The cab started up.

I jumped in, making sure the virus was still securely
within my coat, and then turned around to offer my hand
to the stranger who had just saved my life. It was too late.
The vampire with the Russian sable coat had reached
him. He grabbed ahold of his shoulders and snapped him
back as if he were a rag doll. As we swiftly drew away I
saw his face, his red, frightened eyes as he screamed and
flailed and they drew him into the carriage.

The carriage remained behind, but the driver of the
antique black *calèche* with its unseen occupants cracked
his whip at the horses. We tore through the dark streets of
Florence, the *calèche* with its two large wheels keeping up
with our every maneuver. We passed the moonlit Boboli
Gardens and raced southwest through the outskirts of the
city. We were headed toward Massa Marittima.

For forty minutes we rolled through the dark Italian
countryside. We managed to stay ahead of the black
calèche, but it was a losing battle. Our horses were pulling
much more weight and they began to tire more quickly. In
a bewildered panic our driver informed us that he could
not keep our lead much longer. I looked out the window of
the carriage and saw that the *calèche* was only a few
hundred feet behind us. We had no weapons. We were
powerless against their infinitely superior metabolisms.
There was nothing we could do.

I was about to turn to Dr. von Neefe and make my last
amends when she cried exultantly, and gestured toward
the window. I looked out and saw that, impossibly, the
black *calèche* was slowing. It paused in the middle of the
road as if watching us for the last time and then turned
around. I frantically withdrew my pocket watch and saw
that it was just a little before dawn. They had to turn
back. Soon the sky would be light, and the sun would
begin to shine.

The sun! First god of the ancients. I had never greeted that magnificent and glowing orb with so much rapture and adoration before. Ours was a strange thankfulness, for the world had never looked bleaker. Dr. Weber was dead, and the fates of my two daughters were unknown. The *società* had been destroyed. The image of that flailing man, the horror in his eyes, was still burning in my mind. Our every source of hope had been torn savagely from our arms. We had been reduced totally and utterly. We were so exhausted with shock we could scarcely think or speak, and perhaps that was why the one pitiful flicker of spirit left in us luxuriated so desperately in the sun.

I paid the driver a hundred pounds to continue on to Massa Marittima and he happily obliged. We reached the little village by late afternoon. The sun was intense. The little walled town was lost in time. On the outskirts of the sleepy settlement several glass blowers tended their glowing kilns. Grass grew among the cobbles of the matchbox-sized piazza, and in the shade of a plane tree a bartender had brought a chair to the door to escape from the suffocating heat.

We sat down at a table in one of the little outdoor cafés, just to sit, not to think. Just to sit. *Where was Ursula?* I could barely allow the question to pass through my mind, for the pain that accompanied it was extreme. Out of the corner of my eye I saw a tousled man rise rheumatically, discussing something in a slow, impenetrable dialect with the woman seated across from him. Dr. von Neefe gazed numbly into space, her nails tapping distractedly against her glass.

I gaped lifelessly at the crowd. I felt like a bird or quail who had momentarily outwitted the hunter, only instead of among shadows, it was in the sunlight that I hid. There were half a dozen people sitting in the café and fanning themselves against the heat. Beneath the arches of the portico sat two men, one of them a worker, the other a man in a pea-green waistcoat with a very wide-brimmed straw hat. His back was to us.

I became aware of the sounds of the August afternoon, the hissing of the insects, the rattling of the glasses. I became aware of something else.

"Wait," I told Dr. von Neefe, beckoning her to stop the

drumbeat of her fingers against her glass. Even through
the fabric of her gloves her nails clicked loudly. She
paused and listened. Behind us there was a shifting of
chairs, and I turned to see that the man in the pea-green
waistcoat had stood and was turning toward us. There was
no mistaking the graceful and extraordinary way he
moved, the face. He smiled as he approached. The broad
straw hat cast a shadow over his eyes, but we knew the
eyes all too well. They were blue, icy blue. He carried
himself and his finery with the same enviable panache.
The sun shone brightly on the green of his waistcoat.

The sun.

"Bonjour, monsieur et madame," came the voice of the
gentleman monk. "You look surprised to see me."

"How can it be?" I asked.

He balanced dapperly upon his cane. An opal ring
glinted. "Because nothing is as it seems, *monsieur.*
Everything is an illusion."

"And the sun?"

He squinted in the brightness, adjusting the tilt of his
hat. "Oh, yes, the myth that the vampire is a completely
nocturnal creature. Ah, Monsieur le Docteur, how many
times have I asked you to consider logic? It is true that
our eyes are more sensitive to the day than mortal eyes.
But as you see, we do not wither. Centuries do not
suddenly flake and powder in our faces. As for the myth, it
was started by the vampire themselves very long ago. As I
say, think about it. What better protection could we
provide for ourselves, *non?* Our enemies are so eager to
believe and accept. Imagine their surprise when they
steal into our dwellings in the full of the day, feeling
completely confident that they are going to drive a stake
through our hearts, only to hear the door shut behind
them and find us sitting, smiling in our chairs. Yes, that
rumor, carefully spread and nurtured, has proven to be one
of our simplest and greatest protections."

Monsieur des Esseintes clicked his thumbnail in a
subtle and rapid succession and I realized that was what I
had heard. Against the background of the summer sounds
that remarkable mode of vampire communication had
provided a macabre counterpoint. Even more disarming,
commingling with the sibilance of the insects and the

clinking of the cups against the tables there was the sound of a distinct reply.

I turned to see Dr. von Neefe rapping her nails in a purposeful and alien rhythm against her glass.

How many times had I suspected she was a vampire, but dismissed the thought when I saw her standing in the sun? Had I ever seen her eat? Here and there a pretended bite, but during most of the meals we had shared we had been conveniently divided by the walls of our cells. What other clues had I been given? I had often brushed against her and been comforted by the warmth of her flesh, but hadn't it been revealed to me through the story of the troubadour that the vampire possessed the yogic ability to control their pulse and body temperature? Had she not displayed incredible strength when she had artfully lifted the sewer cover above her head during our escape in Paris? And what of our escape out the window of the train? I had attributed her strength and dexterity to the adrenaline of fear, but what normal woman would have behaved as she did?

I had been accompanied by the vampire all along. They had coaxed me here, tricked me here to this isolated little village. I had fallen neatly and simply into their trap. Her lip curled up in a snarl to reveal her fangs. Her hand reached out. I pulled the virus back.

In a sudden show of rage her gloved hands gripped the sides of the table and flung it upward with such inhuman strength for a moment it seemed to be tumbling toward the sky before it fell and crashed in the roof of a building across the piazza. Screams rose from the crowd as I gripped the satchel containing the virus and broke into a run. I ran as I have never run before, pulling tables and street carts in my wake.

I was only dimly aware of the sounds of the crowd and the excited shouting. I prayed that the milling people might somehow slow down my pursuer. I knew of only one place that suited my purposes. I reached the outskirts of the village and the glowing kilns of the glass blowers. In the tiny courtyard behind the shop were racks upon racks of shimmering vases and decanters of aquamarine glass. There were two or three workmen wandering about and they looked up when I entered their vicinity. In the back against the stucco wall of the adjacent building stood the immense tiled kiln, its maw gaping like the inferno itself.

"Che cosa desidera?" prattled a plump little man in white overalls as he ambled toward me through the racks. I approached the furnace. *"Che cos'e"* he said, smiling and trying to understand. *"Mi dispiace, ma non capisco."* I looked at the satchel. The heat was intense upon our faces. He knitted his brow. It was at that moment that the woman who had deceived me reached the hill and looked down toward the courtyard containing the kiln. Des Esseintes was close behind. They stopped in mute horror as I dangled the satchel before the blazing furnace. They dared not advance.

They had me, but they would not get the virus. I moved closer to the conflagration. My hand was just inches away from the opening of the kiln. I realized that for the sake of human life, for the sake of the world I had to destroy the virus, and yet, out of the haze of my bewilderment, spun a host of uncertainties. *If she had wanted the virus so desperately, why hadn't she just taken it? She had had numerous opportunities. If the vampire could move about in the sunlight, why had the black* calèche *turned back before dawn? Why?* Nothing made any sense. It was all insane.

Out of nowhere came a voice. "Father!"

I turned to see that Ursula had appeared on the hill and was standing about thirty feet from them. She was safe! The sight of her gave me new strength. I looked at Dr. von Neefe. I could not believe it. I had repected her. I had felt for her as I had not felt for any other woman for quite some time. I might have even loved her, but now all that was meaningless. Her ability to communicate through the clicking of her nails indicated that she had been a vampire for quite some time, long before she had introduced herself to me as Lady Hespeth Dunaway. But if she had been a vampire all along, what of Dr. Weber? The *società?* Had they all been lies? And if I had been accompanied by a vampire from the very beginning, what purpose had there been to the terrifying chase, the alleged war between mortal and vampire? Was it possible it was all a deception, an elaborate and stupendous hoax? Why? To achieve what ends? Niccolo's words came rolling back to me: *Never trust the vampire, for everything they say and do is for some other purpose. They will play a cruel and enigmatic "game of the mind" with you and it will be up to you to solve the puzzle, unravel the Gordian knot.* I looked at the devouring flame and in one prodigious flash of understanding I realized. What had they driven Chiswick to do, but to destroy his work? Hadn't they done the same to the engineer at Oxford? What was Hatim's senseless harassment of the woman in the garden if it was not a tactic to fill her with unreasoning fear? What had they nearly accomplished with Cletus, and they were now carrying to completion with me? In a blaze of crystalline awareness I comprehended the fateful emptiness I had experienced in the street outside of Dr. Hardwicke's, and again after Dr. von Neefe had begged me to sacrifice my work and I had refused. When Cletus had failed they had switched the focus of their game to me. They had never wanted the virus. They had only wanted *me* to destroy it.

I pulled my hand away from the fire.

The expression that swept over the faces of the vampire was distinct. They had played the game and lost. In an instant they both turned to flee, and in that same instant the game reversed itself.

Ursula looked at them in confusion.

"After them!" I cried as I charged up the hill. Dr. von Neefe grabbed one of the horses tied up outside the tiny shop and mounted it, while des Esseintes vanished among the buildings. One of the workmen began to run up the hill. I could not believe what I was doing. I tucked the satchel back into my coat and mounted one of the horses. Ursula mounted the other.

"Polizia!" I heard a voice cry. *"A quale punto polizia!"*

It did not matter. Only one thing was important now, to catch these creatures, the last threads of the puzzle before they pulled away from us like kite strings.

I looked in the direction in which des Esseintes had vanished and decided to pursue the woman. Through the outskirts of the village we sped, past the low buildings and the slatted wagons. Just outside of Massa Marittima we collided head-on with a herd of sheep indolently crossing the unpaved road. The horses reared, trying to get by, and I held on tightly. It had been a long time since I had ridden. At last Ursula broke through and just as I

swerved by the last frightened creature, I spotted her. She
had left the road and had reached the summit of an
adjacent hill.

"Up there!" I shouted.

We jerked our horses into the grass. The slope before us
was steep and we had difficulty making the ascent. When
we finally reached the top we glanced anxiously around.
As far as the eye could see lay the fabled green valleys of
Tuscany. To the east stretched the mountains. To the west
unrolled a checkerboard of undulating plowlands and
emerald hills. It was a landscape straight from Leonardo,
atmospheric in its lushness and haunting in the other-
worldliness of its escarpments and groves of cypress. We
spotted her in the distance, a flourish of brown and black
moving along one of the plowlands.

We dug in our heels.

She proved herself a rider of formidable skill, leaping
hedges and walls like a champion steeplechaser. As we
thundered along, I kept my eyes fastened on her.
Everything else was nonexistent. The green unfurled
beneath me, and through my mind flashed the history of
this magical land. These were the hills that had brought
forth Dante. Somewhere in the haze of time they had
belonged to the Medici, and before that the Romans had
built their villas here. It did not end, the story of these
ancient hills. Far, far back in the silky veils of time the
Etruscans scattered a mysterious civilization among
their ridges and strategic valleys. Isolated ravines still
harbored their tombs, and many a farmer's field still
surrendered their broken spears.

She had taken quite a lead on us, but we were driven by
our own individual obsessions. We had to hold on,
somehow draw closer to this impossible creature. She
veered southwest and to my horror headed for a thicket of
pines. Again we demanded more of our poor horses.

We reached the grove and saw a flash of ebony through
the trees. We almost had her. I ducked to miss a bough.
Branches swept against our legs. A lather of sweat
drenched our legs, gluing our clothing to our bodies.
Ursula's horse hammered a jut of rock and went
stumbling. She lurched forward, grappling its neck to
keep from falling. Her head narrowly missed another low-

hanging branch and went crashing through its fringe of needles. We were there. Just a few lengths more. The large woman turned and for a brief instant our eyes met—hers now possessed that same dead scrutiny that characterized the vampire. Neither fear nor pleasure. Her broad white face was frighteningly blank. Suddenly, a dull thud of pain resounded in my chest. The sky somersaulted around me and the next thing I knew I was lying on my back on the ground. My entire body was vibrating. My head was ringing like a tuning fork.

"Father!" I heard Ursula cry.

My horse whinnied.

She came running to my side. "Father, are you all right?"

Was I feeling pain? A wave of strange nausea swept through me. My mouth filled with saliva. I grew suddenly, blissfully tired.

"Father!"

I felt a hand against my cheek. I fought the drowsiness. Was I paralyzed? Had I broken my spine? I flexed my fingers, struggling to pull myself back into the world. In an almost weightless euphoria I sat up. Our horses trotted in a slow canter around us.

If anything was broken I did not yet feel it. In astonishment I noticed Ursula was crying. Tears were streaming down her flushed cheeks.

"We must continue."

"Are you sure? Are you sure you're not hurt?"

I fought another ripple of drowsiness. My nervous system seemed electrified. Everything was still ringing.

We got on our horses and resumed our speed.

We paused when we broke into the clearing. The warm breeze rustled through the cypresses lining the green tunnel of the hills. There was a buzzing of flies. There was another sound: the distant tattoo of hooves.

Was it coming from the west? There was no time to deliberate. We kicked our horses into a run and moved ahead. Over the crest of the hill we spotted her making a beeline through the valley beyond. My thoughts were still clouded, but slowly something began to seep into my consciousness. I had noticed something, but I could not yet articulate it. I ony sensed its vague presence.

The constant pounding of my horse lulled me, tried to
entice me once again into unconsciousness. I fought it. I
don't know how far we traveled. It must have been miles,
for at length in the distance the green velvet shelf ended
abruptly in a vast rocky precipice. My feeling grew.
Beyond loomed the Tyrrhenian, impossibly blue, that
extremity of blue found only in the Mediterranean. Olive
trees embroidered the cliffs. My head swam. Where were
we? I gazed again at the sea. Somewhere beyond the
ultramarine horizon was Corsica, brick-dust and white
stucco slaked with water.

My feeling congealed.

As we sped along the grassy promontory, I remembered.
It was her face. Just before I had fallen I had seen
something in her face.

The olive trees wafted in the wind from the sea. There
was a hint of bergamot in the air. Impossibly, our quarry
picked up speed as she rode to the top of the ridge before
the cliffs and looked back again. Her horse struggled
against its reins, as exhausted by the ordeal as ours. She
vanished beneath the summit.

Our horses could not take it much longer. They
stumbled, snorting as we forced them up the steep incline.
Each inch was agonizing. On the invisible shore the ocean
frothed, licked its wounds, a vast and liquid jewel.

And then, at the edge of the green hills and resting
upon the very brink of the cliffs themselves, we came
upon the villa.

I have read in *The Illustrated London News* of the
discoveries of sumptuous villas in the ruins of Pompeii
and Herculaneum, the villas of Cicero and Hadrian and
the mysterious Villa of the Papyri still buried beneath the
impenetrable silt of Vesuvius and protected in its tomb by
poisonous gases. One of the most impressive aspects of
these villas was their imperial proportions. Often they
covered a dozen city blocks, dwarfing even the palaces of
the Medici, and equaled only by the most lordly homes in
England. As I gazed at the size of the edifice before us I
realized I was looking at such a villa, only preserved,
carefully tended, and protected against the ravages of
time. It was immense. Even the wall that surrounded the
villa was monumental. It was constructed of massive

stone blocks and topped with stuccoed capitals. It towered
twenty feet into the air and wound through hills
enclosing an imposing expanse of land. It did not line the
cliff side of the estate, for the soaring precipice upon
which the villa rested was obstacle enough for any would-
be intruders. On either side of the villa itself the grounds
ended in numerous gardens and terraces, and beyond
stretched the blue Tyrrhenian.

The villa itself was a sprawling complex of white stucco
buildings with roofs of terra-cotta tile. In the Roman
fashion it seldom towered over two stories, and the
anarchical arrangement of its many wings, colonnades,
enclosed courtyards, and vine-encumbered pavilions indicated that it had grown like an ancestral manor,
expanding and distending from generations of additions
and changes. It was engulfed in sinuous masses of vines
and surrounded by stately cypresses, Lebanese cedars,
umbrella pines, and olive trees, all meticulously land-
scaped. The majestic green lawns were also immaculately
kept and huge pots of bergamot swayed in the Tyrrhenian
breezes. Although well kept, the gardens, the arbors and
vineyards, the stables, and the extensive workers' quarters were deathly silent and void of life. Only one figure
sped toward the compound, and one sound, the dull echo of
hooves, broke the tranquil, even desolate calm.

So she was one of Lodovico's emissaries as well. Trust no
one. Nothing is as it seems.

How old was she?

Had she knelt in basilicas of gold? Had she loved before
the first European hand touched silk? Tasted blood before
the first Muslim bowed his head toward Mecca? How did
she fit into the puzzle?

We rushed in, but when we reached the villa we found
her just standing there, the late-afternoon sunlight full
upon her broad white face. We jumped down from our
horses, but then we paused. We did not know what we
should do. I was certain the vampire had never wanted
the virus. From the solemn resignation of her breathing it
was apparent she had given up. She could run no farther.
But she was waiting for something. She wanted us to see
something before we proceeded. What?

We stood there for many long moments, watching,

wondering. She stared back. And then the final realization came to me. I understood what I had seen in her face.
There is an ineffable something that comes from a
woman. An élan. A magnetism that emanates from
within and embues her simplest act with a fascinating
quality—the combing of the hair, the lighting of a candle.
It goes beyond beauty. It comes from young and old. I had
always felt it coming from Lady Dunaway, and then Dr.
von Neefe, from the first day of our meeting to our final
exchange outside of Victoria Station. But now it was
gone. That was what had troubled me when our eyes had
met in the pines. The face was no longer that of a woman.

I was speechless. Was it possible? Incredulously, I
recalled the incongruous hallmarks of her character, her
large frame, her powerful hands, and the deep and
resonant voice. I examined her features. Nothing had
actually changed, the broad cheekbones, the long, black
hair. But the face had lost its alien beauty and was more
stern and mannish. Even the long hair took on a more
masculine cast. She removed her spectacles. No longer
magnified, a new quality came into her eyes. That had
been the purpose of the spectacles all along. Having the
aquiline vision of a vampire, she had had no true need for
spectacles. She had worn them only to conceal what would
have been instantly recognized. Once the spectacles were
removed, her eyes seemed to sink back into their sockets.
With a magisterial gesture she thrust her long, straight
arm before us and began to peel off her gloves. Had I ever
seen her without her gloves? I looked at the hands. I
returned my gaze to the eyes. They were no longer
human. I don't know whether they were the eyes of a
demon or a god, but they were far from human, far even
from any vampire's eyes I had yet seen. Out of them
streamed voices and black thunder. They pulled, like wind
swirling through a tunnel. Across the hand was a scar, a
scar identical in every detail to the blemish I had seen on
the severed marble hand.

"The game is over," boomed the voice. "Won't you come
into my home? Your child is waiting."

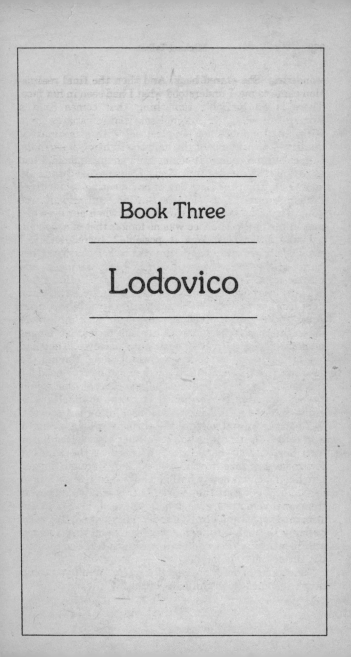

Book Three

Lodovico

XXIV

Was it possible that the legendary one, the oligarch of the vampire had been with me all along? It had to be, for the evidence was before us, and yet I could not accept it, accept that the feminine movements, every feeling and emanation that had conveyed themselves to me, had all been a masquerade. Even as I looked at the unfamiliar individual before us I found it difficult to utter the name, Lodovico.

All of the confusion I had felt, all of the rage and bewilderment swelled up within me as we stood there. I could contain myself no longer. "Why?" I screamed.

He turned and as his eyes passed us by it was as if an actual force swept through our bodies. I could tell Ursula felt it as well from the shudder she displayed. It was undeniable. As I have repeated over and over, I had always tried to understand vampirism as a disease, but I now knew I had been wrong. It displayed certain pathological characteristics, but it was a complexity, an awesome and uncategorizable something that transcended all of the pigeonholes in which I ordered my world. I did not know what it was. I could only say that it was beyond our present realm of knowledge, for something unfathomable flooded forth from those eyes. It is difficult to put the experience into words. It was not a color. It could not be pinpointed in the white or the striations of the iris. It was similar to the luminous hum of energy I had sensed coming from des Esseintes in the orchid conservatory, but it was not a luminescence. It was a distortion, a quality of the air that had its origin in his gaze and ended in the human nervous system.

I looked at Ursula. She was as stupefied by what was going on as I was, but I saw something else in her expression. She was rabid with curiosity. It was more than just bedazzlement. It was as if what was transpiring had some special importance to her, as if the danger of the situation was irrelevant and some other unknown factor of the outcome would somehow decide the very course of her life.

He pushed the door open.

I did not have to consider what to do next. I knew that, blindly, we both had to follow.

Inside we found ourselves in a frescoed anteroom devoid of furniture and sealed off from the rest of the house. Oblivious of our presence, a scurry of human servants rushed in from side doors to retrieve Lodovico's castoff clothing as he strode through. They bowed humbly, as if not wishing to look in his face, and quickly backed away. As the doors shut behind us there was a soft cushioning sound and a rush of air. I wondered what made it necessary for the inner chambers to be so completely sealed off from the outside world. A second set of doors, immense sculpted bronze doors, opened before us with a low whir of machinery. A surge of fresh, cool air enveloped us, and the mellifluous sound of an unknown operatic tenor coming from the horn of a Berliner gramophone. I found it odd that the gramophone was playing. It seemed that someone had just been there listening to it. But that person was gone now. On the floor was a richly woven carpet of the type one might expect to find in the home of the Medici, and the walls were covered with a hodgepodge of old masters in gilded frames.

Beyond this anteroom was the massive peristylium of a Roman villa, a court supported by pillars with a honeycombed dome of leaded glass. I noticed that the glass was tinged blue and the sunlight that flooded down possessed a distinctly aquamarine tint. A fountain splashed in the center of the enclosed garden and everywhere there were birds, most peculiar birds. My attention focused on these creatures, for they were more caricatures than birds. Their large bodies were absurdly out of proportion with their stubby wings and proboscidian faces. They were like oversized turkeys and ambled here and there amid the pillars. I had seen such birds before, but not in any field or zoo. It was with continued disconcertion that I began to suspect they were creatures out of mythology.

A young man in the livery of a servant padded in and

draped our host in a purple toga. Our host's large, strangely feminine hands motioned toward the door at the opposite end of the peristylium. The birds waddled nervously out of our path as we continued.

It was incredible to see the complete and utter transformation of character in Lodovico. Certain aspects of Hespeth—an occasional fragment of a gesture, a flash of the eyes—remained, but this ghost was no longer imbued with her presence. It merely rippled through the creature before me, an empty insect shell.

Even the way Lodovico moved was different. He no longer possessed the deportment of a woman. A myriad of subtle and distinct mannerisms were appearing that had not been present in either Lady Dunaway or Dr. von Neefe. His ambulation was actually transforming, becoming more fluid, like a pantomimist relaxing after a confining routine. Was it possible that he possessed so much self-control that for the months of our contact he had constantly monitored his every play of hands, his every minute twinge of muscle? It had to be, for the lordly gentleman before us possessed an entirely new vocabulary of movement.

We passed through another garden filled with arbors and potted trees. Fountains splashed melodiously amid the vegetation and there were a number of small zebralike creatures, reddish-brown above, blending into white on the legs and marked with dark brown stripes on the head and forepart. It was pure coincidence that I happened to know what they were. I had seen them on display, tattered and moth-eaten victims of the taxidermist's art, at the British Museum. I was reasonably certain that they were quagga, a small South African desert horse that had been hunted by man into extinction. If they were, these were the only living remnants of their species left in the world.

This spurt of thought provoked my memory and I recalled where I had seen the comical and clumsy birds. It had been in *Alice's Adventures in Wonderland*. Alice had just pulled herself out of the pool of tears and found herself standing among an assemblage of birds on the bank. In the assemblage there had been a bird like the ones in the enclosed garden, for I remembered the Tenniel illustration of it clearly. For a few moments I was mysti-

fied, even frightened by the connection, but then I remembered. The birds were dodos, a species of large,
flightless birds from the island of Mauritius that had been
eaten into extinction by hogs, dogs, cats, and Dutch
settlers in 1681. Once again, the vampire had apparently
saved a small population of the creatures from extinction,
and if that were true the ones we had just seen were the
only living dodos in the world. I wondered what psychological trait had motivated him to populate his
gardens with such significant pets.

The door at the end of this garden was also hermetically
sealed, and it opened with a whoosh. We passed through,
and it was here that we began to get a taste of the true
flavor of the villa. To begin, the air was of a decidedly
different quality. It was much drier than in the previous
chambers and possessed that solemn and slightly preser-
vative scent one normally associates with funeral parlors
and museums. The gallery itself was of almost blinding
splendor. The spiring arched ceiling resembled the nave of
a cathedral and was carved in high relief and inlaid with
gold and precious stones. The ornate Corinthian capitals
were also gilded and the columns themselves were of lapis
lazuli. The floor was of varicolored marble chips and
polished to such a shine that it reflected the lapis lazuli
columns perfectly and created the illusion that everything was floating in space.

Other rooms led off the main gallery between each set
of columns and in these rooms, between the columns,
covering the walls and every available inch of floor space
was a treasure trove unlike any I have ever seen in any
manor or museum, church or palace in the world.
Everywhere one looked was an endless expanse of objects,
masklike sconces and sixteenth-century Medici tapestries, ancient jeweled urns and furniture made out of the
horns of Ethiopian sheep. Most visible was a hoard of
stone and marble statuary. Standing amid the macabre
and jeweled objects was a ghostly army of ancient and
silent figures, Roman warriors and Etruscan gods, frozen
nymphs and haunting white goddesses. It was apparent
that these had not been dug up from any hillside or bed of
volcanic ash, but had been perfectly preserved since the
moment of their inception, for many still possessed the

original paint and gilt with which the ancients adorned
their statuary. Here a graceful white Venus removing her
sandal still possessed a garish gold breast band and gilded
pubic hair. There an unknown maiden gazed lifelessly
into space with painted lids and chalcedony eyes. They
stood like otherworldly guardians over the overwhelming
vastness of the objects and artifacts, garlands of carved
agate, stuffed leopards, cameos, rings, brooches,
necklaces, bracelets, chalices, and cups.

I had seen the clutter of the vampire before, but the
wealth in these chambers dwarfed anything I had seen in
the home of des Esseintes. As we strode through we
noticed that the side rooms leading off through the
columns also possessed their stores, vitrines of every
imaginable coinage back through antiquity, gold florins
and sestertii, drachmas, denarii, and talents. Corridors of
endless apothecary jars. Collections of ancient firearms.
Cases of red porphyry and Egyptian glass. Although there
was a certain amount of disorder in the objects, everything had the appearance of being carefully and conscien-
tiously placed. Unlike the rooms of des Esseintes, nothing
had been allowed to grow dusty or decayed. Nothing was
forgotten. Furthermore, nothing seemed to be saved
simply for its monetary value. This was not simply the
depository of a miser. Archimedean screws were given
equal status beside priceless gold ornaments. Ostrich
eggs were apparently as cherished as Greek amphorae. We
were just about to leave when I noticed a peculiar bronze
head with riveted features and a hinged jaw. I recalled des
Esseintes's account of the talking bronze heads of Pope
Sylvester II and Friar Bacon and wondered if this could be
one of those fabulous automatons.

When we left the great gallery the same whooshing of
air accompanied our departure and I realized the climate
in certain rooms of the villa was very carefully controlled.
It suddenly dawned on me that we were in the presence of
a personality who preserved everything, obsessively. For a
moment I marveled at the vigilance the vampire must be
forced to display to keep his treasures from crumbling to
dust. We humans live such a fleeting second in the cosmic
scheme of things we are not overly distressed by the
omnivorous erosion of the centuries. We treat our books as

if they'll always be there. We let sunlight shine upon our walls without fear of fading the ornaments. We get some sense of those erosions in our museums, where things are encased in glass, and humidity is fervidly watched. But if these objects were merely the normal accumulations of a being sixteen centuries old, what precautions must he take to insure that the material world will not fall to dust around him? In a very literal way I realized that Lodovico's home was his museum. I wondered if even the blue tinting of the skylights in the peristylium had some protective purpose.

Suddenly Lodovico turned to us. "I am now going to show you my most prized objects."

We continued on through a resplendent corridor, wondering what possible riches could surpass those we had already seen. I noticed there were paintings by various Renaissance masters on the walls, Titian's and Raphael's. We passed through another door.

It was after passing through this door that we saw what treasures surpassed all the precious metals and wealth of gems that we had already seen. Beyond was another great gallery even larger than the previous, only this one was filled with an endless canyon of books. They towered two stories over the marble floor, bisected by a narrow balcony and scaled by numerous ladders. It was reminiscent of des Esseintes's endless collection only much vaster. There was a second important distinction. Slowly, as I took in the details of the library, I realized it delved even farther back through the gloom of time than the collection of the gentleman monk. My eyes passed from the interminable rows of portfolios and leather volumes, to codices and parchment scrolls. But this was not the end. There was more, much more. Tiers of lead plates and special containers for slabs of inscribed wax. Unending glass catacombs of rolled animal skins and hermetically sealed tubes for papyri. I was dazzled. Perhaps nowhere else in the world could any one man lay his eyes upon a collection such as this. Oh, there were reading rooms in certain libraries where one might examine a scrap of parchment or an ancient table, but again nothing so endless and perfectly sustained as this. Incredibly, I realized that these records, the lead plates and the animal skins, had been kept by the same personality since antiquity. These were the incunabula of a man who had had access to the medieval libraries of Europe, a man who had walked among the Medici. What impossible secrets lay hidden in these walls?

Once again, and for reasons unknown to me, I got the distinct impression that the library had been recently vacated. There were no books resting open on the tables. There were no lingering smells, but still I sensed that only moments before our entry, other feet had scuffed these floors, other eyes had stopped and browsed among the books.

I would have given my right hand to spend even an hour in that library had I not been so filled with exultation at the prospect of at last seeing my little Camille. I looked at Ursula and again I was a little startled to see that she did not seem as enamored by the awesome world we were being allowed to witness. There was still something else troubling her, something I did not comprehend. As we approached the opposite end of the impossible library I noticed that towering high in an alcove over the double bronze doors was a statue of the scribe from the Arch of Constantine.

Lodovico glanced at us cursorily, and once again I felt the influence of his eyes. For the first time I began to understand the full meaning of the control he must exert over Niccolo, the source of Niccolo's powerlessness. What's more, I understood the total immobilization of emotion and thought the ancient prophets must have felt when they confronted their gods; what Ezekiel must have felt when he faced the four beasts of the burning wheel. I was oddly comforted by the fact that at least Ursula trembled before his gaze as well.

We passed through the bronze doors and into another corridor, and at length a familiar sound met my ears. It was distant and plaintive, a rapturous and melodic tinkle. I could hold back no longer. I rushed by our silent antagonist and felt the same electrical tingle of his presence that I had first sensed coming from des Esseintes in the orchid conservatory. I did not pause to wonder what further metabolic control had enabled Lodovico to conceal this aura from us during our previous exchanges. I was much too concerned in reaching the source of the music. I burst through the doors at the end of the corridor.

Inside was a grand salon all in white, with wall panels in high relief. Here and there white busts, as white as the ivory walls, were inset into oval-shaped niches, and the ceiling was resplendently painted by an unknown Renaissance master. One entire wall was filled with glass doors facing a Tuscan columned loggia, and olive trees lined the cliffs beyond. Through their leaves the sun was setting and flooded the room with vermilion. The panes of the glass must have been very thick, for the olive trees fluttered rapidly in the updraft, but not a sound could be heard inside. The room was luxuriously furnished with white chairs and divans. At one end of the room and set in a recess surrounded by pilasters was a mammoth oil painting. The subject was a strange moonstone goddess, naked and embracing a swan. Around her feet were human infants hatching from eggs. Even if I had never seen the painting before; the pearly shimmer, the dreamlike landscape of crags and mossy hills were all undeniably the work of the master, Leonardo da Vinci. As it was, I did know the painting. It was Leonardo's famed *Leda and the Swan,* and it had hung in Fontainebleau until it had vanished mysteriously at the end of the seventeenth century.

At the opposite end of the room a tall cabinet sparkled with a collection of Florentine glass. Before the cabinet sat a long, squarish pianoforte, and at the pianoforte sat little Camille.

There are no words to describe the ecstasy I felt. The moment I stepped upon the fine parquet floor she seemed to sense my presence and stopped playing. She turned her empty ashen eyes in my direction and I rushed forward. I cried as I swept her up into my arms. My outburst of emotion surprised me almost as much as it seemed to surprise Ursula as she entered the salon. Camille's face expressed no emotion, but the tenacity of her grasp, her reluctance to release herself from me, was indication enough of her feeling. At long last I stood her on the floor to get a better look at her.

She was dressed in a blue-and-white-striped frock and

her knee stockings were also white. It was surprising to
me that she had changed so little, although it shouldn't
have been. Her small button nose still turned up a little.
Her chestnut hair curled ever so slightly on either side of
the small white neck. Her pale hazel eyes were as blank
and frozen as a French porcelain doll, but still in some
ineffable way the vacancy of those eyes exuded all that
was innocent in the world. I stood for many long moments
just holding her tiny hands within my hands as she faced
me, when suddenly a thought of utter horror swept
through my mind. With cruel forcefulness I grasped her
head in either hand and flung it back. I opened her mouth
and intrepidly peered in. The relief I experienced was
profound. What I had feared was not there. There were no
tiny sharpened canines. Her teeth were as normal and
pure as a painted angel's.

Nonetheless, the terror I had felt somehow exemplified
all of the doubt and confusion I had suffered. I turned
toward Lodovico, who had positioned himself magisterial-
ly in the most prominent chair. To my continued wonder
something strange was occurring in his eyes. They were
black and smoldering with unknown resources, but I
stared bravely into their depths.

"Why did you take her?" I demanded.

For the first time a passionate curiosity rose up in
Ursula and she too jerked her head toward the vampire. It
was obvious it was a question of critical importance to her
as well.

"Forgive me if I am wrong, Dottore Gladstone, but I was
under the impression you had already figured most of that
out."

To my surprise, the voice that had once been a smoky
contralto was now deep and rumbling, and a rich Italian
accent had blossomed within it. I was about to speak when
something equally mysterious occurred. A quaver passed
through our host's frame. For the briefest of instants his
head tilted back, his eyes rolled psychotically, and the
large hands flexed and trembled. The seizure passed.

I looked in the face. I had previously assumed that Dr.
von Neefe had been Lodovico. That is to say, I had believed
Dr. von Neefe and Lodovico to be the same personality and
that he or she had only put on different superficial

character traits. But at long last it dawned upon me that
this was not the case. The creature who sat before us was
not the same personality who had pretended to be Dr. von
Neefe. I wondered, was this what sixteen centuries had
wrought, a chimera, a cultivated schizophrenia? Was it
possible that when it reached a certain stage of complexity the human brain could not be considered to possess one
personality? Like all things surrounding the vampire I
realized this was but another mystery in an endless chain
of mysteries. Even in my welling of emotion I appreciated
that we were witnessing a mental phenomenon that if
presented to the world at large would have shaken the
very foundations of the fields of psychology and human
behavior. But somehow none of this was mattering anymore. I was reaching a point where it seemed increasingly
meaningless to try to understand the vampire according
to any human labels. I no longer cared whether it was one
personality or a dozen occupying that ancient frame. I
was content merely to know that at this moment
something different occupied those eyes, something that
was neither male nor female.

"You took Camille because you wanted to lure me away
from the virus. You wanted to drive Ursula mad. You
wanted to torment her until she destroyed both the virus
and herself."

Ursula's eyes widened and our host placidly turned his
blazing gaze in her direction. "It is not true, *signorina,*"
drawled the voice. He looked back at me. "It is true we
wanted you to destroy the virus. It is true that we used
your little Camille to lure you away, but we had no
intentions of bringing about the demise of this lovely
young woman. In our game of manipulation and deceit we
only resort to that option when it is our final option." The
large hands spasmodically gripped the chair.

"If you recall, Dottore, from the very beginning I
begged you openly to destroy what you now hold within
your coat. We took you prisoner in Paris, not to draw
Signorina Gladstone into our game, but only to provide
ourselves with time. As your daughter so readily explained to Niccolo, *Camillus influenzae,* like all naturally
occurring varieties of influenza, will not survive forever.
Every ten or twelve years the influenza virus undergoes a

mysterious and inexorable mutation. In ten or twelve
years that deadly demon that you now clutch so dearly
behind your lapel will itself mutate into simply another
harmless strain. We recognized in you something that is
not present in most mortals, a thirst, a voracious passion
for a more ornate world. We had hoped you would be happy
in the home of Monsieur des Esseintes. We had earnestly
wished that for ten or twelve years the world would have
forgotten about Dr. John Gladstone, that through neglect
or spontaneous mutation the deadly *Camillus influenzae*
would pass harmlessly out of existence."

"But Cletus interceded," I filled in.

"Yes," he returned, another tremor passing through his
hands. "Dottore Cletus Hardwicke blindly placed himself
in the midst of things." Lodovico sighed and at the same
moment it seemed another sound issued from beyond the
doors at the far end of the corridor. The vampire paid it no
attention.

"You see, Niccolo made extensive notes on Signorina
Gladstone's character and psychological constitution, and
if left alone we were certain she would allow the virus to
pass out of existence through neglect. Not so with Dottore
Hardwicke. We had studied him as well, you see. We had
studied all of the people in your life before we made our
move, Dottore Gladstone. Il Pensieroso, that one. A
pensive man, tortured by his own self-hatred. He would
have released the virus upon the world within six
months."

I was stunned. I had been so shocked when Ursula had
abandoned the virus. I had been so blind, and yet the mind
behind the furnace of those eyes had seen it in a glance,
had known my own daughter better than I had.

"So you drove Dr. Hardwicke insane?"

"We persuaded him to find his own insanity."

"How?"

"The same way we almost persuaded you, Dottore
Gladstone. As Niccolo told you in the very beginning,
there is a loathing in the human heart for the vampire. It
may lie dormant, but it is always there. Actually, it has
nothing to do with the vampire, really. It is a loathing and
a fear that all humans seem to have for anything that is
not exactly like them or the way they have been taught to
be. If you visit one of your fine British schools you will
discover even your children treat any child who is unusual

or different with medieval cruelty. It does not matter if
the child is different because he has been raised in a
different world, or possesses some genius. If he does not fit
into the pecking order of brutality and sadistic courage,
he is judged an outcast. It is because human beings are
such miserably insecure and frightened creatures. You
may garb your world in decorum and social grace, but you
are still just apes beneath your frock coats, territorial and
fear-driven. It was a simple matter to convince Dottore
Hardwicke that there were dark forces at work that hated
his race even more than he himself did. We pretended to
be after the virus and he crumpled beneath the weight of
his own fear."

"Whom the gods would destroy, they first drive mad, is
that it?" I inquired acidly.

"Most poetic, Dottore," he replied with clinical dis-
regard.

"Is that what you did with all the others, with Dr.
Chiswick and the physician in Liverpool?"

"Yes."

"And everything, the war with the vampire, the train
chase, the capture of the man from the *società* in Florence,
it was all a game, an elaborate deception intended to
make me destroy the virus and perhaps myself in a
paranoiac frenzy?" I was so filled with fury at such a
treacherous and dispassionate imposture that I shouted
out the words, causing Ursula to turn toward me in alarm.
Even little Camille was affected and she hugged my legs
forbearingly. Only Lodovico remained motionless,
unblinking—gripping the arms of his chair like a
Cumaean Sybil.

Again I became aware of a sound coming from the
corridor. It was a clumsy sound, as of something dragging
over the floor. Ursula heard the sound as well, for she
looked toward the door with dread. Whatever it was, it
was approaching. We both remained frozen, watching the
resplendent carved white doors of the grand salon and
wondering what freakish brute maneuvered beyond. It
moved indolently. A nail scratched against the floor.
There was a thud.

I looked at Lodovico with consternation, searching for
some clue as to what was about to happen. But his
expression was stony, almost dazed. Something pressed
against the door.

I turned again, watching with Ursula, as the white door crept open. It moved so slowly I was almost unaware of it, save that the space between the door and its frame was quietly widening. Again there was a slothful scratching and both of our eyes followed the space down to the floor, where we were met with an unexpected sight. There on the floor was a large Galapagos tortoise. To our further surprise, as it slowly moved through the door we saw that it was inlaid with gilt and completely encrusted with jewels. Every inch of the carapace of its back glimmered with rubies, emeralds, diamonds, topazes, opals, and pearls. Furthermore, attached to the bejeweled back was a golden tray sparklingly laden with cordial glasses and a decanter of an unknown liqueur.

"This is Artemidorus," Lodovico introduced. "Would you care for an apéritif?"

Before we could answer, the door at the end of the corridor opened and closed and footsteps, this time distinctly more human, padded down the hall. Artemidorus, the gilt-and-liqueur-laden tortoise, had barely made it to the middle of the room when the door swung open and in strode Monsieur des Esseintes in his pea-green waistcoat and holding his beribboned straw hat in his hands. His expression was solemn, more solemn than I had ever seen in his pale and bony face. He bowed before Lodovico and then turned and gazed at us.

"Bonjour, monsieur . . . mademoiselle."

He turned back quickly toward Lodovico and muttered something in an unknown Eastern-sounding tongue. It might have been ancient Babylonian or Sumerian. I did not know. Then he snapped his knuckles and clicked his fingernails in a rapid and crackling succession. At des Esseintes's appearance the older vampire appeared strangely relieved and lapsed even further into his peculiarly lethargic mood. Although he seemed on the verge of drifting into an almost narcotized state, his mind was still clearly cognizant of what was transpiring. He closed his eyes. His head tipped back limply, but one of his large hands lifted from the arm of the chair and issued a complex staccato of clicks in reply.

The gilded and bejeweled tortoise stopped before Lodovico's chair and turned its head torpidly in our direction. It blinked its large and woeful eyes at us as if wondering if we did indeed want an apéritif. Pondering the life span of the giant tortoises, I wondered how long this priceless monstrosity had been in the older vampire's possession.

"Oui," replied Monsieur des Esseintes, taking up the conversation exactly where Lodovico had left off. "Everything that Dr. von Neefe told you about vampire hunters was a fabrication. There is a Dr. Weber at the University of Vienna, but he, too, is one of our kind. The abduction of the man from the *società* was staged merely for its psychological impact. In truth, the gentleman you saw taken into the carriage in Florence is one of the servants in this grand house. He works in the stables."

"I still don't understand," I said. "All along, from the very beginning, when Lady Dunaway entered my house until we came to Massa Marittima, all you ever wanted was for me to destroy the virus?"

"Oui, Monsieur le Docteur."

"But the time and money you invested. Why such endless sleight of hand? Why didn't you just have Niccolo torch my laboratory, or why didn't you just take the virus from me?"

Monsieur des Esseintes stood looking at us for many long moments as if he were reluctant to answer.

Again the older vampire, who was now deep in some unknown mental state, lifted his hand and emitted a series of clicks. Monsieur des Esseintes turned to us again.

"Hélas, monsieur, this will come as profoundly unbelievable to you, but we have been more truthful with you than you've suspected. When Niccolo first revealed to you that he was a vampire, he told you we disdained killing. I have never dwelled upon the matter, but that is more true than you can ever know. We have lived the bloody pageant of history. There is not one in our number who has not seen a loved one tortured or dismembered at the hands of you and your kind." For the first time since I had known him, Monsieur des Esseintes shuddered. "Books could be written," he said slowly. "Children have had their eyes gouged out. Throughout history the methods of disemboweling, hanging, beheading, breaking with the wheel, burning, flaying, trussing, flogging, cutting off of the ears, hands, breasts, and genitals boggle the imagination." He paused for a moment, once again enveloped in his familiar unutterable calm. "My own

wife, Noemie, was tortured to death during the French Revolution in 1792."

He conveyed the remark simply and factually, as if it were the time of day or a passing amenity, but I suddenly realized that the endless depictions of the woman in farthingales, the numerous statues, and the carefully tended altar of purple orchids conveyed a deep and sustaining bereavement even if the Frenchman's countenance did not. I wondered what vast and unsuspected rancor still coursed through the unmanifested thinking processes of the vampire.

He took a slow step forward.

"It is true that we could have set the torch to your laboratory or murdered you and taken your work, but, believe it or not, Monsieur le Docteur, we are a race more moral and ethical than any species you have yet encountered. Unlike our human ancestors, and you are our ancestors, as distant from us as you yourselves are distant from the lower primates, we have evolved, we have passed into an awareness that is still many centuries from the grasp of your species. We have had enough of violence and killing. We have reached a state where we have realized that force, no matter how morally justified, will only beget force. For a while you believed that we wanted the virus because we wanted to destroy you. I must tell you that for untold centuries we have had the alchemical knowledge to destroy your race, but we would never do that. We see only aboriginal idiocy in the notion of an eye for an eye. Even if the day comes that you hunt us down, that you kill us every one, we will never use our knowledge to destroy you.

"I have told you that there are things you would not understand. It is with little hope that I tell you we would die proudly before resorting to violence, for we have set our sights on a more distant vision. We are lucidly aware that achieving through mere physical force establishes the rules of a game from which there is no escape. When one grants oneself the moral justification to use force, one cannot logically deny it in one's enemies, for all moralities are relative. The dissimilarity between different human cultures alone suggests that one cannot establish universal goods and evils. The enormous disparity between mortal and vampire makes such values a farce. In the end, if we see the wisdom in a world without violence we must be willing to take the first step, to refuse to resort to physical coercion, no matter what the costs.

"That is why we go through such an involved game. You see, we are creatures of pure intellect. We have chosen a weapon we are fully prepared to allow our enemies to use as well—words and illusion. We always play fairly with our enemies. We employ a set of tactics that never forces them or restricts their free will. We are of the opinion that through guile and bluff we can trick an opponent into killing themselves. We do not use airships or guns. Our only weapons are misinformation and confusion. Our only battlefield is the mind."

Could it be true? Was it possible that these creatures, beings who were infinitely superior to the mortal world both in body and science, were duty bound to refrain from using physical aggression no matter what the consequences? It seemed to me the height of folly, but for once I sensed in the blue eyes of the Gallic gentleman that it was the unqualified truth. I had suspected previously that some unknown code of honor was prohibiting them from actually taking the virus from my hands, and now that notion was verified. What other explanation could there be for the fact that Lodovico stood by so helplessly as we escaped from Monsieur des Esseintes's, and as I unrelentingly made my way back to London, back into the middle of their attack on Cletus? At any second on the train he could have reached out and snatched the virus, but he didn't. He didn't because he was constrained by belief, as constrained as the Hindu is not to violate his caste, as constrained as a martyr, who, with a word of renunciation, could save himself from the flames.

"Why are you telling me this?" I asked.

"Because the game is over," des Esseintes replied. "We have tried and we have failed. We cannot start the game anew."

On one hand I was exhilarated by my newfound knowledge. It made me feel I had some power. Here I was standing in their midst with the virus they wanted so desperately, and they were completely powerless to reach out and do a thing. On the other hand, I was outraged. They seemed to consider their intellectual game as somehow noble. In their distorted view of things they obviously perceived their terrifying shams and deceptions as completely sporting, as urbanely acceptable as a parlor game, or a round of chess. Had I not come to understand the vampire better, I might have viewed their sweetly reasonable perception as raw evil. As it was, I did not accept that all moralities were relative. I could never hold that it was somehow more ethical or moral in any way to drive a person insane than to shoot him with a pistol. But some distant part of me seemed to accept his words, or at least intuit that it was not raw evil that spoke, but a complex and ordered intelligence, albeit nonhuman, that, taken within the context of its own existence, was as calmly accepted as any clergyman's faith.

The vampire apparently perceived my irresolution. "Stand witness, Monsieur le Docteur," he said. "Ours is the way of the future. If there comes a day when humanity trafficks with a truly alien intelligence, evil will come not in their sword, but in the unconformity of their logic."

Outside the sunset was beginning to lose its vermilion. The shadows of the slender Tuscan columns grew long within the room and the olive trees still fluttered soundlessly. Only one question remained.

"Why did you want me to destroy the virus?"

With this Lodovico languidly opened his eyes, as languid as the gilded tortoise at his feet, and their black thunder cut through us once again. Another quaver of power trembled through his limbs as he kept those unfathomable orbs upon us. "The answer to that," he said, "lies in your daughter."

On reflex I tightened my hands upon little Camille's shoulders and out of the corner of my eye I noticed that Ursula watched my every movement attentively. I looked back at the Alexandrian scribe.

"That is what drew me to her in the first place. We have ways of knowing the future more accurately than you. We cannot predict the final role of the dice, but we can sketch a passable picture of coming events. For uncounted centuries we have been playing our game. We knew that the time was coming when we would lose our secret influence in the world. We knew that the fates had chosen you to be the unwitting instrument in this dénouement, but we did not know how. When I learned that your child was an idiot savant I thought the unseen wheels had delivered me a sign.

"I have already told you why we wanted you to destroy
your virus. I have told you many times. Because the world
is blind and will use it for destructive purposes only. It is a
sad truth, but it is a truth, indeed, that the knowledge of
the human species far surpasses their wisdom. I do not
know why fate has chosen this to be so, but it is so. It has
been true since the first ape picked up the jawbone of an
animal and swung it as a weapon. That is why we have
done everything we have done. The engineer at Oxford
had come up with the design for a dirigible that possessed
the brushstrokes of genius, but it was a dangerous genius,
a military genius. If he would have released it upon the
world at this time the results would have been devastating. We had to stop him. You may be interested to know
that your Dr. Chiswick had come very close to your own
discovery. He had devised a way of creating endless
biological mutations of the influenza virus. We had to put
a stop to it before he achieved what you did achieve, the
creation of a virus that completely lacks antigenicity."
With this last remark Lodovico underwent another faint
seizure and in the flash of an eye his features were
suddenly feminine.

"Don't you see?" said a voice that once again lacked the
sonorous Italian accent. It was a deep, but more womanly
voice. The voice was oddly disjointed with the countenance, the rumbling eyes. It was Dr. von Neefe's voice, or
at least the voice of the personality that had pretended to
be Dr. von Neefe. Its effect upon me was piercing. I was
swept with a warmth, an almost bereaved longing, but at
one and the same time I was repelled by my own feelings.
It was as if it were the voice of a deceased loved one
speaking through the body of a medium, or the voice of an
oracle coming from the mouth of an entranced priest.

Even as I recoiled the ghost faded away.

"That is why I saw your little daughter as an omen, or
portent," Lodovico continued. "Camille is a creature who
possesses a certain genius, a very special genius, but
completely lacks all awareness or understanding of her
own capabilities. And what is the entire human race if
they are not creatures who possess genius, but are also
bound by their own blindnesses and stupidities? Don't
you see, what is Camille if she is not the perfect metaphor
for the human race? What are your scientists if they are
not idiots savants?"

"That is the work of the vampire," I chided scornfully, "to function as the benevolent overseers of the human race? To scour the newspapers and scientific periodicals and every time you come across an invention or discovery that you deem dangerous in the hands of we mere mortals, you bring your fist down?"

"Never the fist."

"Your game, then. Your game!" I shook my head in disbelief. So that was why the vampire were always associated with centers of knowledge, why Lodovico had been drawn to the scholarly exploits of the Medici, why the medieval vampire of Europe had participated so benignly in the school of Notre-Dame. "How long has this been going on?" I demanded. "How long have the vampire considered themselves the grand inquisitors of human learning?"

"Since the Unknown Men decreed it," Lodovico boomed. "I am going to tell you, Dottore, what I have told few other mortals. I am one of the Unknown Men. There are eight others. We are the undisclosed rulers, the hidden powers at the top of the secret hierarchy of the vampire. Together we possess the combined knowledge of this world." He clutched the arms of his chair, and his dark eyes blazed. "For centuries we have pulled the secret strings of history. You seem to greet our work as mere censorship, but if you knew the gravity of the forces at play, if you knew what holocausts we have prevented, you would understand a glimmer of the sovereign reasoning behind our task. These forces have been discovered before. They were known by the ancients. They were preserved in the library of Alexandria, and that is why the library had to be destroyed. Your history books say the library was burned by the Arabs in A.D. 642. That is not true. It was destroyed by the Christian Patriarch, Theophilus, in A.D. 392. It was a simple matter for the vampire to convince Theophilus that the library contained the works of the devil."

In an awesome flash my mind dredged up all that I knew about the fabled Alexandria. Not the Alexandria of today, but the Alexandria that Lodovico must have known, the Alexandria that remains only in a few crumbling catacombs and pillars and submerged beneath the Mediterranean. I recalled reading of a city whose splendor encompassed no less than four thousand palaces,

four hundred baths, and four hundred theaters. In a
dreadful vision I imagined its library, containing all the
knowledge of the ancient world, in a roaring tower of
smoke and flame against the Egyptian sky. A few short
months ago I would not have believed that there was a
conspiracy that had infiltrated our entire history and
stretched back through the mists of time, but my
skepticism had long since died. I had witnessed enough. I
had seen the stones laid by their hands and I knew of
their influence. I knew there was a second intelligent
species on this earth, that they had mingled with popes
and kings and infiltrated every level of our society. I knew
that there was an entire other history of the world, and
that that was what was being spoken to me now, merely a
page of vampire history. What invoked my fury was that
this was not an age-old dispute, a crime committed by his
ancestors. It was a crime committed by this creature
himself. No doubt it was he who had whispered the words
that had set the library of Alexandria to flames.

"How could you!" I croaked. "How can you dare to say
you value knowledge and then destroy it so carelessly?"

For the first time since I had known him des Esseintes
gaped unbelievingly. Only another series of raps and
clickings from the older vampire seemed to pacify his
perplexity.

"He doesn't know," Lodovico muttered to him. Lodovico
turned to me, shaking his head slowly. "Nothing has been
destroyed, Dottore. For the centuries of our work
whenever it has been necessary for us to keep a certain
discovery from being released upon the world, we have
never allowed anything to be lost. The papers of the
engineer at Oxford, Dr. Chiswick's findings—copies of all
of these things can be found here." His voice lowered to a
reverent hush. "Every word, every arcane fact from the
library of Alexandria has been preserved."

For a few moments I did not understand the implications of his remark. Then it hit me. The parchments in his
library, the wax tablets and animal-skin scrolls. He had
been quite correct when he had said the library was his
most valuable possession. It would be quite impossible to
place any sort of estimate on a collection that contained
all the volumes of the library of Alexandria. What
unknown masterpieces did it contain? What priceless
classics lost to the human world?

In anticipation of my thoughts Lodovico said, "Polybius wrote forty volumes of history. The human world knows of only five."

I could not believe it. He seemed to be gloating.

"Among my volumes I possess the eighty-three missing dramas of Aeschylus, and the one hundred six lost plays of Sophocles."

Everything began to make sense, the dodos and the lost Leonardos. The alchemical inventions and the endless bottles of unknown chemicals. The villa was a museum of the lost. It was a fragile and sealed repository of all the treasures the vampire had looted from history. I was infuriated.

"In God's name, how can you justify keeping these things from the human world, keeping them for yourself?"

"Most of them would have been lost if I had not saved them. You seem painfully unaware that the keeping of books and paintings in one's household was scarcely a common practice until deep into the seventeenth century."

"But the library and the inventions, these things you stole!"

Even des Esseintes was shocked at my verbal attack against the magister, the most ancient of his kind. He glared at me.

"I will admit, Dottore, that there were some selfish motives involved," Lodovico said with a rise in his voice. "We need the human race. As Monsieur des Esseintes has pointed out, you are our ancestors, as important to us as all the evolutionary links that have led to *Homo sapiens* have been to you. The only difference is that your evolutionary links are in the past, while ours are concurrent with us, two separate but interlocked species evolving at different rates. We cannot reproduce. We need you. We need your massive numbers, for only one in ten thousand possesses the genius our forefathers have demanded of the vampire. Our need goes beyond mere reproduction. We are all part of a delicate balance, an incredibly complex interconnectedness that extends from our food chains to the rudiments and building blocks of our reality.

"Not the least important strand of this web is our sociopolitical survival. Throughout the centuries the thousands and thousands of dangerous and abominable things we have kept from the human race, we have kept because we did not want them used against us. Even your deadly *Camillus influenzae,* which would not harm us, we wanted you to destroy because if it were ever released the mayhem that would result in the collapse of human civilization would affect our lives as well. We share your cities with you just as certain insects share the homes of ants. We want them to keep running." He raised his hands. "But you must realize, humanity is as much to benefit by our censorship as the vampire. We were only protecting you from yourselves."

I was livid. Thousands and thousands of things? Even if I disregarded all of the pain and torment they had caused through their endless manipulations, the untold and uncounted deaths of hundreds and hundreds of unknown scientists and scholars. Even if I overlooked the madness of a logic that suggested there were certain blameless ways of destroying the life and work of an individual, I could never condone the blasphemy of their assault on the freedom of learning and discovery.

"It is wrong!" I shrieked. "Even if you have the unabashed gall to say you were protecting us from the horror we would cause ourselves, it is itself a terrible crime against humanity. pompously to keep this knowledge for yourself!"

"There are things you are not ready for. One does not give a child a gun."

"But wouldn't it be better to teach a child to use a gun safely than simply to take it away from him?"

"It depends on the gun."

To my astonishment I noticed that somehow Niccolo had stolen into the room while we had been arguing and was sitting in a chair near the window. Furthermore, the sight of him, of his fragile and beatific countenance, comforted me oddly. I still harbored a great deal of resentment for him, but my hurt was abating. I was beginning to realize the full meaning of the control Lodovico must have over him. I abruptly turned to Ursula, wondering if seeing the angel again had as weighty an effect on her as it did on me. To my continued amazement she seemed not at all interested in the young boy who had once touched her emotions so deeply. Instead, she still kept her eyes trained on me, or more specifically on my hands, which I rested on Camille's shoulders.

I looked at Monsieur des Esseintes. "You, of anyone, must know the ecstasy of a never-ending hunger for knowledge. Can't you see what a sin it is to thwart the unbridled search for knowledge?"

It was a day of new emotions for the vampire, for my importunity appeared to have a slight effect upon the Gallic gentleman. His eyes moved slowly between the older vampire and myself. The search for knowledge was one thing that did have an effect upon des Esseintes's alien emotions.

"Would it make you feel any better, Dottore," said Lodovico, "if I told you that we are not altogether happy with our solution? You may comprehend a particle of what I am saying when I tell you that minds far greater than yours have considered the problem for centuries. We have wrestled endlessly with the very criticisms you yourself have mentioned, and we have made concessions. But in the end we have discovered no other solutions. We have a saying in Italian: *Il meglio è l'inimico del bene....* Better is the enemy of good."

With this last remark he abruptly rose and approached me. "Would you hand me the satchel within your coat?" he asked.

I drew back fearfully.

"*Piacere,* Dottore, surely you must know how powerless I am to do anything to destroy it by my own hand."

"Then why do you want it?"

"I simply want to show you something. After that, you have my word that your work will be returned to you unharmed."

At another time I would never have dreamed of obliging those words. But now, in those black and endless eyes I saw that the older vampire was speaking the truth. I reluctantly withdrew the satchel and handed it to him. He took the packing out and layed it aside until he finally held the sealed Petrie dish in his large hands. He turned it over once, admiring the brown smear of agar containing the virus.

"If released, this would wipe out most of the population of the world?"

"Yes," I returned firmly, not shrinking from the gravity of the possibility.

"And you damn me, Dottore. You damn me because I tried so long to get this from you, to save you from your own stupidity?"

"Yes," I returned again.

He continued calmly to inspect the two interlocking pieces of glass and then leveled one of his unpropitious eyes upon me. And then, in a single swift movement, he lifted Camille's tiny hand and placed the dish within it.

For a brief second I stood frozen in terror as she lifted the closed dish to her mouth, ineffectively licking the glass, and then fondled it with both hands. She began to turn the lid.

I cried out, savagely pulling the sealed dish from her innocent hands. For a moment she looked a little surprised, but then her face resumed its composed and vacant stare. I looked at the Petrie dish in my hand and then back at the smoldering black eyes of the vampire. A grave and bitter expression filled his face.

"Executed well, Dottore. If you had not intervened she would have opened it."

"It means nothing," I said, both stunned and outraged by the display.

"Does it, Dottore?" he murmured, returning to his seat. "I still might ask you: What have I done that you have not done?"

I stood there for many long moments, numbed and vibrating with emotion. I knew that after several hours my mind would be brimming with questions and accusations, but for the moment I was deathly tired of arguing. I did not agree with the vampire, but I knew it was useless to continue. For the first time I started to accept that there were differences between the vampire and myself that would forever remain irresolvable.

I had only two questions remaining. "You mentioned that the time had come when you could no longer secretly influence the world. You said that I was the unwitting cause of this dénouement. Is it because you have failed to trick me into destroying either myself or the virus?"

Lodovico sedately blinked his lids. "That was what we thought initially, Dottore. We thought that somehow, in some way, your virus was going to play a major role in world events, that that was your role in the scheme of things. That was where we made our fatal error."

"Your fatal error?"

"We thought that it was your work. But it was not your work. It was your actions. You see, Dottore, as I have told you, there are forces at work in this universe, forces you have not even begun to suspect, let alone make your first infantile attempts to harness. Since the beginning of the Christian era we have had a hand in history and what has been allowed to evolve. But the times are changing. Things are beginning to grow too fast and in too many directions. You have, indeed, played one of the trump cards of destiny, but our failure with you is merely a sign of the times. A new world is forming, a world that may be dangerously beyond the control of either mortal or vampire. It is up to you, Dottore. We have failed."

With that, and at some unseen signal, both of the older vampire prepared to leave.

"But what, what do you mean it was not my work, but my actions? What was the trump card of destiny?"

"The woman," he said cryptically.

I shook my head, not understanding.

The Italian was obviously reluctant to speak further. "The woman in the garden at 24 Rue de la Glacière," he finally conceded. He shook his head solemnly. "It will not mean anything to you now. Nothing will, but the name Marie Curie will have a more profound meaning for future generations than you can ever imagine."

He continued to walk toward the door of the grand salon.

"But wait!" I repeated. "What is to happen to us?"

The older vampire slowly pivoted and once again turned the influence of his gaze upon us. His eyes passed from Ursula to Camille and finally to myself. "You are free to go," he muttered simply.

I was dumbfounded. "You mean, with everything that we've been through, with everything we know about you, we are free just to walk out of here?"

"There is nothing you can do to harm me," Lodovico returned. "Nothing you say will ever affect me. No one would ever believe you."

He offered what, under other circumstances, might have been construed as a smile. But I knew the vampire well enough to know that it was a hollow action, that his thoughts were really a thousand miles away.

Niccolo led us back through the villa and out into the gardens. As he accompanied us I noticed that Ursula was

not at all observant of his presence, but still furtively
watched my affections for Camille. It dawned upon me
that this was what she had been interested in all along.
There was something about my feelings for my empty
daughter that she did not understand, that she was
burningly desirous of figuring out. In turn, I was baffled
at why she possessed such a morbid and voyeuristic
curiosity. Even after Niccolo had bid us farewell at the
gates of the immense and secluded estate and we made
our way back to some semblance of our civilization, she
remained fixed upon my every movement and gesture
toward the child.

The sun had set and behind us the ancient walls loomed
ominously. After traversing the cypress-covered hills we
came to a dirt road extending toward Massa Marittima,
and a peasant farmer indolently riding in a wagon. He
spoke a little English and offered us a ride. Once aboard
the wagon I turned and looked behind us. In the far
distance the Tyrrhenian was now a vast expanse of black,
and the villa was only a mote of white in the moonlight.
"Do you know who lives there?" I inquired.

"The *padrone,*   Signore Giacomo D'Annunzio," he
replied without notice.

"Do you know who he is or what he does?"

In the bluish moonlight I saw the white eye of the
grizzled farmer turn toward me wonderingly. And then he
laughed, realizing that such a silly question could only be
a joke. "Why, he owns the largest vineyard in Tuscany."

Intrepidly, I asked him if he knew anything about
Signore Giacomo D'Annunzio or the *vampiro,* hoping to
unleash a flood of superstitious gossip from the brain of
this most rustic of creatures. He looked at me with a
strange concern and I realized I had struck a nerve. But
then I realized it was not village rumor that disturbed
him, but me. He could not imagine why I would be asking
such an absurd question. At length, he threw his head
back in a relieved cackle and slapped my knee.

"You do not believe in the *vampiro,* do you, *Signore?* " He
chuckled. He did not wait for my reply. He knew it could
not be.